A Rock and a Hard Place

Anne Sutcliffe

Autism Asperger Publishing Co.
P.O. Box 23173
Shawnee Mission, Kansas 66283-0173
www.asperger.net

P.O. Box 23173
Shawnee Mission, Kansas 66283-0173
www.asperger.net

Publisher's Cataloging-in-Publication
(Provided by Quality Books, Inc.)

Sutcliffe, Anne, 1956-
A rock and a hard place / Anne Sutcliffe.
p. cm.
LCCN 2005931731
ISBN 1-931282-82-X

1. Asperger's syndrome – Fiction. 2. Parents of autistic children – Fiction. 3. Mothers and daughters – Fiction. 4. Psychological fiction. 5. Domestic fiction. I. Title.

PS3619.O93R63 2005 813'.6

QBI05-600132

Designed in Palatino and Emmascript.

Printed in the United States of America.

This book is dedicated to Mark ...

. . . for being infinitely strong, loving, patient, good-humored and resourceful, both when we were living through the most difficult times, and when I was reliving them while writing this book . . . for your wonderful equanimity . . . for being wise enough to see straight to the heart of issues and problems . . . and most of all, for being as unlike Lucy's husband, Simon, as it is possible for anyone to be.

... To Jolyon, Jack and Tiffany ...

. . . for inspiring me, for always being ready to help with their sister, and for making me able to laugh at the worst of times . . .

... and to Jenny ...

. . . for being the lovable pest that she is . . .

... with love

Chapter One

I am, by nature, a very shy person. As a rule, I take to confrontation as readily as I take to highway pileups. It really was not like me to do something like this at all.

And it's not as if Hollie was any more difficult on that day than on any other. After all, people had been telling us for years that she was impossible. They asked us how we coped as regularly as they discussed the weather or the price of training pants. It was simply that there came a moment (it was in the bathroom, when I found my toothbrush in the bottom of the toilet) when I knew we couldn't cope a second longer.

I didn't discuss my plan with Simon, who left for work that morning unsuspecting of what his wife would be up to later in the day. I took Joshua, our seven-year-old, to school, and Lisa, our four-year-old, to preschool. Then I returned home and packed a small overnight bag for eight-year-old Hollie: a change of clothes, a dozen disposable diapers. While I did so, she amused herself by swinging on her bedroom curtains.

As I dropped the bag in the hall, I heard the curtain rod crash to the floor with a bang that made the floor boards shake. Hollie sat, unhurt, among the crumpled folds of fabric, her gaze fixed on a point somewhere in the middle distance. With her shiny blonde hair, her sky-blue eyes and her serene expression, she looked like an angel from a Florentine fresco. When my eyes caught the empty holes where screws had held the curtain rod in place, bitterness burned my throat like acid.

Leaving the mess behind me, I strapped Hollie into the back of the car and drove slowly and carefully from our village of Brackley into the local town, Shalham. She liked car trips, so she sat obediently, without trying to escape from the seat belt. The problems, as I had predicted, started when we reached the school district office.

I parked outside the office building on zig-zag lines that clearly indicated "no parking," reasoning that as I was intending to cause a scene anyway, I might as well start out as I meant to go on.

Then I began to try to extricate Hollie from her seat belt. "Hollie, we're going to talk to a lady who's going to decide what school you'll go to," I explained. I always tried to explain things to her, though she couldn't talk or understand language, just in case she was comprehending more than I suspected. She clung for dear life to the seat belt and tried valiantly to stick the metal end back into the groove. Eventually I grabbed her with both arms around her waist and pulled her up, depending on the element of surprise to make her let go her grip of the seat belt. It worked, but she immediately curled up into a ball on the ground, her arms wrapped around her knees, and wriggled away from me into the middle of the road. I slung the strap of the overnight bag around my shoulder, bent down and began trying to force my hands under her armpits to get her up.

Hollie began to scream as I half dragged, half carried her across the doorstep and into the entrance hall of the board of education building. The two receptionists looked up and frowned when they saw it was me. Not particularly severe frowns, I have to say. I have become an expert in frowns over the six years since Hollie's diagnosis; indeed, I could write a thesis on the subject. These were more the weary, is-it-really-necessary-to-bring-an-actual-disabled-child-into-the-Special-Education-Office sort of frown.

"Do you have an appointment, Mrs. Roseman?" one of them called.

"No," I puffed, heaving a struggling Hollie up the first step.

"Then you can't go up, I'm afraid."

There was no point in replying. I picked up Hollie and carried her in my arms up the stairs as if she were a baby, a position that allowed me to control both her legs with one arm so that she couldn't continue kicking me.

"Mrs. Roseman! MRS. ROSEMAN!"

I headed straight down the hall, then across to the special education department. I passed the desks of various junior administrators and secretaries, who were drinking coffee, talking on the telephone and working at computer screens. All conversation ceased as Hollie and I cannoned across the room.

I gave the most cursory of knocks on the door of the inner sanctum at the far side before pushing it open. Inside was a small room crammed on three sides with bookshelves and row upon row of tall, bottle-green filing cabinets. The fourth wall, directly in front of me, consisted mostly of large windows, all tightly shut. In front of me, at a large desk cluttered with piles of folders, trays of letters and an assortment of stationery items, sat a woman in her mid-forties with short, straight brown hair and no makeup, wearing a black pinstripe jacket and a stiffly collared white blouse. Her jaw was firm and round like a concrete mixer. The polished wooden nameplate at the front of her desk announced in shining, gold letters "Miss Mary Walsh, Assistant Director of Special Education." Glancing up from her file, she saw Hollie and me on the doorstep. She looked down her mountain ridge of a nose at us, and her face swelled with anger.

"I don't think we have an appointment, Mrs. Roseman."

"I don't need one, Miss Walsh. It's been six months since Hollie was kicked out of her school. You keep refusing to make a decision about her future because you don't want to pay for the boarding school placement that she so obviously needs. In the meantime, our lives are being ruined. My marriage is at breaking point, my son has been held back a year at school, and my younger daughter is withdrawn and having problems making friends. I want a decision. Today. Now."

"Mrs. Roseman, we have to arrange meetings, review costs, hold discussions with Social Services. We have to look at budget considerations. We regret that this takes time. If you can just wait . . . "

"I cannot wait! I – we – have waited enough."

I picked up the overnight bag from the floor and placed it carefully on her desk.

"Normally I am a quiet, unassuming person," I went on. "I hate making a fuss. Up until the last year or so I knew how to take no for an answer. But taking care of Hollie has changed me. I am not going to sit quietly and watch my family be destroyed by a lack of action on your part."

Hollie poked at a batch of files sitting precariously at the edge of the desk. They crashed to the floor with an enormous flapping sound, falling in all directions with papers scattering everywhere.

Miss Walsh looked at me, outraged. Any other day over the past forty years I would at this point have been stricken with guilt and begun gushing apologies like water from a garden hose. But I controlled myself. I forced myself to sit down in a deliberately calm, slow manner. I manufactured a serene expression, as if I really was relaxed and didn't have a stomach full of wriggly snakes. In the meantime, Hollie wandered around the room, flicking pens, rulers, staplers off shelves. With an air of great casualness, I crossed my legs. When Hollie picked up Miss Walsh's handbag, Miss Walsh and I eyed each other without blinking, like two gunslingers across from each other in a saloon.

"If you don't stop her" she began, through gritted teeth. But in a second the handbag was upside down and the contents – keys, lipsticks, tissues, tampons, notebooks – had collapsed in a chaotic heap on the floor.

Miss Walsh had tried to lean forward to grab the handbag when she saw I did not intend to move. Now she leaned across the table, her weight on both arms, her expression thunderous. Her hard, round jaw quivering with rage, she practically spat at me. "Would you please take your daughter."

"No, I won't take her anywhere. You've lived with this for one minute. We live with it twenty-four hours a day, every day. Maybe living with Hollie's behavior for a day might concentrate your mind more on making a decision. I will leave her here and be back to pick her up this time tomorrow."

Then I promptly turned and walked through the outer open office again, concentrating on keeping my head high and my back straight, avoiding the gazes of any of the twenty or so people in the office. Voices ceased as I passed once again, and heads from all corners turned in my direction. I could hear the muffled beginnings of sentences from the far side of the room; "That's Mrs. . . . ," "Isn't she the mother of . . . ," "Isn't her daughter one of . . . ," but then either the ends of the sentences faded into whispers, or hands went in front of mouths in a crass parody of discretion. Just as I reached the far side of the room, a switch clicked in my head. I turned, confronted the sea of faces, and opened my mouth. I wanted so much to explain. In my mind I could hear myself saying, calmly and emphatically:

"I am so pleased to have been able to present you with such a spectacle today. I hope you all enjoyed it. Just to let you know, Hollie has autism, which is why she behaves the way she does. Perhaps those of you who have normal children will stop for a moment to consider how lucky you are."

I could even imagine the earnest expression I would wear. But in the end I couldn't get the words out. Although desperation had just forced me into an unprecedented confrontation, I was still the same wouldn't-say-boo-to-a-goose Lucy I'd been for the past forty years.

As I turned to walk away, voices began calling after me. "Mrs. Roseman!" And then again, more loudly, "Mrs. Roseman! MRS. ROSEMAN!"

I couldn't do it, of course. I got as far as the car. I even opened the car door and sat down on the driver's seat and pulled the door closed. A stone's throw away on the main road I could see the unbroken lines of cars inching their way toward the city center. Shoppers with baskets and shopping bags weaved past each other with bored expressions. Cars drove in and out of the reserved spaces in the little cul-de-sac of offices, and immaculately dressed business people strode in and out of redbrick offices with shiny gold name plates.

What was happening to my Hollie? She wouldn't register the fact that I'd gone, but she would notice if everyone started shouting at her. I pictured her standing in some corner, bewildered and lost, papers and files from all the desks strewn across the carpet where she had sent them flying, desperately trying to block out the meaningless cacophony of angry voices around her. As a toddler she had spent most of her waking hours hidden behind a dresser in our bedroom. We had spent years teaching her to trust people. If I left her now in this alien place, where everyone made hostile bellowing noises . . . I leaped from the car.

I pushed open the office door, immediately facing the two frowning receptionists. These frowns were now more you-are-the-scum-of-the-earth sort of frowns, I noted for my research. But this time trying to anaesthetize myself by adding a funny side to the situation didn't help. As two pairs of accusing eyes drilled into me, I felt the full force of their scorn. I didn't so much want the ground to open up and swallow me, as to bury myself in the bowels of the earth.

"I think Social Services has been called," said the older of the two woman, icily.

The younger woman had picked up the phone "Mrs. Roseman is here to pick up her daughter," she said, giving me an arch look. Then she put the receiver down. "Miss Walsh's secretary is bringing your daughter down."

Almost immediately the elevator doors opened, and a middle-aged woman with a limp perm and a stony expression appeared, leading Hollie firmly by the hand. Hollie looked bemused, her gaze fixed at a point halfway up the wall. The woman handed me the bag. "Miss Walsh said there's a letter in the mail. And if this ever happens again, Social Services will be called in."

I took Hollie's hand. I picked up the overnight bag. No one offered to help me with the door, so I pushed it open with my shoulder and ushered Hollie through. I strapped her into her special harness in the back seat of the car and threw the bag into the other seat. Then I climbed into the driver's seat. I put my head in my hands. I wanted to stay there forever, but after a minute or two I sat up and opened my eyes. My vision was blurred. I couldn't feel my arms and legs.

I looked at my reflection in the rear-view mirror. As a child and as an adult I had been afraid of asserting myself, afraid of competing, afraid of sticking my neck out over anything. I almost never got angry or said what I really thought. The nearest I ever came to being uninhibited was when, in rare moments alone in the house, I would put a CD on and sing at the top of my voice to some sixties ballad or seventies rock classic. And now, in just a few weeks, this alien person had moved into my head, a stranger with a capacity for volcanic rage that frightened me.

I spent the evening putting off the moment when I would have to tell Simon about my futile little protest. There were plenty of good reasons for skirting the issue. There was too much noise and chaos during the children's bath time, and a program on TV that Simon wanted to watch while we ate dinner. There was a flooded bathroom carpet to mop up with armfuls of towels. Then there was the final chapter of *Harry Potter and the Sorcerer's Stone* to read to Joshua and Lisa. When I finally summoned the nerve, Simon was getting undressed and I was already in bed.

"My God, how could you do that? Sometimes I think you hate Hollie. You'd do anything to get rid of her."

I swung myself out of bed, my chin set, my fists clenched against each other.

"How dare you say that!" I said, not knowing where to begin to explain the confused, angry feelings that overwhelmed me. "You know she's impossible to cope with at times. You know what a constant job it is looking after her. God, I shouldn't have to explain to you, of all people."

"She's been given to us. We have to look after her."

"But she's destroying us."

"Look, she barely relates to us. How do you think she'd relate to a load of strangers in a boarding school, even in the unlikely event the education people ever agreed to it."

"I don't know," I said, miserably. "I just know that we can't go on."

The following day, Saturday, we had been invited to a wedding. I wished desperately we didn't have to go – I even found myself wishing one of the children would get sick to provide us with a ready-made excuse. But Simon had been a college friend of the groom, David, and nostalgia for his youth mixed with a most uncharacteristic desire to socialize (Simon never normally wanted to go anywhere) had made him determined to accept the invitation.

I was up at eight, changing Hollie's diaper and preparing the children's breakfasts. I scarcely exchanged a word with Simon. Actually there was nothing I could think of to say to him. He showered while the rest of us ate our breakfast and emerged from the bedroom stern-faced, already dressed in his suit, as I carried the breakfast plates to the kitchen.

"I'll clean up here," he muttered. "You get them all ready."

"Okay."

I set about the task of getting Hollie ready first. Dressing her is a bit like painting a bridge. The key to conducting the operation successfully is not only to have everything you need – dress, socks, underwear – on hand before you start, but to try to prevent interruptions. The main problems arise when the phone rings or one of the other children asks you to find a toy they've lost, because you return to find she's stripped everything off and is sitting stuffing one of the socks into her mouth. Then, when you bend down to try to put the socks on her feet again, she grabs your hair and starts to pull it, giggling wildly. And by that time you feel like joining her and pulling your own hair out in frustration.

Today, to my amazement, Hollie was reasonably compliant, perhaps because she was fascinated by the pretty party dress that she'd worn only once before. I strapped her into the car with a bag of chips and a cup of juice, then rushed to complete the rest of the preparations in the few minutes it would take her to consume them.

The bright sunshine was a comfort. I called Lisa, who was collecting the dolls she wished to take on the trip, and dressed her in her pink and blue party dress. I brushed her pretty blonde hair and wiped the breakfast smears from her mouth with a towel.

"Jessica and Jemima need their party clothes too," she said, indicating the dolls.

"Run and get them quickly," I said, taking the dolls from her and packing them in her bag.

Joshua was more obstructive. He hid under his blanket and shouted that he wasn't going to wear the green shirt and new corduroy trousers I had ready for him. He was going to wear the jeans with the knee holes and the ice-cream-spattered favorite T-shirt he had on.

"Why are you under your blanket?" I asked.

"I spilled my Legos. I thought you'd be angry."

I was under pressure. I knew Hollie would have finished her chips and juice. She was probably at this moment escaping from her seat belt and entertaining herself by pulling down the rear-view mirror or ripping cassette tapes to shreds.

"Look, we'll compromise," I said. "I'll pick up the Legos if you put these clothes on for me."

Slowly Joshua's unkempt dark brown hair and freckled face appeared from the further end of the blanket.

"Come on, sweetheart," I said, trying to convey the need for hurry through an air of brisk cheerfulness so that I wouldn't have to begin shouting so early in the day. Slowly he pushed back the blanket and stumbled toward me across an obstacle course of scattered toys.

"Good boy!" I cried, giving him a quick hug before starting to remove the grubby shirt.

Simon took the children out to the car while I threw on a red and white patterned double-breasted dress and slightly high-heeled red shoes. I studied myself in the mirror. I had dark bronze, very curly hair that reached my shoulders, into which, for today, I slipped two red and gold hair clips. Here and there my hair was flecked with grey, but overall it looked shiny and healthy. I applied some eye shadow and a thin coat of mascara to my eyelashes. In general, I wasn't too displeased with what I saw. The lines under my eyes may be more deeply etched every day, but there were no lines elsewhere on my face. I looked surprisingly like a normal forty-ish woman, not at all like a 18-wheeler with no brakes and loaded with dynamite.

I stood on the doorstep watching Simon packing the wedding present into the trunk of the car. He was tall and thin, too thin. His face was gaunt, and these days seemed to be set in a permanent frown (#43, the stoical, down-trodden husband-and-father frown). His hair was badly receding, exposing a wide expanse of white forehead like a chalky clifftop with fault lines. At fifty-two, twelve years my senior, he looked older. He was a quiet, home-loving man, not interested in parties, socializing or climbing career ladders.

All he had ever wanted from life was a job where he could shut himself in a small office with a computer and not have to talk to anyone, and a normal, happy family. He hadn't talked for weeks after Hollie's diagnosis. Heavily pregnant with Joshua, I had lived in an almost silent world with a child who couldn't talk and a husband who wouldn't talk. Eventually he had been prescribed anti-depressants. He was still taking them.

I tried to think of something conciliatory to say.

"I guess we'll have to leave before the mail comes," I said, trying to sound bright and chatty.

"I don't suppose the stupid letter will come today anyway," he said, morosely, without looking up at me.

Simon strapped Joshua and Lisa into the car while I went back to get Hollie's bag of diapers and spare clothes and to lock the front door. I was about to shut the trunk when the mail carrier arrived with a handful of letters. I hesitated, the urge to look through them for the one letter we were awaiting almost irresistible. Then Simon opened his door and called out, "Put them in the bag till later. There's no time now."

"But it's so vital."

"Forget it. Just get in."

Fuming, I shoved the letters in the bottom of the bag and slammed the trunk. Then Simon slammed his door. I climbed into the front passenger seat without looking at him and smoothed out the folds in my dress with deliberately irritating slowness. Then I finally slammed my door. We drove off down the road in silence.

This was the form our arguments had been taking recently. When stress and exhaustion exceeded their normal high-alert levels, snapping at each other was too much effort. Instead we simply conjured this mutual antagonism like some sort of grotesque, shapeless, invisible monster that filled up all the space between us.

I knew I should have felt happy. We were going out, after all, and to a wedding, where I could at least enjoy sumptuous food, look at beautiful dresses, and – best of all – spend time with my best friend, Geraldine, who had just returned from one of her frequent trips abroad. But instead I felt desperately lonely, shut off on my side of the invisible wall of misplaced anger that separated Simon and me. The children were quiet, out of spirits, sensing the tension. The only conversation in the car was between Lisa's dolls.

We had to stop only once on the twenty-minute trip. We had just turned from the highway to a side road when Lisa suddenly let out an ear-splitting scream. Hollie was yanking at Lisa's hair, while Lisa was trying to push her off with one hand and to shield her hair with the other, screaming at the top of her lungs. Joshua also joined in, shouting "No, Hollie, no" and reaching across Lisa to push at Hollie, but his small arms could not even make contact.

Simon stopped the car at the side of the road, leaped out, flung the back door open and grabbed Hollie's hand. He held Hollie's hand with his left hand and gradually prized her fingers off with his right hand, while I comforted the other two, who were now both crying. I could hear Simon rearranging the luggage in the back and lifting Hollie into the rear seat.

Lisa gradually stopped sobbing as he shut the door and walked around the side of the car.

"Look at this," said Simon, and handed me a mouse-sized handful of Lisa's hair.

As we reached Tylney, about twenty miles on the other side of Shalham, I spotted the small church on the hill overlooking the tiny village. We had all begun to feel better. Lisa was dressing one of her dolls for the wedding, and Joshua was building a Lego velociraptor. As Simon stopped the car, just across the road from the church, he reached over and squeezed my hand briefly.

"I'm sorry." "I know you're right about Hollie."

"I love you," I whispered.

"I love you, too."

"I'll take the first shift with Hollie," he said. "You and the kids go and watch the wedding. I'll drive straight to the Windleshire Hotel, where the reception is, because we'll need Hollie's bag at the reception. Then Hollie and I will walk back slowly from there."

We crossed the road and headed toward the church. As we climbed the steps that led up to the churchyard, Lisa holding my left hand and Joshua my right, I was distracted by a curious sight. An old man in a baggy sack-colored coat held together with string, his grey hair long and unkempt, was being helped down the steps by a tall, burly-looking man who had the "don't-mess-with-me" look of a nightclub bouncer. The escort kept his right hand gripped tightly around the arm of the tramp, though he showed no signs of trying to resist. At the bottom of the steps the odd-looking pair turned to the left and disappeared behind the wall.

There must have been two hundred or more people gathered on the gravel path through the churchyard, the gentlemen all in expensive-looking suits and the ladies in the kind of outfits with hats to match that would have come with price tags in the hundreds from exclusive boutiques with French-sounding names. There was a gentle, even rise and fall of polite conversation; guests everywhere, it seemed, had just been introduced to someone they had never met before, or else had bumped into second cousins not seen for twenty years. Then, suddenly, loud female shouts erupted just ahead of us. About four yards away, in the middle of the path, two women began a loud argument, their angry voices cutting across all those placid, muffled conversations, making heads turn in every direction.

I was embarrassed and curious in equal measures. At that point, they must have become conscious that they were making a scene because both women immediately turned down the volume, with the result that none of their words reached me. Gradually all the guests returned to their previous conversations. I alone continued to stare at the two women, partly because they were both very striking-looking women who would stand out in any crowd, partly because one of them was Geraldine.

Geraldine was one of those people who made an impact wherever she went. Usually if I bumped into her at a social gathering (which, in the context of my present non-existent social life, occurred about once a year), I would spot her laughing and talking at the center of a group of admiring men. Today it was another woman she was talking to, a young woman in her early twenties, very beautiful with silky blonde hair that curled lightly on the shoulders of her well-cut jacket, an immaculately made-up face, and eyes like flint. Geraldine had a more striking, angular kind of beauty. She had a lovely, almost elfin face, with classic high cheekbones, and she wore her dark hair in a short, almost cropped style that drew attention to her beautiful features. She wore a green and black mini-dress that very few women in their forties could have carried off as well, with a matching green jacket, hat and shoes.

Cautiously I approached them.

"It's all very sad," the young woman was saying, in a brisk, business-like manner. "But there's nothing I can do about it."

"The old man wasn't doing any harm," Geraldine snapped. "You had no right to throw him out. You don't own the church. You could have just let him stay. I don't suppose he would have been there long."

"Mrs. Haughton does not want to run the risk of any trouble on her daughter's wedding day," the young woman countered, curtly. "And that's all I have to say on the matter."

With that, she turned and marched away, smoothly and confidently on the sharpest stiletto heels I had seen for years. Geraldine stared after her, fuming.

Just then, from overhead, came a loud peel of bells from the bell tower. A few people began to make their way around the side of the church to the door. As Geraldine turned, she saw me and immediately came forward to kiss me.

"What was that all about?" I asked.

"That was a very ambitious young woman called Paula Rochelle, who thinks that being ruthless is a sure-fire way of succeeding in life. I felt sorry for the tramp, that was all. He was just standing among the tombstones. He wasn't begging or trying to bother anyone."

"You look stunning," I said to distract her. She looked at me and smiled, the tension lifting from her face.

"I've had two hours to get ready," she continued. "I expect you've had, what, fifteen minutes?"

"Ten."

"And you always look wonderful anyway, Lucy, even without time to doll yourself up. You should have more confidence in yourself. I don't think you have any idea how attractive you are. In fact . . . "

At that moment a woman's booming voice coming from behind us struck across our quiet conversation. I turned and saw the tall, imposing figure of a woman, probably in her mid sixties, in an elegant silk dress, jacket and wide-brimmed, expensive-looking hat, all of the brightest red. She was the only woman in a group of middle-aged men, and though she was not taller than any of them, she dwarfed her companions with her formidable presence. The group seemed to be having an argument about nautical matters.

"Of course the Titanic was found only recently," one of the men was saying, "within the last ten or fifteen years. For about eighty years, since it went down in 1912, no one knew exactly. . . "

"No, no," the woman exclaimed, dismissively. "The Titanic didn't go down in 1912, it was sunk by a German U-boat in 1940."

The men exchanged glances, and one of them timidly began:

"I think it's quite well known that . . . " but the woman cut in loudly, "We're about to go into the church. I'd better check that everything's going according to plan." Then she marched off, her red shoes gleaming from toe to enormously high heel in the bright autumn sunshine.

"Who's that?" I asked Geraldine.

"Bella Haughton. She's the mother of Philippa, the bride, as you've probably guessed from her spectacular outfit. That young woman you just saw, Paula Rochelle, works for her."

"I've heard Bella Haughton's name before. Not just in connection with the wedding, I mean."

"She's very busy on the city council. A very powerful person. They say she'll be mayor next year."

The crowds around us were thinning as people began to enter the church. The usher directed the children and me to a pew about half way down. Geraldine dashed up and down the aisle exchanging kisses and brief greetings with many of the guests.

"Why isn't Geraldine sitting down with us?" Joshua asked.

"She knows almost everyone," I said, smiling at him. "She's worked in most of the local companies at some time, sorting out their computer problems. And she's just been abroad for a few months, so she hasn't seen her friends for a while."

Like all Geraldine's friends, I accepted her absences during her business trips abroad as just a normal part of life. People who knew Gerry well never blamed her for the "eat, drink and be merry for tomorrow we die" manner in which she lived her life. Problems to do with her family and her past had ruled out a conventional home life for Geraldine, and she had accepted this misfortune not just philosophically, but almost with open arms.

I could see David, the bridegroom, standing in front of the steps to the sanctuary with his best man, looking restless and self-conscious. As the organ chords announcing the bride's arrival reverberated across the pews, he straightened and faced forward stiffly, as if afraid to look around. Geraldine scurried along to our pew and sat down next to me.

The bride walked slowly up the aisle on the arm of an elderly gentleman, who might have been an uncle or cousin, her father having died many years before. They made an ill-matched couple. Philippa was very slight with a thin, pointy face rather like a sparrow, whereas the gentleman giving her away was tall and broadly built.

"She doesn't look very happy," Geraldine whispered.

It was true.

"It's probably the strain of making sure she got here on time, that all the arrangements work out okay," I whispered back.

"Hmm. I think it's more than that."

"Why is she marrying him, then?"

"Because she's afraid she won't find anyone else."

I looked at Philippa. I had never met the girl, but even to a stranger like me, she looked apprehensive, even anxious. As I watched her walk down the aisle, the recent altercations and hostile silences with Simon fresh in my mind, I was dazzled by a sudden insight. Simon had told me that Philippa's father had died years and years ago, when his children were very young. And here she was marrying a man twenty years her senior. Simon was twelve years my senior; had I been looking for a man to fill the role of wise, patient, benevolent adviser that my own father had never occupied? To complicate matters further, Simon had been married before. Had he wanted a quiet, undemanding, stay-at-home wife to replace the flighty, disloyal one? Had we both tried to manufacture roles for each other that didn't fit?

"Who's happy, anyway?" I said, peevishly.

"Not you, evidently. Another row?"

"Yes."

"I'm sorry."

"It's just surface bickering," I added quickly, unwilling to appear to criticize Simon.

"Try not to blame yourself, Lucy. Drop a thousand-ton bomb on any marriage and people will get crushed. You're still suffering from the fallout."

"Well, when do we start rebuilding?"

"Good question."

The vows were exchanged in a quiet, nervous manner, and we sang a hymn. As the register was being signed, Lisa announced loudly that she needed the bathroom. "It's almost over," I whispered, "can you wait?"

The bride and groom walked slowly down the aisle, Philippa smiling slightly more now, and David staring at the ground.

As always at weddings, I had a lump like a cricket ball in my throat. To say that I am emotional is an understatement. I am reduced to tears by the hundred yellow ribbons tied around the old oak tree. I'm a puddle on the floor when Puff the Magic Dragon sadly slips into his cave. So the chances of my remaining dry-eyed at a wedding were negligible. It was partly the sense of occasion, partly that I still hadn't let go of teenage dreams about love and passion and being hit by thunderbolts, even though the cynical forty-year-old me saw them quite clearly as fantasies. I pulled out a tissue and dabbed at my eyes. When I looked up again, I noticed that Geraldine's cheeks were also moist and that she too was quickly wiping her face with a tissue. She glanced at me, and we both burst into laughter.

Bella Haughton walked past our pew at that moment on the arm of David's father, and threw us a thunderous look. Geraldine put her hand up to hide her face while she continued to laugh. I shuddered inwardly. Mrs. Haughton was an awe-inspiring woman, and I was nervous and easily squashed, without Geraldine's take-me-or-leave-me, up-front confidence. I stood there feeling like a five-year-old who has been sent to stand in the corner as the more distant relatives filed out behind the main participants, while Geraldine remained a picture of easy self-assurance.

Simon and Hollie joined us outside the church, where the photographer was badgering guests into awkward groups for the camera. As I looked at Hollie, she opened her mouth and took out a half-chewed mouthful of grass and dropped it on the ground.

"Has she been eating a lot of grass?" Grass consumption was one of Hollie's favorite activities. It was very much a seasonal pursuit, favored during the summer and early autumn. In the winter she switched to carpet padding, and could often be found peeling back the edges of old bits of carpet ready for a good feast.

"She kept grabbing handfuls of it," said Simon, eyeing me warily. "She makes such sudden dives, it's impossible to stop her."

"Oh, I'm quite used to it," I replied. "At least it's not rabbit poo or sheep poo."

Joshua, prowling round the churchyard as a tyrannosaurus, his hands held bent in front of his chest like paws, had made friends with another dinosaur-obsessed boy called Alastair. His mother beamed at me from a nearby group, seemingly as delighted as I was that her son had made a friend. Alastair prowled happily after Joshua while they eagerly discussed whether an allosaurus was bigger than a tyrannosaurus. Lisa, even more amazingly, seemed to be making friends with two of Philippa's small cousins. They were holding hands and beaming at each other while they played "Ring Around the Rosey."

Our friends Jeff and Lynsey knew the way to the reception, so we followed behind them in a group of about twenty people, Joshua and Alastair arguing over whether the allosaurus had lived in the Jurassic or the Cretaceous period, and Lisa and her friends doing little skips as they held hands. Hollie walked holding Simon's hand, and remained meek and placid for almost the twenty minutes it took us to walk to the Windleshire Hotel on the hill at the far side of the village.

The hotel was a frowning Victorian affair, a hodgepodge of Gothic towers and extensions, all built at different times with no thought to the overall effect. Its best feature was the immense and beautiful garden that offered wonderful views over half of Windleshire and Southshire. It sloped away in every direction around the sprawling annexes of the hotel, the expanse of immaculate lawns broken here and there by dominating columns of chestnut, oak and beech trees. The master of ceremonies, a middle-aged man wearing a tail coat, and sporting a mass of thick, black hair, directed us to the garden, where waiters dashed around with trays of sherry and wine.

"It's good you still have a strong base of friends to come back to after your trips abroad," Jeff commented.

"Well, I don't actually," Geraldine replied. "My mother stayed in touch, of course, but the only friend who really did was Lucy." She touched my shoulder lightly and smiled. "A few others wrote, but Lucy was the only really steadfast friend. She's pure gold, isn't she, Simon?"

Simon, jerked out of some distant reverie, was momentarily stumped for a response.

"Yes, er – Lucy is – er – very loyal."

The statement came out as more half-hearted and backhanded than he probably intended, making everyone laugh.

"What Simon means," I said, "is that I'm crabby and bad-tempered – recently, anyway – but if pressed to find a good word to say about me, then, yes, I am loyal." I laughed, but everyone else looked awkward. I hurriedly sipped the last of my sherry.

As we were summoned inside for appetizers, I took my turn watching Hollie. She held my hand peaceably enough, and we walked through the dining room on our way to the garden for a short walk before lunch, passing the bride as she talked to some friends. Hollie reached out, fascinated by the textures and the sheen of the dress's white fabric. I grabbed her hand before she could either touch the dress or try to climb on the bride's shoulders, as she sometimes liked to do even with people she didn't know. To my surprise, her hands were fairly clean.

"No, you can't climb on anyone's shoulders today," I said.

At one o'clock the guests had found their seats at one of the dozen or so large rectangular tables. I managed to finish my appetizer before Hollie became too restless. She wasn't interested in pretty concoctions of prawn and avocado, and though Simon and I gave her our rolls, she had consumed them and was starting to make grabs for other people's rolls long before the main course was served. I finished my glass of wine, knowing it was likely to be the only one I would manage, before taking Hollie's hand and leading her out to the garden.

Back in the wide open space of the main lawn, Hollie did little jumps of joy, then sat down and began picking up small pebbles from the flower bed, fingering them delicately before popping them in her mouth. I knew from past experience she was unlikely to swallow them, and anyway there was no way I could put my fingers in her mouth to remove them without being bitten.

As she seemed peaceful, I wandered away over to the oak tree, where the best views of the surrounding countryside were to be had. When I came back less than a minute later, Hollie was gone. I ran round the corner of the flower bed to find her in another flower bed further down the garden. She had taken her clothes and her diaper off and was sitting among the flowers scooping handfuls of soil into her mouth. Her face and tummy were smeared with dirt, and globules of dirt were stuck in the ends of her hair.

"Oh, Hollie," I said, wearily. Then I took her hand and tried to lift her, but she refused to move, rolling away and giggling uncontrollably.

"Please, Hollie, please, please get up. Up. Up." My voice grew more strident as I became aware of afternoon strollers staring at us wide-eyed. But Hollie rolled herself into a ball, still giggling. I tried to get my hands under her armpits to get her to her feet, but she stayed rolled in a ball.

"Please, Hollie, just this once, do as I ask . . . " I mumbled through gritted teeth, tears of frustration smarting at the back of my eyes. Her giggling got louder. As more people were walking past, conversations died in mid-sentence. I tried to squeeze my hands into Hollie's armpits, but she immediately clenched her arms tight against her sides. Then I tried to pull her back toward me by her arms and her shoulders, but she wriggled away from me farther into the flower bed. She was now almost totally surrounded by rose bushes, their last few withered petals looking so loosely attached that the tiniest breath of wind might dislodge them.

I shuffled forward on to the ground to try to get a better grip. Thorny rose branches snagged at the sleeve of my dress. I painstakingly freed myself without cutting my fingers, only to find that another branch had knotted itself in my hair. This was trickier because I couldn't see what I was doing, and as the thorny twig came away, it pulled several locks of hair with it. This meant I was now trying to reach for Hollie through a matting of hair. Angrily I thrust it behind my ears with my soiled hands, leaving small encrustations of dirt on my cheeks.

I was so angry that the temptation to stand up, confront my viewers and crisply ask for help was almost irresistible. Forty years of training in repressing my feelings and scuttling away from confrontation won the day, but only just. What I had found on several occasions in recent months was that anger made me bold. I grabbed Hollie's right arm with my right hand, thrust my left arm under her chest and pulled her back toward me with one great pull. Then I pushed my hands into her armpits and propelled her to her feet.

"Come on, Hollie, let's go back to the car and get you some clean clothes," I muttered, fixing my gaze like a laser on the ground. I knew what a picture we must make, a frantic woman half leading, half dragging a naked, mud-smeared child. I led her around the side of the building to the car. With one hand clinging onto her arm, I flung the trunk up and grabbed the bag we took everywhere, containing packs of baby wipes and changes of clothes.

I pulled the larger lumps of mud from her hair and brushed as much of the rest out as I could. Then I cleaned her face with three or four baby wipes while holding the back of her head as well as I could in the crook of my left arm to stop her wriggling away from me. I pulled another dress quickly over her head and attached another diaper. This was no easy job, bearing in mind that she was standing up, wriggling all the time, and that the diapers were not quite big enough. Finally, I shook the worst of the mud from the dirty clothes, and whisked them into a spare plastic bag.

Fifteen minutes later, apart from a few small bits of soil still knotted in her hair despite heavy brushing, she was reasonably neat and clean again.

We walked back into the hotel grounds, and oddly enough the first person I saw, several yards away, was the tramp I had seen being manhandled out of the churchyard when we first arrived. This time he was on his own, staring dreamily, without moving, in the direction of hotel dining room.

Hollie and I walked on, no doubt passing many of the people who had been so entertained by her behavior a few minutes before. Once again, I kept my gaze rooted to the ground, refusing to look at them. The virulence of the anger I had begun to feel on such occasions in the past weeks frightened me. I was a quiet, conciliatory person who always tried to see the best in people. Or at least I had been until this embittered harridan had taken up residence a few months before, like Voldemort in the back of Professor Quirrell's head. "Let them go back and titter about us in their comfortable, tidy homes," the Dark Lord muttered from the back of my skull. "I defy any of them to cope any better."

Eventually Hollie settled for a while, pulling the heads from the fuchsias in an immaculate border. I sat on the ground near her, knowing I should stop her, but not ready to fight worse battles. After we had sat there for a few minutes, hunger drew me back to the dining hall, from where I could hear the swelling murmur of conversation and occasional shouts of laughter.

In the dining room the main course had been mostly eaten, but Simon had loyally saved my plate for me.

"Where's Hollie?" he asked, as I picked up my plate of almost cold turkey, potato and broccoli.

"Outside, pulling the heads off the best flowers. I'm going right back out."

"I'll take over in ten minutes."

I moved along a few yards to watch Joshua and Alastair racing toy cars along an empty table in the far corner of the room, giving shouts of excitement when a car either won or shot off the table at an extraordinary angle. Lisa and her two new friends were sitting in a little huddle in the corner of the room playing with Lisa's dolls, which Simon must have gotten from the car. I could have stood and watched Lisa all day. It was such a joy to see her flushed, animated expression in place of her usual pensive, introspective one, but I couldn't leave Hollie for another second.

As I carried my plate back along the aisle to the garden door, a buzz of activity at the center table drew my attention. The magnificent three-tiered wedding cake had just been wheeled in and was now being positioned ceremoniously on a small table covered in a magnificent lace tablecloth in front of the bridal party. The master of ceremonies was talking to the groom and to Philippa's uncle. Then he turned, clapped his hands and said:

"And now, ladies and gentlemen, quiet, please." The master of ceremonies paused, partly waiting for the guests to fall silent, partly trying to build suspense. But in that brief moment, my well-attuned ear caught the sound of scuffing footsteps at the second garden door. Hollie – fully dressed, thankfully, but with brown hands and a mud-smeared face – was skipping down the path from the garden door to the central table. She was a good ten yards from me, and the space between us was barricaded with tables. The aisles between tables were blocked where guests had pulled their chairs out to chat to guests at other tables. Unless I jumped and ran across the tables – which I was on the brink of doing – I had no way of reaching her.

"I now give you the bride's uncle," concluded the master of ceremonies, unaware of the girl dancing ever nearer down the aisle.

"Simon!" I yelled, instantly aware of the pale ovals of a surrounding sea of faces all turned in my direction.

Simon, whose table was only four yards from Hollie, leaped to his feet and began pushing through the lines of guests. Hollie was halfway down the aisle now, giggling loudly.

"Can you please stop her!" I yelled, looking at the people who sat a foot away from her. They looked from me to Hollie, then to each other, and back to me again, mildly curious, each waiting for someone else to respond first, comfortably certain that what was happening had nothing whatever to do with them.

"Oh God," I moaned.

Simon was still several feet away, and the guests who barred his way, stupefied with wine and rich food, did not easily move out of his way. He had to stop to ask each person individually if they could let him through. At this point I could see Geraldine, running from the other side of the room.

I threw my plate on to the nearest table, brushing someone's shoulders to do so. Faces turned toward me, and a male voice called an indignant "Hey!," but I was already running back toward the door I had entered by, down the outside path and in through the door Hollie had used. I ran with no thought to how absurd I must look, my shoes clattering on the parquet floor, one of my hair slides flying off to the side of me. There was no time to be anything more than distantly aware of the sick lurch of horror in my stomach, or to notice that the pockmarked appearance that the room had acquired was created by the throng of gaping mouths that surrounded me. The air of suspense, solemnity and expectation created by the commanding tones of the master of ceremonies, and the consequent interruption of a hundred conversations, lasted just another few seconds. Then the sight of a wild, mud-spattered child and an equally wild-looking woman pounding after her just yards from the bridal table and the impressive wedding cake caught the attention even of those at the far side of the room.

I kicked off my shoes and made a lunge for Hollie, but she was already climbing on the table inches from the cake. A second later I felt a pain like a vast slap across my thighs, though I was only half aware of it, as I threw myself forward on tip toes to try to reach her. The horror I felt was so intense that it seemed to propel me sideways into an alternative universe, a caricature world where my warped vision took in faces so misshapen and contorted with rage that they looked quite alien, and where all sounds meshed together in a grotesque cacophony of bellows and shrieks.

When my vision righted itself, Hollie was already sitting down on the top tier of the wedding cake. What followed had the surreal, timeless quality of a dream. It seemed to take about five minutes for the thick case of icing to crack under Hollie's weight, but in reality it must have been no more than a second. The pillars holding the top two layers slid gracefully sideways, and the three tiers collapsed together with a soft thud. Aware of her throne disintegrating around her, Hollie grabbed at the white iced sides with her muddy hands in an attempt to hold herself steady.

I was distantly aware of the pandemonium behind me. I lunged again, caught Hollie's arm and managed to pull her down on to the table. She fell awkwardly on her side and gave a whimper of pain.

The cacophony had changed to a medley of loud, accusing voices and horrified laughter as people took in the awfulness of what had happened. I was dimly aware of figures moving closer on the other side of the table. Grabbing her left arm with my right hand, I half pulled, half lifted Hollie to the floor, but as I did so, she wriggled away and rolled into a ball under the table. I tried to grab one of hands, but they were too slippery. She evaded me, shifting to the other side of the table where she quickly rose to her feet.

The figures on the other side of the table bellowed "How dare you?" and "Stop there!," while not daring to take a step toward this wild-looking creature. I ducked under the table on all fours and flung my arm at Hollie's foot, but she was adept at escape and side-stepped, giggling. As I climbed out on the other side, Hollie danced away from me, but she had stopped giggling.

Frightened by the loud bellowing and incomprehensibly distorted faces, Hollie looked around for comfort and noticed the beautiful, silky fabric she had wanted to run her hands over earlier. I saw the realization of what was about to happen hit the bride just a second too late. Within seconds, Hollie had grabbed her, and her mud- and cake-smeared hands were all over the white expanse of elaborate dress material as she fought to reach the bride's shoulders.

Chapter Two

"You are clearly insane."

Bella Haughton, the bride's mother, stood on the threshold of the first-floor hotel bathroom where Geraldine and I were bathing Hollie, her gaze singeing my cheeks and my forehead. With her red dress and flaming cheeks, she resembled a red-hot coal. I even had the impression that smoke was blowing from her nostrils.

"I would like to hear what explanation you can offer," she said, her formidable face and grey-streaked hair quivering.

I had just lifted a large towel from the heated towel rack. I hugged it, savoring the soft, warm feel of the material against my neck and chin. My thought processes ran helter-skelter through the crumbling mansion of my brain, throwing up lids, flinging open doors, scouring shelves for the right words. I knew I would never find them. Reluctantly, I pulled my head away from the towel.

"What can I say? I am utterly devastated," I said, with complete honesty. "I have never been so mortified in my life. I am so, so sorry. I only left Hollie for a minute, because I'd missed my lunch and I was starving. But she does these things in seconds."

"A wickedly naughty child like that should be smacked and sent to bed," said Mrs. Haughton, pursing her lips.

I took a deep breath. "Hollie has autism."

"I'm not interested in all these modern excuses for bad behavior," snapped Mrs. Haughton. "She looks perfectly all right to me."

I felt infinitely weary. "You can't see autism. It's not like Down's Syndrome; there's no outward physical sign."

"Well, you should be minding her better."

I looked away from the woman's mean, vindictive face and stared instead at the bathroom door, knowing there was no point in even beginning to explain.

"I just want you to know," she went on in a tight voice, "that you have ruined what should have been the happiest day in my daughter's life and the happiest day of my life. We have dreamed of this day for years . . . "

On and on she went. I stared at the bathroom door, noticing the chips and flakes of paint, the overpowering whiteness of it, till I became mesmerized and my vision started to blur. When she had finished, I turned, forcing myself to meet her gaze, and repeated, "I am just so, so sorry."

"Well, that's hardly going to make up for it," she said, her voice rising unpleasantly. "I want you to take your child and leave immediately."

"We shall, as soon as we've dried and dressed her," I said, quietly.

"Good." She turned and walked away.

I buried my face in the towel. I felt exposed. I felt raw. My family, I myself, had become the butt of other people's derision. To have walked down the street naked would have been, on the whole, less embarrassing. In fact, I felt as if my naked body, with all the imperfections that I tried constantly to hide, had been blown up to giant proportions and festooned around the room. People, everywhere, had seen and tittered.

There were occasional milliseconds of respite over the next few minutes when I would think that there was just a chance that the ocean of shame would one day recede, and that I would eventually recover, but then fresh tidal waves of embarrassment and misery would crash over me once more. Film sequences of deluded ways of escape played briefly in my head. We could move. I could become a hermit. I could get a job, work twelve hours a day and never see anyone, and Simon could be the one who stayed at home. I wished there was some shop where I could go to buy mind armor, self-esteem, a strong inner glow of mental well-being that would stay the same, strong and warm and bright, whatever happened around me. Then I wouldn't care what they all thought.

Geraldine took the towel from me. I lifted Hollie from the sink and Geraldine wrapped her in it.

"I'm sorry you had to put up with that on top of everything else," she said, putting her hand on my arm. "You'll never get someone of that age, who's so totally set in their ways, to understand what the problem is."

"No," I agreed. I felt faint and leaned back against the wall, closing my eyes.

"I hope I never have to see that woman again."

"You won't," Geraldine assured me. "I can't think of any possible way in which you would ever need to deal with her again."

Briefly reassured, I pulled clean clothes out of the bag, and Geraldine held them up to me one-by-one for me to dress Hollie. As I dug around in the bag to locate the bulging sack of dirty clothes, my hand brushed a sheaf of papers.

"Christ! The letters!" I cried, and pulled them out. There were two bills and an autism charity newsletter. The fourth was a large official-looking brown envelope with a Shalham postmark. With an icy, panicky feeling I realized it was almost certainly the letter Simon and I had been awaiting for months.

"Is that it?" said Geraldine, taking the dirty-clothes bag from me and tucking Hollie's mud- and cake-smeared clothes inside it.

I held the letter delicately in both hands. I could not bring myself to open it. I turned it over and put my thumb under the envelope flap, ready to rip it open. In a few seconds I would be exulting in the shiny new future before us. Or I would be lost.

Months ago when Petheril School for children with autism had said Hollie's autism was too severe and they could no longer cope with her, we had applied to the board of education for a boarding school placement for her. In order to learn the most basic skills, Hollie needed consistent, patient teaching every waking moment of the day. Teaching her to eat with a spoon rather than with her fingers, for example, had been a painstaking process that had involved Simon or me sitting at her side throughout every meal with our hand keeping her hand clutched round the spoon; every mealtime, every day for a year. Hollie needed teachers and caregivers who worked in shifts, coming in fresh morning, evening and night to the task of teaching her in a consistent way how to say "hello," how putting on underpants had to come before putting on trousers, and so on. She would learn little, if anything, from brittle, demoralized parents who had come to the end of all their resources.

She needed space, too; exercise calmed her. A school with a gym and a swimming pool and large playing fields where all her excess energy could be burned off was our ultimate dream. But herds of pink, round snorting creatures with curly tails would be flailing muddy trotters between fluffy clouds the day we found a school like that.

I had spent many weeks the previous spring compiling a detailed report explaining the reasons for our request. Since the early summer I had been waiting for the reply, rushing out hopefully any morning that I heard a satisfactorily heavy-sounding thud of mail on the doormat.

The letter had the address of the special education office at the top, together with the printed title "Director: Roger Stevens." The brief letter was from his assistant director, Miss Walsh – the lady I had sparred with yesterday. It said that the department had reviewed Hollie's case, following the decision by Petheril School that her disabilities were too severe for her to remain there, and produced a draft statement of her educational needs, which was enclosed. I grabbed at the pamphlet labeled "draft statement" and turned to the all-important final paragraph, which named the proposed new school. There was no mention of boarding school. Instead the name of Browns School, a local nonresidential school had been typed there, a school with no specialty in autism, a school that took children with every type of disability.

Any remaining sense of having even a vestige of control over my life vanished. Browns School would baby-sit Hollie for six hours a day, after which she would be back home, more frustrated, more hyperactive than ever, to let off steam by swinging from the curtains and sweeping clocks and vases off shelves. I felt as if I were stepping on a sycamore leaf and hoping it would carry me safely across a raging torrent. I wanted to cry but I couldn't. Geraldine snatched the letter and read it.

"Don't let this knock you down, Lucy," she said. "You've plenty of fight in you. You need all of that now. You always said you would request a due process hearing if this happened. That's what you've got to do now."

I nodded, incapable of speech.

"I'll introduce you to a friend of mine, Joel Warnock. He's a financial consultant. You said you would need a top lawyer and other professional expert witnesses if this happened. He can arrange a loan to help you pay for them all."

I was only dimly aware of her words. The walls of the bathroom, Hollie's happy face, Geraldine's grim, determined one, had all dissolved into a watery, formless chaos.

"Do you think they hurried up this decision because of your visit yesterday?"

"No. I think the decision must already have been made, but she couldn't bring herself to tell me face-to-face." I paused for a moment. "Where's Simon?"

"Come on, we'll go and find him."

Geraldine and I walked, one on each side of Hollie, each holding one of her hands. Geraldine carried the bag in her other hand. We found a back staircase so that we could avoid other guests, and in a minute we emerged into the bright sunshine at the entrance to the hotel parking lot.

Simon was standing by the car with Joshua and Lisa, talking to Jeff. I walked up to him, clutching the letter in my hand, unable to speak. He turned and saw me crying. Anger flashed across his face.

"Oh, for God's sake," he muttered. Then he saw the letter. He reached out and took it. He read it. The anger drained from his face. All other feeling drained from his face too. I took his limp hand in mine and squeezed it, but he didn't respond. I glanced round and saw Jeff strapping Hollie into the rear seat with the bag of clothes and Geraldine fitting Lisa into her seat belt.

Simon climbed into the driver's seat without a word. As I slid into the passenger seat next to him, Geraldine bent down and squeezed my arm. "I'll call you," she said.

Simon turned the key in the ignition, put the car in reverse and pulled backwards out of the parking space. He was a careful, thoughtful driver, but, as we shot forward to the head of the drive and turned right on to the main road, he crashed the gear shift from second to third, and we careered all the way to the first major intersection at almost twice the speed limit. Whenever I dared to glance at him, his expression was the same. His jaw jutted forward in a grim, set manner; his eyes looked glazed, empty.

On the highway, he veered rashly from lane to lane. It was as he cut too sharply from the fast to the slow lane prior to taking the next exit that I cried out, "Watch out for Hollie." I could hear the bags in the back falling on her, seated alone in the rear seat.

"Me? Me watch out for Hollie?" he cried in a choked voice. "It was your turn to watch Hollie back there, so why couldn't you damn well do it? I took my turn in the churchyard."

"I'm sorry, I only took my eyes off her for a few moments. I was starving . . . "

"What a bloody catastrophe!"

I was silent while I searched for words.

"Look, you know as well as I do that it's impossible to watch her every second. We need help, we've got to have help . . . "

"Well, there's not going to be any help now, as you know." He glanced at me, then snapped, "Oh, for God's sake, crying's not going to help. We've just got to – got to . . . "

But what we were going to do next obviously evaded him too, for he never finished the sentence.

During the rest of that terrible drive home, and for the early part of the evening, Simon and I said almost nothing to each other. The events of the day were so appalling that after a while I could not believe they had actually happened. I experienced an unreal, set-apart feeling, as if everything was occurring at a distance from me.

Unfortunately that numbness came all too quickly to an end.

Simon read Joshua and Lisa the first chapter of *Harry Potter and the Chamber of Secrets*, then went up to his study to work on some business program on the computer. Overtired, Joshua and Lisa played loud games with each other in their bedroom for about half an hour, then began bickering and snapping. Within ten minutes, however, they were both asleep, slumped across their blankets with an undergrowth of plastic dinosaurs, dolls and dolls' clothes all round them. Hollie would be awake till at least midnight, but I put her in her bedroom at about eight o'clock as I always did, with her special gate in place, so that we could keep her in her room while still being able to check on her constantly.

I washed the dinner plates and cleaned up the kitchen and the family room, and all the time Hollie was at her gate, rattling the bars, reaching her arm out to grab me when I went past. I brought her drinks, toast, an endless supply of chips and crackers, but everything I offered her she threw on the ground. Three times she removed her clothes and her diaper and urinated on the bed. The third time, at five to midnight, as I was changing her sheets, I said to her, "You'd better not do this again, Hollie. I've got no more clean sheets."

Then, with an icy flash of realization, I saw that this was how I was going to be spending the rest of my life now that boarding school for Hollie was ruled out. Every day she was bigger and stronger and harder to carry to the dinner table or the car. Every night she was awake for longer. How would we cope when she was twelve or fourteen? More panicky still, how would we cope when we were fifty-five or sixty?

I replaced her special gate, added the wet sheets to the overflowing laundry basket and walked into the family room. Then I turned the lights off, opened a window and looked out into the dark garden and the scattering of stars in the sky. For months I had had the feeling that I was living on the margins of life. Something would have to change soon, or I would go out of my mind. Some good news had to come from somewhere, or I would do something awful.

I made Simon some hot chocolate, poured myself a brandy and sat in front of part of a late-night movie on television. At one thirty I went to bed, knowing I was too keyed up for sleep. When I eventually dropped off, my sleep was disturbed and intermittent. I dreamed I was going down a large flight of steps toward a dark tunnel in the midst of a crowd of grey-suited, blank-faced people, a crowd so tightly packed I could hardly breathe. All around me I was jostled by knees, elbows, people's shoulders digging into mine. I kept being shoved from behind and crashing forward into the grey overcoated backs of tall men in front. I felt hemmed in, desperate for air, longing to float up and away. But the sky was rapidly disappearing behind us as the crowd jostled me down into the darkness of the tunnel.

Suddenly I found I was screaming, but no one was responding or apparently even hearing me. I screamed until I was so submerged in the crush of grey, blank-faced people that I no longer had air enough to scream and could only stare upwards and backwards at the one, tiny, rapidly disappearing speck of sky.

The following day Simon took Hollie up to the park for a long walk to try to work off some of her boundless energy. Depression settled on me like a physical weight. I had to force myself to shower and to make the children's breakfast. Even brushing my teeth was an effort. It was as if the carpets and floorboards had rotted overnight and I had to wade everywhere in thigh-deep mud. I brought the Duplo train set down from the attic and helped Joshua and Lisa piece it together so that they could make the most of the time before Hollie came home and dismembered it.

Geraldine stopped by briefly. She said she had come to have coffee with me to try to lift my spirits, but within five minutes she left, commenting that she had thought of something else she could do that would be more helpful to us. An hour later she called and said she had been to see Joel Warnock, the financial consultant friend she had mentioned the day before. He had cleared a space on his calendar and could see me at his office at half past nine in the morning.

Geraldine was stern with me. "You've got to keep fighting, Lucy."

"I haven't the slightest glimmer of fight left, Gerry."

"Well, find it. Don't just lie down and let them steamroller over you. Do what you always said you would do if this happened. You request a due process hearing. You build a case. You get experts to assess Hollie and write reports. You can win. You will win."

"Gerry, I can't even face walking to the freezer to find fish sticks for the children's lunch."

There was a momentary silence on the other end of the phone.

"Lucy, you're not letting go, and I'm not letting go of you. Remember all those times when we were in our teens and twenties and I thought I would die? Do you remember?"

"Yes, I remember." Most of the members of Geraldine's family had died early deaths from a ghastly inherited disease, and when she was younger, Geraldine had been sure that she would be one of them. Now that she had reached her forties, it looked as if she was safe.

"Well, you never allowed me to mope. You galvanized me into life on many occasions. It's that way you have of trying to find a funny angle to even the worst things that happen; it's what I loved most about you when I first got to know you.

I'm going to do the same for you now. I'm going to kick your butt until you start to move. Do you want me to come and pick you up and drive you to Joel's office tomorrow?"

"No, I'll go. I promise."

"Good. I'll call you afterwards and see how you got along."

Hollie spent most of the afternoon having four or five baths. I never knew whether to be pleased or sorry when she was in the bathtub. At least she could be checked on easily, and, once the toilet paper and shampoos were removed, only limited mess-making potential remained. She might lie happily for ten minutes or so without needing attention of any sort. Other times she kept turning the hot tap on, and I would speed in and out of the room every few minutes, turning it off so she didn't scald herself, only to hear her turning it on again when I was barely halfway back down the hall. Sometimes we didn't hear her when she turned the taps on, and I would come in to find Hollie standing astride the brimming bath with the bathroom carpet flooded with two inches of water.

That night it was harder than ever to shut my mind off so that I could fall asleep. Requesting a due process hearing was now a necessity. But what if we lost? I wandered through the house in the early hours unable to rid myself of this fear. In an attempt to find comfort, I pulled *The Magician's Nephew* off the book shelf. Rereading the Narnia stories, favorites from my childhood, might not solve the problem of my sleeplessness, but it was the best form of night time comfort I could think of even today.

Waking up had been hard on many mornings, but waking up this Monday morning was verge-of-battle hard. I had to force myself out of bed. How many glasses of brandy had I had last night? Too many. My limbs were leaden, my head felt as if it were stuffed with black cotton wool, I had a thudding headache, and my tongue seemed glued to the roof of my mouth.

I fed and dressed the children, handed Hollie over to the bus driver, and then went to the bedroom to try to find some clothes that I could wear for my appointment with Joel Warnock. I went through all the clothes I had worn to work ten years before, and found that either they were too small, or else hopelessly old-fashioned (blouses with shoulder pads, and the like). In the end I settled on a cream roll-necked sweater that looked quite dressy when worn with my one stylish brown-and-black patterned jacket, and black pants.

I took Joshua to school and Lisa to preschool, then drove to the center of Shalham and parked in a multi-story parking garage that Geraldine's map suggested was within a couple of hundred yards of Joel's office.

The offices of the Peterson Warnock Partnership were in a three-story building at the end of a small area lined with immaculate offices. According to their expensive-looking nameplates, most of the businesses seemed to be architects, accountants and attorneys. The floor of the foyer had a pattern of grey, light pink and light-blue paving stones, in the middle of which was a rectangular brick-walled pond with water lilies, gold fish and a fountain. There was not a speck of litter to be seen anywhere.

The gold metal nameplate that read "Peterson Warnock Partnership" was immediately to the left of a varnished mahogany door. I tentatively pushed the door open and entered. To the right was a waiting room with comfortable yellow armchairs. To the left was the reception desk, behind which sat an immaculately groomed secretary. She had gleaming, faultlessly applied makeup and sleek blonde hair tied in a pony tail with a bottle-green clasp that matched her bottle-green,\ double-breasted blouse. On her scrupulously tidy desk I could see neat piles of papers, a computer screen and a telephone.

"Hello, may I help you?" she asked, with professional friendliness.

I told her my name and said, "I have an appointment with

Joel Warnock for half past nine," in a small voice. I felt shapeless and fuzzy in that brisk, orderly environment.

"Please take a seat over there, and I'll see if he's ready for you," she said. She pointed toward the small reception area of yellow armchairs positioned round a glass coffee table covered in magazines.

I walked slowly across the floor, telling myself I should be cultivating a more dignified way of walking, while my shoulders remained rounded and hunched and my ego could have been mistaken for a piece of fluff on the carpet. I proceeded to sit down on the edge of the chair, picked up a woman's magazine, and flicked through it. There were pages labeled "fashion" where broomstick-thin models draped themselves over richly decorated beds and armchairs in eccentric combinations of clothes, then a section devoted to accessories, followed by a feature on new looks for kitchens and bedrooms. I glanced away while I struggled for several seconds to remember what color my kitchen was painted, then I resumed my reading. It was like looking at a catalogue advertising life on Mars. For a few enjoyable minutes I was lost in an imaginary world where in my luxuriously appointed bedroom, I sorted uninterrupted through shelves of belts, scarves and shoes in my large well-organized closet, searching for the perfect match for one of my sleek designer-label suits.

The receptionist returned a couple of minutes later.

"Mrs. Roseman, Mr. Warnock is ready to see you."

I stood up, pulled my sweater straight and patted my hair. The receptionist led me down a wide hallway past a thickly carpeted staircase to a gleaming white door at the end. Then she knocked and pushed the door open. I crossed the threshold and heard the door shut behind me. I was aware of my feet sinking in a thick sandy-colored carpet.

The room was remarkably attractive for an office, business-like but comfortable, spacious and light, with windows on two sides. On a large mahogany desk to the right stood wooden trays of letters and a wooden desk organizer containing pens, pencils, rulers and paper clips. Beyond the desk in the center of the room were four armchairs in a circle surrounding another glass coffee table, overlooked on the left by bookcases that stretched to the ceiling, and on the right by smaller bookshelves that lined the walls as far up as the window. At the end of the room in a small conservatory area, all glass, stood four wicker armchairs, upholstered with large pale-cream cushions.

Standing behind the desk against the sun streaming through the window stood a man, who looked to be in his mid-thirties with classic high cheekbones and a firm, slightly prominent chin. His thick, light brown, rather long hair was brushed to the side, drawing attention to his high forehead. The dark grey pinstripe suit he wore emphasized his considerable height, and he carried himself in a very upright, dignified fashion, with his broad shoulders pulled back. He was gazing straight at me. I stared at him too, partly because he was surprisingly handsome, but mostly because there was something quite appealing about the questioning, slightly amused expression in his eyes. Embarrassed, I glanced away for a moment. When I looked back, he was walking to meet me, holding out his hand.

"I'm very pleased to meet you, Mrs. Roseman," he said. There was just a trace of an Irish accent.

I enjoyed the feel of his large, strong hand enclosing mine as we shook hands.

"I'm pleased to meet you too," I mumbled.

His intense grey-green eyes studied me for a few moments, then he ushered me forward to the armchairs.

"Would you like coffee or tea?"

"Coffee, thank you."

He pressed a button on his telephone and requested two coffees.

I sat down in what I hoped was a dignified manner. I was very conscious of trying to make a good impression. I had been aware before I came that this man could be a huge help to us in our campaign, but suddenly it seemed even more important than ever that I make a good impression on him.

A minute or two later there was a knock on the door, whereupon the receptionist entered carrying a tray made of some light-colored wood and decorated with an immaculate lacy white cloth. She placed it on the table, consulted me on my preferences for sugar and milk, then poured milk from a delicate white jug, and handed me an elegant porcelain cup and saucer. She put another cup and saucer in front of Mr. Warnock, then picked up the tray and left the room.

Finally, Joel Warnock sat down. I was aware of him looking at me as he picked up his spoon and started to stir his coffee. I felt very strongly drawn to look at him, and when he picked up his coffee cup, I risked a glance. After a moment he looked over at me, and I glanced quickly away. We continued to play optical ping-pong like this for several moments.

"Thank you for agreeing to see me so quickly," I said, looking intently at my coffee cup. "I know you fitted me in specially. I – I mean, we – really appreciate it. We are in – well – a very difficult situation. It's hard to know where to begin to explain it."

"That's all right. Geraldine explained about your daughter and about the school district refusing to pay for her education. You sounded as if you needed help urgently. Please explain exactly what you want me to do for you."

"Because our request for Hollie to go to boarding school has been rejected, we need to take our case to the due process hearing. Although this step in itself does not cost anything, to have any realistic chance of winning, we have to pay for expert witnesses either to examine Hollie and write reports or to appear at the hearing and give their assessments of how difficult she is to manage and why she needs this boarding school placement. It can cost £1,000 a day for a top lawyer or expert on these matters to appear at a hearing, and almost as much for an experienced independent educational psychologist. We also have to pay for the time they spend preparing the case. The opinions of these expert witnesses are often what sway the panel at the hearing. To have any realistic chance of winning, we need money to pay them."

"I see. Please write down for me which particular experts you will need to consult, and a very rough estimate of how much you expect them to cost."

I took the pad of paper he offered, thought for a few moments, then wrote down some names and figures. Joel took it from me and studied it.

"I see. So a loan of up to £20,000 would seem to be required.

How much do you feel you could comfortably repay a month?"

"A hundred. Possibly £150. I mean, if we won the case, I could get a job afterwards, which would help. I can't at the moment. No nanny or babysitter would take Hollie."

"Okay." He wrote some more, thought for a few minutes. Then he looked straight into my eyes. My insides shifted slightly.

"Feel assured that I will get you this loan. You can go ahead and make arrangements to consult your experts. I will arrange the loan at a rate that you can repay. I want you to have no worries on that score. I know you have a heavy load to carry, and I am glad to be able to take at least that small burden off you." He paused and added, "Very glad."

I dropped my gaze. I found it difficult these days to look people in the eye, but I knew that it was important that I look at him now. I forced my eyes up to meet his gaze.

"I'm so grateful," I said. "I'm just so grateful." Then I looked down, embarrassed at my own emotion. Gratitude, that's what it was. That was why I was experiencing this strange, fluttery sensation. My insides seemed to expand with it, like warm air in a balloon.

But gratitude alone did not account for it. I fumbled around trying to find the explanation. Recognition came suddenly, as if I had just walked around a corner and bumped into a well-loved friend who'd lived abroad for years. It was joy. Happiness.

"Thank you so much," I mumbled. When I was finally able to look up, he was writing again. He started to speak, without looking up, and I cursed myself for embarrassing him with my display of emotion.

"I'll have my secretary call you when everything is arranged. Then you'll have to come and sign some forms. It might be a good idea if you could give me the names of some of your experts when you've made arrangements with them. It will make the case all the more solid and credible to the businesses I approach."

He put his pad and pen down and stood up.

"Yes, of course." I stood up, too. As I turned to follow him toward the door, an idea struck me.

"There's just one thing I haven't asked," I said. "How much will you charge?"

"I won't be charging a fee," he said. I stared at him. He met my gaze full on. I could feel tears pricking the rims of my eyelids. He looked down.

"I'm a father. I have two sons of my own. There but for the grace of God, and all that."

"I can't thank you enough," I said. He was busy with the pad of paper on the desk, so I took advantage of the opportunity to look at him. He was extremely handsome, in quite an unusual way. I badly wanted to know more about him.

"How old are your sons?"

"Twenty-one and sixteen."

"You must have been married young."

"Too young. They have different mothers. Neither of my marriages lasted."

We both felt slightly embarrassed at this revelation, so when he held out his hand, I shook it without either of us looking at what we were doing.

"Goodbye."

"Goodbye, Lucy." I glanced over and caught him giving me a thoughtful look.

I turned, walked forward and pulled the door shut behind me. I passed back along the corridor with a sensation of gliding rather than walking.

My heart felt light as a sunbeam for the rest of the day. I don't know what inspired me more: the knowledge that this powerful, successful man was going to help us, and that the money we needed to pay in connection with the hearing was almost guaranteed, or the memory of him and of how he had acted toward me.

I had walked almost all the way back to the car before I realized that gratitude and happiness still did not fully account for the buoyant feeling inside me. The aura of loyal, loving unavailability that I had carried successfully for fifteen years had somehow been permeated. I was smitten with this man. I stood stock still beside the car as I absorbed this fact. After a minute or two I opened the door. This is a bit awkward, I thought. I sat down heavily in the driver's seat and slammed the door shut. This is very, very awkward.

By evening the uplifted feeling began to evaporate a little as the Hollie-checking-routine ground me down again. I went to bed just after midnight when Hollie began to look as if she were settling. After tossing and turning for half an hour or so, wondering if I should get up to check if her eyes had finally closed, I fell asleep myself.

Hollie woke at five, and I awoke too. She seemed peaceful, but I still couldn't rest. I listened as her noises – the foot banging on the wall, the crashes as the toys got flung off the top shelf – gradually quieted. I lay there for a long time afterwards, knowing I should get up to check if she had gone to sleep again, knowing I had no chance of going back to sleep myself unless I did check, but still unable to move from the suspension-bridge weight of exhaustion.

My memories of Joel began to seem absurd. He was simply a kind man who wanted to help us, and it showed just how out of touch with reality I had become that I had even for a moment blown my straightforward business meeting with him into anything more significant.

Eventually I forced myself upright and into my slippers. I flopped across the bedroom and along the hall. By now Hollie was fast asleep, wrapped in her blanket on top of the dresser. As I stared into her room I could see the grey dawn through the gaps in the curtains. I didn't want to see it. Today would be a repeat of yesterday, and tomorrow would be the same, and the next day, and the next.

Back in the bedroom, I found Simon awake, staring at the ceiling.

"What are we going to do?" he said.

I lay down next to him and took his hand.

"We request a due process hearing."

"How long will that take?"

"We'll probably be given the date in three months or so."

"I suppose it will cost a lot of money."

"All the people I know who have won their cases have spent thousands, I'm afraid. You have to pay for lawyers and experts such as psychologists to appear and give their opinions."

"We have to do it. We're not living at the moment." As he spoke, he turned on his side, away from me.

For a few minutes we both lay, silent. It hadn't occurred to me before that he, too, was at the limit of what he could take.

"I suppose we'll have to borrow through this friend of Geraldine's. My parents have said they can't afford to help us. So have yours."

"Mr. Warnock said he'll help us as much as he can," I said. "He's not even going to charge us a fee."

I reached across the curve of Simon's back. I couldn't reach his hand. Instead I stroked his arm. He reached up his other hand and held mine for a minute, then let it go.

"There'll still be a loan to repay, however much he helps us," he mused. "We'll be in debt for years to come. We're only just making ends meet now." He pulled himself to a sitting position, stood up and stretched. Then he walked over, parted the curtain and looked out at the dawn.

I contemplated the grey half-light and thought, there's nothing like facing the earliest moments of a new day when you've hardly got the energy to get through the next half hour. It's a feeling that I imagine must be akin to being on the brink of battle when the only weapons you have are a few sticks and stones. It induces a kind of inspired, lunatic bravado. You want to hurl yourself at the day, but not think about it too much because the odds against you are just too high to contemplate.

I got out of bed and walked over to where Simon was standing. I looked into his face. "It's like you said. We have to do it."

We put our arms around each other and held each other for a long time.

During the rest of the week I sank further into depression. It wasn't just the hopelessness following the determination letter. I felt worse partly because I knew I should be very active, researching the hearing process, contacting experts and autism organizations, and trying to locate other parents who had been through it. I should be throwing myself into all those activities every spare minute. But I wasn't. I couldn't. Just getting Hollie dressed, fed and out to her bus each morning required the most enormous effort. I had to drag myself to preschool and school with the other children every morning, and, in the afternoon, an even more gargantuan effort was required simply to get a meal served.

The following Saturday afternoon Joshua and Lisa wanted to ride their bikes, so I shut and bolted the front gate and carried their bikes through to the front yard so they could ride up and down on our short concrete drive. I shut the kitchen door and the back gate firmly, so that we weren't providing escape routes for Hollie. Then I came back into the house and checked that she was still where she had been a minute before – lying on Lisa's bed – before taking a cup of coffee up to Simon, who was working in his study.

I carried the lunch plates through to the kitchen from the dining table, then looked in on Hollie again. This time she had pried open Lisa's collection of beads and was running her fingers through them, then letting them drop one by one down the side of the bed behind the radiator. I stood on the doorstep, utterly divided. If I stopped her, as the part of me loyal to Lisa knew I should, Hollie would no doubt move on to some even less congenial activity – throwing toys down the toilet or tearing pages out of books. The pragmatic side of me won. I would leave her for now, and pull the bed out and pick the beads up later, when Hollie was in the bathtub or eating a snack.

I put the dishes in the sink, then checked on Hollie. I washed the plates, checked on Hollie; washed the silverware, checked on Hollie; washed the plastic cups, checked on Hollie. Then I began a quick tidying of Hollie's bedroom. I had just finished replacing all Hollie's various building bricks in their different containers in between further frequent checks on her, when there was a knock at the door.

I opened the door, and to my astonishment found Joel Warnock standing there. Unbelievably, he had Hollie firmly by the hand.

"But –" I gaped. "She was dropping beads down the radiator. I only checked on her a moment ago."

"I was driving up the road to leave some forms for you and Simon to read and sign. I found her running in the road, dodging between the cars."

A white haze of horror formed in front of my eyes. "Running around . . . But how . . . In the road. . . I'd just checked on her."

"Could one of your other children have left the door open?"

"Yes," I murmured dizzily. "That must be it."

I ran past him. There was the front gate, with four-foot high vertical wooden bars, still securely bolted. It was almost certain she hadn't climbed out that way. The fence between our front yard and the next-door neighbors' was only two foot high, however. We had raised and strengthened the fence in the back to prevent Hollie from escaping, but as she was never allowed in the front yard unaccompanied, that extra – and very expensive – precaution had seemed unnecessary.

I looked down to the side of the house. The back gate and the kitchen door stood wide open and, beyond them, Joshua and Lisa were playing with a ball in the back yard. I ran forward and pulled the garden gate shut.

Then I dragged myself back to where Joel and Hollie were standing on the front door step.

"You're right. Joshua and Lisa must have left the garden gate open when they brought their bikes back through. They're playing in the back yard now. She must have gotten over that low fence there."

I stared at Joel. Up till now, I had had a sense that I was keeping my grip on things – just. But these occasions when Hollie fell into danger despite my constant vigilance were hurtling my way more and more frequently, making illusory any sense of being in control. Every time these things happened, I would tell myself "things can't get any worse" or "we've turned a corner now and things will start to improve." Such clichés were oddly comforting. They implied other people had been through such times and come out the other side. But things just kept on getting worse.

"I checked on her just a minute ago. I've been checking on her every minute. I always check her every minute."

Joe Warnock looked at me sympathetically.

"I'm not criticizing you. No one in their right mind would criticize you. You can't be vigilant every second. And you can't allow for mistakes others might make, especially children."

I reached forward and took Hollie's hand from him.

"What can I say? 'Thank you' is hardly adequate."

I looked at him, his tall, muscular frame carried in that dignified pose that so clearly conveyed self-assurance and strength of character. Casual clothes suited him even more than the sleek, well-cut suit he had worn on Monday. The striped soccer shirt, black leather jacket and jeans showed off his well-formed, masculine frame. I was momentarily overpowered by a desire to finger his leather-clad shoulders, run my hands down his arms and touch his broad chest. Then reality reasserted itself. What was I, a married woman, a mother, doing fantasizing about this man?

"Thank you," I said, still staring. "Thank you so much." I wondered how he'd react if I added, "You haven't been out of my thoughts since I met you."

I collected myself. "I'm so sorry, I'm being rude. Please come in."

"Just for a minute, then." He stepped over the threshold. "Let me give you these." He handed me a batch of papers. "Maybe you and your husband can look through them and sign them over the weekend. If you drop them back to me early next week, we can get that loan formally processed in a few days."

"That would be wonderful. Thank you."

He looked away. "Well, I know how important it is."

Hollie tugged loose from my hands, and dashed away into the house. I gazed after her.

"Well, I'd better be on my way," Joel murmured.

I wheeled around without thinking and burst out, "Oh no, please, don't go!"

He turned and looked at me. His eyes were glinting. I made an effort to at least appear composed. "Can I offer you a cup of tea? I mean, you've come all this way . . . "

"No, I must go. I have an appointment on the other side of town in twenty minutes."

I forced myself to look into his eyes. "Thank you," I said. "I know you've worked hard for us."

"That's all right. I haven't found it too hard. After all, the incentive was there. You've . . . er," he coughed and looked away. "You've . . . er – both . . . er – been very much in my thoughts over the past few days."

He suddenly turned and walked away from me, without glancing back, as if afraid he'd said too much.

It was almost unbelievable, but this charismatic, handsome, successful man seemed to like me. I refused to be fooled, however, and kept telling myself it was just a slight passing interest, a tiny matchstick flicker that would be gone in the first suggestion of a draught. But I allowed myself to indulge my fantasies for a day or so. Outside, the September nights were drawing in while inside the gloom of hopelessness stretched on without end. Joel was a fantasy, a daydream, but surely I could be allowed that one illusory northern light in the polar winter darkness.

Sunday was a grey day that promised rain, with a biting wind that made it seem more like November. Geraldine called me at nine. "Do you still want to go?" she asked.

We had arranged to take Hollie to the coast for the day. The intention was that Simon would have a chance to unwind a little, and that Joshua and Lisa could have a few hours of uninterrupted play without fear of Hollie drinking their paints or trampling on the train set.

"Yes, let's go," I said firmly.

Hollie loved the beach. She loved wading – wading for Hollie invariably meant head-to-foot saturation. And she loved skipping around on wide expanses of sand, jumping in the waves, and running; plain running. She could run for miles and use up large amounts of her vast reserves of energy. An adult had to run with her, of course, so that she didn't get lost or duck under the waves, but that was a price worth paying for the joy, the calmness and, above all, the tiredness that ensured.

I picked up Geraldine at ten at her luxurious apartment in the center of Shalham. I pressed the buzzer on the outside door, and soon she looked out the windows and waved. A minute later she strolled out the door. Even for a walk on the beach, she looked stylish and well dressed in her favorite ski jacket, padded and very warm, and expensive black jeans. I wore an old pair of corduroy trousers, thick knee-length winter socks and Geraldine's old ski jacket, which I had rescued from a bag of clothes she was taking to a charity shop.

"Thanks for coming," I said, as she strapped herself into the passenger seat.

"There's no need to thank me. I've been looking forward to it. I worked late most nights last week. I can't wait for a breath of sea air."

For the first leg of the trip we discussed Geraldine's work. The roads were clear, we were making good progress, and I felt surprisingly relaxed. So, when the highway crossed into Southshire and Geraldine mentioned a lovely coffee shop she knew in nearby Hursham, I said, "Let's give it a try."

The café was small and cozy. Ferns, spider plants and monsteriosas dangled shiny, healthy looking leaves from plant boxes along the walls, and faded sepia prints of Edwardian gentry standing outside country mansions decorated the walls. Eight or nine wooden tables were laid with white lacy tablecloths and gleaming silver cutlery. An elderly couple were eating tea cakes in the window seat, while a couple with a toddler in a high chair were having coffee and cake at another table. We chose a table by the wall, but away from the plants, where I could sit on the outside of a double seat to discourage Hollie, on the inside, from escaping and running around. Geraldine and I drank cappuccinos and Hollie munched chips and sipped juice.

"So has Joel sorted out the final details of the loan?" Geraldine started.

"He has. There are some forms for us to sign, and I've got some more details to give him as soon as I can – names and addresses of experts, that sort of thing. It's all just to prove that we're honest and above board, wanting the loan to help us with a lawyer for the due process hearing."

"Has he said what his fee will be?"

"He said he won't be charging us."

Geraldine raised her eyebrows. "I thought he might charge only a nominal fee, but I didn't expect that."

"He said he has two kids of his own."

"Yes, he's got two boys from two different marriages. One of them lives in France with his mother, who's French."

"Does . . . er," I paused, trying to find the right tone of mere casual interest. "Does he have a girlfriend?"

"He must. He always has. And there are always others interested in him. That Paula Rochelle is definitely after him. He'll have trouble getting away from her; she's persistent."

"But she's not going out with him at the moment?"

"Not as far as I know. But she's definitely working on it. She wouldn't be right for him, though. He's an extremely complex man. He gives the impression of being very extrovert and sociable and a good laugh – and he is – but I think a lot goes on in his head that most people never see."

I felt as if a clown were juggling flaming torches inside me. There was a question I had to ask, but I had to make it sound part of a normal, casual chit-chat between friends.

"Did you – have you ever, I mean," I mumbled into silence, realizing I didn't sound in the least casual and innocent. Geraldine was looking at me suspiciously. I was saved from awkward questions by Hollie's sudden decision to climb around the back of the seat behind me. In a second she had escaped into the main part of the restaurant and was making a wild dash for the kitchen area behind the cash register.

We reached Limewater Bay on the Southshire coast just before midday and parked in a half-deserted seafront parking lot. While Hollie loved the open air, she felt the cold, so I wrapped her in a vest, thick shirt and fleece as well as her winter coat. We crossed the parking lot, looking around at the little town spreading up the hill to our right, dotted with hotels and guest houses. Clustered on the flat level ground behind us was a further spread of seafront houses, cafés and beach shops, many of which were shut in preparation for the coming winter. There was a piercing wind, and some distance out in the bay thick, grey clouds hung so low that they merged with the battleship-grey sea.

"There's a sea squall about to blow in from the looks of things," I commented, apprehensively.

"Never mind, let's make the most of it while we can," Gerry responded optimistically.

We clambered carefully down the slippery, mossy stone steps to the beach and turned to the left. I stared in amazement. "The tide's a long way out."

"Fall tides," Geraldine reminded me.

A vast expanse of sand was exposed, far beyond the end of all the breakwaters, stretching a hundred yards to the sea to our right, and into the hazy distance down to Fennel Bay a good mile or so away. Hollie kept holding my hand for a while, then she pulled free and skipped a few yards ahead of us. To our right the larger waves crashed on the sands, then became low frothy waves that skimmed farther across the beach, before becoming even tinier flat waves that met, crossed each other, and traveled even farther inland. Some board surfers in wetsuits were riding the larger waves, and farther out windsurfers sped elegantly backwards and forwards. A few family groups flew kites – box kites, and dragon- and bird-shaped kites with magnificent streaming tails – and sand yachters raced backwards and forwards when they caught the wind in their sails.

Geraldine and I talked about Simon and about her various boyfriends. After that we walked in silence. Then we went on to discuss the consultations I was supposed to be arranging with the experts who would help us at the due process hearing, and Geraldine nagged me about making myself get down to calling them. The one important subject that we both skirted was that of the wedding disaster.

The rain held off despite the heavy grey clouds, but as we walked, the fog gradually seeped across the landscape. As the wind died down, the mist settled into every nook and cranny, making everything wet, clammy and oppressive. When finally we couldn't see more than about fifty yards ahead, we agreed it was time to turn back and head for the town.

Turning Hollie around was not so easy, however. She had a fixed idea in her head that we were going in one direction, and she didn't intend to change. I tried to lead her gradually toward the sea, rather than turning her immediately around, so that it wouldn't seem quite so much like a complete change of direction, but each time she turned decisively back to the direction in which we had been headed. When eventually I succeeded in turning her, she took off back down the beach.

"I'll go after her," Geraldine said gently. "Then we'll find somewhere for us all to have lunch."

The drizzly mist seemed more enclosing than ever. Wrapping my coat and my scarf round me tightly, very slowly, I walked the few yards to the sea. I bent down and watched the water rippling round the sides of my boots. I took my gloves off and let the wavelets run over my hands. The shock of the icy cold was a momentary distraction.

The mist had lifted slightly, so I could now see the grey wavelets skimming across the sand all the way down to the beachfront shops and cafés. I watched the tombstone-grey waves surging relentlessly across the sands. There was the slightest suggestion of movement in the air. A breeze was picking up and pushing the mist back, out to sea.

In a small, half-empty beachfront café to the west of town, the three of us ate fish and chips and drank hot, cheering tomato soup at a table by the window.

"The trouble with being forty," Geraldine said, "is that suddenly all one's opportunities seem greatly reduced."

"My opportunities certainly seem reduced."

"I suppose I should – well, I do feel grateful to still be alive," said Geraldine.

"What particular opportunities are you thinking of?"

"Well, I suppose you won't believe I'm finally saying this, but it would be quite nice to get married. Or at least to want to get married. But the trouble is, I can't imagine ever wanting to marry anyone. I mean, to get married you need to feel thrilled to the core with someone, as if you can't possibly imagine life without them."

"How do you know the feeling exists?" I asked.

She looked rather shocked. "Well, didn't you and Simon – ?"

I answered her question before she could finish asking it. "It's hard to see my relationship with Simon clearly. I love him very much. He gives me a quiet, calm sense of security; in fact, he is the center of my life. I know I'd be lost without him, both on an emotional and a practical level."

"I suppose you're too busy cleaning up to have time or energy for great passion."

"That's it in a nutshell."

We both laughed.

"Seriously, though," I added. "Much as I love him, it's always felt a very – well, domestic-relationship, even in the early days. It would be nice to feel the sort of passion that you hear people talk about just once, before I die."

"Heavens, Lucy, what's brought this on?"

Geraldine was looking at me, stunned. I was on the brink of telling her what was in my thoughts. And then Hollie, reaching out for one of the collection of plastic toy bricks I had put on the table for her, knocked her glass of juice over. Crimson liquid washed over the table, then streamed over the sides, soaking our knees.

"Time to go, perhaps," I said, reaching in my backpack for a wad of paper towels.

Geraldine called the next afternoon.

"So what have you done today?" she asked, pointedly. "How many experts have you called? How many autism organizations have you consulted?"

"Er, well, to be precise . . . "

"None?"

"Exactly."

"What on earth is the matter with you?"

How could I begin to explain my lethargy to someone who had never experienced it? I dragged myself to school and preschool in the morning, and I plodded like a lump of blubber between my endless chores each evening, fueling myself with brandy. In spite of Joel and his kindness – as the days had passed, though I couldn't stop thinking about him, I had seen quite clearly that he was simply being kind – there seemed not the slightest spark of hope that we could ever win.

"Gerry, we will never – we can never win. Us, two people, two parents whose every waking moment is taken up with one autistic child, how can we take on and win against a whole education system that can marshal armies of lawyers, psychologists and experts at no personal expense? It's crazy to even contemplate it. I just don't have the fight any more."

"Well, it looks as if I'm going to have to play the Arab, then."

"What on earth are you talking about?"

"The Arab who lights the fire under the exhausted camel. I heard it on a documentary once. In the desert, when a camel is too exhausted to carry on and collapses on the ground, a trick some Arabs use is to light a fire underneath it. That makes it get up."

"I'm not surprised."

"Well, I'm lighting a fire under you now. I've located an independent educational psychologist, someone who's well recommended. Her name is Beth Johnson. She's had a cancelation for this Wednesday, and I've made an appointment for you to see her. She lives in Hatfield. Do you want me to take you?"

"No, I'll go."

The next afternoon, Tuesday, my parents stopped by. They only lived about fifteen miles away, just over the border in Southshire, but we saw them rarely. My father had always been a very distant figure. He was a university professor in history, and I had grown up close to a university campus in the east of England. Acknowledged expert he might be, but he had never been much good at actually teaching his subject. He enjoyed hiding away in his study and writing his books, but he hated giving lectures, and, most of all, seminars and tutorials.

My parents were in our area on a tour of antique shops. They loved antiques and spent much of their time poring through the shelves of antique shops, looking for objects of interest. My father said, as always, a quick hello to the children, and then wanted to be talking about his subject, his studies, or what he had found in the day's round of the antique shops. He did not have the patience or the interest to listen to the children. My mother enjoyed them, but in small doses. Like Simon's parents, they were both uncomfortable around Hollie and had as little to do with her as they could.

"The local school district has turned down our application for Hollie to go to boarding school," I told them, after we had sat down with our cups of tea.

"What a shame, dear," said my mother, settling her plump body comfortably in the armchair and patting her little grey bun to make sure it was still securely in place.

"It's a disaster. I spend my time watching her or clearing up after her. It's affecting the other children, quite apart from driving Simon and me mad."

"We know it's very difficult for you, dear."

"Last night I spent two hours cleaning feces from her bedroom. I had to clean not only the bedclothes, the toys and the floor, but the curtains and the ceiling."

My mother looked at me blankly. "It'll be a good thing when you get a new school arranged for her," she said, looking very comfortable and content.

There was simply no way of making people understand. In fact, my attempts to explain and make them understand only served to make me feel even more distant and shut off from those around me.

Time to stop flogging the dead horse. Time for a complete change of subject. I took a sip from my mug of tea and asked brightly, "So what bargains have you found today, then?"

My mother instantly came to life.

"We found an eighteenth-century vase and a silk Victorian screen for only fifty pounds."

My father added: "There's an antiques fair at a hotel in Shalham next week, so we may be down this way again then."

"Look at this, dear."

My mother pulled a package wrapped in brown paper out of her large all-purpose bag.

My heart sank. They had actually brought a valuable, no doubt breakable, item into our house – the House of a Hundred Daily Breakages.

"It's lovely," I said quickly, as she unwrapped a shiny, flowery vase. "Perhaps best put it away. You never know what might happen with Hollie around."

Joshua was standing at my elbow, looking at me nervously. "Mom, Hollie's taken her diaper off. There's poo all over the floor in her room."

The number of incidents like this, involving mess and destruction, was growing every day. The feeling I had had, that I was just about keeping on top of it, was being gradually eroded. I felt swamped. Even though I cleaned and disinfected Hollie's room whenever an incident like this occurred, I was starting to feel that her room was a health hazard.

The antique vase had been repackaged and my parents were quickly on their feet.

"We'd better get going before we get caught in the rush hour," my mother said.

They hastened along the hall and grabbed their coats. My father glanced into Hollie's room with a look of distant curiosity, as if he were looking at a picture in a magazine. In the meantime my mother already had the front door open and was calling goodbye to the other children.

The next day, after taking Lisa and Joshua to school, I drove to Hatfield to meet Geraldine's independent educational psychologist. This woman had assessed a large number of autistic children and appeared at their hearings to back the cases for these children receiving educational services of one sort or another. On Monday evening I had sent her a copy of the draft statement, together with copies of all the reports we had on Hollie. She was going to show me where the statement was unsatisfactory, and how we could use its faults to argue that the district was not meeting Hollie's needs. The drive took about two hours. It was a sunny, late-September day, almost an Indian summer. I was uncomfortably hot with the windows shut to keep out the highway noise.

Mrs. Johnson was not at all what I expected. She was small and slim with dark hair flecked with grey that fell below her shoulders, and she wore a floor-length pink dress with lacy patterns on the sleeves and around the hem. I guessed she was several years older than me, for her face was deeply etched with lines, especially around the eyes. I was suspicious and even slightly prejudiced. She didn't look the way an educational psychologist should look. Not, of course, that there is a particular way that an educational psychologist should look. I mean, one has an image of a librarian as someone in a tweed skirt, flat shoes and horn-rimmed spectacles. Perhaps the educational-psychologist look would be that of an ex-hippy, a woman in a cheesecloth dress draped in beads who would have appeared to have strayed from some anti-Vietnam protest march circa 1968, with a husband in a caftan and open sandals. I realized I would have preferred someone neater, smarter, wearing, if not a suit, an I-mean-business outfit of some sort.

"Hello," she said brightly. "Come in."

I caught a brief glimpse of two reception rooms, quite small and dim looking, with armchairs strewn with flowery cushions with thickly tasselled edges, and tall bookshelves lining the walls. As she led me down a dim passageway, my heart sank even further as she called cheerily behind her, "I'm out of coffee, I'm afraid. I can offer you herbal tea – jasmine, blackcurrant or orange pekoe."

But to my surprise, as I reached the end of the passageway, I was dazzled by bright sunshine. She had led me to the door of a small garden. The side borders were screened by bushes and by climbing roses and clematis, which bloomed all along the fence. There was a grassy area at the end of the garden, but nearest to me was a small stone-flagged terrace. In the center a large round pine table was overhung by an apple tree laden with fruit. Sunshine pouring through the branches and leaves made intricate shadows on the table and the ground below. Mrs. Johnson gestured me to a chair and shoved piles of books and papers aside on to another chair. Then she went to make the tea.

I sat down reluctantly with a sinking feeling that I had wasted a day and the best part of a hundred pounds on this vague-looking woman. But I gradually found I was enjoying the warmth and brightness of the sun. Here, in the cozy warmth of this small terrace, with the sun pouring down between the branches of the apple tree, there was nothing I should be doing, and for the first time in weeks I felt relaxed.

I found myself wondering whether Joel was in a business meeting at this moment, or traveling to one of his offices. I wished intently that I had a better knowledge of his job so I could picture more clearly what he might be doing. Then from nowhere came the most intense fantasy. I had a strong image of him bending down and kissing me, kissing me in a way no one had ever kissed me before, gently at first, then forcefully. I imagined him caressing my cheeks and my hair, then bending to kiss my neck.

"Here's your tea." The voice was friendly, but it cut like a knife through all that golden fantasy. Mrs. Johnson placed a cup of heavily scented, orange-colored tea in front of me. Then she sat down next to me, lifted some papers, which I recognized as Hollie's reports, off the pile, and placed them in front of us.

"This is a photocopy I've taken of your daughter's draft statement," she said, briskly. It was marked all over with blue highlighter pen, asterisks and comments.

In the next thirty minutes I was forced to make a complete about-turn in my appraisal of Mrs. Johnson. Her comments were observant and shrewd. Her summary of how she viewed Hollie from the reports she had read was accurate and well-rounded. In front of me she rewrote the draft statement, listing Hollie's strong points and areas of greatest difficulty, then proceeded to stipulate in a further well-honed paragraph how these needs would most comprehensively be met. The original draft statement, which we had known to be inaccurate and unbalanced, appeared now as a hodgepodge of illogic and irrelevance.

"I think that gives you enough ammunition for now," Mrs. Johnson smiled, a lock of hair falling in front of her face.

"It certainly does. I'm extremely grateful." I gathered all the papers up in my bag, then wrote out the check. As we walked back along the corridor, which seemed dimmer now, Mrs. Johnson said, "I'm going away to Scotland for a few weeks, but I will check any messages you leave on my voice mail."

"I've always thought September was the best time for a vacation," I said, making conversation.

"Well, it's a sort of vacation, I suppose. My marriage has just broken up, and I need some time away, a change of scene."

"Oh, I see," I said, awkwardly.

As I drove the M25 highway back toward Shalham, I thought about Mrs. Johnson and her husband, Geraldine and her boyfriends, and Simon and me. All these relationships were minefields. My affair with Joel might only be happening inside my head, but I still had to be very, very careful.

I had a nightmare afternoon and evening. Hollie broke the locks on the kitchen cupboards and grabbed a bottle of liquid detergent. I found her in her room trying to drink it, detergent having been emptied in pools all over the bed. I didn't panic. This sort of incident happened so frequently these days that I had long stopped panicking. I smelled her breath, which was fairly clear, so I didn't think she could have drunk much. I gave her a drink of water, filled the bathtub and deposited her in it while I stripped her bed and piled the clothes in the washing machine. Then I brought towels and stomped up and down on them where most of the liquid had been spilt to try to absorb it. I finally brought clean clothes and a diaper and put them in the hall near the bathroom while I ran into the kitchen to throw the towels into the washer with the rest.

When I came back, Hollie, dripping from the bath, was standing on the pile of clean clothes and diaper, urinating on them. I deposited her back in the tub and threw those clothes in with the others into the washing machine. When I came back to the bathroom, Hollie was standing with both feet in the toilet bowl. She had thrown the soap from the sink in and was standing on it, enjoying the feel of squishy soap under her feet.

I finally managed to serve Joshua and Lisa burnt fish sticks and chips at six o'clock. They sensed my mood and ate without complaining, though they drenched every mouthful in tomato sauce and left more than they actually consumed.

The rest of the early evening continued the same way. It was bright and sunny, and Joshua and Lisa played for hours outside, riding their bikes and playing golf with plastic clubs. But even if it had rained, I felt certain that their innate sixth sense, which told them when times with Hollie were particularly difficult, would have led them to play quietly in their bedrooms. The only conversation I had with them was when I asked them which video they would like to watch before bed.

"*Pinocchio*, please, Mom," said Joshua.

My heart sank. I knew what was coming next, because we had this conversation every time they watched *Pinocchio*. I wasn't going to lie to them any longer.

"Mommy?" asked Lisa.

"Yes, darling?"

"Hollie will be a real girl one day, won't she?"

I turned away from them both and began hunting through the piles of videos.

"I don't know, darling. Perhaps not."

There was a stunned silence.

"But . . . " said Lisa.

"Mommy, you've always said Hollie would be a real girl one day," Joshua said, accusingly. "You did, you did."

"I know. We can hope, can't we? And pray . . . "

When Simon came home, I gave him a brief summary of the

day, then told him I was going out for a breath of fresh air to calm myself down a little. On an impulse I grabbed the car keys as I walked out of the door, got into the car and drove down the road. It was half past nine, and dark. At first I thought I would drive up to the park and look out at the view of the lights of Shalham, but instead I found myself driving to the main road, which was fairly quiet at this time of night.

I had a thundering headache; the pressure on me was almost like a physical weight. It was a windy, chilly night, but I rolled the windows down, wanting to feel the force of the wind on my face and in my hair, to feel some strong physical sensation to distract my thoughts from the suffocated feeling inside. I wanted to listen to loud music with a pounding beat, something striking enough to shut out all my thoughts. I found a tape, stuck it into the tape player and turned the volume up very, very loud. When the first guitar chords and drum beats boomed in unison and the piano tinkled up and down the scale, I turned the volume up even louder. I spiraled up the ramp to the freeway, as the music slowed slightly, and the guitars moved up and down the scale slowly, building anticipation for the singer's cue. The guitars and drums boomed again, and the singer began singing, his voice full of an intensity that almost matched my own.

"There's evil in the air and thunder in the sky and a killer's on the bloodshot streets."

Higher still I turned the volume control as I slipped from the slow to the middle lane. I had the road to myself as the music from the chorus exploded out of all the windows. I was shouting the words of the chorus in unison, sixty miles an hour building to seventy, thumping my hands on the steering wheel, shaking my head.

A handful of cars passed me on the other side of the road, but nothing on my side. There was just me streaking along in the darkness buffered from everyday thoughts by these wondrous thundering chords.

"I know that I'm damned if I never get out, and maybe I'm damned if I do . . . "

I screamed, shaking my head from side to side and up and down.

It had begun to rain slightly, the most dangerous time for driving, I knew, but still I built my speed, eighty miles an hour, ninety. To my amazement, the only car I had seen on my side of the road passed me at that moment, coming from nowhere it seemed, since I was deaf to all outside sounds. I was a careful driver, normally slow and cautious, and I had never driven like this before in my life. A hundred miles an hour, a hundred and ten. The drizzle and the rain on my face refreshed me.

It was raining harder now. A hundred and twenty miles an hour. Had I gone mad? Perhaps . . . But it felt terrific. Then the skid began. I swung the steering wheel to the other side in a panic, and lost all control, swinging round and round, aware of bright lights ahead of where I was, spiraling furiously toward the bridge over the highway.

I stopped trying to move the wheel. I didn't scream. It was all happening so fast. There was a blissful, liberating feeling of an outside force having control over me, deciding my destiny. Round and round I wheeled, dizzy, the pounding chords and the screaming brakes joining in a cacophony that filled the night.

The wheels slowed. I spiraled to a halt. Ahead and all around was the amber cloud created by the lights of the freeway below the bridge. I had come to a standstill a foot before the metal fence of the bridge.

A car rocketed past in the fast lane. As it passed me, lights flashing and siren wailing, I realized it was a police car. I leant forward with my head in my hands, and the only thought I was aware of was of Joel, "Did you think of me once, just once today . . . "

Chapter Three

Over the next few days, Joel kind of gate-crashed my head. Waking or sleeping, he was there. Snippets of our brief conversations played continually through my mind, interspersed with memories of the way he turned his head, his dignified posture, his deep voice with that faint trace of an Irish accent. I was so busy every moment of the day, and indeed half the night, that there wasn't time to indulge myself with these fantasies. But he was always in my mind somewhere, a glimmer in the growing darkness.

I got through the next couple of weeks by forcing myself to think just one day ahead at a time. I knew we couldn't continue to exist as we were much longer. But the alternative, that we could take on and win against a whole education system, which had unlimited funds and access to an endless supply of experts who could be brought in to back its case, well, that seemed even more impossible. Even parents with a reasonable armor of confidence had balked at that possibility.

After all, I just wasn't someone who made things happen. I had been so shy and ineffectual when I was at school that I sometimes wondered whether other people could even see me. Afraid to stick my neck out, afraid to assert myself, afraid of competition. What a prey I was for bullies until I met Geraldine and she began to fight my battles for me. My confidence had edged forward a little since then, but assertiveness was still as foreign to me as gondolas and paddy fields. Okay, I had tackled the assistant director of special education, Mary Walsh, but that had been my one moment of brashness in a lifetime of caution, and probably had something to do with Lord Voldemort moving into the back of my head and laying me open to unaccustomed fits of grouchiness and spleen.

It was hard enough just getting out of bed in the morning and facing the mountain that had to be climbed each day, just with day-to-day caring for Hollie, without contemplating an unwinnable battle against a powerful government body. Yet without that battle, and an almost unimaginable victory, life would very soon be unbearable.

The dilemma was so insoluble that each time I contemplated it, I returned to my living-just-one-day-at-a-time approach. I was so assiduous at sticking to this blinkered-vision approach that Hollie's birthday, which fell on a Sunday on the last day of the month, crept up on us almost without me realizing it.

Thursday afternoon Lisa and I went into Shalham after play-group to buy Hollie's present, and had great fun looking at baby toys in the Early Learning Center before we finally decided on an activity table. It had buttons to press that made sounds or turned on lights, plastic lids to flip, shapes that could be moved around to form patterns, and different-shaped holes where triangular or square shaped bricks could be inserted.

Friday morning I shopped for the party, to which the four grandparents were invited, and in the afternoon, Lisa helped me make the cake.

The night before Hollie's party was overpoweringly hot. I had just finished reading Joshua and Lisa a bedtime story when a loud crash from the bathroom where Hollie was having one of her frequent baths brought me running to see what had happened. Hollie was standing in the tub, and a basket of bath toys that had been standing on the top of the sink was now upside down on the floor, toys scattered across the carpet. There was no point in clearing it up, only to have her do the same again, so I kicked the toys into a pile gently with my foot. The air in the bathroom was oppressively humid, so I moved over and tried to open the large bottom window. It had been a long time since it had been opened, so I had to punch the woodwork with the palms of my hands until eventually, very creakily, it opened. As I secured the catch, I looked out past the walls of the house next door at a mass of greenery where bushes and trees from several gardens stood tall.

It was that golden time in the evening just as the sun was beginning to go down, the landscape illuminated with the sort of balmy, caressing light that could have shone straight from Heaven itself. The greenery was lush and vibrant, a beautiful wilderness that seemed empty of people, and yet there were sounds and smells that showed that not very far away people were living quite a different sort of life. The wonderful aroma of sizzling barbecued meat, together with the distant sound of conversation and laughter, took me straight back to the days of going out, and of conversations with friends that did not revolve around broken furniture, stained sheets and placement hearings.

I felt an ache of longing for that distant time. I wondered, too, about what Joel might be doing. Probably he was sitting in a garden somewhere drinking wine with friends. Or dining out at an expensive restaurant with a glamorous girlfriend – someone like that pushy Paula. The only thing I could be certain of was that he would not be standing alone staring out of his bathroom window.

I pulled myself back from my daydreams and headed back to the kitchen to put the finishing touches on the birthday cake, shutting the bathroom window as I left before Hollie could be expected to escape through it.

Hollie's party was due to start at one o'clock on Sunday afternoon. At five to one I was bringing plates of sandwiches and jugs of fruit juice and lemonade from the kitchen to the dining room, and Simon was doing some last-minute tidying of toys in the yard. Joshua and Lisa were running from the family room windows to the front door and back again, watching out for the arrival of the grandparents, while the birthday girl was crouched in the corner of the room, with only her bottom sticking out from under the curtain, banging two plastic bricks together.

Suddenly Lisa began shrieking, "Here they are! Here they are!"

As I walked to the back door to shout for Simon, I heard

tires on the front drive, and then the sound of car doors opening and shutting. I plodded back down the hall, opened the front door, and Joshua and Lisa dashed out like greyhounds. Geoffrey and Veronica, Simon's parents, were stretching after their drive from Southford, and extricating bags from the back seat, but they quickly deposited them on the ground to hug the children. Veronica was tall, thin and elegant in an expensive-looking pink and yellow summer dress and matching pink shoes. She had curly light brown hair and a still-handsome face with a strong bone structure. Geoffrey was also tall, a distinguished-looking man with glasses and a grey beard.

Simon had followed me out, and there was a moment or two of kisses and hugs and handshakes.

"Lovely to see you," said Veronica, bending to kiss my cheek. "How well you look, Lucy."

"Thank you."

"Good to see you," Geoffrey chorused automatically, giving me the quickest of pecks on the cheek.

As we were ushering them through the front door, there was another shout, this time from Joshua, and I spotted my parents slowing down, ready to turn into our driveway.

All four grandparents entered the dining room together and, standing to the side in front of them, I saw them look around in trepidation for Hollie, and then noticed the flashes of relief when they couldn't see her.

"Here she is," I said, with artificial cheerfulness. I walked over and pointed to where she crouched.

"Hello, Hollie," the four grandparents cried with false brightness, almost in unison, not moving from the doorway. I had a strong sense that if Hollie had turned, risen and walked toward them, they would all have backed away, as one, down the hall. I walked up to Hollie and bent down in front of her. Imposing myself between her and the curtain, directly in her line of vision, I gently lifted her chin and cupped her face in my hands, trying to make her still her swiveling gaze so that she could look at me.

"Hello," I said, brightly. Then I commanded: "Look. Look."

We had worked on this lesson for half an hour or so every day for the past few months. I would give the simple command "Look," then reward her with a potato chip or a favorite toy whenever she obeyed, even for the merest second.

Sometimes I varied the game by putting candies right in front of my nose so that she was forced to look at me, even if only for a second, as she reached out to take the treat. Now she flashed me the quickest of glances.

"Good girl!" I cried, in excitement. Then, keeping my voice calm and reassuring, I added, "Hollie, Grandma and Grandpa Roseman and Granny and Grandpa Graham are here. They have presents for you."

Hollie's eyes flickered from side to side, then back down to the bricks again. She was obviously not going to move. I sensed the outpouring of relief from the cluster of grandparents by the door.

Then Simon weaved his way between them and, failing to spot Hollie and me, called cheerfully. "Help yourselves from the buffet here. We'll have presents and cake after lunch."

We sat in the shade of the apple tree, enjoying the hot September afternoon while eating sandwiches and salad. Every few minutes Simon and I took turns seeking out Hollie from under the dining room curtain and trying to persuade her to eat some lunch. Sometimes I lifted her bodily to show her the spread on the table, and sometimes I put plates of sandwiches and chips in front of her. But every time she shoved them contemptuously away. Seated with the grownups under the tree, Joshua talked a little about school, the lessons he enjoyed most and the friends he played football with. Lisa brought out pictures she had drawn and models she had made at preschool.

Veronica talked to my mother about her four other grandchildren, the children of Simon's two brothers, and about the problems they gave their parents with tantrums, petulance, and their constant need to be taxied everywhere. In the meantime Geoffrey and my father discussed lawnmowers.

I consumed my plate of food, speaking very little and, as soon as I had finished, came back inside. Sometimes it was easier to be with Hollie all the time than to run back and forth checking on her. I bent down in front of her and made one more attempt at lifting a sandwich up to her mouth, but when she pushed it away, I said, "That's it with lunch, Hollie. I'm going to get your birthday cake ready now."

I picked up some of the dirty plates and carried them with me to the kitchen. Behind me I could hear a soft patter of footsteps, which I presumed was Lisa coming in to find more treasures to show off to her grandparents. But, to my amazement, it was Hollie who appeared on the threshold.

"Hello, Hollie," I said. She was staring up at the ceiling, beaming. I got the plastic cake box down from the cupboard, lifted the cake out and located the box of candles in one of the drawers. As I emptied the candles on to a plate, I glanced around again. Hollie was still beaming happily at a spot on the wall somewhere just above the back door. I began placing the nine candles on the cake, trying to judge the distance between them so that they were equally spaced, when I glanced around and found Hollie standing right beside me. I expected her to grab my hand to lead me to something she wanted me to get her, or to scavenge for bits of food on the counters, but instead she came up to my left-hand side and stood there. I glanced at her and found she was staring straight into my eyes.

This, in itself, was remarkable, since Hollie had probably only looked at me about a dozen times in her whole life, but more amazing still, she was smiling. I dropped the candles without another thought, bent my knees so that my eyes were on her level, and held her gaze, beaming at her in return. I was afraid at any second she would look away, but the intent look continued. I put my hands out, resting them lightly on her shoulders, and she permitted the touch. Terrified that the moment would pass, I willed her not to look away, and she didn't. Indeed, she began giggling in delight at her achievement.

"Hello, Hollie," I said, softly. "It's been a long time since we've seen you."

There had been precious moments like this before, times when one of the children would shout, "Mom, Hollie's looking at me," or "Mom, Hollie's laughing." Each time the whole family would drop whatever they were doing and come running, as they would to see a shooting star. But I knew immediately this one was subtly but vitally different. Hollie was shaking with excited laughter, not just at her amazing achievement, but because she was aware of my excitement too, and delighted that she had pleased me. She had never shown awareness of other people's feelings before, and the effect on me was similar to a total eclipse of the sun. All the traffic lights in the city had gone green at the same time. All that faulty wiring had suddenly, miraculously, reconnected itself to produce this one shining moment.

And then it was gone! The metal door clanged shut, the drawbridge was raised. Entry forbidden. Hollie stopped smiling, and her eyes glazed over until all that was left was the familiar blank stare. Unaware of me now, she picked up one of the candles and stuffed it into her mouth, moved it around once or twice to see if it tasted better in other parts of her mouth, then picked it out and dropped it on the floor. I remained where I was, my knees bent, my hands falling by my side where she had shrugged them off her shoulders. "Bye for now, then, Hollie," I said. "See you next time."

She had retired back inside the fortress, and it might be six months before she found another opening. I put plates, knives, spoons and mugs on a tray and I filled the kettle. As always, on these rare occasions, I felt an absolute conviction that if only we could find the right school for her, Hollie would find more of these little apertures and chinks in the fortified walls that surrounded her.

Simon appeared with a pile of dirty lunch plates as I was positioning the last candle on the cake.

"Hollie was looking at me, really looking at me and giggling," I cried. "She beamed and got excited. She knew it was a clever thing to do."

Simon's face lit up. "Really? That's amazing. I wish I'd seen. Where is she now?"

"Back behind her curtains with her bricks. But I'm afraid she's gone back into herself now. I'll quickly light the candles, then I'll bring the cake in."

Simon went back out to the yard and began summoning the guests back to the dining room while I quickly lit the candles. As I picked up the cake, cheerful voices and slow, unhurried footsteps approached the door. The four grandparents, now seated in a group, were ready to go through the whole birthday charade with us.

Simon glanced through the door and smiled when he saw the lighted cake.

"Come on everyone," he cried, trying to fire enthusiasm in the waiting group.

"And Joshua and Lisa, try not to sing too loudly, we don't want to alarm Hollie."

"Happy birthday to you . . . " he began singing in an exaggeratedly cheerful voice. As the grandparents obediently joined in, Simon went over to Hollie's corner and tried to pull her gently to join the group, but she took no notice. Eventually, he put his arms around her waist, and lifted her around until she was facing the room. She didn't look at anyone, but the cake with its lighted candles immediately caught her attention, and she came over and stood by me, staring at it mesmerized.

As everyone finished singing, Joshua and Lisa began chorusing "Blow, Hollie, blow," making blowing sounds and gestures to show what they meant. But Hollie took no notice, merely continued staring mesmerized at the cake. After a few minutes Simon said, "You two help Hollie to blow them out." Not needing any further encouragement, Joshua and Lisa blew until, in two seconds, all nine candles were snuffed out.

Hollie had no interest in the cake now that the lights had disappeared, and tried to run from the room.

"Hollie, it's time to open your presents," said Joshua, amazed to see her starting to run away. Simon looked harassed as he caught her and carried her struggling back into the room. He sat on a high-backed dining chair and kept his arms firmly around her waist.

"Quick, pass me a present someone," he said, tersely.

I passed the activity table. It looked like a lovely, large, enticing present. Simon put his hands on Hollie's, and tried to pressure her to tear the wrapping paper, but she wriggled and struggled. Then he clamped his arms harder around her waist, his expression grim, and began ripping at the wrapping paper himself to show there was something of interest inside, but Hollie struggled to such an extent that he was forced to let her go. She ran from the room. A couple of seconds later there was a splash, and I knew she had gotten back into the bathtub.

"Here, you two unwrap it," Simon said, wearily.

Joshua and Lisa raced to unwrap the activity table, and for several minutes they were absorbed pressing buttons, pushing shapes into holes and making pictures light up and bells and hoots sound. Then both sets of grandparents handed over their presents, and Lisa opened them. One was a touchy-feely book of shining papers and textures, and the other a large ball that made strange noises as it rolled about.

"Thank you," I said. "Hollie will enjoy both of those, but it will take her a day or so to get used to having them around. Then I'm sure she'll look at them and enjoy them."

I made a pot of tea, while the four grandparents sat on the dining chairs around the buffet table and discussed vacations.

"We went to Guernsey as usual," my mother said. "Two weeks in St. Peter's Port – lovely."

"We went to Malta in April, and we're going to Tunisia on Tuesday. A lovely hotel with views over the beach. It's a little off the beaten track, and since we're not quite at the height of the summer, it shouldn't be so crowded."

"Where will you go next year?"

"Oh, we're being very adventurous next year. We want to try Bermuda."

Geoffrey finished his tea, turned to Simon and said, "Can I take back that saw I lent you?"

"Of course. It's in the garage."

As everyone finished eating, I cleared cake plates away in between checks on Hollie, who lay for a long time in the tub, rather in the manner of a crocodile, with just her eyes, nose and the top of her head showing. I poured further cups of tea, and handed them around.

Joshua came in, "Where's Hollie? I thought I'd show her the ball."

"In the tub."

"No, she's not."

"What?"

I ran to the bathroom. It was empty. Then I flew into Hollie's bedroom. Again, no sign of her. I rushed into the dining room. "Simon, I can't find Hollie," I yelled. "I've checked downstairs."

Simon raced upstairs while I raced into the yard. Still there was no sign of Hollie. As I came back, I noticed that the garage door was open to the road. My heart immediately sank.

I raced into the dining room, just as Simon came back from upstairs.

"The garage door's open," I said. A look of horror flashed across Simon's face. Then I remembered something.

"You went to the garage to get the saw, didn't you?" I asked, turning to Simon's father.

"Yes, I took it straight out to the car," he said. "No point in carrying it through the house."

"Did you shut the garage door again?"

"Well, I can't remember." He looked slightly annoyed. "What's all the fuss about? Perhaps I didn't."

"Hollie's almost certainly escaped through it," Simon said. "You all stay here with Joshua and Lisa, please."

Simon and I ran out of the door and through the garage, shutting every door as we came to it. When we reached the road, we looked at each other.

"You go to the left, I'll go to the right," said Simon. We started to run, but even as I turned out of the yard I knew it was hopeless. She could have run into any of the back yards, and I'd never see her. She could be in a hedge, or behind a parked car. She might be anywhere. After running hard for a couple of hundred yards, I turned and jogged back down again. Simon had done the same. We looked at each other blankly.

"No sign?" I asked.

He shook his head.

We came back into the kitchen. All the grandparents' eyes turned toward us.

"I'll call the police," I said.

But just as I picked up the phone, there was a knock at the door. I opened it. There stood one of the helpers at Lisa's preschool, holding Hollie tightly by the hand. Hollie was completely naked.

"Thank you, thank you, thank you" I repeated, like a needle stuck in a record groove. "I was just about to call the police."

"She was running down the center of the road," she said, friendly but with a slight air of accusation. "It was lucky there were no cars coming."

"One of our guests mistakenly left the garage door open," I said, taking Hollie's hand and leading her back inside. "I thought she was in the tub. I'd checked on her only a minute before. Thank you so much."

I shut the front door and collapsed against it for a moment with my head in my hands. How long would it be before someone would be carrying back her dead body?

It was just after five when my parents began to collect their bags and suggest they should be leaving. Veronica and Geoffrey immediately said that it was time they started on their trip home, too. Veronica and my mother both called "Bye-bye, Hollie" across the length of the room in bright, tense voices, while my father packed bags into the car and Geoffrey collected his sunglasses from the garden table.

Standing in front of the porch, Veronica gave me a quick kiss on the cheek and said, her face full of sympathy, "It must be so difficult for you, with Hollie, I mean." Then as Geoffrey strode out behind us, her expression snapped to one of slight impatience to get through the formalities and be off. "Must go, dear," she said, hugging Simon, and then Joshua and Lisa. "So much packing to do for Tuesday. It's such a worry, making sure we don't forget anything important."

My mother followed immediately. My father patted Joshua and Lisa on the head and muttered "goodbye," then went to start up the engine. My mother bent toward me and kissed me on the cheek. "Thank you for a lovely afternoon, dear. We may stop by to see you later in the week, but I can't be sure. We've got to get the business of this new lawnmower sorted out. Your father's quite worried about it. If we don't hurry up and find the right one, the grass will be too long to cut."

"Of course."

Simon and I stood with Joshua and Lisa waving them all out of the gate.

Joshua grabbed a soccer ball and started kicking it around, and Lisa tried to grab it from him, giggling. "Come away from the road," I said hurriedly.

"They're still so full of excitement," said Simon. "Perhaps I'll take the three of them to the park for half an hour while you clean up."

"That's a great idea."

While Simon strapped the younger two into the car, I went to get Hollie from beneath the dining room curtain. She had found the box of paper tissues I'd opened earlier and was pulling them out quickly one by one and sending them flying in the air.

"Hollie going out!" I said, putting on a bright, excited tone. "Going out!" She continued thrusting her hand into the tissue box, tissues floating to the floor all around her like giant snowflakes. There was no point in trying to take her hand to encourage her to her feet; she would just pull away from me. Instead I put both hands under her armpits and tried to lift her to her feet, but she kept her legs bent and refused to take her weight on them. I tried a second time, with the same result. As I put her down, momentarily tired out, she immediately wedged a foot through the leg bars of one of the chairs and grabbed the table leg tightly with both hands.

"Hollie, you like the park. You love it." I said wearily. Then I added, despairingly, "Oh, how I wish you understood me."

Simon walked briskly into the room and stopped almost in mid-stride, looking at us. I sensed his briskness evaporate.

"I'll take her feet, you do her hands," he said. As he tried to unwedge her foot, Hollie immediately wedged the other one tightly around another bar of the chair. I pried the fingers of one hand off the table leg, then held that hand tightly with my right hand while I tried to pry off the gripping fingers of her left hand. Immediately I held each of her hands tightly in mine. Simon had managed to extricate both her feet and now held one foot in each hand. We carried her through the house in this fashion to the front door, but as Simon put her legs down to grab her shoes, she darted away from me, collapsing into a tight ball on the ground.

"I suppose I'll have to leave her."

"But she loves the park. And it helps to tire her," I cried, furiously.

"Well, it's not my fault," he snapped.

"I know, I know; I'm sorry."

"So I'd better just take the other two, then."

"Yes, I suppose so."

I walked back to the dining room, and as I did so, I heard the sound of the car door slamming through the open windows. My nerves pulled tight with annoyance and frustration, I picked up the cake plates and crashed them down on the kitchen countertops. Then I began furiously emptying garbage into the can and piling the plates into the sink. Bored with the tissue game, Hollie found my purse, which I had unwisely left on the mantelpiece, opened it, and begun spilling the coins into a haphazard pile on the floor, enjoying the clattering sound as each one fell.

She had just moved back to the brick game behind the curtain when there was a loud knock at the door. I walked slowly back along the hall, feeling annoyed at being bothered when there was still so much work to do. I opened the door. Instantly all thought – about the work, Hollie's birthday, even of its being Sunday – was banished. Joel was standing there.

"Hello," he said, looking at me intently. "I've brought a present for Hollie." He was holding a gift wrapped in shiny, silvery blue wrapping paper. He was wearing his black leather jacket, a black tight fitting tee-shirt and jeans.

"That's extremely kind of you," I said, full of wonder. "Come in, please."

He stepped over the threshold and pushed the door shut behind him. He was only two feet away from me. I noticed how the sleeves of the jacket creased on his muscular arms. His forehead was shiny with sweat.

"How did you know?"

"Her date of birth was on several of the reports you gave me."

I turned and began to walk back down the hall, with Joel following me.

"I don't know how she'll react," I said, as we entered the dining room. "She often tosses new things aside, and then comes back to play with them later when she's gotten used to them."

Hollie was almost completely hidden by the curtain. I lifted the curtain and said, "This is Hollie," looking from Joel to Hollie's curved back and bottom, which was all he could see of her. I tried pushing my hands under her armpits and lifting her, but she just kept her legs bent, refusing to stand, forcing me to take her whole weight.

"Hollie, stand up," I said. Again, I tried to raise her to a standing position, but again she refused to take her weight. I tried shifting her around so she at least was crouching facing Joel and I, but she immediately scrambled back into the corner.

"Would you like to give her the present?" I asked.

Joel was looking uncomfortable.

"Perhaps it would be better if you did," he said.

I did as I had done earlier, trying to implant myself between Hollie and the wall, but she moved her head so that it was resting on her knees to avoid having any contact with me or the strange object in my hand.

"Hollie, it's another present for you," I said, trying to lift her head and grab her hands to make them unwrap the present even though she was refusing to even look at it. But she whipped them away from me.

"Hollie, look, look," I cried, and began unwrapping one edge of the present. She scrambled back into a ball, hedgehog-like. I finally stood up, slowly. "I'm sorry," I said. "I'm sure she'll like it later when it's unwrapped. It takes her a while to get used to new things."

"Never mind. Give it to one of your other two, perhaps." Joel was still looking perplexed. I noticed his hair was slightly tousled. I wanted to run my fingers through it.

"How are you?" he asked, speaking the words not as an empty phrase, but as if he meant them.

"Not too bad. Tired."

"We will win, you know. You mustn't worry."

He was still standing about two feet away from me as he said this. As his gaze met mine, the expression in his eyes subtly changed. The social guardedness that one wears like a film over one's eyes with near strangers was blinked away, and the look we were giving each other was questioning, asking for signs of what the other was thinking.

All of a sudden, he took a step toward me. For a second he lingered right in front of me, inches away, well within my personal space, giving me a smile that was amused and at the same time faintly provocative. I wanted him to stay exactly as he was, so close to me that I could see how the skin crinkled at the corners of his eyes, and yet, at exactly the same moment, the urge to step away from this overpowering closeness was almost irresistible.

I returned his smile, basking in the delicious sense of danger. Then, to my simultaneous disappointment and relief, he stepped back, took an envelope out of his jacket and handed it to me.

"This is an invitation for you and Simon to my fortieth birthday party in October. I hope you can come."

"Thanks, we'd love to," I said. I looked at his thick, wavy hair that had scarcely any grey, and added in my thoughts, "And I'd love to run my fingers through your hair."

"It's at my house, on the other side of Shalham. I'll give you directions nearer the time."

"That's great. Thanks." I want to run my fingers across your neck and across your chest. I want to squeeze your arm muscles.

"It'll be quite a bash. You may not know any of the guests. Apart from Geraldine, that is."

"That's great. She finds it very easy to meet people. She can introduce me to people." I want to nuzzle your cheek and your neck. I want to dart my tongue into your mouth.

"I'm still wondering whether to have a live group playing or perhaps just a d.j. After all, we don't want the music so loud we can't talk."

I want to take your tee-shirt off and look at your broad chest. I want to undo the zip of your jeans and take them off very, very slowly. Or perhaps quickly . . .

Heavens, what were we talking about? Was it still music?

"Yes. Er, no."

Joel was looking at me strangely, and no wonder. A woman who appeared sensible and intelligent enough, but who couldn't follow a simple straightforward conversation about parties and music.

"Sorry, you must think I'm insane," I said, quickly. "It's fatigue. I keep losing the thread of conversations."

"Of course." He smiled, sympathetically. "I've done that before now, when I've worked late into the night for several evenings running."

There was a short silence.

Desperate that he might take it as a hint that he should leave, I burst out, "Would you like a cup of tea? Or coffee? Or a glass of wine?"

"No, thanks, I'd better be going."

At the door he turned to me. "I hope you can come to the party. But I'm sure I'll see you before then."

All of a sudden he leaned forward and kissed me on the cheek, putting his hand lightly on my arm as he did so. I wanted to throw my arms around him and hold him like I'd never held any man before. I didn't, of course. But I sensed he read my thoughts, for his smile was conspiratorial.

"Let me know if you can come to the party."

"Yes, yes, of course."

And he was gone, walking speedily back down the driveway.

For the rest of that day, and throughout the next, I felt strange stirrings inside, tiny blips on the steady line of the hospital monitor screen that had previously shown all inner life to be non-functioning.

Tuesday morning it occurred to me that I could call at Joel's house that evening to formally accept his party invitation. Once the idea had taken hold, I couldn't get rid of it. I kept trying to decide whether it was something that a normal acquaintance with normal social feelings would do, but I found I had lost all objectivity and wasn't capable of deciding. The fact was, I felt impelled to do it.

When Simon came home, I said I needed to go out for a short while for a drive "to calm my nerves." It's not that much of a lie, I told myself as I darted into the car, slammed the seat belt into its fastening, put the car into gear and veered right out of the driveway onto the road. Actually, you're a whopping great liar, I told myself as I reached the main road. A visit to Joel was more likely to inflame my nerves than to calm them.

The light was just beginning to fade as I pulled into the driveway of the address on the invitation. Waves of sickness were charging about uncomfortably in my stomach. A short curved drive led up to the front of a white-painted house with a heavy oak door. I rang the bell, then stood back, away from the doormat. No reply. No sound of footsteps. I rang again. Still no reply. I began wondering whether to sit in my car for a few minutes or even drive away, when I noticed that the side gate was open. I peered in and saw Joel toward the back of the yard with his back to me.

I stood for a minute or two just staring at him, until he turned and saw me.

"Come in, Lucy."

I took a few steps forward.

"I'm delighted to see you," he said.

It was a cloudy evening, and a chilly early-autumn wind was blowing the first of the dropped leaves around. Joel had been gardening, and was evidently warm from moving wheelbarrows of garden waste from all over the large yard to the spot where we stood, where he had been building a bonfire.

"You haven't said anything yet," he said, smiling.

I coughed and found my voice. "No, sorry, I didn't mean to be rude. I was just coming to accept your kind invitation."

"I'll get some drinks. Red or white wine? Or perhaps beer?"

"Oh, I don't know if I ought to be drinking . . . "

"One glass won't do you any harm." He turned and walked toward the house without another word. I sat on the low wall behind me and watched the breeze nuzzling at the leaves of the mature oaks and chestnuts beyond the hedge at the bottom of the yard. To the left was a wheat field. The stubble had remained after the harvest, waiting to be ploughed back into the soil in readiness for another crop next year. Rough spikes of straw spread over the wide hump of hill like a scene from an African savannah; indeed I half expected to see giraffes and wildebeest grazing in the distance.

All along the sides ash trees and sycamores displayed their firm, gnarled, knotty bark. Their leaves were only lightly tinged with yellow while they awaited the full onset of autumn. There was hardly a hint of their innate potential to transform to their full tangerine, scarlet and golden glory. Crows cawed loudly from the depths of the woods, and regiments of starlings produced a background cacophony from distant telephone wires where they waited for the signal to fly south. Summer might be over, but every living thing still seemed to be brimming with the most vibrant life while waiting for the full propulsion of the planet along its most distant loop from the sun.

Joel soon returned with two glasses and two bottles, one red and one white.

"Which would you prefer?" he said firmly, as if I had no choice but to have one or the other.

"White, please."

He poured a brimming glass, and put the bottle down on the ground. Then he reached out his hand to offer me the glass, and as I took the glass he moved his fingers so that for a second they skimmed over mine. When he removed them, I felt hugely disappointed. He poured himself a glass and lifted it up toward me.

"To you, Lucy. To you winning your case."

I drank. He drank. He took several sips, looking at me frequently. He picked up the bottle and began automatically topping my glass up, adding – in a tone I did not feel I could refuse – "Have some more."

"Well, really, I'd better not."

"Have you had dinner?"

"Sort of. I had some pizza with the children."

"Then you'll be okay to drive on two glasses."

He filled his own glass and took another sip. I had a sudden image of him saying "Come to bed" in exactly that commanding tone, and I giggled out loud.

"What are you laughing about?"

"I couldn't possibly tell you."

"You don't laugh very much, do you, Lucy?"

I realized he was right. I had a tantalizing sense of the life he lived, so different than mine. Sunday afternoons when I was picking up bits of Hollie's portion of chicken and potatoes from the carpet, he would be sitting laughing and drinking wine with friends in a sun-filled garden. The image was intense, but gone as fleetingly as a face in a car under a highway bridge.

"No, you're right. I don't."

He was staring at me intently with that characteristic amused look on his face.

"Why are you having a bonfire?" I asked. "I don't see you as a keen gardener somehow."

He laughed. "No, I'm not. But I have various things that need disposing of."

I looked at the pile of old bits of wood.

"Are you just going to set a match to that?"

"I see you've never lit a bonfire, Lucy. Let me show you what you do."

To my amazement, he removed the wine glass from my hand, placed it on the ground, and took my hand and led me gently forwards. I shivered again. He watched me and smiled that conspiratorial smile once more. Then he bent down and pulled me gently to a squatting position.

"You take some of these bits of twigs and dried leaves and tiny branches and build them into a wigwam shape. Then you put larger twigs and very small branches on top. Like this."

He gave me a handful of larger twigs. "Put them on this small pile here," he said, as he quickly put together the twigs and branches. I did as he said, watching him intently.

"Now we'll scrunch up bits of newspaper to put all around the pile. Here, you help." He took a couple of old newspapers from the low wall to my left and handed them to me. "Tear them up, then scrunch them into tiny balls."

Once again, I did as he said, enjoying the tearing sensation, and scrunching up the paper into rough balls.

"Now scatter them around the pile," he said.

Joel came very close to me on my right side. I was about to pick up a scrunched-up ball. He took hold of my hand, newspaper ball and all, then jerked his hand forward to indicate a throwing gesture. He pulled more newspapers down from the wall behind us, and as he did so, his left hand momentarily brushed my shoulder. My throat was completely dry.

"Come on," he said, "let's get this fire going."

He picked up balls of newspaper and flung them on the pile. I also picked up a newspaper ball and flung it on the fire and then another and another.

"Now the bigger pieces," he said. He took hold of larger branches and began propping them over the top of the pile.

"You, too."

I picked up pieces of wood and lay them over the top of the bonfire. Each time Joel picked up a piece, he came over and stood just a couple of inches away from me before balancing it on the top of the pile.

"And now we light it," he said, squatting down to pick up a box of matches.

"Come closer so you can see."

I moved forward, squatted down. He slid close to me, putting his left arm around me so that I was totally encircled in his arms. The birds stopped singing, the wind went dead. I wanted to move my fingers slowly across every inch of his neck, and across the slightly roughened, five-o'clock-shadow area up to his chin. His face was just inches from mine. I gazed into his eyes and shivered. He held my gaze and smiled, as if reading my thoughts, then handed me the matches.

The voice from behind us was sharp as a foot snapping a twig.

"A good way to keep your clients busy, Joel."

The voice was loud, penetrating and female. Joel turned and slowly raised himself to a standing position, while I jumped to my feet in shock.

I had met this woman once before, but it took me a moment to recognize her. She was just as beautiful as when I had first met her, with her long blonde hair falling loosely on her shoulders, and as elegantly dressed – in a stylish black blouse that looked expensive and possibly French, and well-cut black and grey striped trousers. On this occasion, however, she was not involved in a virulent exchange, though there was a slightly surly edge to her tone that put me on my guard.

Joel exuded ease and charm.

"Lucy, have you met Paula, Paula Rochelle? Paula is public relations officer for Bella Haughton, whom you may have heard of. Bella is one of the most influential people in Windleshire, a top city council member who is assumed to be a future mayor of Shalham. Paula, this is Lucy Roseman, a new client of mine."

I felt I should shake hands, and took a couple of steps forward, but Paula made no move to approach me or hold out her hand.

"Hello," I said, smiling to ease the tension.

Paula answered with a cool nod.

Joel went on talking in his easy way.

"Bella Haughton is in the process of opening her ancestral home, Welshney Castle, to the public. It's a grand and very ancient manor house on the edge of Pershore Forest, about five miles northwest of Shalham."

"That sounds interesting," I said, politely. "When will the castle be open?"

"In December, we're hoping," Paula said briskly. "And that's what I've come to talk to you about, Joel," she added, stepping toward him with a conspiratorial air. "Yet more problems with the Chapman Brothers loan." Her eyes were heavily made up, with shiny, dark-grey eye shadow, eye pencil drawn thickly around the lids, and heavy-duty mascara. She fixed them resolutely on Joel.

"I was hoping I could talk to you about some problems that have cropped up," she said.

The hint was too obvious to ignore.

"It's time I was getting back," I said quickly.

Maybe Paula had not just set her sights on Joel; maybe they were actually already an item.

Joel threw me a concerned look. "I'll walk you to your car."

"No, don't worry. I'll make my own way. You sort out those problems with Paula."

"Goodbye, then, Lucy. I'll see you soon."

"Goodbye."

I tried to meet Joel's eye, but he had already turned toward Paula and was listening intently to a detailed explanation she was giving, accompanied by elegant hand movements and little, tinkling, feminine laughs.

I woke in the early hours. Almost before I was fully awake, I was thinking of Joel. I remembered his grey-green eyes gazing at me with a look of amusement, and I felt suddenly full of light and energy. If someone like Joel could like me, really like me – hopeless, awkward me – then perhaps, after all, I was worth something. And if I was worth something, if I had some valuable inner qualities, then maybe, after all, I was someone who could have an impact. Maybe, just maybe, it was worth proceeding with the due process hearing.

I climbed out of bed and walked to the bathroom, where I splashed my face with cold water. Then I made myself a cup of coffee and took it to the dining room table. I pulled my notebooks and files from the bookcase, placed them in neat piles on the table and sat down to begin planning our strategy. I was going to do as Geraldine had said. We were going to build a case.

I worked solidly for an hour, planning a list of contacts to call later in the day, other parents of autistic children, members of independent advisory bodies, autism organizations.

At six I went back to bed. As I passed Hollie's room, I could see her fast asleep. As usual, she had pulled the mattress off the bed and was lying with just her head on it, the rest of her body wrapped in her blanket on the floor. I climbed into my own bed and fell promptly asleep.

I felt galvanized and determined. Indeed, what I felt could almost be described as euphoria. I brimmed with the stuff. I wished I could siphon some of it off and store it in bottles so I could use it when reality brought me crashing down again. This man, this amazing, larger-than-life man had awakened feelings in me I didn't know it was possible for me to have. And he liked me. It was just – well, it was mind-blowing.

Hollie was picked up by her school bus at eight, after which I took Joshua and Lisa to school and preschool, respectively. I raced back, eager to start, made myself some strong coffee and sat down at the table. My first act was to write two letters, one formally rejecting the local school board's proposal, and the other an appeal for a due process hearing. I then called various friends who were parents of autistic children and began the long task of trying to locate other parents who had been through this process. I spoke to representatives of independent educational agencies for children with disabilities, who advised me on the legal process involved in the appeal. At just before midday I left to pick Lisa up from preschool, my head swimming with facts and information.

That evening, when Joshua and Lisa were asleep, in between changing Hollie's sheets and plying her with drinks and chips, I called phone numbers I had been given that morning and talked to parents who had had successful due process hearings or parents whose children were now at excellent boarding schools. They were all very generous, giving me their time and offering to send me copies of information that had helped them.

The next morning I began calling possible schools, asking about their approaches and methods, trying to find one that even vaguely corresponded to the idea we had in our minds for Hollie. The people I spoke to were all caring and conscientious, but these schools used the same traditional approach as at Petheril, where Hollie had regressed so badly. Somewhere there must be a school where the teachers believed children with more severe disabilities could make progress, and where they pushed and pressed and motivated them until they did so; a school that utilized a program of vigorous physical exercise to burn off all that hyperactive energy, and to spark all the happiness-inducing endorphins in the brain, making the children calm, cooperative and ready to learn. The following day, Thursday, I called more schools.

The bubble of energy and euphoria carried me through the week, enabling me to get through an incredible workload. Without it I would have struggled even to get meals on the table. I knew there was no chance of anything ever happening between Joel and me (I couldn't even bring myself to think the word "affair"). I was a nice girl, I was loyal, I had been properly brought up with a strong sense of right and wrong. I loved my husband very much. But I got such a buzz of excitement from knowing that, unbelievably, this totally extraordinary man found something to like in me. I began to find myself entering a state of mind that I had never experienced before; I felt calm, relaxed; I felt able. I felt as if I was someone who could achieve something.

Toward the end of the week I started telling myself that I needed to get back to normal, to believing that Simon was the center of my existence again. But I was reluctant to do so. The trouble was, getting back to normal was getting back to not coping. But in the end my dilemma was irrelevant. Normality simply refused to return.

I didn't waste too much time blaming myself. I was in an extremely unusual predicament, so I was entitled to use any extremely unusual methods that helped, I reasoned. When you're about to be swept away by a raging torrent, you don't question whether you're right to hang on to the one branch that forms your lifeline.

I was glad, in the end, that I couldn't get back to normal, as my old self would not have coped with what was to come. Hollie's behavior seemed to be deteriorating, if possible, and not just gradually, but frighteningly quickly.

On the Saturday following her birthday, she climbed up to the top of Joshua's bunk bed, got her foot behind the free-standing shelf unit full of toys that stood next to the bunk beds, and pushed. The entire shelf came crashing to the ground. The jigsaw puzzles survived, though the boxes were rather squashed, but the jar of marbles was smashed and the elaborate Duplo castle that Simon and Joshua had built the day I took Hollie to the beach was broken into fragments. And scattered among the marbles and handfuls of Duplo I found thousands of broken sea shells, which were all that remained of the giant seashell collection Joshua and Lisa had put together on a trip to the beach in August.

It wasn't malicious. It wasn't naughty. I'm sure Hollie never even made the connection between the piece of wood that swayed back and forth against her foot when she kicked, and the monstrous crashing sound and the tears and shouts that followed. She had simply liked the feel of the wood against her foot.

We had no more started to recover from this episode when, on the following day, Hollie escaped for the first time over the back fence. I could see her for several minutes playing in the neighbor's yard, but she didn't even glance in my direction when I called for her to "come here." The neighbor was out and her gate locked. I went to get a stepladder, calling for Simon to come and help. But by the time he and I had carried the stepladder to the back fence, Hollie had disappeared. We eventually found her in one of the yards that adjoined our neighbor's, but only after the neighbors on either side of us, and most of the people who lived in the cul-de-sac at the back, had been notified and compelled to help us with the search.

Then on Monday, problems with her school bus began. Hollie, who had always sat like an angel for the entire length of her hour-long ride to school, suddenly began escaping from her seat belt and trying to run up and down the bus, or to lie flat in the middle of the floor. The plump, bespectacled aide, who must have been pushing seventy, and who claimed to have great experience working with autistic children, told me about the problems in great detail, and with more than a hint of an accusing tone, as if the way that Hollie behaved was somehow my fault.

On Tuesday afternoon she informed me that the bus driver had had to stop the bus to help her to get Hollie back into her seat, and that this had made them late for school. She said that they had ordered a special harness for the next day; she hoped that, with Hollie reined in by a complicated set of tight straps, the problems would end. But no, by Thursday night, she was informing me that Hollie Houdini-like had contorted herself out from underneath the complicated new contraption, and proceeded to slither about the bus licking dust from the floor.

By Friday afternoon, I was dreading the arrival of the bus. I made baked beans on toast a few minutes before she was due home, and put them in Hollie's place at the dining table, in the hope that instant nourishment would discourage her from climbing on cupboards to get hold of chips and cookies. When I heard the familiar chugging of the diesel engine as the bus slowed to a halt outside our house, my heart plummeted. I wondered wildly for a minute if I could find a friend who could accompany me on the walk down the drive so that I would have a friendly face to look at while I was harangued with the list of Hollie's misdemeanors. But there was no time, and anyway, it was a crazy notion.

I could see Hollie's happy face and the glower of the aide even at a distance.

"Hello," I said, manufacturing a false brightness intended to keep my own spirits up as well as to try to disarm the other woman as she descended from the bus. It failed on both counts. A fat leg and plump foot in an absurdly inappropriate high-heeled shoe hovered in mid air for a moment before landing, then with a grunt the woman levered her other foot to the ground and imposed her bulky figure in front of me.

"She's been escaping again," she said, in a hostile tone, with no preface or greeting. "And she's been trying to slide into the seats next to the other children, and get under the seats. Twice we've had to stop the bus for the driver to help me."

Hollie jumped down from the bus, her clothes dusty, her hair matted with dirt. I reached out and tried to take her hand, but she evaded me and ran toward the house. I started to run after her, but the woman called me back angrily.

"I haven't finished yet."

"I'm sorry, but I can't leave Hollie alone in the house."

"Well, you should know that if this happens on Monday, we'll turn the bus around and bring her straight back."

"You can't do that. The district has a responsibility to provide transportation for special needs children to get to their schools."

"Not if they're a danger to everyone else," she said, shortly.

"She's autistic. That's her special need. You still have a responsibility."

The reality of what she was saying slowly sank into my consciousness. "I couldn't cope with having her at home all day."

"Well, that's what may happen," she said, clambering heavily back on to the bus and slamming the sliding door shut.

I walked out of the bright autumn sunshine into the gloomy interior of the house. Every day, it seemed, I was becoming more isolated, as the ranks of those who had any contact with us at all retreated further and further into the distance. If the bus people refused to take Hollie to school (surely they didn't have the right?), she would be at home with me all day.

But there was no time for panicking. I shut the front door and dashed through the hall to check on Hollie. When I had put her meal in her place at the table, I had done it expecting that I would enter the house with her and be able to lead her to her seat. But as I looked from her bedroom to the family room, to the kitchen, there was no sign of her. And, oddly, no sign of her dinner either. Icy fingers squeezed my heart as I remembered that I had put the wading pool out for Joshua and Lisa, so I leapt from the family room door to the garden.

Joshua and Lisa were standing, laughing and pointing to the paddling pool. Hollie was lying in the pool, fully clothed. But the water surrounding her, clean just ten minutes before, was a murky, orangey brown, dotted here and there with small globules. My first thought, that she had filled her diaper and that the contents had escaped, quickly changed when I saw her plate floating upside down beside her.

Lisa looked at me and pointed back at the pool. "Baked beans!" she laughed. "Hollie put her baked beans in the paddling pool!"

I smiled weakly, but said nothing. I pulled the plug on the wading pool, then went to the kitchen to turn the oven on, taking a bag of chicken nuggets from the freezer and emptying them on to a dish. Through the window I could see that Hollie – not so comfortable now that the water level had diminished – had climbed out and was busily stripping her wet clothes off, dropping them wherever they fell as she jumped about. Then she spied the sandbox, climbed in and began scooping fingerfuls of sand into her mouth. Never mind, I told myself, at least the sand would keep her occupied while I cleaned out the wading pool. I brought out a dustpan and brush and began sweeping up the soggy baked beans, then scooping out the more watery mush with a sponge.

As I brought the dustpan and brush and soggy sponge back through to the kitchen, I heard someone dash through the family room and across the hall. Wearily I dropped everything and ran to find Hollie, plastered from head to foot in wet sand, jumping about the empty tub, a dusting of sand and mud marking her trail through the house.

"Okay, I'll run you a bath," I muttered, putting the stopper in and turning on the taps. But as I quickly washed the worst of the mud and earth down the drain, Hollie scampered out again, and I heard her rattling about in the kitchen. Suddenly, the sound of a large quantity of something spilling over the kitchen floor reached me. I decided to ignore it and quickly finish cleaning the bathroom. But a minute or two later, I was forced to come when Lisa started to cry loudly from the kitchen. She had slipped on the wet floor. When I arrived, Hollie, who was tall for her nine years, was sitting hunched up in the kitchen sink, with both taps on. She had thrown out the dishpan, which had been half full of water, so the kitchen floor was swimming with water and also with soggy Rice Krispies, now spread everywhere from the box that she had pulled down from the upper shelf. I came from cleaning the bathroom and began immediately to clean up the water and mushy cereal from the floor. I wrapped Hollie in a towel and quickly put a diaper on her before she could add to my problems by peeing on a bed or a chair.

"Mommy, I'm hungry," called Joshua.

The urge to snap at him was almost overpowering. "Can't you see I've got enough to do," I wanted to shout. But I resisted. None of this was his fault, for heaven's sake. I threw the tray of nuggets into the oven, then pulled the brandy bottle from the cupboard, poured a few drops into a cup and took a sip.

Simon wouldn't be back from his meeting until midnight, and by ten I was exhausted, plying Hollie with juice and snacks, putting new diapers on her, and removing the old, discarded ones along with her wet clothes. When Joshua and Lisa called out, asking for a drink and a story, all I could do was snap "Go to sleep." I relented, of course, and took each of them a drink and promised I would read them a story "in a few minutes, when Hollie calms down a bit," hoping against unlikely hope that Hollie would indeed be calmer and less demanding in another few minutes, so that I could honor my promise. But the next moment a crash brought me running to Hollie's bedroom. She had flung her juice cup from where she was sitting on top of the dresser, the lid had been knocked off, and there was a pool of juice in the middle of the floor.

I mopped it up, then walked into the kitchen, thinking I should begin clearing up, but the ramparts of dirty dishes, saucepans and bottles of juice and milk on the countertops disheartened me so effectively that I went instead to tidy our bedroom. But as I entered, the two-foot-high mountain of clean, dry clothes waiting to be put away fought me off even more successfully. I could have put them in the linen closet, so that they would be hidden away for a bit longer, except that I'd just cleared them out of the linen closet a few hours ago, so that I could cram in a few more of Hollie's clothes.

The two dirty linen baskets overflowed with Hollie's soiled clothes. So the first job should probably be getting on another load of washing. I went to the bathroom to check that there were no more of Hollie's discarded clothes on the floor, and was immediately driven back physically by the stench from the diaper bucket, whose lid would not fit snugly, since it was crammed to overflowing.

Standing just outside the bathroom door, I sank slowly down the hall wall until my bottom was on the earth-and sand-sprinkled carpet. I just didn't know where to begin.

Joshua had given up calling out and fallen asleep, but I could still hear Lisa's tiny voice calling, "Mommy, can I have another drink?" so nervously, so uncertainly that my heart melted. God, what sort of monster mother was I that I couldn't even find time to give my long-suffering youngest child a drink?

I took Lisa a drink, and sat and sang to her, stroking her hand, until gradually her little eyes closed. Then I came back to the hall and stood with my head bowed. I just did not know what to do. After a minute or two the thought permeated my inner darkness that what I most needed was to talk to someone. But there was no one I could call at eleven o'clock at night, and no one I could have talked to, really talked to.

I needed something solid in the midst of this turbulent inside world. I needed something concrete and strong in that outside world of confident indifference. I needed someone who came forward when the rest of the world was stepping back. I needed . . . But I couldn't put a name to it. And what did it matter, anyway? I was alone. I walked in defeat to the kitchen where I poured myself a brandy, knowing that no amount of brandy would dull my awareness sufficiently to remove the feeling that I was skimming on a mere leaf over the surface of mountainous seas.

The next day was the day of Joel's fortieth birthday party. In the morning I couldn't face the thought of going, but by the afternoon I felt vestiges of enthusiasm. Not that I had much expectation of being able to talk to Joel. Over a hundred guests had been invited, and it occurred to me that it was even possible that Paula would be his official partner and hostess. But at least I could look at him from time to time, and feast my eyes on his handsome face when there was no one to observe me. And it was that rare treasure, an evening out.

The babysitter, Carolyn, came at seven to allow us time to get ready. I left her reading a story to Joshua and Lisa, and keeping half an eye on Hollie, who was sitting in the middle of the dining table, swinging the light fixture back and forth on its cord.

I walked quickly to the bathroom and shut the door before I could be trapped into worrying about what Hollie might do next. I showered and washed my hair. Then I took my silver party dress out of the back of the close. I gazed at it in admiration for a minute or two before slipping it over my head. It was beautifully slim fitting and had a lovely satiny sheen that made it feel smooth and silky on my skin. I dried my hair and applied some makeup. Then I looked in the mirror. For once in my life my first thought was not the coal cellars under my eyes, or how pale my skin looked. For once my bronze curls didn't look too wild and frizzy. I looked at myself and thought, "You don't look too bad; in fact, you actually look good."

Simon came in. He flashed the quickest of glances at me.

"Hollie's trying to swing on the light fixture in the dining room," he said, proceeding to hunt in the closet for a pair of trousers.

I seethed. I didn't know whether I was cross about the fact that he couldn't be bothered to compliment me on my appearance (he probably hadn't even noticed) or frustrated that babysitters didn't have my built-in early warning system – always on amber alert – to tell them when Hollie was about to leap into mischief. (How could they have? Mine had had nine years of fine-tuning.)

Carolyn, the babysitter, looked up and smiled. "You look nice," she said.

Disarmed by her obvious sincerity, I smiled back. Then I looked around for Hollie, who was no longer on the table. After a few moments I spied her on the floor. She had gotten hold of Lisa's felt tip pens, and was putting them in her mouth one-by-one and biting off the ends. I bent down to remove them, but Hollie clung on to them with a grip of iron. It took several minutes to pry them all from her fingers and replace them in the box. Then I stood up and looked at Carolyn, whose attention had returned to the storybook she was reading. I contemplated asking her pointedly to keep more of an eye on Hollie, but in the end I refrained. I was so deeply grateful for her compliment to me, so hungry for reasons to feel good about myself that, on this occasion, I couldn't bring myself to risk damaging the friendly atmosphere. Clutching the box of ruined felt-tips, I returned in silence to the bedroom, where Simon was putting on his sports coat.

We could hear the noise of party music as we turned onto the road where Joel lived. Guests' cars were parked on almost every inch of space in the road, all along the sidewalk, and crammed in front of Joel's house. Christmas lights hung across the exterior, and garden lamps lit each side of his drive. We had to park almost a hundred yards away, and as each footstep brought me nearer and nearer to the house, I felt my nerve seeping away. By the time we reached the front door, I had convinced myself that I would not be able to think of one interesting comment or subject of conversation.

Geraldine opened the door, looking sophisticated in a black sparkly cocktail dress. She kissed us both.

"Oh good, I was afraid you'd chicken out and not come," she said.

"It was a near thing," I muttered, as Simon walked off to hang up his coat.

"We're not having any of that sort of talk," she said, briskly.

I smiled. "That's what you always used to say to me at school if I ever said I was afraid of something."

"Is it? Well, there were so many times when you were afraid of things. Not like now, eh?"

I laughed. Geraldine was looking to each side of her. "Where's Paula? She was greeting guests as they arrived."

I was determined to know the worst. "Gerry . . . "

"What?"

"Are Joel and Paula an item now?"

"I think so. Well, sort of. She'd like everyone to think so, anyway. Why, what's it to you?"

"Oh, no matter," I said, breezily. "I was just curious."

"Ah, there she is," said Geraldine. "I think perhaps we won't interrupt her just now."

Paula was standing a few feet away in the middle of the

hall, holding court at the center of a group of some half-dozen men. Her mane of shiny blonde hair was swinging over her shoulders, and the scooped neckline of her red floor-length dress was showing just the right amount of cleavage. She oozed professional confidence and ease.

"What line of business are you in?" one of the men was asking her.

"Public relations. I help to organize conferences and exhibitions and special events for small firms that don't have their own public relations department. At present I'm working for Bella Haughton, one of the local city council members. She's in the throes of opening her historical house to the public. I'm helping to organize the publicity and the opening ceremony."

"There've been a couple of unfavorable stories in the press, haven't there, about the plan to open Welshney Castle to the public?" asked one of the men.

Paula was smiling, but there was just a hint of intransigence in her voice and her gaze, when she responded.

"There have been a couple, yes, but they've been far outnumbered by the many favorable articles. And those who wrote the unfavorable pieces will find they won't be invited to the opening in December. As it will be the biggest local story for a very long time, they will regret it." She looked around as she spoke, and momentarily – though it was probably my imagination – I thought that she caught my eye.

"You see, those who oppose me always come off worst, one way or another." She laughed that tinkly melodic laugh of hers, and all the men who surrounded her laughed as if she had just cracked an enormously funny joke. A large party of seven or eight guests had just appeared.

"Anyway, gentlemen, please excuse me," she went on. "I must greet the new guests."

"There's a most delicious-looking spread of food in the dining room," said Geraldine, quickly. "Come and look." We hastily crossed the hall in the direction of the dining room while behind us Paula was exchanging bright greetings and air kisses with the new arrivals.

The dining room was large, but it was so packed with people that we could barely move. Geraldine became almost immediately embroiled in a conversation with a group of men, and I saw Simon moving off through the thicket of people toward the drinks table at the far end of the room. I was uncertain what to do. Please someone, some nice, friendly person, come and talk to me. I couldn't see anyone I knew, and I couldn't hang on to Geraldine all evening for support. Please please please pleeeeeeeeeeeeease. I quickly cobbled together a nonchalant expression so that anyone who saw me would think that an incredibly glamorous man was in the process of getting me a drink, and not that I was remotely in need of someone to talk to.

Suddenly inspiration struck. I could fill a plate with food – that would make me look well occupied for a few minutes. I moved through the crowd of people and stood staring at the magnificent arrangement of cold chicken pieces, salmon with cucumber and tomato, quiches, salads, cold meats and cheeses, garnished dips and exquisitely shaped rolls.

"Go on, take a plate and fill it up," said a deep voice to my right. I flicked my head around, but even before I took in the sight of Joel standing beside me, the sound of his voice sent shock waves through me as if I had suddenly come smack against a delightfully cushioned but still hard brick wall. His intent grey-green eyes were fixed on me. I had intended to be very cool and controlled, but I couldn't prevent a smile from breaking out that curved every muscle from my chin to my forehead. He wore black jeans and a white polo neck shirt that showed off his muscular arms and chest. The urge to reach out and run my fingers through his thick hair where it curled on his neck was almost irresistible.

"The trouble is, I've never been able to eat and talk at the same time," I said, still beaming.

"Well, you'll just have to spray it at everyone then," he retorted.

I broke into laughter. He beamed at me, and then began to laugh himself. I shook with laughter until my insides began to hurt, and even then I couldn't stop. The walls and barricades that years of chronic anxiety had raised in my head exploded, and all the tension rushed out in a great whoosh of air. Soon another guest touched Joel's right arm and spoke to him, and he was forced to turn away. I stood there enjoying that post-laughter sense of exhilaration and contentment that makes you want to do nothing but lie in a hammock in a South Sea paradise.

I filled my plate with salad, cold chicken and salmon, then walked – or, rather, glided – over to where Simon was sitting, beer glass in hand, talking to Geraldine and a group of others. Everyone was eating, so I pulled up a chair and joined the edge of the group nearest to Simon and Geraldine.

I glanced around, but couldn't spot Joel's tall frame in the crowd. But even if I couldn't look at him, I could at least talk about him.

"Do you work with Joel?" I asked the middle-aged slightly grey-haired man sitting to my right.

"Not directly," he replied. "I'm an investment adviser so I have worked with Joel on some short-term projects."

"Gerry, how do you know Joel?"

"I had a temporary contract with his company a year or two back."

"Is he good to work with?"

"Oh yes," Geraldine and the investment adviser chorused in unison. They both laughed.

"He's extremely professional, hard working and a very clever man, but he's also good at people management," said the investment broker.

"He gets a long way just with charm," smiled Geraldine. "He exudes warmth and friendliness, and people feel at ease with him. But he can be very distant when he's not in the mood. He's a very complex man."

"How have . . . " I began, but the group were getting up to take back their dinner plates and choose desserts. I joined them. When we came back, the conversation took a new direction. I could hardly keep returning the subject matter to Joel, so instead I ate my dessert, frequently flicking my head around to see if I could catch sight of him, but I never did. Behind us the plates, serving dishes and food tables were being cleared away.

The lights gradually grew dimmer, the music became faster and louder, and people began to dance. I glanced around for

Joel, and still I couldn't see him. Nevertheless, for some uncanny reason my expectations of seeing more of him remained high. I had a strong intuition that something significant would be said or done before the evening was out.

After a few songs the music changed to disco music, the kind I had danced to in my teens and twenties. Simon must have caught me glancing around.

"Are you okay?" he asked.

"Oh yes."

"Let's go and dance," he said, still eyeing me uncertainly.

"Can you remember the last time we did this?" I asked as he led me to the dance floor.

"Not since we were first married, I think."

We found a reasonable-sized space on the edge of the dance floor. Simon danced in a quiet, restrained manner. The dance floor had once been one of the few places where I felt confident, and in my youth I had been quite uninhibited in my dancing. I very much wanted to dance that way now and let off steam a bit, but I felt awkward and self-conscious because it had been so long. My dancing was cautious and bland, but at least I could be fairly certain of not looking ridiculous. When Geraldine and the others in the group came to join us, and the little space filled up, I stopped worrying quite so much, and my moves became more fluid.

A couple of times I saw Joel dancing, mostly with Paula, but sometimes with other guests; of course, he was an excellent dancer, performing with an easy, rhythmic grace.

After a while, I saw Simon talking to Joel, and I went to join them. A few minutes later, Geraldine came over, took Simon by the hand and whisked him off to the dance floor. Making the most of an unexpected opportunity, I shifted to the seat next to Joel that Simon had just vacated. He looked at me without blinking for a moment or two. "Hello, Lucy," he said.

"How long have you been planning all this?"

"A few weeks and months, though in a way I've been planning it all my life, since I've always wanted a really big birthday bash with all my friends and family, and never had one."

"What about your wedding? Wasn't that a big family party?"

"Both my weddings, you mean. Yes, I suppose so. But, well, you know weddings. They were both very formal, and both were organized by my brides' parents. You couldn't exactly let your hair down."

"So have you succeeded this time? Have you got everyone you want here?"

"Pretty well. Some school friends, some university friends, dozens of people I've worked with. My two boys, my brother, my two ex-wives."

"Your ex-wives? Are you – do you . . . "

"Look" he shifted his head slightly with a look of exasperation. "I really don't want to talk about them."

"Well, what do you want to talk about?"

"How about music? Do you like my choice in music? I've been raiding my friends' CD collections over the last couple of weeks to record it."

"Yes, very much. It's been excellent."

"Have I missed anything? Anything you really like, I mean?"

I took a long drink from my glass of wine. I had lost count of how many glasses I had had, but I didn't need to worry because Simon was driving home. I was in that floaty, dangerous state of inebriation where you feel you can say anything you like and get away with it because you are inviolable.

"Well, there's one track I've always really liked, that's good to dance to."

"Oh?" he smiled.

"Do you remember 'Light my Fire," a song by The Doors from the sixties?"

"Of course." He looked thoughtful, as if he had to make an effort to remember the words, when it was quite obvious he knew what they were. "Oh yes." He fixed his eyes on mine hypnotically. "Light my fire, light my fire . . . " He didn't blink. I threw my head back and laughed. I couldn't remember when I had ever enjoyed myself so much. He laughed too, that deep, infectious laugh that was so characteristic of him. I pulled my head straight and met his eyes, and we both laughed again.

"Any others?"

"Well, yes. There's that Bob Dylan song, 'Lay, Lady, Lay.'"

He was staring at me, if anything, even more intently.

"Ah, another good one." He recited the words of the chorus very slowly, holding my gaze with his. Neither of us blinked. I shivered visibly. I pictured us alone in a room, me lying across a huge bed with gleaming brass rails and ruffled silk sheets, because he had commanded me to.

I was burning to touch him, and couldn't stop myself from reaching out and touching his arm very lightly.

Immediately he slipped his arm around me, bent toward me and kissed me on the cheek.

"You've no idea how beautiful you are," he said. "Especially when you smile and laugh. I'd like to make you laugh more."

Afraid of showing too much feeling publicly, I reached my hand down to squeeze his leg under the table, meaning to touch it just above the knee. But I discovered, with an equal mixture of horror and delight, that my hand was a lot further up his leg than I had meant it to be. I realized I had two alternatives. I could withdraw it quickly in obvious embarrassment, perhaps apologize, and we would undoubtedly spend the next minute or two fumbling about in awkward attempts at conversation, not meeting each other's eyes. Or I could leave it where it was. Brazen it out. Really, there was no decision to make. I left it where it was. I had to struggle hard to restrain myself from bursting into laughter. Keeping my hand there, I decided to risk a glance at him out of the corner of my eyes, to see with what degree of anger or indignation he was greeting my presumption. The look he was giving me was hard to describe. I would have said – except that I couldn't quite believe it to be possible – that his eyes were full of an intense longing.

My feeling of recklessness started to ebb as I spotted Simon and Geraldine returning from the dance floor. Simon gave me an uncertain smile as he approached.

"Come on, love, let's go and have another dance," he said.

I had no desire to do anything except stay exactly where I was. But I had no choice.

"Yes, let's," I replied, forcing a smile. Simon took my hand and led me on a circuitous route between guests who sat talking and laughing in groups around tables piled high with empty and half-empty wine bottles and discarded wine and beer glasses.

The dance floor was so full now that it was impossible to dance without knocking into people or feeling elbows or hands jabbing you as you moved. Nevertheless, it felt good to dance again. I enjoyed the beat of the music, the easy rhythmic movements and the sense of the world outside the walls of the room seeming faraway and half forgotten. How many years had it been since we had done this, I pondered, as I glided about the dance floor, smiling at Simon, and smiling at strangers whose eye I accidentally caught.

This mood lasted until I spotted, at the very edge of the dance floor, Joel dancing with Paula. Not dancing as the other couples were dancing, some feet apart, but so close to her that their arms touched almost constantly. But if the amount of touching was unpalatable, it was nothing compared to the way they were looking at each other, or, more specifically, Joel was looking at Paula. It wasn't just that his eyes seemed wider than usual; it was as if, as far as he was concerned, there was no one else in the room but her. I didn't like it. I found it so distressing that the image of him looking at her in that way plagued me throughout the ride home, which we undertook about twenty minutes later, in all the wakeful moments of the night, and throughout the following days.

Chapter Four

What a loving mother. The kind of warm, loving mother who all but pushed her child, at exasperation point, into the very last place in the world she wanted to go. That's me.

I had to do it. I had to do it because, even worse than the gut-ripping pain of inflicting this misery on my child, was the fear of the solitary, forlorn adult she could become if I didn't force her into it.

Lisa's hands were clasped over her face, hiding her eyes, her nose, her mouth, her cheeks, as we began the walk from the car across the parking lot to the community center where her preschool was held. She could, of course, see nothing, so I held her left forearm with my right hand to guide her, while in my left I carried her bag. I aimed at a tone of bottomless love and patience. An air of brittle self-restraint was the nearest I came to it.

"It's okay, Lisa. You love it when you get in there."

"No, I don't."

"Yes, you do," I urged, still trying to maintain a slightly cooing, reassuring tone, though the pressure of my anxiety made me sound more like a strangulated pigeon.

Last Monday Lisa had walked into preschool with her hands over her nose and mouth, peeping over the tops of her fingers. On Tuesday she had remained like this for half an hour, even though I had stayed to encourage her to join in songs such as "Row-Row-Row Your Boat," which required hand movements. Then from Wednesday onwards, she had insisted on covering the whole of her pretty little face, and I had guided her as if she were blind, in turn, being comforting and encouraging, then firm and snappy.

It was a bright, blustery autumn day, and the air was mild.

"I expect they'll take you to the swings and slides today," I said, enticingly.

"I don't want to go."

"But you enjoy the painting, and the songs. And you like that little girl, Isobel."

"No, I don't."

"What is it, Lisa?" I stopped and turned the little fist-covered face toward me. "Why are you hiding your lovely face?"

"I don't want them all to look at me."

"They'll look at you much more if you keep your hands in front of your face."

"Take me home, please, Mommy."

What was I to do? Like Joshua, she was quiet and shy and needed encouragement to make friends. Simon and I had never been able to give the two of them much experience of playing family games or going on family expeditions to castles, museums or theme parks, because we had been too busy guarding Hollie or clearing up her messes. And, gradually, over the months and years, the prospect of taking Hollie on such an outing with her brother and sister had come to seem too hazardous.

The result was that Lisa had had little chance to learn how to interact with other children. I had tried to spend the time when Hollie was at school doing activities with Lisa, trying to give her the attention she had so greatly lacked, but it was hard to counteract the effect of her early isolation. Six months ago I had hoped joining preschool would help, but the counselors told me that she was timid and quiet and distant with the other children.

Should I take her home, or should I force her to stay? I shut my mind to the fact that I was driving Geraldine to the airport later in the morning, and considered what was best for Lisa. The fact was that she had to stay. In less than a year she would be starting school, and she would then have no choice. If I took her home now, she would learn the lesson that running away from a problem was an acceptable solution, and it would be that much harder in a year's time to learn that she could no longer run away. I had no choice.

But what was the right approach? Perhaps I should tell her that in a few months she would be starting school, but I didn't want to frighten her. No, surely the best approach was to continue encouraging her and reminding her of how much fun she could have.

I tried to pull her hands from her face, but they remained resolutely clamped there.

"Darling, it's good for you to go. And I know you enjoy the songs and the painting, and playing with the Play-Do."

"But the other children always come along."

"Yes, but you must try to play with them. Say something nice about what they're painting. And can't you play with the other girls in the shop and the hospital corner?"

"They're not my friends."

"Isobel's your friend. I know she likes you very much because her mommy told me. That's why she's asked you to go for lunch today."

That was the final straw. I heard the sobs before I saw the tears.

"No, Mommy, you come and get me."

Her shoulders heaved, and she sobbed and sobbed. Steeling myself, I put my hands on her shoulders and pushed her gently the short distance to the concrete staircase. Down the steps I guided her, and along the corridor to the main hall where the supervisor sat checking off the children's names on the attendance list.

"Hello, Lisa," she said cheerfully. "What's the matter?"

Carol, one of the helpers, appeared at this point, picked Lisa up in her arms and carried her over to where the children were listening to a story.

"She's still saying she doesn't want to come to preschool, and I keep trying to emphasize how much she enjoys it when she gets here."

"We're doing our best to get her to join in with the other children, but she's very reluctant."

"She's supposed to be going for lunch with Isobel today, and she's saying she doesn't want to do that. But it's the first time she's ever been invited to someone's house, and I very much want her to go."

"Well, we'll keep trying to encourage her. But it's hard to get her away from the Play-Do table and the painting. Did you know, she only paints in black and white?"

"Yes, I know."

Geraldine seemed almost as dejected as Lisa when I went to pick her up. Normally she was enthusiastic, even excited about her trips abroad, but I sensed the change in mood immediately when she answered the door.

"I'm all ready," she said, evading my eye. She handed me the large shoulder bag that represented her hand luggage, while she herself picked up the suitcase. As I opened the trunk for her to lift in the suitcase, I thought again how out of spirits she seemed. She looked as immaculate as ever in a cream silk top, tan suede jacket and brown and tan silk scarf, her makeup faultless, her hair glossy and carefully styled. But she looked pale, and there were heavy shadows under her eyes that I didn't remember having noticed before.

"Are you okay?" I asked, as we shut the car doors and put on our seat belts.

"Fine. How was the school run?" she asked crisply.

"Depressing. Joshua just hates being in his new class. The teacher and the principal decided in the summer, you remember, that Joshua should repeat second grade. All his friends have gone up into third, he knows no one in the class and has made no new friends. We argued against the idea when it was first proposed. Now all our fears are being borne out. Joshua is becoming more withdrawn than ever, and losing that tiny little bit of confidence that was growing inside him over the summer term."

"Can you do anything more? Protest again that he should be with his group?"

"That's what we're going to do. I'll write another letter to the school and ask for a meeting to discuss the effect it's having on Joshua."

"How are things with Lisa?"

"No better. I try to be upbeat with her, but it's terrible. She keeps walking into preschool with her hands over her face, saying she doesn't want people to look at her. I tell her, people are going to look at her far more if she walks in looking as strange as that."

"Are the staff supportive?"

"Oh, yes. At the moment, anyway. The leader told me she's never known another child to behave in that way. Plenty of children cry when they're left for the first few days, or even weeks. But no child has ever walked in trying to pretend they're invisible."

"How impossibly hard. For you, I mean."

"Yes. Sometimes I get – well, bitter and angry. Why can't just one part of my life go well?"

There was silence for a minute or two as I negotiated the traffic. As I pulled out from the shoulder between two trucks on the slow lane, and then into a gap in the middle lane, Geraldine suddenly said:

"I don't want to go."

"I can't believe I'm hearing this. You've always looked forward to your foreign trips. You've always had itchy feet if you stayed in one place too long."

"I know. I seem to have changed. Perhaps it's the onset of middle age." She gave a forced laugh.

"Come off it," I said. "You're the last person who'll ever be middle aged. You're the most open-minded person I know, always full of enthusiasm for everything you do, always open to new ideas, always reluctant for things to stay the same for too long in case you get stuck in a rut."

"Hmm. Perhaps I was like that. But – you won't believe this. I'm beginning to think that all I want to do is find the right man and buy a nice house, and all that."

"I never thought I'd hear you say that."

"I know. Would you believe it; this morning, while I was waiting for you to come, I was planning what colors I'd paint all the rooms if I had this ideal house."

"There's nothing wrong with that. It is exciting, planning your first proper home."

"But it's so – so middle aged."

"Perhaps you've hit on the answer there," I said, smiling to show I was joking. "Perhaps you're having a mid-life crisis."

But Geraldine wasn't smiling. She was frowning, and her head was bent.

"It's partly a question of age," she said, seriously. "But" – she broke off and thought for a moment, "It's other things too."

I glanced over at her. She had turned away to look out of the window, a determinedly absorbed expression on her face, as if the trees and the fences and the tall ramparts of the reservoir were suddenly fascinating. It struck me for the first time that her makeup was not just impeccably neat, but more thickly applied than usual, and that she was wearing foundation, blusher and eye-liner, all of which were new. The words "Are you sure you're okay?" formed themselves on my tongue so distinctly that I could almost taste them, but I swallowed them. Her bright, sharp gaze continued to laser on to some 18-wheelers traveling on a side road.

We said very little while we found a space in the parking lot at Heathrow, loaded a cart with her two cases and wheeled it across the connecting bridge to Terminal 2. In line at the check-in counter, I said, "You could come home weekends."

Geraldine looked thoughtful.

"I'm tempted to, actually. But it seems a perfect opportunity to explore Lake Geneva and Lake Como, and the Italian lakes. And I might do a bit of work on weekends, too. Then perhaps I could come home earlier."

In the departure lounge, as we hugged each other, Geraldine's spirits seemed to sink even lower. Her determination to honor her commitment was like a slab of concrete, rock hard but grimly devoid of spirit or enthusiasm. As she pulled away and turned to walk down the departure corridor, the words fell out of my mouth, unbidden.

"Are you really okay?"

She turned back to me, her flight bag swinging on her shoulder. "I don't feel so good. Actually, I've not felt good for a few weeks."

Sharp slithers of ice pricked up and down my spine. I stared at her without speaking, and my mouth dropped open. She looked at me, then for the first time that morning she laughed.

"Don't you worry about me," she smiled. "You've more than enough to worry about without worrying about me, too. I'll be back in early November. Back with the Beaujolais Nouveau. In fact, I'll bring back a case."

As I stood watching her disappear into the crowds, I couldn't help but worry about the prospect of Huntington's, that awful inherited disease that she had so far seemingly resisted. No, I told myself firmly, it wasn't that. It was a virus. It was overwork.

I was just crossing the main concourse of the departure terminal, on my way back to the parking lot, when a hand touched my arm. I turned, and then stared in disbelief.

"Is it really you?" I asked, stupidly, unable to take my eyes off him. It had been a constant fantasy of mine over the past weeks, dreaming I might bump into him at various locations in Shalham. I had known, of course, in my heart of hearts, that it was virtually impossible. I mean, how often did I go to city pubs and wine bars, and how often did he, with two almost-grown-up sons, undertake the school run? But now, incredibly, it was happening.

Joel looked perplexed.

"Who were you expecting?"

"Oh – er – no one. I was just seeing Geraldine off on a business trip."

I eyed his small suitcase.

"Are you going somewhere exciting?"

"No, I've just been somewhere. I went to Bordeaux for the weekend to see my younger son. He lives there with his mother."

A host of questions flashed through my mind, but I couldn't decide which were acceptable, or which to ask first, so I settled for augmenting the impression he no doubt had of me as a complete simpleton.

"Oh," I said

He looked at me, and smiled again.

"Are you planning on going straight home?"

"Well . . . I hadn't really thought beyond seeing Geraldine off. I thought her flight might be delayed, so I didn't make any plans. A friend's picking Lisa up from preschool." I looked at his thoughtful expression.

"Why?"

"Oh, just a mad idea."

"What idea?"

"I just thought, it's such a beautiful day, we could go for a walk somewhere, just for an hour or so."

I gaped at him. Unfortunately, he misread my expression.

"No, too short notice. I expect there are other things you've got to do."

"No, oh no," I said, hurriedly. "Nothing that can't wait. What have you got in mind?"

"Do you know the Shalden Garden in Bramshott?"

I consulted my mental map of the villages west of Shalham.

"Yes, I know it."

"How about meeting there in about half an hour?"

"That's okay. In fact, that would be great."

I found my car, unlocked the door and swung myself into the driver's seat. I drove between the endless rows of parked cars, down ramps and other endless rows of cars until I emerged through the dusty black opening of the parking deck, out into the dazzling autumn sunshine and the mild fresh breeze. I darted between the 18-wheelers and vans on the M25 and exulted in the open fast lane of the A543 as it turned south between the gently rolling hills, the sheep fields and ancient woods that formed the leafy backdrop of the expensive, executive houses of north Windleshire. I finally exited left on the side road that led to Bramshott.

The Shalden Garden was a privately owned garden of about twenty acres that was opened to the public a couple of days a week at certain times of the year. The roads had been relatively quiet, so I arrived and parked in the small parking lot with ten minutes to spare. There was no sign of Joel, so I brushed my hair and checked in the rear-view mirror for makeup smudges.

Two elderly women in thick woollen overcoats and boots crossed the parking lot, paid their money at the small kiosk and pushed through the turnstile. The wind swept up dead stems, twigs and newly fallen leaves from beneath the trees at the end of the parking lot. I opened the window and sat listening to the swishing of the tree branches and the rustling of the leaves scudding across the asphalt, and found myself thinking what a good meeting place this was. Discreet. Out of the way, surely, of anyone either of us might know. And then I realized what I was thinking. Heavens, what on earth are you contemplating . . . ? It's just a walk, I told myself, just a walk with a friend.

I stepped out of the car, pressed the locking button and approached the turnstile and the printed notice of prices and opening times. Then I turned.

Joel was striding toward me. He had put on his leather jacket. He was staring at me intently as he strode toward me, and his gaze, like a long tongue, seemed to lick, caress and penetrate every part of my insides.

"Hello." His voice was deeper than usual, and very shaky.

"H-h-h." I failed to get the words out, and after a few seconds gave up trying. He took my right hand, which was a fist of tension, firmly in both of his, pulled it gently flat, then stroked my fingers and my palm. A few yards away an elderly couple made their way across the parking lot to the kiosk, but they were looking ahead to the garden entrance and taking no notice of us.

"Come on." Gently he took my hand and led me toward the kiosk. He pulled coins from his pocket and pushed them under the grill. The bespectacled elderly gentleman on the other side smiled and said, "Good afternoon. I hope you enjoy your walk."

"Thank you." I pushed through the turnstile, beaming with delight and pride at the old man's obvious assumption that Joel was my husband.

Grass lawns spread to the left and right of the path, without a weed or sprig of clover to mar their immaculate perfection. We ambled between them, then around a raised stone bed of exotic shrubs and bushes. The path threaded through a gap in a line of yew trees to a more open grassy slope, dotted here and there with taller trees. To the left the garden sloped up a short hill between flower beds where two gardeners were pruning some drooping rose bushes. To the right the garden stretched down to a long, rectangular ornamental pond dotted here and there with water-lilies. The other walkers had turned to stroll past the worn roses or to explore the immaculate edges of the pond. The elderly couple who had entered the garden just before us were standing staring over the wrought-iron, waist-high fence at the enormous goldfish. A group of middle-aged women in anoraks and quilted coats were approaching the pond from another path. A young mother pushed a stroller up the hill between the lines of jaded rose beds while a toddler in an over-sized coat tottered at her side.

In contrast to these visitors, Joel and I chose neither path. Instead we crossed the grassy slope toward a cluster of trees.

"There's a small waterfall in this direction," Joel said. "Let's see if we can find it."

The path led in among clumps of oak, ash and beech trees, gradually becoming thinner and more overhung with brambles and overreaching branches. I was just beginning to think it would come to a halt in the middle of some thicket, that Joel was wrong and that we would have to retrace our steps, when suddenly it opened out into a sunny clearing. We were at the bottom of a rocky bank, down which a small stream flowed, rippling over giant boulders and small rocks into a large pool at the base, from which it filtered outwards and on through the trees.

"There are stories that a hermit used to live here, over a thousand years ago. He was supposed to inhabit a cave somewhere behind the waterfall, but no one's ever been able to find it."

"Just a legend, I suppose. It's a shame. On a day like today the idea of living in the wilderness seems lovely. Most of the year it would be awful. But it's a lovely, romantic dream, to think of people living wild all those centuries ago."

"It has been done more recently, you know," Joel said. "Surely you've heard the story of the wild boy of Pershore?"

I shook my head.

"He lived in Pershore Forest, just a few miles from here on the other side of Shalham. You'll know it because Hollie's school grounds back on to the edge of it."

"Yes, I know it, but I've never heard of this wild boy. Who was he?"

"He lived about a hundred and fifty years ago in one of the local villages. The story goes that he ran away from home, and slept in the woods. The forest was a lot bigger and wilder in those days, of course. He lived wild in the woods for many years."

"How was he found?"

"I don't know. But I know that when he was found, he was almost like a savage. He could no longer talk, and he lashed out at people trying to help him."

"What an amazing story."

We turned from the waterfall and followed the stream into an area of thicker undergrowth and foliage, between chestnut trees and sycamores laden with orange and amber leaves that looked as if they needed only a touch of wind to bring them flying down. A few yards ahead was a large clearing, and as I followed Joel out of the protection of the trees, a strong gust of autumn wind caught large strands of my corkscrew hair and blew them across my face. Before I had a chance to push them away, I could feel Joel's fingers, strong and gentle, on my cheeks, brushing the hair aside.

Ever so carefully he redirected each strand to its proper side. Then, the job done, he continued to stand there, his face just inches from mine, his fingers caressing my cheeks and my forehead. I just stood there. Afraid to move, afraid almost to breathe in case it prompted him to cease these beautiful, rhythmic movements.

Then in one swift movement, he slipped his hands around the back of my head, bent forwards and kissed me lightly on the lips. He remained standing there, just inches away, and smiled. Then he bent forwards again, slipped both arms around my back and pulled me firmly toward him, brushing my lips with his lips and his teeth in little movements that were half kisses, half nuzzles, half licks. I seemed to come alive with tremors and quiverings in every part of my body.

Eventually, it was the wind that, having brought us together, quickly broke us apart. I could feel half-dead leaves carried on gusts across the clearing pattering against my face, my hair and my clothes, and it was the sense that something other than leaves was catapulting against us that made us break away from each other and turn to look.

"What are they?" I asked. The fragments were roughly the size as leaves, but black and grey, more crumpled, slightly burnt looking at the edges.

"Bits of newspaper," said Joel. "Someone must recently have had a bonfire somewhere near, and the bits of newspaper they used as kindling have been caught by the wind."

Handfuls of the scraps came hurtling toward us for another minute or two, and were blown into the thickness of the woods behind us. Joel caught one. He opened it out, then he shot me a mischievous smile. "Look."

He handed it to me. The fragment contained the remains of some newspaper headline of days or weeks before, but only one of the words could be made out. Joel looked at it again, then read the word out loud.

"Passion."

We looked at each other in a conspiratorial manner, then both burst into laughter.

We walked back hand-in-hand along a path that bounded the right-hand side of the woods. The brown curves of the newly ploughed soil lifted like undulating waves, gleaming in the sunshine. In the hedgerows to our left, juniper berries, rose hips and a few remaining blackberries, voluptuously round, shiny and succulent, hung temptingly on thorny stems from out of the tangled mass of twigs and foliage. We crossed the stream on a wooden bridge and saw the water rippling pure and clear over soft, round pebbles that gleamed like precious gems in the stray sunbeams poking through the forest canopy. We walked back to the main part of the garden across a meadow of autumn crocuses that were just beginning to wilt and that appeared to have split themselves down the middle in their ardent attempts to stretch their velvety purple petals toward the light.

We said goodbye as we reached the entrance kiosk. He said nothing about any future meetings; indeed, his manner became suddenly very crisp and business-like as if he had moved on already in his mind to the client meetings he was holding later that afternoon.

To my surprise, this coolness did not lessen my joy. I couldn't believe how full of energy I felt. I could have jogged all the way home and still have had the week's worth of energy that

I needed to get through the day. I felt invigorated. Above all, I felt powerful, as if I could achieve anything.

When I got home, I parked the car in the driveway, made myself a sandwich and a cup of coffee in the kitchen, then spread my files and notebooks over the dining room table. I crammed a few mouthfuls of sandwich into my mouth while I studied the notes I had made the previous days during my telephone conversations with parents who had succeeded in winning boarding placements for their children. Then I drew up lists of tasks for the next few days based on their advice.

I needed reports from all the specialists who had assessed Hollie, and I made a list of them. We needed a lawyer, and we needed the advice of disability agencies. Above all, I needed to throw myself into what would no doubt be the most frustrating, time-consuming, but ultimately most vital job of all – finding the right school. I made a rough division of the jobs into lists for the following days.

When I had finished that, I had almost two hours left before I had to pick Joshua up from school. Two hours was a wealth of time. I moved the telephone onto the table, studied my list and picked up the receiver. The first name on the list was that of Hollie's pediatrician. I remembered the bleak, grey January Friday seven years ago when I had sat in her consulting room while the words this kind, humane woman was uttering – without being able to meet my eyes – floated in and out of my consciousness, not quite registering.

"I think we have to accept . . . communication disorder . . . autism . . . lifelong . . . incurable," while a little golden-haired cherub clattered around the room, obliviously pulling toys noisily from boxes. I dialed the number and spoke to the secretary.

Next, I called the clinical psychologist who had visited in the first months, and made an appointment for her to visit us. I wrote a letter to our doctor, asking for a brief letter of support. I also called our visiting nurse and asked her to call. She had known us since Hollie was born; she had applied for free diapers for us when Hollie was three, and put me in touch with local charities that had given us small donations from time to time. She had a glimmer of an idea of the chaos we lived in; she would support us.

By the time I left to pick up Joshua, I felt a deep sense of satisfaction at what I had achieved, which in turn ignited a small candle flicker of hope inside me.

All the time I was at the school, and at Isobel's house to pick up Lisa, I treasured this sensation. It was hope – precious, precious hope – but it was something more than that. It took me a long time to identify the feeling because it was something entirely new. I realized that it was the beginning of some kind of self-belief. I, who had always been so ineffectual, so afraid of sticking my neck out, I could take action, I could do these things that would help. I treasured the sensation inside me, almost as if I were a few days pregnant and no one but I knew.

I realized that this embryo of self-belief, if I could keep it alive and help it to grow in the coming months, would be of inestimable importance in the trials to come. Later that evening, I had a foretaste of the help it would be. My sister-in-law Fiona called to discuss the fiftieth birthday party for Simon's brother Daniel, to be held in November. Veronica, my mother-in-law, had called her with an idea for a combined family present, and she wanted me to call Rachel, Daniel's wife, to see if she liked the idea.

"I think it's a good idea for a present," I said. "But I've been on the phone most of the day, trying to make arrangements with our pediatrician and our clinical psychologist and lots of other experts to do assessments of Hollie for our upcoming due process hearing." I paused for a second, aware that as far as Fiona, and indeed the rest of the family, was concerned, I might as well have been describing the mechanics of a lunar landing. But I carried on resolutely: "I've still got a long list of parents of autistic children to call for advice on how to get a child into a special boarding school. Would it be possible for you to phone Rachel?"

I could sense Fiona swelling with indignation on the other end of the phone.

"Well, I'm very busy too, you know. I've got my cousins coming for dinner tonight."

I felt the familiar wave of weariness and frustration. It was impossible to explain to people who hadn't been through it themselves exactly what it was like, coping every day with everything that arose from having a child like Hollie. Now, for the first time, with these vestiges of self-belief, I seriously contemplated trying to explain to Fiona. I opened my mouth to begin, but habit and conditioning had too strong a hold.

"Yes, of course, you've got a dinner party. Of course, I'll call Rachel."

I had less time on the other days. Each morning, by the time I had spent up to an hour trying unsuccessfully to pry Lisa's hands from her face, I had little more than an hour left.

However, I was determined to make the most of every minute. On Tuesday I wrote out a list of names of recommended lawyers, together with phone numbers and any comments that individual parents had made about them. I had just brought the phone to the table together with a fresh mug of coffee when the phone rang.

"Hello, is this Mrs. Roseman?" asked a bright, friendly female voice.

"It is."

"My name is Ruth Taylor. I've just been appointed your social worker. I know you've been asking for a social worker for a long time. I was wondering if I could make an appointment to visit you and Hollie."

For a few seconds I couldn't think of anything to say. I'd forgotten how long we had been asking for a social worker.

"That would be . . . would be wonderful," I faltered. "We need . . . oh, it's too hard to explain, there's so many problems. I'm at . . . well, I'm not exactly at the breaking point, but . . . "

I had been at the breaking point, as I now saw clearly, and I would be still if it wasn't for Joel. Thanks solely to him, I had taken a step back from the edge to a place where I could see more clearly and begin to think and plan effectively, instead of lurching from one crisis to another. Inspired by his belief in me, I had started to take action, and I was discovering powers and talents I had never dreamed of.

"You feel overwhelmed by your daughter's problems?" asked the social worker.

"Yes," I said, surprised at the open acknowledgment of our problems by an establishment figure. "I'm completely overwhelmed."

"Let's set a time for me to come then," she said gently.

"Today? Tomorrow?"

She laughed. "I could come Thursday afternoon."

"About ten past four? That's when Hollie's bus returns."

"Four-ten it is then. I look forward to meeting you both."

"Thanks. Thanks very much indeed."

I replaced the receiver, still not quite able to believe my own ears.

On Wednesday morning I wrote a letter to Joshua's teacher, requesting a meeting with both her and the principal, to ask once again if Joshua could be returned to his third-grade class. He was not settling in the new class, and could not understand why he had been separated from his friends. After that I returned to the task of researching possible schools for Hollie. I had allocated a whole notepad to this investigation and jotted down on separate pages the names of schools specializing in autism mentioned by other parents, so that I could add comments and opinions on each one as I came across them. Representatives of autism organizations and of special education agencies I had consulted the previous week also went on the list.

I began phoning the schools on the list, asking for brochures and talking to their administrators about their educational and therapeutic approaches. Nearly all offered the same sort of traditional approach as Petheril, one that had not suited

Hollie. None of them grabbed my attention and made me think, "This is exactly what Hollie needs." And perhaps this was a good thing, since they all had waiting lists and no possibility of placement for two years or more.

Thursday morning I had an appointment to visit a boarding school in Southshire. It took about an hour to get there. I was kept waiting for half an hour after my arrival. When the director finally showed me around the school, I quickly realized that its character was almost identical to that of Petheril, only with a small boarding department.

Later that day as I walked out to meet Hollie's bus, an elderly Volkswagen Beetle pulled up alongside. Hollie leapt happily out of the bus, and the aide heaved her fat calves toward the step and handed out Hollie's school bag, muttering grumpily, "She's wasn't too bad today."

I didn't want to get into a conversation with her. "Thank you so much," I said briskly, taking Hollie's hand. I was about to run back to the house when a young woman climbed out of the Volkswagen.

"Mrs. Roseman?"

"Yes?"

"Ruth Taylor." She held out her hand. "I'm your new social worker."

"Oh!" I smiled. "I am so pleased to meet you."

I released Hollie, and we shook hands. Ruth Taylor, probably only in her late twenties, had a dark, page-boy hairstyle, a thin, pretty face and an effervescent manner.

"I'm pleased to meet you, too," she said, with a warm smile. "And this must be Hollie." She bent down and tried to meet Hollie's wildly wavering gaze.

"Hello, Hollie. I'm Ruth. I've come to talk to your mom about your new school."

Hollie arced her gaze about as if absorbed in watching a formation of flying saucers. Then she turned and made a sudden dash for the house. I started to run after her, while Ruth hurried by my side.

As I entered the through front door, there were loud angry cries from the family room. Joshua was holding Hollie tightly by both arms and yelling, "Don't knock any more down." He had put down his plastic dinosaur world map and carefully set out all his model dinosaurs in their proper places, the brachiosaurs among the trees, the plesiosaurs in the water. Hollie had hurtled like a comet through their midst.

"I'm sorry, darling," I said to Joshua, taking Hollie's arm and holding her tightly away from the dinosaur map.

"She probably walked on them by accident," said Ruth, who had followed me in. "She can't have seen them."

"No, she did it deliberately," I corrected her. "Not maliciously, of course. She wasn't intending to be mean. She just thought – if you can call it thinking – that they weren't in their proper place because they're not meant to be on the floor. And that made her uncomfortable."

"I see," said Ruth, genuinely interested to learn. She bent and began to help Joshua put the dinosaurs back in their places.

It was a bright day, so I brought two mugs of tea into the yard, and we sat on the wooden bench watching Hollie stuff stones, earth and handfuls of grass into her mouth. Ruth said:

"I think you are absolutely right to look for a boarding school. I don't see how you can ever have time for Joshua and Lisa when your life is like this. I will write a report supporting your case, and I'll make sure you have it by the end of next week. In the meantime, you haven't found a school yet, and even when you do, realistically, there may be a long delay before Hollie can start. You need help now, after school. I'm going to talk to various organizations, for example, the Joan Davis Foundation, which sometimes supply care workers and helpers. It is imperative you have help after school every day."

"After-school helpers," I repeated, hardly able to believe my ears. Hollie had moved farther down the garden and was now thrusting handfuls of sand from the sandbox into her mouth.

"Assuming I can find people, which I should be able to, they will watch Hollie for you, allowing you to cook and do things with the other children."

"Where are your wings?" I smiled, and she laughed.

Just then Lisa came out of the kitchen door and walked over to where we sat. She knelt down and put her head on my lap. I stroked her hair for a few moments. When I looked up, I saw that Hollie had stripped all her clothes off and was starting to remove her diaper. For a second I stayed relaxed, telling myself it was a mild day and she wouldn't come to any harm running around naked for a few minutes.

"Is that mud all over her bottom?" asked Ruth, curiously.

I looked more closely. Then I leaped to my feet and, Lisa careered suddenly backwards.

"No, it's not," I said grimly.

Hollie was climbing up the slide on her hands and feet, her filthy bottom facing me. I sprinted thirty feet, then leaped to grab her arms as she was just turning on to her feces-encrusted bottom, ready to slide down. She pulled away from me, making loud protesting noises. I had to maneuver very carefully to pull her while simultaneously arcing my own body backwards to avoid smears of poo from her mucky bottom.

When I returned a few minutes later, after cleaning Hollie and depositing her in a freshly run bath, Ruth had washed up the tea mugs and was pouring juice for Joshua and Lisa. She turned as I entered the kitchen, rinsed her hands under the tap and dried them on a towel.

"I'd better be going now. I'll give you a call when there's some news about those helpers. In the meantime, good luck with your hunt for schools."

"Thank you for everything you've said, and for your help. I'm so grateful."

"Just one more thing," Ruth turned toward me as she was putting on her jacket.

"Can you and your husband get out more, go out with friends, go for drinks, go to the cinema? You need a break."

"No ordinary babysitters are prepared to look after Hollie. We did have one once, but Hollie pulled a dresser over while she was here, and the babysitter said she didn't feel she could cope. Carolyn, who babysat for us last Saturday, was somebody we found through Hollie's school. She's been specially trained, she costs a fortune, so we can only ask her occasionally."

"Won't your family help?"

I laughed. "They're even more terrified of her. Certainly, they're too scared of her to give us any hands-on help with her."

Ruth frowned. "I'll think about that. There's another organization I know of that may be able to help you." She turned and walked a couple of steps still deep in thought, then she came back toward me.

"I'll call you next week when I've done some work on this." she said. "I promise I will find you help."

Friday morning Lisa was a little more settled at preschool and consented to remove her arms from in front of her eyes when one of the helpers took her on her lap and cuddled her. I came home, made myself coffee and sat among my books and files staring at the blank sheet of my notebook.

So far I had not come across any boarding schools that had anything other than a very traditional approach to teaching autistic children. I knew there were schools in America that had the same ideas and philosophy as we did, which incorporated frequent sessions of vigorous exercise into their schedules to work off the children's hyperactivity and reduce their anxiety levels. I sipped my coffee and contemplated, with some degree of seriousness, the possibility of trying to get Hollie into one of those schools. But what about the flights there and back for three terms a year? And if we thought it was going to be difficult getting the school district to pay for a boarding school in this country, to persuade them to pay for a school in the States was totally absurd. I laughed at myself for having spent even five minutes considering the idea. Then, on a whim, I called the National Autistic Society and asked to speak to one of their counselors. I don't know why I did this. They had already sent me a list of schools, and there didn't seem a lot more that they could do.

I was put through to a friendly sounding adviser named Martin. I described our problem and gave brief details of our search and of our hopes, expecting him to say – as all the other experts did – that we were wasting our time. But what he said knocked me sideways.

"There's a school being built at Newshire that has exactly the approach you're looking for."

"Pardon?"

"It's a boarding school called the Leo Kanner School. It's being built by the Special Schools Society. It proposes to offer a regime of vigorous exercise during the day. The facilities are meant to be outstanding, a gym built especially for that purpose, art room, music room and a state-of-the-art swimming pool and sensory room."

Waves of panic began to rise in my stomach. It was too good to be true. I'd never be able to get hold of the phone number. It would already be over-subscribed. The authorities would refuse it out of hand. I couldn't wait for the information, for the contact details. I wanted to be on my way to visit it right that second.

"You don't have the phone number, I suppose?"

"I do." He read it out.

"I can't believe it. Thank you. Thank you so much."

I replaced the receiver and sat for several minutes staring at the piece of paper in front of me. It looked like an ordinary number, just a set of digits, like any other phone number. But I had a strong feeling in the pit of my stomach that at last I was on to something. Then, almost as the seed of hope was being planted, I became shaky and panicky again. The trouble was, hope didn't seem to be able to come on its own. Once I began to hope, there was the immediate possibility of it being dashed, in which case, slipping back into the former dark desolation would seem worse than if I had never left it.

I picked up the receiver and dialed the number.

"Leo Kanner School. May I help you?" a woman answered.

My nerves ganged up to throttle my voice. I managed only an indistinguishable noise.

"Hello," said the woman. "Is anyone there?"

"Sorry. Yes – er – my name is Mrs. Roseman. I have a severely autistic daughter. I'm looking for a school for her. I very much like the sound of what I've been told about your school. My daughter is very hyperactive and destructive. I think your approach would help her."

"Would you like the director to talk to you? Or perhaps you'd like to make an appointment to come to see the school?"

I wanted to dive down the telephone line right there and then.

"I'd love to, as soon as we possibly can. When can we come?"

"We're arranging appointments two days a week at the moment. But I must warn you . . . "

She went on to explain that most of the school was a building site at present, that we had to bring heavy-duty walking shoes just to look around. The hub of the school, the administration block, was a country mansion that had been renovated and refurbished, but the rest of the school – the school buildings, the residences, swimming pool, gymnasium and staff accommodation – was being built from scratch.

"We ask all visitors to remember that the school will look nothing like it is at present once it is finished."

"Of course. When is the earliest appointment?"

"Well, it so happens we have a cancelation for next Wednesday at eleven o'clock."

"Please book it for us. We will be there."

The receptionist asked for some details, particularly about Hollie, and promised to send a brochure and map of how to find the school. I put the phone down in a normal manner, and then suddenly I was on my feet, leaping about and shouting "Yes, yes, yes!" punching the air with my fist. For several minutes I jumped up and down dementedly, then I jerked my head around quickly in case there was anyone walking up the driveway who might see me.

After a few minutes I sat down, flushed with excitement, and called Simon at work.

"Simon Roseman."

"It's me."

"Oh, hello," he said, dully.

"I think I may have found a school for Hollie."

"Oh, yes."

"It's in Newshire. It's called the Leo Kanner School. It's just being built. Its philosophy is based on the idea that lots of vigorous PE reduces the children's hyperactivity and anxiety and makes them calmer and readier to learn. It could have been built for Hollie. And Simon" – I choked on the words in my excitement. "It has places now!"

"That's great," he said, in a humoring tone.

I felt as if I'd just run a race and won, only to find the cheering crowds, the judges and race officials holding the trophies and the bouquets had all dissolved in a mist.

"Simon, have you been listening to me? I'm not calling to tell you the electricity bill has arrived. I've called to tell you that our prayers may have been answered."

"I'm really pleased . . . "

I was shaking with anger.

"I don't understand why you're not enthusiastic. It sounds perfect. It sounds like a dream come true."

"It does sound perfect. But I'm afraid that even if it is the perfect school, it will also be exactly what you describe – a dream. We will have to persuade the district to pay for it. A place at a school like that will cost a fortune. They'll never agree to it. We just can't win."

"Well, we won't get anywhere if we admit defeat before we've even started."

"I'm sorry," he said, with slightly more feeling. "I agree, but I don't want to get too enthusiastic and I don't want you to get too enthusiastic because it almost certainly will never come to anything."

"But you'll come to look at the school? You'll take the morning off?"

"Oh, yes."

'You'll go through the motions to please me," I added, in my head.

I came off the phone and slumped back in the chair. There had been times at school or at work, or in the early days of my marriage, when I had tentatively wondered whether I knew the answer to a problem when others didn't, but I had stayed silent, thinking other people always knew best. How startlingly the roles were reversed now. In Hollie's case I knew, with a rock-hard certainty, that I was right and everyone else was wrong, Simon included. He at least could be on my side, he at least could be pleased when I'd achieved something. I shouldn't always be so alone.

Simon's attitude might more sensible and realistic but I had to cling to my heady, unfounded optimism if we were to have the slightest chance of succeeding.

Later in the afternoon, just as I was calling Lisa to get her shoes on for the afternoon school run, the phone rang. It was Ruth Taylor. "I've come across a service organization called Carers First, whose helpers look after ill and disabled people in their own homes so that caretakers can have a break. They should be able to do the odd bit of babysitting for you, and they might be able to help out in the holidays, too."

"It sounds almost too good to be true,"

"There is help out there that can at least take the edge off your problems. You shouldn't have been on your own this long, Lucy."

I got off the phone and helped Lisa with her coat and shoes. As we drove the short distance to Joshua's school, I contemplated the difference that a few days had made to my mood. I had felt desperate. Now I felt empowered.

I felt so driven, in fact, that the next morning – Saturday – I couldn't settle. I felt fluttery and on edge, and I kept looking for little windows of time – just ten minutes or so – when the children were occupied in some way so that I could complete another task on the list and regain some of that same feeling of power. The windows didn't come, of course. However, after lunch, when Hollie seemed to be playing relatively peacefully with some plastic building bricks, and Joshua had gone to play with his friend up the road, a quite different, but equally rousing idea sprang to mind. The children had been given some Disney Store gift certificates the Christmas before that were about to run out, and it occurred to me that it would be fun to take Lisa into Shalham and choose something from the shop together.

It was not an idea that would ever have occurred to me a few months before because the prospect of leaving Hollie, even with Simon, would have seemed unthinkable. But now, in my new frame of mind, I grabbed at it. Simon agreed.

"Hollie seems peaceful enough," I said to him, as Lisa and I put our shoes on.

"For the minute," he said, rather grimly.

"I know that could change any second," I admitted.

"Don't worry. You go," he said, giving me a tired smile. "Enjoy yourself. I know you don't get out much."

I expected to have to sit in a long line of Saturday afternoon shoppers waiting for spaces in the Abbot shopping center parking garage, but we were lucky, with only two cars in front of us, and half an hour after we'd left home, Lisa and I were descending to the shopping floor in one of the glass-fronted elevators.

The next hour was a happy window-shopping jaunt in which we stared at all the tempting exhibitions of toys in various toy shop windows, and considered which of them Hollie and Joshua and Lisa herself might like for Christmas. In the Disney Store we held up various outfits against Lisa before deciding on a shiny sparkling princess outfit, along with a book for Joshua and a soft baby toy for Hollie.

After that we went to the café in the center of the shopping complex, where I let Lisa select the table and choose what drink she wanted. We then both stood and eyed the cakes in the display cases; after Lisa had made her choice, I got her to sit down while I chose mine.

That was when it happened. I turned and saw a man probably in his mid-thirties passing the food display cases as he headed for the exit. It was the way he looked at me that grabbed my attention. He was looking – no, staring – in my direction, with a look that could not be described as anything other than admiration.

Immediately I turned my head around to look for the glamorous, leggy blonde who had to be standing six inches behind me, but there was no one there. It appeared, though it just seemed unbelievable, that the man was looking at me. Me. I turned back to him, wide-eyed with disbelief, and as I did so, he raised his eyebrows in a quick movement, and shot me a mischievous smile. I managed a rather awkward smile in return before sitting down at to our table where, two minutes later, dazed, I gave the waitress our order.

Lisa and I drank our drinks and ate our cakes and talked about what Daddy and Joshua would say when they saw her in her new dress. For so many years, going shopping with a daughter had seemed an impossible dream, and now it was actually happening. Every minute or so I reached out and touched her arm or stroked her hand or her cheek. She was so precious.

On the way back to the parking lot, we passed a toy shop that sold expensive wooden toys. In the window was a magnificent three-story dollhouse. Lisa had plenty of toys and lots of dolls, but she had never had a dollhouse. We stared at it for quite a while until, from nowhere, an idea occurred to me. If the social worker was able to provide those after-school care providers, I would have more time to do things with Joshua and Lisa.

"Lisa," I said, feeling as if I had just stepped into someone else's life, "we could make a doll's house together."

I watched as her face was transformed by a smile. "Mom, that would be wonderful."

I stood looking at the dollhouse and making plans for its construction. We'd need extra thick cardboard, a craft knife, a special ruler for cutting along . . . we'd have to go to an art shop. Could I glue the pieces or could I cut them so that they would slot together? An idea flickered in my mind. I was sure I had seen a dollhouse magazine among the vast array of magazines in the bookstore.

"Let's go and get a book on how to do it," I said, excitedly.

I took Lisa's hand, and we both began to skip. We skipped along and out of the shopping center, both giggling, while I concentrated hard on ignoring all the glances thrown my way. We crossed the road and passed down through an arcade on to the street where Smiths bookstore was situated. I soon found the hobby section, and then spotted the doll-house magazine, while Lisa glanced at the cover of a comic book about princesses. My initial flick-through showed nothing but glossy photos of antique dollhouses, but with more careful study I found exactly what I was looking for – a practical dollhouse built in an open-plan style with no out-side walls, so that children could sit and play on all sides of it. Feeling heady with excitement, we went up to the cashier and handed over our coins.

I whizzed around the supermarket on my way home, and when I came home to a bundle of Hollie's soiled clothes piled against the bathroom door, I wasn't even fazed. I thrust them into the washer, unpacked the shopping, amazed to find myself singing as I did so. Both Joshua and Lisa came to stare at this almost unknown phenomenon of Happy Mommy. They went away again, carried on with their games for a moment or two, then returned, giggling, as if they couldn't believe what they were hearing. Even Simon came and stood leaning against the kitchen doorway, shaking his head and smiling.

"You can't sing 'Scarborough Fair' and the 'Canticle' together on your own," he said, laughing. "You need a Garfunkel."

"I know," I said, beaming back at him and carrying on with my appalling singing.

This guiding star of hope led me through the weekend and into another week of study, analysis, visits and telephone calls, culminating in that longed-for pinnacle, the visit to the Leo Kanner School.

I drove my brain like a Victorian workhorse. I forced myself into a state of dogged intellectual concentration so that I was productive in every moment I had available. On Sunday evening, while Simon worked in his study, I skimmed half of a turgid autism textbook. On Monday morning, with the children at school and preschool, I sat in the library and wrote ten pages of notes on approaches to autism. And yet, brimming though my head was, another thought had been trickling along underneath, refusing to be forgotten: The wild boy of Pershore – the little boy in Victorian times who had run away and lived for years by himself in the forest. I couldn't forget him. I pored through textbooks, listing ideas, but every few minutes I would come up from the depths of concentration to the surface of normal awareness, and find myself wondering about him.

After a while, I stood up, stretched and wandered over to the local history section. There were only half a dozen books covering the history of Windleshire. I skimmed them, but found nothing related to what I was looking for. I considered asking one of the librarians. Being Monday, there were very few people present. Indeed, there was only one other person in the entire non-fiction section, a distinguished-looking man in his sixties with rather long, iron-grey hair and a thoughtful, intelligent expression, who was studying from a pile of books and folders and taking notes.

I went to the front desk and spoke to the librarian, a lady who, though well into her fifties, had a round, girlish face, and friendly, open expression.

"Let's take a look through the local history section," she said. "But I'm afraid we've no more books on the subject in the back that aren't on display. If you've looked through them all, we may not be able to find anything more."

"Thanks very much for looking."

I followed her back to the end of the aisle, where she pulled each title out and either glanced at the cover or flicked quickly through the book. Then, just as she was putting the last book back, she noticed the distinguished-looking man. She raised her eyebrows, turned to me and whispered: "Come over here a moment."

We moved back through the racks of books. In a low voice she said, "If you want to know about local history, John Chard is the man to ask. He came to live here a year ago when he retired, and he's researching a book on local history. He's already done various talks with slides for the local Women's Institute and the Royal British Legion, which everyone has praised highly. Let me introduce you to him."

"That would be great. Thanks."

I walked behind the librarian, feeling awkward, as she approached the large square table where Mr. Chard was working. He was intent on his reading, a pen in his right hand while his right forearm rested on a large notepad.

"Excuse me, Mr. Chard. I'm sorry to disturb you, but this lady, Lucy Roseman, is interested in finding out about one particular aspect of nineteenth-century local history. We can't find anything about it in the textbooks, and I just wondered if you might be able to help her."

He looked up and rested his thoughtful grey eyes on me. There was no trace of annoyance at being disturbed in the middle of his work. Instead he looked curious.

"What is it you want to know?" he asked in a deep voice.

I glanced toward the librarian, but she had already turned and walked away, so I swallowed my embarrassment and began: "I wanted to know about the wild boy of Pershore. He lived for many years in the forest a hundred and fifty years or so ago . . . "

"Oh, I know the story. It's true you won't find much about him in books here in Brackley library, but Shalham library has some books that mention him. What exactly do you want to know?"

"Where he lived, how he lived, how he survived. Everything, really."

"Well," he paused and glanced around. "They wouldn't normally allow us to talk here, but since there's no one else in this section, I'll tell you some of what I know. Please sit down."

He gestured to a seat. I pulled the chair out and sat down opposite him.

"What do you know about him?"

"That he ran away from home. That he lived wild in the woods for several years. That when he was found, he had become so wild that he'd forgotten how to talk."

"Those things are true. No one knows why he ran away from home, but he was thought to be about eight at the time. After he'd been living wild for four or five years, some farm laborers taking a shortcut through the woods found him. There'd been rumors of a boy living wild in the forest – there'd been odd sightings before, and food had been stolen from people's kitchens, as well as clothes off washing lines."

He broke off and looked at me.

"Why are you so interested in this story?"

"It's just sort of captured my imagination. I have – you see – I mean, it's hard to explain . . . " Hard as I'd thought about it, I'd never latched on to a set of handy phrases with which to explain Hollie to strangers.

"Let me begin again," I said. Mr. Chard sat back in his chair. He had a very piercing gaze. The skin around his eyes crinkled, as now, for the first time, he smiled. "Take your time."

"We have a severely handicapped daughter. She's autistic. At the moment I'm spending all my time studying autism and researching schools. She's being kicked out of her present school, and we not only need to find another school – one that will meet her needs – we also have to persuade the school district to pay for it." I paused and smiled. "That sounds completely irrelevant, but it's not. I think I was taken by the story of the wild boy because it was a mystery, something fascinating that provided an escape from all my endless research. I can't justify spending time reading novels because that's not real, it's not helping my daughter. But the wild boy was real, and, well, it's a romantic story."

"I understand."

"Perhaps the wild boy wasn't found because he didn't want to be found," I said, thoughtfully.

"Perhaps not. But it's unusual – very unusual – for boys of that age to run away from home. They might think they want to, but they wouldn't actually do it."

"Perhaps he was very unhappy at home. Perhaps he was beaten."

John Chard looked skeptical. "It's possible. While there are no detailed records about the family, they were thought to be gentle, respectable people. Of course, appearances can deceive."

He looked at me intently.

"Where did he . . . " I began. But at that moment an elderly man with a walking stick hobbled along the aisle and began surveying books directly to our right. Then, seconds later, a plump middle-aged woman in a red coat and black fur-lined boots came puffing around the corner, putting her handbag on the table next to me while she too began to study the lines of books.

"Here . . . " John Chard tore off a square of paper and began writing on it. "This is my home address and phone number. Come and see me if you want to discuss this further. I'm out a lot of the time doing research for my book, so perhaps you'd better call first. It's up to you."

"Thanks." I took the piece of paper and tucked it into my purse. "I'd love to."

I glanced down at his large notepad. His neat, sloping handwriting had covered nearly the whole page, and there were several other sheets already torn off spread over the desk in front of him.

"How wonderful to be able to spend your time researching and writing a book," I mused wistfully. "And to be able to do it at your own pace, without the pressure of a hearing date looming before you."

He looked at me kindly. "I'm sure you'll have plenty of time once you've won your hearing to follow your interests and hobbies."

"I don't know about that. In fact, I doubt very much if that will ever happen." I was embarrassed to find that tears were squeezing from beneath my eyelids.

Seeing my confusion, he smiled once more. "You seem a young woman of great resources and strength of mind. I'm sure you'll succeed in whatever you set your mind to."

He did not know me at all, but his kind words lifted me a little. I smiled.

"Do, please, come and see me if you want to know more about the wild boy," he smiled. I've all sorts of books and bits of information about him at home. I'd be glad to show you."

"I promise I will. Very soon."

Chapter Five

Things, at last, were moving my way. Or so I believed.

The hopeful feelings I had enjoyed over the past few days carried me through all the before-school chores the next morning. I glided out to the bus with Hollie and her bag, and the bus aide's dour expression had not the slightest impact on me. My positive mood even infected Lisa, who, for the first time in weeks, went into preschool without her hands covering her face, but held in little cautious fists under her chin. Indeed, it lasted all the way to Welshney Castle – Bella Haughton's home – where it finally crumpled.

Joel had made an appointment for me to talk to Paula Rochelle, who was working there while on her temporary contract with Bella Haughton. He thought she could advise me on getting press coverage for our story, in order to put further pressure on the district to agree to our case. It was something that was hard to imagine, our story in the local newspaper or in a magazine article, but I was prepared to consider absolutely any course of action that might help.

I parked on the large rectangular drive in front of the house, then crunched my way across the gravel to the front door. Within a few seconds it was opened by a middle-aged woman in a smart blue suit and an impeccable flicked-back hairstyle.

"Hello, I'm Lucy Roseman. I have an appointment for ten o'clock with Paula Rochelle."

"Oh yes, Mrs. Roseman, please come in. I'm Linda Poole, Mrs. Haughton's secretary."

I followed her as she walked across a gloomy hallway to a small office that contained a light wood desk.

"Paula's expecting you," Miss Poole said briskly. "I'll call to say that you're here."

She pressed a buzzer. There was no reply. She pressed it again, then frowned in puzzlement.

"I was talking to Paula only five minutes ago. She must have gone out of her room for a few moments. But I know for certain she's expecting you, so I think it's all right for you to go on up." She led me to the door of the room. To the left of where we stood, a grand oak staircase led upstairs.

"Just go straight upstairs. Paula's room is the third door on your right."

"Thank you."

The thick red and gold carpet muffled my footsteps as I slowly climbed the stairs and began to make my way along the corridor. The first door on the right was shut, but the second door stood open, and I could hear raised voices coming from inside. Bella Haughton's precise, piercing tones were unmistakable. Paula, though her voice was quieter, was speaking with equal firmness and conviction. What was I to do? It was too awkward for me to step forward and announce my presence, but I didn't want to retreat downstairs again either. Yet if I was found as I was, I might be thought to be eavesdropping. In the end the decision was taken away from me. The subject of the argument, as soon as I grasped what it was, held me rooted to the spot.

"It's only six weeks till the formal opening of the castle to the public," Paula was saying. "I must have your final agreement to this guest list for the ceremony so that the invitations can go out."

"You have my agreement to it, as far as it goes," Bella replied. "But there are a few more names I want added – a few more council members and journalists. Above all, I want John Chard's name put back on the list. I don't know why you've taken it off."

John Chard? He was the distinguished gentleman who had sat surrounded by library textbooks, recounting the story of the wild boy of Pershore. How did Bella know him?

"John Chard is establishing a reputation as an excellent local historian. He's had articles published in magazines and newspapers, and he is just about to complete a book on local history that I gather has already been accepted by a renowned publisher. He is exactly the sort of person we want to have invited to the opening ceremony."

Paula sounded exasperated. "But, as I've explained to you, he is a loose cannon. I met him at the opening ceremony for the new Shalham library, where he lambasted all the council members present because the completion of the building was six months behind schedule. He speaks his mind – to everyone. He has no inhibitions about saying what will make him unpopular, and he is not afraid of offending people."

"Well then, he can speak his mind openly about the magnificent castle that the public will be able to view for the first time."

Paula was evidently struggling to remain patient.

"But it is just possible that he might find some angle of the event that displeases him, and if so, he will make sure everyone knows about it. He's known for blasting people publicly at such events."

Was she really speaking about the man I had met yesterday, the man who had talked about his subject with such charm and insight?

Paula finished, "It could be embarrassing if he made a scene."

"What reason could he possibly have to do that?" Bella asked, scornfully. "I'm sure he'll applaud what we're doing. He might even write something complimentary in his articles. He knows a lot of people, and I'm sure he'll pass on good opinions of us."

"I'm far from sure he'll do that," Paula muttered.

"His name is to be put back on the list regardless," Bella commanded.

Paula spoke with weary determination. "Even if you continue ignoring my advice on every other matter, I really think you should heed my advice on this point. It is imperative that we not ask John Chard to the opening. If he feels any criticism and voices it publicly, it will be extremely damaging."

"Rubbish! His name is to be put on the guest list, and that is final."

If Paula made any reply, it was in such a low voice that I couldn't hear it. Nothing more was said that I could hear. However, I could imagine her pretty face looking angry and frustrated as she bowed to the opinion of her employer.

After this angry exchange, I dreaded Bella discovering me more than ever, but luckily she must have returned through some inner door to her own office, so I was spared running into her. After a minute or two Paula appeared through the doorway. An expression of shock flashed across her face, then she seemed to remember.

"Ah yes, Lucy. Sorry to keep you waiting. Please come in."

Paula's office was like its owner, pretty, feminine and business-like. It had a light ash, L-shaped desk, with a computer screen and keyboard to one side. There were a handful of well-cared-for plants on the windowsill, a box of tissues and a bottle of Perrier on the desk. I sat down where Paula gestured, in the guest chair.

It was then, while looking across the desk, that I saw it. I felt stung inside. A photo of Paula and Joel taken at some sophisticated function. They were gazing at each other, but the photo was taken at such an angle that Joel's face was obscured, and all that was showing was his hair as he bent his head toward Paula. I thought it was a strange photo to put on display, for it seemed to be announcing Paula's apparent ownership of Joel, rather than celebrating his character and individuality. I looked quickly back at the plants, trying to pretend I hadn't seen the photo.

Paula sat down behind the desk and spoke in a crisp, no-nonsense manner.

"Have you considered contacting any local magazines or newspapers to see if they are interested in your story?"

"I haven't, no."

"Newspapers are interested in exactly this sort of human-interest story. I can imagine a title that goes something like 'Parents battle to help handicapped child.' Try to imagine a photo of you and Hollie in the paper, along with selected details of your story. Would you be happy with that?"

"I think I could accept it, for the sake of building our campaign."

"Good. Let's think of some ideas for people to contact, while we have coffee."

Paula left the room. I heard her turn a switch in a room off to the right, and the coffeemaker soon started to hum. While she was gone, I feasted my eyes on the photo of Joel. It was so clearly him, even with his face obscured; the dignified, upright bearing that was so distinctive, the light brown hair, worn slightly too long. In the background I could hear Paula stirring the coffee mugs. I stared at the photo again, trying to imprint the image of him on my mind, so that it would remain there for the rest of the day, then I quickly averted my gaze just as Paula re-entered the room.

Twenty minutes later I came away clutching a list of the names of local journalists, and a script that Paula had concocted as a brief introduction when phoning them. I drove home and added them to my list of possible helpful contacts, then whisked off to pick Lisa up from preschool.

Our appointment to visit the Leo Kanner School was set for the next day. I had circled the date in red felt-tip on the calendar, though there had never been any question of my forgetting about it. I had been practicing mental strategies to make the time seem to pass more quickly. For example, I had been doing a mental countdown each day – four days to go, three days to go . . . Then I would try to remember some event that had occurred four days ago, or three days ago, some event that was so fresh in my mind that it seemed as if it had only just occurred. That way, the amount of time that had still to elapse before the day of our appointment would seem more bearable.

Now, unbelievably, the day was here. While Simon drove, I reviewed the campaign, as it stood, for winning Hollie a place at such a school. I had kept detailed notes, but only as a back-up – I had a clear mental picture of all the strands of the campaign, of where I was in relation to each piece of research, of the calls I was expecting, the calls that still had to be made, and the aspects of our own submission to the review board that still needed rethinking and re-planning. I was more dedicated than the most dedicated career person because the need to win overrode everything else. Not to win was unthinkable.

I could not contemplate our present life continuing. If we lost, the intolerable tension, the bickering and snapping and resentful silences that existed between Simon and me would permeate our relationship entirely. All that anger and bitterness would eat into the few remaining moments of goodwill and affection until we loathed the sight of each other. We would both be too exhausted, too depressed to prevent it.

There would never be uninterrupted time for Joshua and Lisa. The inability to concentrate that they both already displayed would become exacerbated, impeding any chance they had of making progress at school. They would grow up thinking that the deepest relationships that one could form with another human being would consist of a few snatched moments of affection scattered throughout weeks of stressed-out preoccupation, and that all conversations ended after a minute with cries of "Oh no, what's happened now?" and "Tell me later after I've cleared up this mess." And they would go away resigned to the fact that the magic time "later," when they would be able to tell me whatever it was, would never actually happen. And in the evening, as I bathed Hollie or stuffed sheets into the washing machine, I would hear them calling for a drink or a story with that weary air of resignation until, exhausted, they fell asleep.

No, such a nightmare existence was unthinkable. But flashes of this grim future haunted me often in the daytime, strengthening my determination.

I had a strong intuition about the Leo Kanner School, a feeling that the approach it offered was different from that of every other school we had come across, and very much in tune with our own ideas. I was desperate to see it, desperate for it to be right, and yet afraid that, perfect though it might be, something would happen to prevent it from being the school for Hollie. It could be full already. Hollie could be considered too difficult even for them. Most likely of all – indeed, it was the most certain thing in all the world – the school district would refuse even to consider it.

I had to keep a grip on my fears as we negotiated the route to the school, Simon driving and me following the map, for the ninety minutes that the trip took. For the first half of the drive I was eaten up with anxiety, only too aware of the vital importance of this visit, but after about an hour we both began to relax a little. As we journeyed east, leaving the outskirts of London and then Readbury behind, I began to enjoy the sight of the sunshine falling on the autumn-colored leaves of the woods that clothed the hills and valleys. Simon and I began talking, about his work, the self-serving ways of his superiors, and the projects that interested him most.

Eventually a sign pointed left for the Leo Kanner School, and we turned off the road to confront a magnificent set of wrought-iron gates towering some fifteen feet in the air. We called from the telephone box to announce our arrival, and the gates slowly and smoothly swung open. A receptionist made us coffee, which we drank in a lovely sunny room overlooking fields of sheep, while waiting for the director to finish showing the previous couple around. After about twenty minutes, I heard a bright, confident female voice talking to the receptionist, and then a woman entered the room, smiling widely and offering her hand in greeting.

"Hello, I'm Jill Pearson, the director." She was a vivacious, dynamic woman in her late forties, very attractive, with thick dark hair falling almost to her shoulders. "I'm pleased to meet you," she added, as she shook my hand and then Simon's, her lively tone suggesting that she meant it. She placed the files and pads of paper under her left arm on the table, then said briskly, "Please sit down and tell me Hollie's story, when you first realized something was wrong, her education so far, and what she's like now – what upsets her, what she enjoys, how she relates to others."

To my surprise, Simon answered before I could. "She was diagnosed very early, at eighteen months," he began, proceeding to describe the first worrying symptoms that had led us to seek help, and the way her behavior had deteriorated even faster as she approached the age of two. I could tell he was excited and impressed. I was impressed, too. It was the first time I could remember someone connected with a school asking about any of these facts.

"It sounds very much as if Hollie would be an ideal pupil for us," Jill Pearson proceeded to say. "Let me describe the school's philosophy to you. To begin with, since we specialize in taking a children at the more severe end of the spectrum, our aim is to understand why difficult behaviors appear, what events trigger them and, if possible, to try to prevent those triggering events from occurring."

She went on to describe the organization of the school day, and how it was structured to prevent the anxiety at any sort of change that was so characteristic of most children with autism.

"But where our approach differs most prominently from that of other schools is our attitude to physical education. We aim to provide five or six sessions a day, swimming, running, PE, cycling, gymnastics, the aim being to work off the children's excess energy and to provide a method of release for all their pent-up anxieties and frustrations, so that they are calmer and more receptive for learning. And as I'm sure you know, vigorous exercise triggers a feel-good factor – all those endorphins charging around the body give the children a real high. And if they're happier, they're more receptive to learning. Shall I show you around the site?"

"Yes, please."

We walked across the grassy courtyard to a two-story, red brick building.

"This will be the education unit for seven- to eleven-year-olds," Jill Pearson said. "The builders finished here a few days ago, and the decorators have nearly finished. The carpets will go down some time next week. Let's take a look at one of the classrooms."

The room was L-shaped. The main body of the classroom was spacious, with white walls and large picture windows that looked out over peaceful, non-distracting fields. The bottom part of the L was a seminar area.

"This will be for one-to-one work," Jill Pearson said, following my gaze. "Every child will have an hour of one-to-one work each day." She turned to look at the main section of the room.

"There will be a work station for every child, set up so that they divide the room up into smaller sections. This part of the room" – she gestured to a corner area away from the windows – "will be allocated for circle time; there will be chairs for six children, one teacher and two or three assistants."

We followed Jill back across the courtyard to another new building where the decorators had finished.

"We'll go upstairs and look at the library first," she said.

The library smelled deliciously of pine furnishings, new carpets and new books, and featured interesting alcoves where books on various subjects were housed, furnished with small-scale seating units where one or two children could sit comfortably without feeling crowded by others. The smell of new pine units and carpets met us downstairs, too. The art room already had painting tables, easels and a large double sink unit; the theatre was already equipped with chairs. There were teaching rooms for domestic science and speech therapy, there was a playroom outfitted with soft play slides, steps and tunnels.

The first sight of the sensory room left us momentarily speechless. I had seen sensory rooms before; typically, they had perhaps two or three sets of flashing lights and appeared as if they were hardly ever used. This was a sensory suite, for it was really two rooms, and it was in a different league than anything I had seen before. There were light-up panels on the walls, large walk-in boxes where the walls and the ceilings lit up, and areas where the floor was criss-crossed with light beams.

"The purpose of the sensory room is to reward children when they make an attempt to communicate. Autistic children love toys that light up. Thus, the teacher operates the equipment so that different effects light up to reward the children if they have made a particular sound or spoken a word, or accomplished some achievement that is difficult for them."

Next we toured one of the residences. The bedrooms each had two beds, were beautifully decorated, and were carefully laid out with the closets positioned across the center of the room, so that each child felt they had their own space. The large living room area looked out across a beautiful garden and grassy lawns toward some woods.

Across the playground we went to the sports center. The large gym already had been equipped with ropes and ladders, and even had a climbing wall; the swimming pool was large, and there were spacious changing rooms. Jill operated a switch; lights flashed across the ceiling and music sounded from speakers on the walls. "More sensory equipment, you see," she said, smiling at our amazement. "We want to reward the children everywhere in the school for special efforts and achievement."

I looked her directly in the eye.

"Please tell me you have spaces left. Please tell me you don't already have a waiting list."

"No, there are spaces left still. At the moment, anyway. But we're receiving applications from school districts all the time."

Simon and I had lunch at a fast food restaurant on the way home.

"It was better than I expected," Simon said, when I pressed him.

"Go on, it was a lot better than you expected. Admit it."

"Yes, all right," he smiled. "I can't really believe we've found it."

"I'm absolutely staggered we've found it," I said, cutting off a piece of sausage and tomato. "In fact, I'm staggered it exists at all."

I could hardly contain my excitement. I tried several times during the late afternoon to call Mary Walsh, the special education administrator, but, as always, she was in a meeting or "on the other line." Excitement gave an extra urgency to my planned visit the following day to the London attorney who had been so highly recommended by the other parents. Simon left later than usual for work so that he could do the school run, enabling me to catch the 8:45 train and be at the lawyer's Wimbledon office by 9:30 a.m.

David Greenham was a plump, bespectacled man in a sharp navy pinstripe suit. His eyes were wise and kind, but his mouth was firm and his chin protruded in a slightly aggressive fashion. I guessed he was a kind man, sympathetic to the plight of the families of autistic children for whom he had won striking victories, who could nevertheless be tough when required. We went over the details of our plans for Hollie, the Leo Kanner School, the district's objections and how we could counter them, and how a due process hearing might run. I came away after an hour fired up by his agreement to represent us – at a nominal charge – and his request to be told the hearing date as soon as we had it, so that he could put it on his calendar.

Once home, I was so full of excitement that I just had to call someone. I didn't want Simon's pessimism, and I was too afraid to call Joel at work, so instead I phoned Geraldine, in Geneva.

"We've got a lawyer! I can't believe it! We've got a top lawyer. He's never lost a case."

"That's amazing, Lucy. Forgive me for asking, because the last thing I want to do is dampen your excitement, but what about the cost? Lawyers usually charge a fortune."

"He's requesting a nominal fee, just £500 total. I think he charges a lot more for most of his work, but he sees parents like us as a special case."

"That's fantastic. You're on a roll now; you can't lose. I knew if you showed a bit of fighting spirit, events would start to turn your way."

"Thanks, Gerry, you're wonderful."

"I'm so pleased you managed to turn yourself around. I was so worried a few weeks ago when you seemed to be dying without a fight. I so admire the strength of mind that made you turn yourself around."

I came off the phone and punched the air with joy for a second; then almost immediately the phone rang. It was a young woman, named Karen Hinton, who worked for Carers First, the support organization for caregivers that the social worker had contacted on our behalf. We talked for more than ten minutes, about the social work course she had completed and the other children she had worked with.

"If you'd like to help us occasionally with Hollie so we can go out in the evening, we'd be very glad to have you," I said.

"I'd be delighted to help. We'll have to make the arrangement week by week as my schedule often changes, and I'll have more work at varying times."

"That's fine. Perhaps we could aim for you to come a couple of times a week, and we can discuss times for the following week on a Friday or Saturday when you have more of an idea of what will be happening."

"Why don't I come and do a trial run one evening next week, just for a couple of hours?"

"That would be great."

Before hanging up, we agreed on a time for Thursday of the following week.

Was it really happening? Were events really beginning to move my way? Following this conversation, I almost began to believe it. Perhaps, as Gerry had said, I was on a roll of success, and there was now a momentum, which meant that events would continue to move irresistibly in our favor, right up till the big day itself.

I was beginning to feel like a person who could have an impact. All my life I had seen myself as weak, negative – a bystander, even a victim, certainly not a major player. This new sense of power, that I could actually make things happen myself, produced quite a heady feeling.

I celebrated by going shopping. Friday morning I drove into Shalham for no more worthy a purpose than simply to look around the shops. For myself. For me. It was almost unheard of. It had been years since I had gone shopping with the sole purpose of choosing clothes for myself. I had bought myself the occasional sweater or pair of pants over the years, but only if something I had seen had caught my fancy while on the hunt for something for the children.

At first I looked – just for fun – in the windows of more expensive boutiques, and also in shoe shops, places where I had no intention of actually spending any money. Then I browsed around Shalham's main department store, Fowler and Harries, where I refused point blank to submit to the inner impulse telling me I should be in the children's department. Today I was here for myself.

I flicked through racks of garments and opened up dozens of sweaters and tee-shirts folded neatly on shelves. I even tried on a couple of pairs of jeans and some fancier pants, but there was nothing about them that made me feel I had to have them. Perhaps I was simply out of the habit of shopping; I'd forgotten what suited me. Maybe it was an age thing. Maybe after the age of forty, that exquisite wave of pleasure that came from slipping a sweater over one's head and thinking, wow, that really does something for me, maybe that just didn't operate any more. Maybe, like the urge to plaster the walls with Duran Duran posters or go out with glitter on my cheeks, it had gone forever. The urge to make the best of myself, to embellish my good points and diminish my bad ones, might have slipped away with my passing youth. It was a melancholy thought.

But as I was putting the jeans back on the rack, I spotted a purple and black roll-neck sweater on a shelf. A plump assistant showed me to a dressing cubicle, and I slipped the sweater over my head. The gentle V-shape created by the roll-neck suited my face; the soft mauve color added color to my cheeks. It looked and felt wonderful. It was slightly shimmery, and too dressy for daytime wear, but what the heck. I'd just been to a party. It was just possible I could talk Simon into agreeing to a dinner party in the near future. I looked at myself from all angles, and instantaneously a wave of that old shopping thrill washed through me. Yes, absolutely yes! I wasn't too old for it.

I had coffee and a doughnut, taking quick peeks every minute or so into the plastic bag that contained the sweater in its generous folds of tissue paper as I did so. Half an hour later in Dobbs, the other department store in town, I spotted a blue and brown top with elegant flowing sleeves. It was equally impractical, equally unsuitable for daytime wear. But I snapped that up too. I felt great.

Reality returned, in the afternoon when, back at home, I resumed my attempts to get hold of Mary Walsh over the phone. I had persisted in trying to call her over the past few days, and she had persisted in having meetings whenever I chose to call. Hollie's caseworker, Margaret Watson, spoke to me on each occasion, with an air of weary irritation, making it very plain what a nuisance I was. I felt tempted to say that I intended to make myself much more of a nuisance until they gave me some real help with Hollie, but I resisted, remembering the fiasco at the special education office a few weeks ago. I took to calling at unusual times, and eventually the tactic paid off, because, at five o'clock on Friday afternoon, I caught her.

"Oh, it's you, Mrs. Roseman."

"Yes, it's me," I said, forcing myself to sound bright and assertive. "I wanted to let you know about the Leo Kanner School in Newshire, which we visited on Wednesday. It's the perfect school for Hollie."

I quickly listed all the wonderful facilities, and particularly the aspects that would suit Hollie.

"Did you say the school isn't even open yet?" Mary Walsh asked, coldly.

My heart sank. "Yes, it opens in January."

"Well, there's no way we would consider a new school like that. It's too new and has no track record. And, once again, Mrs. Roseman, we cannot pay for boarding school for your daughter."

I hung up snarling with rage. How could they keep dismissing us like this? How could they refuse to see what an impossibly difficult child Hollie was? Almost immediately the phone rang, so close to me that it made me jump. I picked up the receiver.

"Hello, Mrs. Roseman? It's Miss Campbell here, Joshua's teacher."

"Thanks for calling. Is it about my letter?"

"Yes. Can we arrange a time for you and your husband to come in and talk to us? Mr. Anderson, the principal, will also be there, just to explain things. Is there any time next week that would suit you? Any afternoon, any time after school."

"Well, I have a babysitter coming on Thursday, so any time after about seven o'clock."

"Thursday it is then. Seven-thirty."

I put the phone down. I put my face in my hands. How was I to persuade Miss Campbell, and more important, Mr. Anderson, the principal – set firm as they were in their entrenched beliefs – that it was imperative that Joshua rejoined his old class?

In spite of these less-than-promising conversations, I still felt on a roll of success. Elaine Davis, the first of the two after-school caregivers that the social worker had found, started work, arriving at four o'clock on the following Monday, just before Hollie's bus. I guessed she was in her late forties, and she had a practical, down-to-earth manner that impressed me. She asked all sorts of questions about Hollie, and talked to Joshua and Lisa about their interests and their friends. She came out with me to meet the bus, and said, "Hello, Hollie" with real interest, trying hard to catch her eye, even though Hollie's gaze was wavering all over the place.

"What would you like me to do?" she asked. "Remember, I'm here to do whatever is most helpful to you."

"If you'd take Hollie to the park before it gets dark, it would be most helpful," I replied. "The more exercise she gets, the earlier she gets to sleep at night, which makes our evenings easier."

"Fine. That's what I'll do then."

While Elaine was at the park with Hollie, I was able to sit down with Joshua and help him do his math homework, and also to listen to him read his book and test him on some spelling words he had to learn. I couldn't remember the last time I had been able to give him such a long, uninterrupted spell of attention.

After an hour I got out the train set and let him play with that while I located the dollhouse magazine and all the materials Lisa and I had bought for constructing the dollhouse. We pulled out the thick cardboard, the metal ruler, the knife and the glue, and put them neatly on the table. I studied the design, then drew the lines of the plan on the cardboard with the ruler and pencil, while Lisa watched excitedly.

"Are you sure this will make a dollhouse?" she asked at one point, looking at the confusing array of lines and measurements.

"It looks very complicated at the moment, I know. But, yes, darling, it will make the most wonderful dollhouse."

I placed the cardboard on top of an old wooden board. Then I took the carpet knife and began cutting the cardboard along the side of the thick metal safety ruler, telling Lisa to keep her fingers well out of the way. At the end of another half hour, I had cut out most of the lines, and slotted the four walls and two floors of the house together.

"Next time we'll stick on the second-floor rooms, and then we can wallpaper and carpet it," I said, as I hid the house structure safely away at the back of the closet in our bedroom. Lisa watched me, jumping up and down with excitement.

"I can't wait! Can we do it tomorrow?"

"We'll see."

My sense of a growing momentum of success was damaged on Wednesday when Lisa displayed a worrying return to her old disturbed behavior. She walked into preschool again with her hands held tightly over her face, and refused to move them for half an hour, despite my entreaties and Carol's gentle encouragement.

On Thursday I had arranged with Isobel's mother for Isobel to come home with Lisa from preschool to have lunch with us. When I picked them up, Lisa and Isobel came racing out hand-in-hand. I made a delicious lunch with chocolate and strawberry ice cream as dessert and, when the games with dolls and toy kitchens started to drag after an hour or two, I brought the girls to the kitchen and occupied them with making chocolates. I was determined that the visit should be a success.

For some reason, fatigue seemed to hit me harder than ever that afternoon. All the weeks of planning for the hearing, all the months, years, of poor sleep seemed to come to a temporary head, and I longed for the arrival of Sheila, the second after-school care worker, who was to come on Wednesdays and Thursdays. She failed to arrive, and I could get no reply from the contact at the Joan Davis Foundation when I called them after an hour to see if there was any news, say, of a car breakdown or sudden family illness.

Any sense that I had any grip at all on events slid further away as the evening came. Karen Hinton came to baby-sit for the first time, so that Simon and I could attend the special meeting at Joshua's school. Our appointment was for seven-thirty, and at 7:15 we left Lisa in bed and Hollie playing in her room, posting toy bricks and shapes down the back of the radiator. Joshua was wandering about disconsolately, unable to settle.

We had to wait ten minutes outside the classroom. When Miss Campbell saw us sitting there, she went to get the principal, a tall, broad-framed man with thick dark hair and a dark beard. Mr. Anderson looked as if he could be quite alarming, but in fact he had a gentle manner and the children were not abnormally in awe of him. He had no people skills, however. He had no understanding of parents' feelings, no memory or awareness of family situations, and didn't even know the names of most of the children in the school.

"Ah, Mr. and Mrs. – er – Roseman," he said, quickly glancing at his papers as he entered the room. "Please sit down."

Simon and I sat on one side of the desk, and Miss Campbell sat on the other. She was an experienced teacher in her early thirties, with an authoritative, no-nonsense manner.

"I gather you've written a letter objecting to our decision to keep Joshua in second grade," Mr. Anderson began.

"Yes, I said, feeling my hackles rise at his complacent manner. "Joshua, as we've explained before, has a younger sister of four who is in preschool. He also has an older, nine-year-old sister who has severe autism. It is the company of his peers that he needs to help to give him some social confidence and to encourage him to take part in normal activities for seven-year-olds. If there is a choice, he should be with older children whose example is more likely to encourage him to try new activities. What he doesn't need is to spend time with younger children. At home he spends all his time with a sister who can't talk and a sister who is unnaturally withdrawn. He needs – he desperately needs – friends of his own age. He needs the self-esteem that would bring him. And he needs to be challenged."

The principal began to talk in his gentle monotone, reiterating with an air of great patience all the arguments he'd produced in his letter.

"It will be good for his confidence to be one of the older ones in the class. He will seem much better at lessons than the other children, he will enjoy coming first in tests and exercises."

"But he needs to be brought out of his shy little shell, and that's not going to happen when he's in with a group of children he scarcely knows. I can't get across to you the damage his sister's autism has done to his social skills. Can you imagine what it must have been like, spending his early years in the permanent company of a child who cried when he went near her, or at best ignored him? How could he learn to have confidence in his ability to make friends, how could he learn to play properly, and to interact, with that sort of example in his face all the time?

"This spring and summer he began to have that confidence for the first time with his friends from his old class. He's made friends, they have been to play at our house, and he had begun to look forward to going to school. He had begun to find that some children do like him – that not all children cry when he goes near them. And what do you do" – I was fighting back the tears now – "you want to take that away from him. Something we've fought long and hard to build. You have no idea what you are doing."

Miss Campbell looked irritated.

"It'll be the best thing for him, you wait and see. Being top regularly will do no end of good to his confidence. It will be his chance to shine."

"Have you been listening to me?" I asked, tears of frustration in my eyes. "Coming top in tests – well, it will be an illusion anyway, since he's so much older than the others. But above all, it's a poor consolation that he might come top in a few tests if he's lost the tiny little nugget of confidence he was beginning to develop. He's suffered more than most children, he's lived with permanent insecurity, with the permanent fear of losing all his belongings, of anything that is his being smashed, of thinking that the child who he spends most of his time with wants to cry when he comes near her.

He needs the bit of confidence that was beginning to come from suddenly realizing he had friends."

Miss Campbell's exaggerated show of patience suddenly snapped.

"Well, I'm sorry, it's a numbers game," she burst out. "We can't have some classes too large and some too small; we've got to have thirty-one children in each. And Joshua is the one chosen to be with the younger group because he's the most immature. It's the funding. It's the requirements. That's it. It's a numbers game."

I was furious.

"I can't begin to explain the damage you are doing," I choked. "You and your numbers game. If it's a numbers game, choose any one of the other children in his former class. They are all more privileged and advantaged than him; they all have comfortable secure homes with normal families; they're not faced with chaos each night when they go home. Choose one of them."

"I'm sorry. This is the decision we have made," said Mr. Anderson, maintaining his artificially gentle tone. Nothing I had said had made any impact on him; in fact, I doubted he'd even taken it in. He had made his decision, and he would simply carry on reiterating his reasons for it in a tone that he universally used to defuse – as he saw it – angry and emotional parents, without ever empathizing with their point of view.

I stood up, tears flowing freely down my face now, not troubling to stop them.

"Hollie's autism has been a tragedy for the whole family. Joshua has already been hugely damaged by it. You have done him extra damage with this decision, but this time the damage was entirely avoidable."

I walked out of the room, Simon following behind. I sensed his awkwardness and embarrassment as we walked back along the corridor and out through the main entrance.

"I think we could have done it without making such a scene," he said.

"I don't," I snapped. "I think making a scene was exactly what was required. I'm sorry that it's done us no good, but I'm not sorry for any other reason."

On Friday I felt extremely low. I felt it would take only one further tiny setback, before I would once more slide down into the old mire of hopelessness. I was weighed down by an impossible load, and people from other areas of our lives, who could have given me a hand up, conspired instead to press me down further.

I felt as if I was clutching on to sanity and normality only by my fingernails.

In the afternoon, the second of the new helpers failed to turn up for a second time. It felt worse, far worse, than if they'd never come at all. I had started to rely on this small respite, this brief alleviation of the load. I had started to feel what it might be like sitting for a concentrated period helping with homework, or beginning fun projects such as the dollhouse. Hollie too was now expecting to be taken to the park for a walk immediately after her return on the bus, and she started to scream and kick when I kept removing her shoes and coat and pulling her away from the front door.

Two days in a row they hadn't come. I tried to call the Joan Davis Foundation contact person, but there was no reply. I left a message, but no one returned my call. Anger and frustration consumed me, corroding all good feelings, all pleasure in Joshua and Lisa's little sayings and doings, all patience and restraint in relation to Hollie. I snapped and chided, and cleaned the messes by sloshing water about and slamming things into their proper places. I was plagued by fantasies of myself as a lone member of a besieging army, attacking a gloomy hulk of a citadel, with slits for windows, where I never saw a face or a real person. But all the time, vast armies hid inside, waiting for me to tire, while they rained down on me spears, arrows and cauldrons of boiling oil.

It was a dreadful afternoon and evening, even by our standards. Hollie was crying as I helped her off the bus. The aide told me with a mean look that she had started to cry about five minutes before, for no apparent reason. She continued to cry almost solidly, all afternoon and nearly all evening. I made her favorite snack, pasta, beans and cheese, and when that didn't work, all vows about not giving her sugary, stimulating food went out of the window, and I found myself offering her chips, sweets and chocolate cookies. However, all she did was take one in each hand and hold them there tightly so that the chocolate melted down her arms, through her fingers onto her tee-shirt, and onto the toys, sheets, armchairs, and anything else she came into contact with.

I offered her drink after drink, in different sorts of cups, lidded beakers, unlidded beakers, just in case it was having the wrong type of cup that was upsetting her. I filled the tub, but, most unusually, she didn't want a bath. I changed her diaper, checked the tapes weren't sticking into her, then put a video on that she sometimes liked to watch, ignoring the justified protests from the other two who had been watching children's TV. I put a toddler's music tape on the cassette player, then I tried a melodious classical tape that sometimes soothed her, but nothing worked.

When Simon came home at half past seven, we stood in the kitchen and thought through every possible factor that could be upsetting her, while she ran up and down the hall and cried and cried.

"She rubs her feet sometimes as if they're bothering her," Simon said after we'd sat in the hall for twenty minutes just watching Hollie run up and down.

"Help me to hold her," he said, and we both grabbed her the next time she ran past. I held her struggling upper body and Simon bent her legs so that she was forced to sit. Then I set her on my lap, while Simon massaged her feet. She lay quietly for a few seconds, looking pleased, then leaped up and began screaming again.

A few minutes later, I said, "She seems to be rubbing her legs now, as if they are bothering her."

"Yes, perhaps something is irritating her skin."

Simon ran a bath while I undressed her and helped her in. Unlike earlier, this time she lay quietly, enjoying the water's comforting warmth.

I felt a pang of recognition. "I couldn't get the usual washing powder at the supermarket," I said to Simon. "I bought a different one instead."

"That must be it," Simon said. There's something in the powder that irritates her skin."

At ten past midnight, tucked in bed, Hollie's eyelids began to waver, then to dip, then slowly to close. Simon and I looked at each other and breathed a sigh of relief.

"Of course, we still don't know that it was that," I said wearily as I climbed into bed next to Simon. "It could still be that she was just very hungry, past hunger, but so uncomfortable that she no longer realized that it was hunger causing the problem. It's happened before."

"As usual, we'll never know."

The next morning, the mystery over the non-appearance of the two helpers was solved. The explanation arrived with the mail. We received a letter from the Joan Davis Foundation explaining that neither of the two felt able to cope with Hollie. They were both experienced with special needs children, but she was too difficult. I put the letter on the kitchen counter, and looked over at Simon, who was trying to force Hollie back to her seat in the hope that she would eat a bit more breakfast.

"Those helpers aren't coming again," I said, dully.

"Which helpers?"

"You know, the Social Services ones who came this week after school."

"Oh, those." Hollie slumped down on the floor beside her chair. She picked up a felt-tip pen that had been lying there and started sucking the tip of it.

"Hollie, please eat some more," Simon said, exasperated, lifting her up under her arms. She allowed herself to be lifted, but her feet were limp so that she took none of her own weight. Then as soon as he had eased her into the chair and let go, she slumped back on to the floor again.

"Oh, Hollie," he muttered, blinking his eyes shut.

I felt as if I were enclosed in walls of ice. Everything seemed very hard and very cold. I felt set apart, unable to connect with the world around me. The colors were dulled. Even the milk at the bottom of Joshua's near-empty cereal bowl looked as if I could knock my fingers on it.

I walked through the hall and into the family room, uncertain what to do. I had half a thought of calling Geraldine in Switzerland, but there didn't seem a lot of point to it. If it had been a weekday, I could have called Ruth Taylor. But even if it had been a weekday, there wouldn't have seemed much point in that either, or in anything.

There were books on the floor that Hollie had pulled out of the bookcase, and all the plates and plastic toy food from Lisa's toy stove were spread across the carpet. I didn't know who had done it, and it didn't seem to matter. For a second I contemplated bending down and clearing it all up. Then I thought, what's the point, there'll only be a different mess here in a few minutes.

Joshua and Lisa were watching a Saturday morning cartoon, an American one that I hadn't seen before. They were watching it because it was on, with bored expressions; it was an ugly, violent show, in which people whacked each other with giant sticks all the time. I contemplated the effort involved in turning it off, listening to the outpourings of protest, and then redirecting them into some more worthwhile and satisfying activity. Then I left them to it. If only I wasn't so tired . . .

That afternoon Simon had to do some work on a computer program project. I packed Hollie's large bag, strapped the children into the car and drove them to a large indoor playground where there was soft play equipment, climbing frames, slides and trampolines. I unstrapped them all, and aided them to the front door of the play barn. One of the play helpers looked at me apologetically.

"It's very full, I'm afraid."

Children were running, sliding down slides and having ball fights in almost every tiny corner of space. The noise levels, the shrieks and shouts of excitement hit me like a wall of sound. Already, I could see Lisa's hands beginning to slide from her chin to her cheeks, then toward her eyes.

Joshua said miserably, "I came here for Bobbie's birthday. I'm not going to be able to sit with Bobbie any more."

It took me one second to make up my mind.

"Thanks, but I think we won't stay," I said, and turned them all around and marched them back to the car. The rain began as I turned the key in the ignition.

"What are we going to do, everyone? We can't go for a walk."

I didn't expect a reply, and I didn't get one. I couldn't face going straight home, so we ended up just driving around. I drove through the outer villages on the edge of Shalham. Some were pretty with old thatched-roofed pubs and village greens, some were little more than housing developments.

As we drove down a country lane on the edge of one of these villages, we suddenly found ourselves at a gate that marked a dead end. A sign above the gate read: "Disley Airfield. Keep out."

Disley Airfield had been quite famous in wartime; clusters of bombers had flown from here to fight in the Battle of Britain. We had a good view of it from the car, through the windshield, in the rain. All it consisted of now was a mass of broken-up bits of concrete, half obscured by overgrown grass and weeds. The aircraft hangars lay derelict, the side walls crumbling, great gaps showing in the roofs. Tall fences topped by row upon row of barbed wire barricaded them off. Life had moved on elsewhere, to the local villages and housing developments, to the roads where people now traveled in cars, to the stations and nearby airports. It was bleak and empty, a grey concrete void. I sat at the wheel staring out of the front windshield for over ten minutes, mesmerized, until Joshua said quietly,

"Mommy, can we go home now?"

Chapter Six

Over the next few days Hollie became more frustrated and destructive than usual, and did everything with a frantic excitement like a mechanical toy that has been wound too tightly. Each night, it seemed, she fell asleep just a little bit later – not until one or two in the morning. And by the time I finally got to bed, I was so overtired that I couldn't unwind. Sleep came in chaotic snatches, punctuated by tense, wakeful intervals. I continued to spend most of those dark hours in Narnia. To get myself to sleep, I lay imagining comforting images from the books, actually playing the scenes out in my mind as if I were watching a film. When I was awake, too tense and uptight to sleep, I read. I had already got as far as *The Voyage of the Dawn Treader.*

My spirits were lifted at the end of the week by Geraldine's return from Geneva. I had convinced myself that a month away, invigorating scenery and a challenging project would have revived her old exuberant spirits, but when I stopped by to see her Sunday afternoon, I sensed from the moment she answered the door that nothing had changed.

I leaned forward to hug her. "Hi, Lucy," she said, forcing a smile. Her face was pale, and her hair was flat in places and spiky in others, as if she hadn't put a comb through it all day. Normally she wore smartly casual clothes, even on weekends, but today she wore faded black leggings and a stretched and baggy old sweater.

She led me into the family room and stood by the coffee table uncertainly, as if she was not sure what to do next. After a few moments, she said, "Coffee? Or tea?"

"How about some of that Beaujolais Nouveau you promised to bring back?"

"Ah yes," she said, deadpan. "I'll open a bottle."

I made myself comfortable on the sofa. But as I glanced around waiting for Geraldine to return, other disquieting signs prevented me from feeling completely at ease. There was a thick layer of dust on all her state-of-the-art electrical equipment, the television, video, the CD player, the speakers. The newspapers splayed out untidily over the coffee table were over a month old. I reminded myself that she'd been back in the country less than twenty-four hours, but this thought failed to console me. I knew that the real Geraldine, the girl I had known for almost thirty years, would have had the apartment precisely as she wanted it within hours of her return.

She padded back into the room on her bare feet with a bottle of wine and a cork screw. Perching on the edge of the armchair opposite me, she unwrapped the black metal wrapper, punctured the cork and started half-heartedly pushing in and twisting the coil of the cork screw.

"I expect you're still tired from the flight," I said. Surely it could only be an hour's flight, at the most, from Geneva?

"Yes, I am very tired," she said. Her voice and her movements were automatic. The coil of the cork screw was twisting around and around, but making little headway into the cork.

"Why don't you get some glasses," I chirped. "I'll open the bottle."

"Okay."

I could see it hadn't even occurred to Geraldine to produce glasses. While she fumbled in the glass cabinet in the corner, I pushed the coil of the cork screw deep into the hole in the cork and hooked it out. Crumbs of broken cork clung to the slight condensation on the side of the bottle. Geraldine set down two glasses in a tiny space in the morass of newspapers and slopped red wine into each of them.

"Cheers," I said, holding up my glass.

"Cheers."

But I had only suggested the wine in an attempt to revive some of her old exuberant spirits, and since the plan was obviously failing, I had no more heart to drink it than she did. We both took sips, as in my head I played with different methods of approaching the subject of her health. I finally decided to be straight.

"Before you went to Geneva, you said you'd not been feeling very well," I said quietly. "Are you feeling any better?"

"No. I still don't feel right." She took a sip of wine and pushed it away.

"When I was away, I threw myself into work and managed not to think about it too much. And even when I wasn't working, the different surroundings, being able to walk around the lake, to see the mountains from every part of the town, and to hear the cow bells on the hillside, lifted me out of myself. But now that I'm home, I've had to confront it once more."

"How exactly do you feel?"

"Totally lacking in energy. Tired. Dizzy. I can't stand still in one place for more than a few seconds without feeling faint. I've never known anything like it."

"It could be a virus." I took a couple of sips of wine, but the taste was bitter, and I didn't enjoy it. "Some viruses can make you generally low for a longish period," I added. Was this true? I had no idea. I was making it up as I went along, trying to think of anything that might elevate her spirits.

"I suppose so." She picked up the wine glass again automatically and shifted slowly back in the armchair. She took a sip, then immediately leaned forward and returned it to the center of the coffee table.

"That's also strange, you see, I seem to have stopped enjoying alcohol."

"You really must be ill," I teased.

She managed a perfunctory half-smile.

"What are the symptoms of – you know, what you're afraid of," I hedged, not wanting to speak the name of the disease in case it somehow made the possibility more real.

"Of Huntington's? Well, I don't know too much about the early ones. I know about the later stages, of course, from my dad and my uncle and my two cousins."

"It's not that, you know," I said, forcing a hard edge of certainty into my voice that didn't sound all that convincing. "It's very late to be developing that. It's much more likely to be a virus."

"Yes, I'm going to keep telling myself that."

She stared dully at the mess on the coffee table for a few seconds, then seemed to give herself a mental shake.

"So, any more news about the due process hearing? I don't suppose you've had a date, yet?"

"Yes, we have, as a matter of fact," I said eagerly. "The third of December, just three weeks away. We got a letter yesterday. First thing tomorrow I will have to get busy, calling the lawyer and the educational psychologist to make sure they keep the day clear."

"How are you feeling about it?"

"I have completely contradictory feelings. I can't wait to get in there and present my case. And yet, at the same time, I'm dreading it. I mean, what if – what if I do it badly?"

"You won't." She made an attempt at a smile. "You seem different, Lucy. You wouldn't believe how much you've changed over these past few weeks. I've known you for almost thirty years, and during that time you've almost always been afraid, afraid of confrontation, afraid of going out and getting what you want, afraid of failing. Now, for the first time in your life, you don't seem afraid any longer. You're standing up for yourself and making things happen. I'm full of admiration, and, frankly, amazement."

I couldn't prevent a smile that stretched from ear to ear. It was true. In recent weeks I had discovered that I *could* change my circumstances, that I *could* make an impact.

Geraldine was looking at me intently.

"What's brought about this change?"

"Well, I've had some things go my way recently. Finding the Leo Kanner School. And then there's finding our marvelous team of experts – the lawyer, the psychologist. And other parents who've been through this have given us loads of helpful advice."

"Yes, I know. But so many things have been against you, and yet with each new difficulty, your spirit seems to rise."

She studied me.

"I don't get it, Lucy. I'm delighted, but I'm also utterly mystified. How can you have been so tentative all your life, so easily discouraged by the smallest setback, and then, suddenly, in such a short time, acquire such spirit?"

I swerved my gaze away, seeking inspiration. None came. Then it occurred to me that I could offer part of the truth. I turned back and met her gaze head on.

"It's desperation, Gerry. The stakes are so impossibly high. If we don't win on the third of December, it will be the end for my family. Oh, we may not divorce right away; we'll probably co-exist for another few years for the sake of the children, bickering all the time and seething with resentment toward each other. Every moment of the day I'll be up to my neck in Hollie's mess. She'll take ten seconds to make a mess somewhere, and it will take me ten minutes to clear it up, by which time she'll have made a hundred more messes somewhere else. I will never, ever catch up.

"And Joshua and Lisa will grow up unable to concentrate or apply themselves to anything because they've never been taught how to, failing at school and not believing there is any reason for anyone ever to want to love them or spend time with them. Any time I feel tired, Gerry, any time I need inspiring, I just have to contemplate that all-too-possible nightmarish future."

We kissed goodbye at the door. But even as she turned away, I saw the puzzled look return. She might understand my determination, but she still couldn't understand the intensity of my fighting spirit, or the good humor and cheerfulness wrapped up in it. Nor could she understand why these enormous obstacles seemed to bring all kinds of previously hidden strengths and aspects of my personality to the fore, rather than instilling a kind of grim doggedness.

As I drove home, I offered up thanks for what Geraldine had referred to as my spirit. I was now surviving on four or five hours of very disturbed sleep a night. The hearing was only three weeks away. Yet instead of being paralyzed with anxiety and exhaustion, I had boundless energy. I was staggered by my own efficiency. Over the past few days I had continued to work closely with the lawyer and the educational psychologist, to add well-developed arguments to the reports, find answers to problems and get a multitude of other jobs done quickly.

I took Hollie to the hospital the following Tuesday to consult her pediatrician. The children's clinic waiting area was large, about the size of a badminton court, and the groups of chairs were divided into three small squares, each with a central table spread with magazines and children's books. In a small adjoining room, with a wall built entirely of glass, was a playroom stocked with toy stoves, cars, dollhouses, musical instruments and a wealth of other toys. I took a seat against the back wall with the playroom directly in front of me. Immediately to my left was the reception area, where two receptionists sat half hidden behind a tall counter; just on the other side, a corridor led a few yards to some double doors, just out of sight from where I was sitting.

I had to wait an hour past our appointment time. This wouldn't have mattered that much if I had been with Joshua or Lisa, as they would have sat quietly with me or played within easy view in the playroom. Hollie, on the other hand, became obsessed with running up and down the small length of corridor between the reception desk and the double doors. From my position on my chair in the waiting room, indeed from the viewpoint of any chair in the waiting room (I tried them all), I could not see the farthest end of the corridor by the double doors. Consequently, I had to jump up every half minute to keep checking that she had not gone through the doors.

Toward the end of the hour, a young, harassed-looking mother came in with a baby in a stroller and a grumpy toddler in tow. She negotiated the stroller around the side of the chairs in front of me, and as she did so a bag of toys, books and diapers that was half sticking out caught on my chair and fell off sideways with a thud. The toddler started to wail, and the baby immediately dropped her bottle of milk and began to cry, too. The mother looked for a second as if she were on the verge of tears herself.

"I'll get it," I said, quickly, I scrambling to pick up the bag and reposition it in the center of the stroller shelf.

"Thanks," she said, automatically, with scarcely a sideways glance. Then she began retrieving the baby's bottle and lifting the kicking toddler onto a chair.

I looked around the corner for Hollie. She wasn't there. Quickly I scanned both ends of the corridor. Still no sign. Keeping a tight hold on my fear – after all, I had been in this situation so many times before – I flicked my gaze quickly from side to side again. I scurried through the waiting room, checking under the chairs, behind strollers and in corners, behind and under magazine tables, and in all the eccentric positions where she was quite likely to have hidden. I also flashed a quick glance around the playroom, and I checked in all the stalls of the toilet. There was absolutely no sign of her. Then, and only then, did I allow myself to panic. I knew the procedure well enough by now. Once I had checked all the likely places, and then all the highly unlikely places, nothing remained but to cast off all dignity and ask for help.

"My daughter has disappeared," I said to the two bowed heads of the receptionists, both poring over paperwork. Then, trying to prevent the critical looks that I knew were about to be offered me, I quickly added,

"She's autistic; she has no sense of danger. I've been following her up and down the corridor for an hour, and not let her out of my sight. I was only distracted for ten seconds."

The receptionist, a woman of about fifty, with tight blonde curls, looked up at me instantly, with a gaze that was not unkind. Then immediately she looked to my right; a dignified, kind-faced lady in her fifties was standing exuding an air of calm authority. It was our pediatrician.

"I was about to invite you to come in," she said. "Where did you last see Hollie?"

"She's been running up and down this bit of corridor. I've been following her most of the time. I've kept her in sight the whole time. I only took my eyes off her for ten seconds to help a woman who was struggling with two babies."

"Could she have gone through the swinging doors at the end?"

"She's shown no inclination to do so until now. But, yes, I suppose she could have."

We both ran down the corridor, pushed the doors open and quickly scanned the large vestibule. Ahead of me was a corridor crossing at right angles, leading to dozens of other wards. Beyond that was a large staircase. To my left and right were two sets of elevators giving access to all five floors of the hospital.

"Oh my God," I cried, "If she came out here and the elevator doors were open . . . "

"We'll tell the security people," said the pediatrician calmly.

We marched back to the reception desk, where at a glance from the pediatrician, the blonde receptionist immediately called the security office.

"Don't worry, Mrs. Roseman," said the pediatrician, in her soothing, comforting way. "They have television monitors showing all parts of the hospital. They'll find her very quickly."

It seemed like an eternity that the doctor and I waited at the reception desk, staring at the phone, willing it to ring. In reality, it must have been about five minutes before it rang;

the receptionist listened for a moment, then gave me a thumbs-up while she talked for another few seconds. When she put the receiver down, she said Hollie had been found wandering around the basement. The security people had spotted her on the monitors and gone to bring her back. In a minute I heard the elevator doors and then the swinging doors open, and promptly a security officer entered, holding Hollie tightly by the hand.

I didn't stop shaking for the rest of the hour that I spent in the pediatrician's office. We went over all the aspects of Hollie's challenging behavior, and she agreed unreservedly to write a report for the hearing, describing what she had seen.

The following day, an outreach worker from Petheril School, a lady called Joanna Reed, came to visit. She was in her late forties, very tall and thin, with quick, bird-like movements. She perched on the edge of the armchair and took sips from the cup of coffee I made her. She spoke in a brisk, disjointed manner.

"Mrs. Atkinson was wanting to know how you are getting along in your search for another school for Hollie. As you know, Mrs. Atkinson has said that Hollie can stay at Petheril until you find a place at another school, but it has been six months now, and she was wondering what progress you have made. The problem is, we have a huge list of children waiting to come to Petheril, and we really need Hollie's place as soon as it can be arranged."

"I assure you, Simon and I are doing everything we can to speed matters up. I spent a long time looking around at schools until I found the right one. Now the school district people are refusing to fund it. We are trying our best to persuade them; in fact, we have a due process hearing coming up in an effort to make them accept the necessity of a boarding place for Hollie. The date has been set for Monday, the third of December, about three weeks away. Hopefully we'll have the result by Christmas."

"That's good. Mrs. Atkinson will be pleased," Mrs. Reed continued. "I know she wants this sorted out as soon as possible so that the place can be freed. There are so many other autistic children waiting to come, you see, all stuck in placements that are highly unsuitable, because they're unhappy or being bullied or not making any progress."

"I'm sure Mrs. Atkinson will understand that it is vital that we find the right place for Hollie," I said. "Otherwise, we'll have to go through the same thing all over again in a year or two."

"Oh yes, of course," Mrs. Reed said. She took a couple of sips of coffee. "I have a fair bit of experience of hearings myself. That is to say, I know of a few families going through due process hearings at present. If I learn of any details that might be of interest to you, I'll let you know."

"Please do."

The next few days followed the same pattern. I saw the social worker again, I saw the doctor, and I interviewed Hollie's teachers. The clinical psychologist spent two hours at our house following Hollie around, observing her behavior and its effect on the rest of the family. At the same time I continued to have long telephone conversations each evening with other parents already expert in these procedures.

Toward the end of the following week, I was quite stupefied by the mass of information I had acquired. I had collected so many facts, arguments and points of detail that my mind was fogged with it all. By Thursday I felt I could not even dredge up one more rational thought, let alone pick up a pen and set it down on paper.

That night I had an extremely vivid dream about the wild boy of Pershore Forest. I pictured him as he might have been when he first entered the forest as a child of about eight. Then, in a few short moments, it seemed, he was older and wilder, with long, bushy hair, a mud-encrusted face and ragged clothes. Where had he lived? How had he lived?

Presumably he had stolen clothes and food from cottages bordering the woods, and then foraged for seeds, nuts and fruit. I imagined his terrified, half-mad eyes when his rescuers caught up with him.

The next morning I sat at the dining table with my notes in front of me, but my mind skimmed senselessly over them as a faulty needle skims over a record on an old-fashioned turntable, back to the story of the wild boy. Why was I so fascinated with him? Was it because I too wanted to run away to a simpler life where I was responsible for no one? Or was it simply an entrancing story? Whatever the reason, I couldn't put it out of my mind.

I made a snap decision and slammed my books shut. John Chard was the person who could tell me more. Not only was he writing a book of local history, he had issued me an open invitation to call on him at his house if I wanted to know more.

John Chard lived in Winnersh, a couple of miles south of Brackley, in a small, newly built bungalow, a hundred yards or so down a lane off the main square. I parked by the low wall in front, and walked through the neatly kept garden to a porch overhung with the branches of a dormant climbing rose. I rang the doorbell, feeling rather awkward, certain all of a sudden that he had made the invitation out of politeness and that he would not be pleased to see me. Soon I heard footsteps in the hall, and the door was opened wide. John Chard stood there, looking as imposing as I remembered, with his tall, broad frame, large forehead and thoughtful gaze. A surprised but genuinely welcoming smile spread across his face.

"Hello, Lucy. What a pleasure to see you. Please come in."

Once inside, he shut the door and took my coat.

"I'm so sorry to be bothering you, but I haven't been able to put the story of the wild boy of Pershore out of my mind. I'm up to my eyes in preparing for our hearing for our autistic daughter – it's only just over a week away – but I just couldn't think straight any more, and –"

"And you thought it might help you to clear your mind if you had a break and thought about an entirely different subject, such as the wild boy, instead?"

"Exactly."

"I'm sure you're right. I'd be delighted to talk to you about him. Let's sit down."

He led the way across the dim hall and opened a door at the far end that led into a large, bright room with wide picture windows and a patio door facing a stone-flagged terrace. Beyond this, a long back yard with a neatly trimmed lawn and wide flowerbeds – now just mounds of earth – lay dormant in the dim late-November light. I stood by the patio doors imagining how verdant and beautiful it would be in the summer when the hedges would screen it from the neighbors' eyes and the sycamore and apples trees would be in leaf, while John disappeared to the kitchen to make coffee. He returned a few minutes later with a large tray, which he placed on the wooden coffee table.

"It's lovely out there in the summer," he said, following my gaze. "I have large potted plants and clematis and climbing roses growing up the trellises."

"I can imagine."

I turned and seated myself on one of the luxurious armchairs opposite to John. He pushed a delicate china coffee cup toward me, took a sip from his own, then took some papers from a plastic folder on the tray. There were photocopied pages of very old-looking texts – newspapers and official-looking registers – and some typed sheets.

"These I typed myself," he said, handing them to me, "and they will go toward the book. The other pages are copies I've taken of public records in the villages of Winnersh, Brackley and Pershore. And these – he flicked through to some more pages – "are copies of various accounts of the period, referring to the wild boy."

I took the pages gently in my hands. I wanted to delve into every word of this treasury of information, but I couldn't sit here for the two hours that would take, nor could I ask to take them home with me. John would need them, and there were already volumes of far more urgent material awaiting my attention on my dining room table. I would have to glean what I could over a half-hour of coffee and make the best of it.

First came an artist's picture of how the boy had looked when he was found.

"That's just the artist's impression based on descriptions from those who saw the boy soon after he was found. He didn't see the boy himself, and it was painted several weeks later, so it may not be that accurate."

The boy looked about thirteen or fourteen with brown hair that fell to his shoulders in matted locks. He wore a ragged coat that reached just below his hips, with what appeared to be great tears and blotches of mud and dust all over it. Under the coat was some sort of leather vest – it was hard to see clearly – with possibly some sort of shirt beneath that. His trousers came to just below his knees, and were torn and shredded at the end. His whole figure was hunched, his back bent and his arms hung rather loosely forward, almost in a traditional caveman fashion.

"His name was Adam Smithson," John said. "He was the youngest son of the village blacksmith. He had two elder sisters and two elder brothers, so he was very much an after thought, or an accident. His parents must have been forty or so when they had him."

"Do you know how he reintegrated after he was found? Did he settle down to life with his family again? Did they manage to carry on as if nothing had happened? Surely not?"

"Not really. All his brothers and sisters were much older than him, and three of them married and left home during his time in the forest, so he came back to aging parents and a home with no other children. Not the best of circumstances to help a child who had been through such an extraordinary experience. Not surprisingly, the records show that he couldn't talk after he was found – after all, he'd had no contact with humans during the time he was lost."

"Did he ever reintegrate properly?"

"It appears not."

"It must have been the huge stress of being separated from people and living wild for so long at such an impressionable time of life. The shock was too great for him to cope with."

"Yes; he couldn't readjust again."

I glanced through some of the papers, but partly I was still so stuffed with facts from my own research, and partly I was so conscious of sitting in a stranger's house taking up his time that I couldn't concentrate. Half an hour flew past as I studied them.

The clock on the mantelpiece suddenly chimed loudly. I looked up and saw it was almost noon.

"Heavens, I've got to go. I'll be late picking up my daughter from preschool," I said, leaping to my feet. "Thank you so much for the coffee, and most of all, for your time. I've very much enjoyed it."

"So have I," John said courteously.

In the hall he helped me on with my coat, waved away my thanks and, as I walked back down the path, called after me to visit him again.

That night I fell into a deep, exhausted sleep the moment I curled up in the blanket. It didn't last, unfortunately. It was only a short while before I woke again, and I then spent long hours shifting around, trying unsuccessfully to stop my thought processes from running about at breakneck speed, so that I could fall asleep again. I pictured myself standing up to make my contribution at the hearing, only to find I had left all my notes at home and that I couldn't remember a single word of my prepared speech. I saw myself being dull. I saw myself speaking in a droning, deadpan voice. I saw myself failing to get across even a hint of what it was like having to be vigilant every second of every minute of every hour of every day. I imagined David Greenham and Beth Johnson giving shoddy performances, whereas the district's expert witnesses were slick, clever and utterly convincing. I foresaw, in a word, failure.

I turned on my flashlight and opened *The Voyage of the Dawn Treader.* I forced myself to empty my mind of all daytime events and concentrate on what I was reading, but the story of Lord Rhoop and his torments on the Island of Dreams disheartened me further, even though I knew the book backwards. When I did drop off again, it was to feverish, unsatisfying sleep, and I awoke just after seven feeling wretched, knowing I had to face another difficult day on just two or three hours' sleep.

Later that day we were to attend a Roseman family party. Even Simon was reluctant to go, being almost as exhausted as I was, although he was able to muster at least some genuine interest in his brother's fiftieth birthday celebration.

I absolutely did not want to go. I so much did not want to go that I could feel Lord Voldemort waking up and muttering in the back of my head. I hadn't heard him for a few weeks. Events, after all, had at long last been moving my way, and I had been positive, and sometimes even happy. This bitter, resentful side of me that had begun rearing its ugly head in the summer, and that I was struggling to suppress, was yet another of the ruinous side-effects of the cataclysm that had hit my family.

I struggled out of bed at eight o'clock, slumped to the bathroom and deluged my face with handfuls of cold water in an attempt to shock myself into wakefulness.

As I returned to the bedroom and started to dress, Simon sat up and put his feet into his slippers.

Lord Voldemort was muttering more loudly, this time not out of the back of my head, but out of my mouth: "What is the point in Hollie and I going to this party? I won't be able to talk to anyone. I'll follow her around, trying to prevent her from destroying valuable ornaments or knocking people's dinners into their laps. No one will offer to help. I'll simply watch other people enjoying themselves for four hours, and be more exhausted than ever when we come home again."

Simon thought about this for a couple of seconds. "We don't really have a choice. They don't understand about Hollie being a reason for not going. And I'll help you with her."

I took a deep breath.

"I know you'll help. I wasn't getting at you when I said no one will help. After all, you'll have Joshua and Lisa to watch. I mean, no one in your family will offer to help. They're all too afraid of her."

I ate a bowl of cereal quickly, and drank two cups of strong coffee while I threw spare clothes, diapers and toys into Hollie's special bag. Eventually, after I'd been up about half an hour, I felt the adrenaline-fueled, overstimulated state of mind that had been my mental framework for the past few weeks begin to kick in and push back the fatigue, just as a powerful incoming tide conquers a river current in an estuary. I drank another two cups of strong coffee to ensure it stayed firmly in place, while I brought Simon coffee and made breakfast for the children.

Simon showered, dressed and made himself toast while I rushed about, tidying Hollie's bedroom, changing her diaper and dressing her, all the while sensing his gaze on me. Eventually he said:

"Are you okay?"

"What do you mean?"

"You seem very preoccupied."

"Well, there's so much to be done, so much to get ready to take with us."

"I didn't mean that. I mean, you've been very preoccupied over the past few weeks."

I froze. What was he doing, suddenly taking notice of me after months – years – of scarcely being aware of me?

"It's really not a good time to talk," I blustered to give myself time to think."It's never going to be a good time," he said thoughtfully. "You're always so busy. We're always so busy."

I bent over the dishes and began quickly sponging down plates, my face turned away.

"I'm sorry if I've seemed preoccupied," I said carefully. "I've just gone into overdrive, preparing for the hearing. It's so absolutely imperative that we win."

"Yes, I suppose so."

He sounded relieved. I turned my back and made a show of drying my hands, and then throwing towels and cups into Hollie's bag while I tried to calm myself. He'd noticed. He'd noticed I'd been different. I'd deflected him for now, and I hoped against hope that the solid excuse of my preoccupation with the due process hearing would serve to explain away any future strange moods that he witnessed. But I would have to work harder at appearing my old self.

We were away from the house by half past ten, with all the spaces in the back seat between the children crammed with toys and games, a bag of candies, chips and snacks on the floor in front of Hollie. We had been driving about five minutes when Simon amazed me by saying: "Why don't you try to sleep? I can see how tired you are. I'll watch Hollie while I'm driving."

"I don't think I'll be able to; I'm too wound up. But thank you." I turned to look at him and found myself unexpectedly reaching out to pat his leg. He was being so thoughtful and so – well – affectionate.

"Lean your seat back and try," he insisted.

I did as he suggested. As I put my head back and shut my eyes, I started to think about Simon, and how all of this might be affecting him. He was the most loyal and loving of men, and devoted to his family. True, our love for each other had never been – well – passionate, but it was solid and real.

My thoughts drifted back to when we had first met. I had been twenty-four or twenty-five, shy and awkward with men, and the two relationships I had had that had lasted as long as even a year had been with men more awkward even than me. Simon had been in his late thirties, with one failed marriage and two failed long-term relationships behind him. That first marriage had been an aberration; he had married his childhood sweetheart at nineteen, only to find, at twenty-one, that she wanted to be out at discos and nightclubs with her friends, not sitting quietly at home in front of the TV with him.

But the other two failed relationships provided definite warning signs, if only I could have read them: the two women had simply got bored. The relationships were obviously going nowhere, and they weren't interested in just being house managers for a man who didn't want to socialize and whose favorite way of spending an evening was operating a computer. However, I had not been clear-sighted. I had been looking for a father figure. I saw it now so clearly. My own father had always been such a distant figure, wrapped up in his books and studies, and he had always displayed intense irritation whenever I tried to ask him questions or to intrude on his time.

So when had I realized that Simon wasn't a replacement father, that as a person he was almost as flawed as my real father had been? Merely a matter of months ago. For years I had been impressed by his air of maturity and knowledge, guided by his opinions on almost everything. But he had caved in before the opinion of the principal of Petheril School, and agreed initially that Hollie should go to an unchallenging local school, and it was I who had seen clearly, immediately, that that would break us. Other people were not, by definition, wiser than I was.

In this crisis, there had been no one to help me except me, and I had been forced to dig deep in myself to find resources that, without this challenge, I would have said, categorically, I did not possess. It was a lonely, but oddly liberating sensation.

Daniel Roseman's party was being held at a hotel outside Dalton that had an annex adjoining a large dining room. The buffet was set out on tables against the far wall of the dining area where sixty or seventy guests were already milling around, helping themselves to glasses of wine, sherry and fruit juice as well as plates of food, which they were carrying to groups of tables and chairs set out in the annex.

When we arrived, Geoffrey and Veronica immediately came out to kiss us all. They talked a little to Joshua and Lisa, and said hello to Hollie in artificially bright, loud voices.

"It must be very difficult. We all feel so sorry for you," Veronica said, giving me her usual look of intense pity and sympathy. I could feel Lord Voldemort stirring in the back of my head, carping at her assumption that these sympathetic platitudes were all that was required of her. He hissed: "Go on, say it. 'Yes, it's very difficult, but it would be less difficult if people like you would help more.'" I told him to shut up, and hastily concocted a smile. Then, to my utter amazement, I heard him saying, not just in my mind, but perfectly audibly:

"You always say that."

Veronica had already half turned away, her sympathy duty done for the day. Now her head flicked back toward me, her mouth open in astonishment. I wasn't good at confrontation; indeed I was lousy at it. Every rational thought in my head would flee in panic, if ever I was forced into one, and I would stutter and fumble inarticulately on a sea of churning emotion. "Well, if I always say that, it's because it's true," she countered, "We all realize it's very difficult for you."

"If you realize how difficult it is, perhaps you could offer to watch Hollie for half an hour this afternoon to give me a break," said Lord Voldemort, who was having an absolute field day.

Veronica's face was a picture of affront.

"Me look after Hollie? Oh, I couldn't cope. And she's your child. I looked after my children when they were young."

"You had normal children. It's just a matter of luck, just the luck of the draw, whether it was us or another couple, or you fifty years ago, who were unlucky enough to have an autistic child."

Veronica swelled with horror. Simon was looking at me as if I'd gone mad. He grappled for a lifeline to stop himself from being submerged in this churning sea of anger.

"I'll watch Hollie for a while later so you can have a break."

"There you are," said Veronica, in relief. "That's all right then; you'll be able to have your lunch. And now, if you'll excuse me . . . " she said loudly, quickly turning away before I could protest that Simon's offering to help was not the answer, since caring for Hollie was always our responsibility.

He looked at me, aghast. "What on earth's got into you?"

"I'm sorry. I don't know what came over me. It's just that I'm sick to death of all the insincerity."

"I'm warning you, Lucy, please don't go upsetting my family, particularly on an important occasion like today."

"I'm so sorry."

I turned away then, because Hollie was sticking her fingers in a plateful of little quiches to the consternation of a group of old ladies who were standing around watching her and tsk-tsk-ing to each other. I grabbed her hands, wiped them with moist wipes and pulled her away without meeting the eyes of the curious onlookers.

Simon, true to his word, relieved me for half an hour while I grabbed a plate of cold chicken, some salad and a roll and some cheese. Joshua was playing cars with his cousins, Ian and Ben, while Lisa sat at one of the tables, desultorily scribbling in a coloring book, while she secretly watched her slightly older cousins, Chloe and Hannah, talk about music and pop stars with some other older girls. I sat down at a table with my two sisters-in-law, Rachel and Fiona, who were discussing the problem of coping with naughty children in supermarkets.

Rachel, the mother of Chloe and Hannah, looked very elegant in a green, long-sleeved dress, her auburn hair, which normally fell almost to her shoulders, piled neatly on top of her head. She always looked too heavily made up, but today she looked more so than ever, because she had chosen to wear a bright red lipstick.

"Hannah still tries to put too many things in the cart, candy and toys and stuff like that. I have such a battle explaining to her that she can't have everything she wants, and to make her put things back."

"Ben keeps running off down the other aisles, and I'm forever chasing after him, telling him to stay near me," added Fiona. She looked equally elegant in a green pants suit and white blouse, her brown page-boy hair glossy and impeccably styled.

I finished the plate of cold chicken and salad, and began buttering the roll and slicing the cheese onto it. I could hear Voldemort in my head grinding on about Hollie, who nearly always screamed and refused even to enter the supermarket. Many, many times I had been forced to drive home again without the supplies we needed, in the hope that she would be more amenable another day.

"And it's so difficult getting to put the shopping away once we're home, when they keep running and asking for drinks, or wanting me to get toys down for them," continued Rachel. "Luckily I can mostly shop while they're at school now. It's just during school vacations that we still have problems."

"The worst problem I have with Ben is getting him to come home after we've been out somewhere," Fiona went on. "He's just so difficult. He'll often start to have a tantrum because he wants to stay – at the fair or the swings, or wherever we are. I try to negotiate and remind him of all the toys and games he can play with when he gets home," said Fiona.

I muttered at Voldemort to be quiet, as he had got me into enough trouble for one day.

"Joshua was like that once," I said, trying to sound chatty and conversational. "And Lisa can be like that. I think it's quite normal behavior for young children."

"Oh no," said Fiona, scornfully. "Ben's tantrums are particularly bad."

"Tell her where to get off," hissed Voldemort. "Shut up," I hissed back. "Go on," he goaded, "tell her that her children are angels in comparison with Hollie, who can never be reasoned with, bribed or cajoled." I stuck a lump of bread and cheese in my mouth and almost choked on it.

Rachel went on, "and it's so hard getting them to go to sleep at night. They keep getting out of bed and coming into each other's rooms, and playing and talking and laughing. I have to shout at them sometimes."

"Yes, I really had to tell the boys off last night," replied Fiona. "They got a box of crayons and felt-tips and the drawing paper, and I found them well after they were supposed to be asleep, drawing in a book. And then, once they'd gone to sleep, I found they'd been drawing on the woodwork on the door. It's hard scrubbing felt-tip marks off paint work at ten o'clock at night, just when you're dying to sit down and have a bit of time to yourself."

At that point I lost it. I put the roll slowly down on the plate. I looked meaningfully from one to the other while Voldemort enunciated perfectly audibly:

"It's also very hard scrubbing feces from curtains and ceilings and door knobs at midnight."

His tone was perfectly chatty, as if he was lobbing in a shuttlecock, not a cannonball. They stared at me in silence as if I were an alien who had just that moment landed from outer space.

"It must be."

"Yes, indeed."

Then they turned toward each other, exchanged an arch look, and gave slight smiles, relieved – as they thought – to have put an end to that bit of abnormality.

"And the trouble is," went on Rachel, "if they go to sleep late, it's so hard waking them up in the morning."

"Yes. They're tired and grumpy."

Neither of them could think of much more to say to follow this. Voldemort had effectively bombed the conversation into smithereens, and all it could do was struggle on for a minute or two until it finally died. After a few more trite phrases about their children's exasperating behavior, the two women fell into silence. I made an excuse about going to choose a dessert, and they nodded and said they would do the same.

I had had a mere three mouthfuls of cheesecake when Veronica interrupted my conversation with Simon's cousin and his fiancée to inform me that Hollie was knocking silverware onto the floor. I turned away without a word and went to find Hollie, who was standing at the end of one of the long tables, where plates were still half laden with food. A pile of clean knives and forks gleamed under the bright overhead light in a messy pile on the floor. Simon had reached her first and was holding her right arm firmly. Hollie herself was squirming and making loud complaining noises.

"I'll watch her now," I said.

"Are you sure?"

"Of course. It's your family. And you can still keep an eye on the other two."

For the next couple of hours I followed Hollie around the dining room and the annex, grabbing her arm if she reached out to snatch precious-looking ornaments or steaming coffee jugs. People kept leaving the garden door open. After a while I gave up trying to shut it, and followed Hollie out into the mild November afternoon. She trotted around the garden, then stood for brief periods staring into the middle distance at nothing in particular.

Each time we re-entered the dining room, the social groupings had changed, relatives in the circles of armchairs and dining chairs had mixed themselves up and moved around to talk to other relatives, against a backdrop of constantly refilled tea and coffee cups. A few people smoked, others sipped brandy or liqueur, and many looked close to dozing off. I felt pretty well invisible.

Eventually, the fact that Lisa was drooping with fatigue penetrated Simon's party enjoyment, and we said our goodbyes and left.

That evening Simon took Hollie for a walk by flashlight on Shalham Downs while I bathed the other two, read them a story and sang them some songs. They, at least, were tired; Lisa's eyelids were drooping as I finished the story, and Joshua was lying quietly with his head on the pillow. But when Hollie came in ten minutes later, she skipped along the hall, making energetic whooping noises.

I took one look at her beaming face as she made excited leaps in the air, and burst into tears. Hollie carried on leaping while Simon stared at me in bewilderment.

"What on earth's the matter?"

I grabbed a handful of tissues and sobbed into them.

"I don't know," I wailed. "It's everything."

Simon sat down slowly on the armchair opposite. It was the third time that day that someone had looked at me as if I were an alien creature that had just that moment landed from outer space.

"You're exhausted."

"That's part of it. And it's the pressure. Only just over a week . . . everything hangs on us winning. What if I get my speech all wrong? What if I get confused and don't explain things properly? What if David Greenham or Beth Johnson get struck down with flu? I couldn't bear it; I just couldn't bear it."

I could feel the movement of the sofa cushions as Simon sat down next to me. He took my right hand, cupped it in both of his hands and squeezed it.

"You're exhausted," he repeated awkwardly. "That makes you feel as if you won't cope. But you will. I know you'll do a wonderful job."

He patted my hand with his left hand, and stroked my forearm with his other hand. I looked up and managed a watery, unfocused smile in his direction. I began trying to explain it, to myself, as much as to him. "I am exhausted, and the pressure is unbearable . . . "

"Is there anything I can do? Anything I can get you?"

A future, perhaps? A clear conscience? Some sort of gagging mechanism for Lord Voldemort?

"But it's not just that. It was so soul-destroying today at that party, not being able to talk to anyone, just watching everyone else talking and enjoying themselves. And it'll be like that from now on, if we lose. Any time anyone feels obliged or brave enough to ask us to an event, that is how it will be. The waiters had more conversation with the guests than I did."

"I'm sorry. I should have relieved you more. Are you so tired you want to go to bed? I'll stay up with Hollie."

"No. No, thanks." And then an idea formed in my mind. "But I might go out in the car for a while, just drive around, get some fresh air and try to unwind. I've a splitting headache. I feel if I have to clear up one more mess or do one more load of washing, I'll go mad."

"Yes, of course. I know how you've been enjoying your drives recently."

Simon was still looking helpless and ready to agree to anything that might pacify me.

"It's just . . . " I began, still trying to unravel my confused feelings. But Hollie, who had been leaping about in the hall, came running in and was tugging at Simon's arm.

"She's probably hungry," I said wearily. "She didn't eat much real food at the party."

"No, I know. You go."

I tried to smile, but I couldn't quite look him in the eye, and my smile felt crooked and forced.

I didn't wait around to see if he needed help with Hollie. I looked in on Joshua and Lisa as they lay asleep, tucked their blankets around them more snugly, and lightly stroked their cheeks. Then I turned and walked upstairs to our bedroom and pulled the door closed, so that Simon wouldn't hear me changing my clothes. I threw off the baggy track suit, dropped it in the bottom of the closet and pulled on the blue and tan clingy shirt with the long wide sleeves, new from my recent shopping spree, together with a clean pair of navy trousers, all inside a minute. I brushed my hair, grabbed my coat, my purse and my cell phone, then dashed down the stairs and straight out of the front door, locking it quickly behind me before Simon could think of any alternative suggestions.

I drove fast, quite unlike my normal careful self, taking corners too quickly, overtaking other cars on even the smallest straight stretches. I knew exactly where I was going. I covered the five-mile trip to Joel's house in about twelve minutes. His road was empty and silent. There were no dog walkers, no cars turning into or out of drives. The only person who could be seen, in fact, was Joel himself, who was getting out of his car as I turned into the drive. He stared at me, dumbfounded, for a moment, then pulled the car door open and touched my arm gently as I climbed out.

"Hello." His voice was deeper than usual.

"Hello." We held each other's gaze, neither of us blinking. Finally, he took my right hand and clasped it tightly in both of his.

"I can't tell you how good it is to see you," he said.

"I'm sorry, you must think it's odd my coming here. I've just had the most impossible day. There was this family party, and Hollie behaved, well, like Hollie always does, and no one offered to help – as usual – oh, I can't explain it in a nutshell, but it was just awful . . . "

"I think everyone who meets you is full of admiration for how you cope."

"Do you think so? Even if it's true, I don't know how much help admiration is, really. I don't know why people can't think, 'There but for the grace of God go I,'" I said. "That's what I would think in their position." Hours before, when I had had the same conversation with Simon, I had felt unbearably lonely and weary. Now the problem of other people's indifference seemed like a frustrating quirk of human nature, something I had to tolerate and make the best of, not something to waste my energy getting annoyed about.

"I mean, it's just a matter of luck whether it was us or another family who had a severely autistic child. And I know that, if it had happened to someone else we knew, I'd be so grateful it wasn't me that I'd be more than willing to do a small amount to help."

"That's not how most people see it," Joel said, stroking my hand. "They don't see that it could have happened to them.

They just see it as your problem."

"I know. I'm sorry, I didn't mean to burden you with this. It's just that today it all seemed too much."

"Come and have a glass of wine," he said.

He opened the front door, but there was no light in the hallway. I hesitated under the light in the porch, waiting for him to switch it on.

"The bulb's gone, I'm afraid," he said. "I know where there's a flashlight. Just come in while I shut the door, then I'll find us some light."

I stepped forward. The front door was shut behind me, and I was plunged into darkness.

I began to panic. What was I doing here, in this house, in the pitch black, with this man whom I really knew very little about? I heard Joel's footsteps striding away, then a lamp went on in the living room across the hall. There was no sign of Joel. I wondered whether I should follow him, but it seemed presumptuous to do so when I hadn't been invited. For a few moments there was total silence. Then I heard a flicking sound, and a second later Joel had reappeared in the lighted doorway, this time holding an old-fashioned lantern containing a lighted candle.

"I used this last Christmas when a group of us went caroling," he said. "I'll leave it as a hall light until I can find a spare bulb."

He placed it on a table that stood against the wall. Then he turned toward me. He seemed taller than ever, his shoulders broader; the shadows seemed to accentuate his cheek bones and strong jaw line. The flickering candlelight from the lantern behind him was reflected on the creases of the arms and shoulders of his leather jacket. I had always wanted to run my hands across his arms and his shoulders. Now I reached out and touched the smooth leather of his left fore-arm just above the elbow. I ran my fingers down the sleeves to his wrist. Then, very lightly, I touched the back of his hand, feeling the curls of downy hair, the large rounded bones of the knuckles. I glanced up. He moved toward me, slipping his arms tightly around my back. Then, with both arms held tightly around me, he pulled me hard against his chest. I put my arms around him and held him back, as hard as I could, dimly aware of how very, very long I had wanted to do this.

He loosened his grip slightly and said, "Come with me."

I stared at him. "What? Where?"

"To the garden. There's something I want to show you, before we have that wine. Something magical in the sky that we won't see again for a long time."

Joel led me through the shadowy hall and the living room softly lit with two small lamps, and out of the patio door. As we crossed the patio, he reached out and took my hand. "Careful of the step onto the grass," he said, "It's easy to trip in the darkness."

I took the step carefully, but he still kept hold of my hand.

"I'm surprised you don't have outside lights, like you do at the front."

"I do. But I switched them off. Otherwise we won't be able to see the flying horse."

I laughed. "I haven't the faintest idea what you're talking about."

"I didn't think you would." After a minute or two the darkness no longer seemed so impenetrable. The sky was sprinkled with stars and a thin sliver of moon hung above the western horizon. We crossed the garden, past where we had stood for the bonfire a few weeks before, until we were at the farthest point we could be from the house without getting under the overhanging branches of the woodland at the bottom. There Joel stopped. Still he held on to my hand, but with his free hand he pointed into the sky. My heart thudded in my chest. My mouth was completely dry. I guessed his was too, for when he said "look," his voice was hoarse.

"That's it," he said, his voice full of wonder. "The flying horse of autumn. Pegasus. It's the autumn constellation."

"Ah, now I understand."

"Look, there's Andromeda, and there's Pisces. Pegasus is in between."

"I don't remember my Greek legends as well as I should."

Joel stood closer to me. I was having trouble drawing my breath. Now he had both my hands in his hands, and was gently squeezing them. His voice was very deep.

"Pegasus was the flying horse on which Perseus rescued Andromeda from her chains."

I laughed, but the laughter was cut off when he suddenly covered my mouth with his, and began kissing me, wrapping his arms around me so tightly that I could hardly breathe.

After a time – it could have been seconds or minutes, I had no idea – we broke apart and looked at each other. There seemed to be so much to say, and I didn't know how to begin saying any of it. So I said the very last thing I actually wanted to say.

"I should get back."

"What about that wine?"

There was nothing I wanted more than to sit down very close to Joel and drink wine. But, being that close to him, would I be able to resist the temptation that was already almost irresistible . . . ? I had to force the words from my lips.

"Er – I think I'd better not."

He looked at me intently for a moment or two. "Okay."

He walked close beside me, holding my hand, as we crossed the garden and made our way back through the dimly lit house. He paused with his hand on the front door. Then he turned and smiled at me, a smile at once knowing and suggestive, and yet as gleeful as that of a child. I could sense his excitement reflected in his taut, slightly quivering cheeks and his quick breathing.

Outside, by the car, he pulled me close to him again.

"Please come back soon."

"I will. Very soon."

I glanced back as I drove off and saw him standing in the porch light staring after me, tall and certain, at ease with himself, while the bushes shifted slightly in the icy breeze and Pegasus reared up over his head.

Chapter Seven

As the next few days passed, I seemed closer than ever to losing my grip on real life. I felt like a very old person with some debilitating geriatric condition who had started to become confused, unable to tell day from night, or even to understand where she was. With Hollie staying awake longer and longer each night, I took to rewriting my notes and studying autism textbooks well into the early hours while I watched over her, since it seemed silly to waste the time. And, even when she did eventually sleep, I couldn't still my overactive mind. I would lie there hour after hour, reading (it took just four nights to complete *The Silver Chair*), tortured by nightmare hearing scenarios. A heroic act of will was then required each morning to get out of bed and get on with the preschool routine.

Once all three children were at school, I would come back, lie on the sofa and try to sleep. But exhausted as I was, I would be lucky to remain unconscious for twenty minutes before waking with a terrible sense of panic and foreboding, certain that there was some vital detail requiring instant action. And I was forgetting things, lots of things. I could drive the younger two to school, and find I had forgotten to make Joshua's lunch. I would go into shops and not be able to remember what I needed to buy. I would start conversations with mothers in the school playground and forget mid-sentence what I had been about to say. Most worrying of all, I would get in the car, only to find, two miles down the road, that I couldn't remember where I was going.

On Thursday I had just woken up in a panic from one of these unsatisfactory catnaps when the phone rang. It was Joanna Reed, the outreach worker from Petheril School.

"I wanted to tell you about a family I met the other day who've just been through a due process hearing. I thought you might want to know what they said."

"Yes, definitely. What was the child's disability?"

"Cerebral palsy, but I didn't think it would matter that it's a different disability."

"No, I'm sure you're right. It's the experience of the hearing that's relevant. I'm just trying to put my notes together for our hearing on Monday, to make sure everything I say carries as much force and conviction as possible."

"Look, why don't you come for a cup of tea at my home, say, tomorrow about five. I can fill you in on what happened at this other family's due process hearing and you can run through your speech in front of me, do a kind of dress rehearsal. Have you someone who can watch the children for an hour?"

With just half of my mind on what Joanna was saying, I exchanged details with her – her address, the time we would meet, the fact that I would only have an hour before I would have to return home to relieve Karen Hinton. The idea of a dress rehearsal appealed to me; a dress rehearsal for a real-life performance, now only four days away.

The next day, just after five, I parked in front of Joanna's house on the north side of Shalham. She greeted me enthusiastically and sat me at the large, pine table in her bright kitchen while she made tea.

"Have you a nice weekend lined up?" I asked, just to be conversational.

"Actually, I have several extremely large piles of work that I've brought home, planning for staff training days and curriculum meetings. And I shall probably have to go into school both days for most of the day."

"Do you have children of your own?" I asked.

"I have a daughter of twenty-one who's at Oxford," she said proudly, "studying medicine. She'll no doubt call me either tonight or tomorrow night. And then next Sunday I'm going up to take her out for lunch." She seemed to read the unasked question in my head, for she added: "I was divorced from my husband six years ago. He sees our daughter separately."

"Oh, I'm sorry."

"You needn't be," she added, with sudden venom. "He was having an affair. I think people who have affairs when they're married are the lowest of the low."

The attack was so sudden, it sliced straight to my heart. She didn't know what she was saying, of course. And, after all, I had only kissed him, even if it was a very passionate kiss. Nevertheless, the sense of betrayal of myself and those closest to me seemed to scoop out my insides.

"Still, you didn't come here to hear my views on adultery," Joanna said, comfortably, taking a sip of her tea. She looked thoughtful for a minute, and I had the impression she was trying to remember exactly why she had invited me.

"Oh, yes, I was going to tell you about this other family's experience at their due process hearing. I don't want to put you off, but it wasn't very encouraging," she said cheerfully. "Their son has cerebral palsy, and can't walk or talk very well. He was going to a local primary school that had a special needs unit, but he wasn't making much progress. The family asked for him to be sent to a special school that deals only in cerebral palsy, just over the border in Southshire, a school with a wonderful reputation that does a lot of successful therapy. He'd have boarded there during the week. Anyway, the hearing was held just the week before last."

"And what was the result?" I asked, breathlessly.

"They lost, I'm afraid." Her face became mournful for a moment, but the solemnity was only skin-deep; the disappointment hadn't touched her own life at all, and her job required her only to relay information in a brisk no-nonsense way. Besides, she was someone who simply always had to be talking.

"They spent quite a lot of money on it as well, I gather, paying for a private educational psychologist to appear at the hearing to support them."

"They lost?" I faltered.

"I'm sorry, but yes. I thought it best for you to be aware of all the facts."

The tea was too milky, and yet bitter to the taste. I pushed it away. I instantly revised the initial impression I had had of Joanna being a thoughtful person. Anyone with any real wisdom would have seen that, instead of putting me in possession of all the facts, her warning would serve only to frighten and unnerve me, and thus make it even more likely that we too would fail. I felt shaky and feeble. Had I wasted the last six months? Should I have put my energies, instead, into seeking some other sort of help? But what other possible source of help, apart from praying for miracles, could I have found?

And then, because Joel was always there in my thoughts somewhere – at the back of my mind if daytime practicalities pushed him temporarily from the forefront – an image and an awareness of him flashed into my mind's eye.

"It doesn't mean you'll lose, Lucy," I could almost hear him saying. "Try to learn from this."

"What were the problems?" I asked. "I mean, why do they think they lost?"

"I don't know the details."

It was on the tip of my tongue to ask why exactly she had invited me there, since she knew so little, and everything she had said had been so discouraging.

"I know the mother was very nervous, and felt she spoke timidly and not as if she really believed what she was saying."

"Thanks for the tea." I stood up and picked up my keys. "My babysitter will have to go soon," I lied.

"Don't you want to go over your speech in front of me?" Joanna Reed asked, her face full of consternation. "That's what we decided on the phone."

"I think perhaps not," I said decisively.

Someone who could have told me such a distressing tale on the eve of our own due process hearing was unlikely to be able to offer the constructive wisdom and discernment I was seeking.

"Hollie's class is going for a walk in the woods this afternoon," Joanna said, as she showed me to the door. "You know the school grounds verge on Pershore Forest, don't you?"

"Yes."

Pershore Forest, that large area of ancient land that stretched from the Petheril School almost as far as Shalham Common, was where the wild boy had lived. Once again, I began to wonder about him.

I stopped by Geraldine's on the way home. I was aware that there had been an odd role reversal over the past few weeks, and that it was me who now seemed to be working to bolster her spirits at regular intervals, instead of the other way around.

"Hi," she said, listlessly, when she saw me. I surveyed her pale, strained face as she shut the door behind me.

"Have you seen a doctor?"

"Why, do I look that bad?" she snapped.

"No, no, it's just that you seem worried."

I followed her to the kitchen and sat on one of her pine stools while she switched on the kettle.

"After all, if it's a virus, the doctor can give you something to help."

"No, she can't. Antibiotics are no good for viruses."

"Well, I don't know," I said, helplessly. "At least discuss it with her. She might think of some quite different explanation that neither of us has considered."

"Maybe."

She obviously had no intention of doing it.

"Have you just come to visit the invalid?" she said tartly.

I stared at her. I had never heard her make such an acid comment before. She caught my glance and looked away.

"Sorry," she murmured.

I tried to think of something to say to change the subject, and leaped at the first thought that came to mind, which was the party Paula Rochelle was holding the following day to celebrate the imminent Welshney Castle opening.

"I wondered if I could borrow a dress for Paula's party tomorrow?"

I was astonished at myself. Until the words were out of my mouth, I hadn't realized I had any serious intention of going to Paula's party. After all, there would be little opportunity to talk to Joel, and I was too exhausted for small talk. Geraldine's face brightened.

"Are you going?" she asked, more cheerfully. "I'll go too, then. I wouldn't have bothered, but if you're definitely going . . . "

I had always avoided parties – not that I was ever exactly deluged with invitations for them these days – and obsessed as I was with the thought of the hearing on Monday, I was even less inclined than ever to go. But it seemed I was now under an obligation.

"Come on then," said Geraldine, sounding much more cheerful. "Let's go and choose our outfits."

The following night I stood at the bathroom mirror applying eye shadow and mascara. Hollie sat in the tub behind me, water up to her shoulders, chewing on the bathroom sponge and dropping discarded mouthfuls over the side.

"Why did Paula invite us?" Simon called from the bedroom.

I stopped dead with the mascara brush against the lashes of my right eye. It was a question I should perhaps have anticipated, and I could hardly reply that Joel had probably pressured her to invite us. I marshalled my thoughts quickly as I walked back to the bedroom and slipped the tubes of makeup into a drawer.

"I mean," Simon went on, "Was it just because we're clients of Joel? I can't believe Paula invites all his clients to her social events."

"I suspect she feels sorry for us," I said truthfully. "She thinks we're cooped up here with our handicapped child, and that we never see anyone."

"Is there any particular reason for the party? A birthday or something? An engagement?"

It was as if a wall of ice had crashed on top of me. Would Joel one day marry Paula? I couldn't bear the thought. Of course he wouldn't. He had two failed marriages behind him already, and he'd told me when I'd seen him a week ago that he was happier now than he'd ever been. And yet . . . and yet . . . I knew in the core of myself that we could not carry on much longer as we were.

"I think," I began, cautiously, feeling about for explanations, trying to convince myself as much as Simon, "that the party is mostly intended for all those who've been working toward the grand opening of Welshney Castle, to help them let off steam after all their hard work before the big public opening ceremony next Tuesday. And also, Paula herself has had overall responsibility for the publicity over the opening, and it's been a big coup for her and her company. I think she wants to draw attention to her input into the project and show off her public relations abilities. She's very astute. Everything she does, she'll be doing with an eye on how it might further her career."

"You're no doubt right," said Simon, taking his sports jacket out of the closet and slipping it on.

The offices of Thompson Associates, where Paula was a junior partner, were housed in a large brick building overlooking the low ruined walls and scattered blocks of stone that were all that remained of Shalham Castle. The clamor of conversation and music reached us as we crossed the road. As we climbed the stairs, the noise increased, and so did my trepidation. I was desperate to see Joel, but afraid of showing too plainly in public what I felt.

What if I commanded my features to remain impassive, but they totally disobeyed me, and little glows and flickers and flames of delight broke out all over them?

A smiling receptionist, impeccably dressed in a maroon dress and matching jacket, greeted us at the door, checked our names on the list and offered us a glass of wine or sherry. Paula, who was talking with a group of recent arrivals just behind the reception desk, turned to greet us. She gave me a look that was hard to read. On the surface she greeted us as she did all the guests, with a very professional ease and charm. But I sensed that her eyes narrowed and hardened when she looked at me.

"How lovely you look," she said, with one of her most professional smiles.

I knew I looked fantastic in Geraldine's dress, but I couldn't believe she was trying to make me feel good about myself. I sensed she had a hidden agenda, and that there was something she was trying to conceal from me, at least until she found the right moment to reveal it – the moment when she felt it would inflict the greatest pain. Certainly, she had a coy, almost smug expression, the reason for which no doubt would soon be apparent.

"How kind of you," I said, automatically, adding – quite truthfully – "you look stunning."

And she did. Paula would have looked good in any outfit, not just because she was young and had that lovely elfin face and silky blonde hair, but also because she carried herself with such confidence and poise.

The office's main function room was straight ahead, already crowded with people. I could hear the sound of many voices laughing, exclaiming, or loudly vociferating agreement or disagreement. But one voice, louder, more penetrating, more arrogant, stood out.

"Is Bella Haughton here?" I asked, horror-struck.

"Yes, of course," Paula replied. "The party is partly for all those who've been involved in the Welshney Castle project, so Bella would be invited."

"Yes, yes, of course," I said hurriedly, trying to work out whether, in this seething mass of people, it would be possible to avoid for the entire evening being seen by Bella.

"Would you like me to introduce you?" Paula asked. Was she sensing my discomfort, and trying to exploit it?

"No, oh no," I blurted out.

I squirmed inwardly while Simon stood swaying awkwardly from side to side. There was no escaping giving an explanation for my outburst. It was just a question of how to dress up the partial version of truth about the wedding that I would have to offer so that it didn't seem quite as awful. Perhaps I could make it sound as if Hollie had merely grabbed a chunk of wedding cake, or bumped into the bride and spread a few cake crumbs on her arm.

"We have met Bella before," I said slowly and carefully, "but we didn't hit it off very well. I'll explain what happened another time if you're interested, but now isn't really the time."

Paula looked wary, but she spoke casually, just as if I was passing on a piece of light-hearted gossip. "This all sounds fascinating! You'll definitely have to fill me in another time."

"She's a very powerful person," I said, thinking aloud.

"Oh, she's powerful all right," Paula replied, and her enjoyment of my discomfort was more pronounced. "She's one of the top city council members, and everyone's expecting her to be mayor next year. Definitely not someone to alienate." As Paula finished speaking, I could hear Bella's clipped, precise diction and penetrating tones emanating from the other room.

"So it's a foregone conclusion that she'll be mayor?" I felt a surge of resentment at the ease with which a woman who made snap judgments based on ignorance and prejudice could cut a swath through the opinions of vast numbers of powerful people, in order to get exactly what she wanted.

"Not totally," Paula replied. "But something major would have to go wrong for her not to get it."

At that point Paula turned and began greeting the next arrivals as they picked up their glasses of sherry from the tray on the receptionist's desk.

Geraldine glided elegantly over to greet us, looking eye-catching in her crimson cocktail dress.

"I'm so glad you came," she said, kissing me. "Let me introduce you to some people."

I looked around surreptitiously for Joel, but I couldn't see him. Then I followed Geraldine. A minute later I found myself talking playgroups and schools and children with June, a colleague of Paula's from Thompson Associates, while Simon discussed software and spreadsheets with June's husband. After a few minutes, exhaustion, hunger and stress conspired to make me feel sick and dizzy.

"Are you all right?" June asked.

"Sorry, I'm feeling a bit faint," I muttered. "I've hardly eaten all day."

"Let's go and get some food then," she suggested. "I've not eaten either."

I followed behind June and her husband, Simon and Geraldine, as we made our way between clusters of newly arrived guests. I searched all the faces, but still there was no sign of the only one I wanted to see. We walked across the reception area to the dining room. To the left of the door a man was standing on his own holding a glass of red wine, calmly observing everything that was going on around him. He was probably in his mid-thirties, tall, with a round, handsome face and thick black hair; he wore a blue, open-necked shirt and brown leather jacket. His dignified, erect posture enhanced his air of easy self-assurance.

I glanced up as I was about to step into the room, and my heart plummeted. Bella Haughton was striding majestically out of the dining room. She wore an emerald-green silk dress and matching shoes so highly polished that they gleamed, and she held a brimming glass of wine elegantly in her right hand. She didn't appear to see Geraldine, Simon, or June and her husband. Her gaze, like a prison searchlight, was focused entirely on me, and the expression in her eyes was as haughty and contemptuous as she could possibly make it.

In those seconds Bella seemed to became taller, just as I seemed to shrink alarmingly, like a shadow under the mid-day sun.

Afraid, absurdly, that I might disappear altogether, I tried to force a polite greeting from my lips, but all that emerged was an unintelligible mumble.

"Hello," she said, somehow managing in her tone to make me feel small, while simultaneously conveying that I wasn't quite important enough for her full-blown contempt. I felt myself withering, and I shrank sideways toward where Simon stood, instinctively reaching for a place where I felt valued and safe. Then a switch seemed to click in my head, and I suddenly saw my cowardliness for what it was. "I am no longer going to be so easily intimidated," I told myself, and I stood my ground. I drew myself up, and felt myself filling out again, like a parched plant that has just been watered. I straightened my back and squared my shoulders. I looked her in the eye.

"Hello," I said, loudly. I sensed amused interest from the round-faced man in the blue shirt, who was watching the altercation eagerly.

Bella scowled at me, and made as if to open her mouth to speak, but I turned away quickly and marched through the door of the dining room, congratulating myself inwardly on my assertiveness. In the dining room, where three large tables were covered with the most mouth-watering spread of food, I concentrated on filling my plate with portions of quiche, pork pie and spoonfuls of elaborate salad. I carefully avoided the gazes of Simon and Geraldine, who exchanged a few awkward smatterings of conversation as they explored the buffet tables and collected brimming glasses of wine. Simon, his plate full, then fell into a more prolonged conversation with June and her husband, as they retraced their steps away from the tables and back across the reception area.

"Come on," Geraldine said. "Get another glass of wine and let's go back to the party. Whatever you do, don't let her get to you."

"I'm not, actually," I said, rousing myself and smiling. "She did make me uncomfortable to start with. But then I decided I'd had enough of it."

"I could see that. Well done, you. I was nearly going to . . . "

But Geraldine, articulate, quick-as-a-flash Geraldine, had stopped mid-sentence and appeared to have forgotten what she was about to say. We had just passed through the dining room door and into the reception area, and she appeared, for the first time, to have noticed the handsome man with the blue shirt who had witnessed my antagonistic encounter with Bella. He was being greeted by three other men, but he appeared to be only half-listening to what the group was saying, for he peered around at us, particularly at Geraldine, as we emerged from the buffet area.

In the main party room Geraldine and I went straight over to where Simon stood with June and her husband, and a group of others. Once more I shot a surreptitious glance around the room. Where on earth was he? Simon was holding his dinner plate in his left hand while he talked into the mobile phone in his right. He slipped it back in his pocket and shot me an anxious look. "I've just called home," he said. "Karen's having problems with Hollie. She took off Hollie's special gate because she said she felt it looked unkind, shutting her in like that. And now, Hollie's come running out and is rushing all over the house, and she can't get her to go back in."

"We'd better go." I said.

"I suppose so. I'll get the coats." He turned and walked off into the reception area, followed by Geraldine, while I quickly swallowed a few more mouthfuls.

Simon and Geraldine were waiting for me in the reception area.

"We've been thinking," said Geraldine. "Why don't you stay?"

"I can go back and sort out Karen and Hollie," said Simon. "It doesn't need both of us, and you need a change of scene, something to take your mind off Monday."

"If Bella's presence is worrying you, we could go to the pub for a drink," Geraldine added.

I looked from one to the other. Geraldine's expression clearly challenged, "For heaven's sake, take this opportunity. Stay and enjoy yourself for once." Simon looked relieved to have an excuse to go. If he didn't go out socially for five years, he wouldn't miss it. Once he'd seen Karen off and succeeded in calming and settling Hollie, he would be happier with a beer in his hand and his feet on a cushion than he ever would be here.

I realized I had made up my mind.

"All right."

"Good girl," said Geraldine, clapping me on the arm.

"Shall I take a taxi so you can have the car?" Simon asked.

"No. You take the car – you need to be back quickly. I can get a taxi."

Simon turned to go. "I'm sure I won't be that long," I called after him.

When Geraldine and I turned around after calling goodbye, we were astonished to see the round-faced, black-haired man directly in front of us, looking from one to the other of us and proffering glasses of wine.

"I'm glad you decided not to go," he said, glancing at me, but turning almost immediately to glance at Geraldine. Evidently pleased with his admiration, she eyed him playfully, with a slight air of challenge.

"We were thinking of going to the pub actually," she said, raising her eyebrows at him.

"I know. I wondered whether, since Bella's presence is definitely worrying me, I could go with you."

"You've been listening to our conversation," Geraldine cried, breaking into a laugh.

"I couldn't help but hear that part," he said, smiling as he turned from Geraldine to me. "How have you managed to fall afoul of the grande dame of Shalham, then? I saw her giving you one of her famous demolishing stares."

"It's a long story. My daughter caused a bit of – er – havoc at her daughter's wedding." I became very embarrassed as I spoke, realizing yet again how impossible it was to provide an adequate explanation of Hollie's behavior in a couple of sentences. "We tried our hardest to prevent it from happening. She couldn't see that what she'd had to put up with for a few minutes, we have to live with twenty-four hours a day, every day."

"Bella is not a woman known for her tolerance and understanding," he commented briefly.

"You sound as if you're not one of her greatest supporters, either," said Geraldine.

"My name is Martin Wiseman. I'm a reporter for the *Southern Evening News*. I interviewed her a year back about some of the plans she had for the district council. She didn't like the piece I wrote, basically because I didn't sing her praises enough. She called my editor to complain." He took a couple of sips of wine, then gave a cheerful laugh. "The editor gave her short shrift." He recounted the story with an air of amusement, but with no trace of anger or resentment, as if Bella's arrogance was just an interesting foible.

"Does she not still resent you for it?"

"It's long enough ago, and she's fallen out with so many people over the years that I'm sure she can't remember who was responsible for each particular dispute. I tell you what . . . " he smiled easily at each of us again, "why don't I buy you two ladies a drink in the Castle Arms across the road, and I'll tell you some more interesting stories of Bella's mismanagement of people."

But once we had crossed the road and found a booth, we found ourselves discussing topics of far more interest than Bella's arrogance.

Martin bought a round, then Geraldine, then me. By the time Martin bought his second round, we had gone beyond common politeness and chit-chat and were giving each other our real opinions.

"Why do you let someone like Bella get to you?" Martin asked me. "You're not a child. You're a mature, attractive, intelligent woman. You should be able to say to yourself, okay she doesn't like me, but it's what I think of myself that matters, and I don't need the good opinion of someone as arrogant and prejudiced as she is."

"Yes, that's true," I said. "Why have I never seen it as clearly as that before? I've spent half my life worrying about the opinions of people who couldn't matter less to me."

"You've just wasted time and energy," he said. "You can't make everyone like you, and, God, wouldn't it be boring if everyone did like everyone?"

"You should be able to think 'screw them,'" said Geraldine. "That's what I do."

"That works for you, Gerry, I know, but I need another way to deal with it."

"This is all something you've been learning for yourself, Lucy, in recent months," Geraldine said thoughtfully.

"How come you understand people so well? Do you understand everyone as well as this?" I asked Martin.

"Some sort of understanding of people is a necessary requisite for the job," Martin replied. "I've worked in journalism or public relations all my life. I know there are many public relations people and journalists who muddle through, with no real understanding or empathy for other people. But I don't think you can do the job properly if you don't have some sort of empathy. I can see, for instance, that Geraldine has perhaps a bit too much of a 'screw them' attitude. What's brought that about, Geraldine?"

Geraldine looked rather nettled at the sudden shift of focus on her.

"I have that attitude because I get fed up with people criticizing me for my actions and behavior when they lead nice, safe, normal lives and don't have the first idea of what I've had to live with."

Martin sat back against the wall, his posture suggesting that here was a man at peace with himself. He took a swig from his beer, "So what have you had to live with?"

Geraldine flashed a glance at me.

"Gerry's had to live all her life in the knowledge that she had a chance of dying before the age of forty. Huntington's disease runs in her family, and all four of her relatives – her father, her uncle and two cousins – who contracted the disease died unpleasant deaths at an early age. The chances were fifty-fifty whether she would inherit her father's genes and die of the disease, or her mother's genes and be safe."

"I decided the only way to live with this knowledge was not to worry about the future and make the most of the time I had," Geraldine added. "So I've always had a living-for-today philosophy. I've lived well and never saved a penny. I've dared to do things other people perhaps would not have dared to do because there's always the thought that I might be dead in a year, so what the heck?"

"And other people don't like this?" Martin asked, gazing at her intently.

"I say what I think, often. They don't like that, women especially. And people don't seem to like the fact that I've never stayed with a man for longer than a few months. They don't think I should be behaving like a nineteen-year-old when I'm forty." She gave a bark of laughter. "Actually, I think they're jealous. The people who criticize me are the ones who seem most trapped in stale marriages." She turned to Martin.

"And are you going to judge me for the way I live?"

"Not if you're considerate and don't ride roughshod over the feelings of the men you go out with. There's no excuse for selfishness."

"Actually, I think there is some excuse for selfishness, if Gerry is ever selfish," I chipped in. I spoke heatedly, fiercely even, and they both turned to stare at me.

"Gerry's always thought she had to pack eighty years of living into thirty, or at best forty, years of life. I think that being in an impossible situation justifies breaking rules."

"And what rules have you felt justified in breaking, Lucy, from your impossible position caring for a severely handicapped child?"

Martin turned his calm, all-seeing gaze on me.

"None," I snapped. "I'm very happily married."

"Why should you assume I might think otherwise?"

I looked away stonily and swigged down the rest of my wine.

"Lucy's too busy cleaning up shit to have time for any naughtiness," Geraldine laughed, but she gave me a quizzical look all the same.

"How come you're so good at cutting through all the clap-trap and getting straight to the heart of issues?" she asked Martin.

"He's not cut straight to the heart of any issues with me," I said, grumpily.

A moment's awkward silence followed.

"I think perhaps I have," Martin said quietly.

"Er – I'll get another round," Geraldine cried, leaping to her feet.

"Not for me," I said. "I'd better get back to help Simon."

"Really?" Geraldine looked searchingly at me.

"Definitely." I'd had enough probing questions and revelatory insights for one night. Besides, it was perfectly obvious that Martin and Geraldine were all eyes for each other and wanted to be on their own.

"Shall we help get a taxi?" asked Martin, concerned for my welfare.

"No, I'll be all right," I said, smiling at the ease with which he talked of "we."

I swayed slightly as I stood up. Dazed and deafened by the cacophony of a hundred conversations, jostled by the arms, elbows and backs of the crowds of Saturday night drinkers, I struggled to put on my coat.

"Are you all right to leave on your own?" Geraldine said, standing and resting her hand on my arm.

"I'm fine," I said, gruffly, and gave her a quick peck on the cheek.

"It's been – er – fascinating meeting you," I said, turning and giving Martin a quick smile.

As I walked, rather uncertainly, back through the pub, it was obvious that the Thompson Associates party must have finished, for many of the people whom I had seen at the party were now assembled at the bar. I was just about to push the door to the street open, when it was pushed in the other direction and Paula came in. She instantly adopted that slightly sneering, smirking expression that she had been putting on recently whenever she saw me.

"Oh, hello," she said, looking very superior.

"Hello, Paula."

"It's a shame Joel couldn't make it to the party," she said, eyeing me beadily to gauge my reaction. I willed my expression to remain neutral.

"Yes, it is," I said, trying to manufacture an air of polite interest, while simultaneously conveying the impression that it didn't really matter to me whether he came or not.

"He's so snowed under with work at the moment," she said airily. She was parading her intimacy with him. I had to accept that they probably were going out together. On the other hand, the very fact she was trying so hard to rub my nose in it and make me jealous showed that she was far from certain of him.

I feigned another look of polite interest.

"He's having to get a lot of work done today, since he has to fly to Boston on business early tomorrow morning."

She'd got me this time. The panic showed clearly on my face. Joel going away? I couldn't stand it. For how long? Please, please let it not be for too long.

"It's a shame he can no longer help arranging that loan for you."

"What?"

"He told me he was writing to you. He's got so much work on, something had to give."

"He can't do that that," I cried out. "He can't let us down now. The lawyer, the educational psychologist, they're all booked. He knows this is life or death to us."

I could see the enormous pleasure it gave Paula to have broken through my veneer of politeness.

"I'm sure he's very sorry about it," she said glibly. "No doubt he'll explain it all in the letter."

"How can he? How can he explain a betrayal like this in a letter?"

Paula gave another superior smile. I said nothing more but turned and raced away from her, thrusting open the door.

"He won't be there," she called nastily. "He was planning to stay in a hotel near the airport tonight."

I raced out into the freezing night air, down to the taxi stand. Jumping into the first car, I asked the driver to go straight to Joel's house. When I got there, I leaned against his doorbell for about twenty seconds. How could he? How could he do this to us? There were no lights on, and no car in the drive. Why had I come? If he really was staying in the airport hotel, as Paula had said . . .

But just then he opened the door. I signaled to the taxi driver to go.

"How could you?" I snarled.

"How could I what?" He looked utterly confused.

"How could you just drop the arrangements for our loan when you knew how important it was to us?"

"I don't know what you're talking about. The loan is all arranged. The money's in your account."

In that moment I saw the truth. Paula had lied simply to torment me.

"Come in," said Joel, still looking confused. "Sit down and tell me what this is all about."

As I entered the hall, which was again lit by the ancient lantern, he took my hand in both of his.

"How could you possibly think I would let you down?"

I could feel tears smarting under my eyelids. "I'm sorry, I'm sorry. I saw – er – someone in the pub after the party, and she said . . . I shouldn't have listened."

He led me by the hand across the hall and into the living room. There were newspapers spread out on the long sofa, and two small suitcases stood ready by the side of the armchair.

"Are you . . . are you going away?"

"In the morning. Just for a couple of days."

He gave me a searching look.

"Sit down."

The room was mostly in shadow, lit only by a small lamp by which Joel had been reading the newspapers, and a log fire, dying down now, which made slight hissing and spitting noises. On the round coffee table was a bottle of red wine and a solitary glass.

"I'll fetch another glass," he said, throwing a couple more logs on to the fire. He moved off into the shadows behind the sofa and soon returned with a second glass. I noticed for the first time that his feet were bare. He poured wine into my glass. As he handed it to me, I noticed the five o'clock shadow area around his chin.

"Thanks." I took one sip, then several more. He sat down on the thick rug in front of me and drank from his own glass. Sweat on his forehead gleamed in the firelight.

"Do you think I don't know how important this is?"

I put my glass down. "I know; I know you do." Tears were running down my cheeks now. I wiped them away roughly with my knuckles. Then he stood up. He looked at me very intently for a few moments, and I met his gaze without discomfort, without feeling I had to look away. He pulled me gently toward him, and I sat down beside him on the hearth rug.

"Do you remember your other three visits here?" he whispered. "We lit the bonfire on one of them."

"How could I forget? The second was your fortieth birthday party."

"I remember you at that party. I remember you standing looking a bit lost in that huge crowd of people you didn't know. I remember you dancing very tentatively with Simon, not realizing how many men were watching you and thinking how beautiful you were."

"What?"

He laughed. "I wish I could have been a fly on the wall at some of the other parties and discos you and Geraldine went to when you were younger. Geraldine's the one they would have been talking to, but you're the one they would have been fantasizing about but afraid to approach."

I smiled vaguely.

"You don't believe me, do you? But I'm sure you can remember some occasions when that happened."

"I remember the third occasion when I came here. Last Saturday night."

"I kissed you."

"You kissed me."

He moved forward until he was right next to me. Then he was taking me in his arms and giving me long, passionate kisses. As the fire curled its tongues of flame around the logs, he lifted off my sweater and my bra and began very gently to stroke and nuzzle my breasts. The room was in darkness apart from the tiny lamp and the light from the fire, which made dancing, weaving, shadows on the walls and ceiling. Naked, I raised myself on to my knees and lifted off his sweatshirt, before undoing his pants.

After we had made love, Joel lay, still naked, against an enormous blue cushion propped against the base of the armchair. I sat between his legs with the back of my head resting on his chest, and he stroked my breasts while we talked.

"I love you," I said. "I fell in love with you when I first met you. I never believed that could happen. I mean, I didn't use those words, even to myself. But I realized right away that you were in a different league than any other man I had ever met."

"I used those words to myself, when I first saw you. You're the only woman I've ever been in love with. I've loved other women, but I've not been in love before. The two are completely different. I never realized."

"I can't leave Simon and the children. It's impossible."

"I know."

We were silent for a long time.

"What about you and Paula – is that a long-term relationship?"

He pulled away from me slightly, looking puzzled. "I'm fond of her. I don't know what will happen to the relationship, though. I don't love her. I suppose it might be possible to love her, if it weren't for you. But I've no plans to get married again or have more children, or anything like that."

He nuzzled my neck. Then we began kissing again, deep, long kisses.

Eventually I noticed the time, which was past one in the morning.

"Oh dear. I'd better call for a cab."

"Don't go."

"I've got to."

He turned away. But my mind was already on what Simon might say about me returning home at two in the morning.

I awoke the following morning, basking in my memories of the night before. I was aware of guilt, but as yet it was something I knew in my head rather than in my heart. It was only when I heard a noise from Hollie's bedroom that the full significance of the day hit me. Sunday, the second of December, the eve of the hearing. It was only half past seven and no one else was awake yet, but I got up immediately, showered and dressed. After all, here was perhaps half an hour when I could read through my notes once more, refine them, hone them, and think desperately of extra possibly winning details.

But though I made myself extra strong coffee, and spread my notes and files neatly across the dining room table, with a fresh notepad in front of me, I couldn't concentrate. I could tinker with a few amendments, maybe rethink the order of my argument. Calling Geraldine to see if I could read the speech in front of her might be of some use. But sitting here any longer in front of my notes was pointless. My gaze careered across the text like a car whose brakes have gone, until eventually I hit a full stop head on without having absorbed the sense of even a word. I gathered up the notes, slammed the files shut and returned them to the cupboard.

The plan for the day – Geraldine's plan, the product of her kindness and thoughtfulness, suggested the evening before – was that she would take the five of us for a long exploration of Pershore Woods after lunch. I hadn't the heart to tell her that no amount of exercise would enable me to sleep that night, and that Hollie, sensing the unusual degree of tension and trepidation around her, would be equally indefatigable. But at least being surrounded by the midwinter starkness of the leafless trees and breathing the freezing air would freshen my mind and my thoughts for an hour or two. It might even enable me, for a few moments, to see the world as everyone else saw it, instead of through the obsessive tunnel vision that showed me only tomorrow. Tomorrow.

We met Geraldine at two o'clock beside a large, ancient chestnut tree near the boarded-up woodland café.

"A good march is what we all need," she said, cheerfully. "I've got the most awful hangover from last night."

"Lucy deserves one . . . ," Simon said, as she moved over to peck him lightly on the cheek. ". . . after her trip to the pub with you. But she doesn't seem to have one."

"I probably do," I said, with a bitter laugh. "I just can't distinguish hangover from all the rest of the clutter in my head."

We walked up a gentle slope, Hollie jumping and leaping from the joy of being outside, until we reached a large treeless crater of dirty, greyish-yellow sand about fifty yards across.

"What do you think created this, Joshua?" Geraldine asked. "A meteorite, way back in the past?"

"Thousands and thousands of years ago," Joshua replied. "Perhaps in the time of the dinosaurs."

"Perhaps."

For a few minutes Hollie ran back and forth nearby, but then she began diving down other paths.

"I'll go after her," I said to Simon, since I was too churned up to walk calmly. When I came back after a slightly longer run down one of the other paths, Geraldine was asking how long the hearing would last.

"Please," I begged, my voice sounding strange and tight, "please, can we talk about anything other than that? I want to try my best not to think about it, just for this afternoon."

"Fair enough," said Geraldine. "It's a momentous week for a lot of people. It's the Welshney Castle opening ceremony on Tuesday."

"It's an odd time of year to hold the castle's public opening," said Simon, "I mean, in December, just before Christmas."

"I believe Bella has ideas about the grotto being a good place for a Santa's grotto."

"You're very quiet, love," said Simon, after a minute or two of silence.

"Yes, you are, Lucy. You look all done in. You must try to have a quiet evening tonight," Geraldine said.

They were both staring at me anxiously. I couldn't bear meeting their eyes, feeling their kindness and generosity thrust at me like this. I had to look away. I felt like the lowest form of life.

"I'll cook dinner tonight, love, and put the kids to bed. You just relax on the sofa."

"It's all that preparation and research," said Geraldine. "All that dashing off to look at schools on top of coping with Hollie. It's too much for you."

I stared at the ground. "You must both excuse me," I choked. "I won't be a minute."

There was a path off to the right a couple of yards ahead. I dashed headlong into it, scarcely looking where I was going; thorns and twigs snagged at my coat and my hair as I ran. The trees grew so thickly together in this deepest part of the wood that the tiny shreds of sky, like stained glass windows in the roof of a cathedral, provided only a gloomy, inadequate light, out of which the long, empty branches reached like dead arms to ensnare me. I ran and ran, until I felt I had expended some of the horror and self-loathing. Then I paused and got my breath back until another wave of self-disgust sent me pelting off again.

Soon I found myself at the end of the path, at a dead end that consisted of a thicket of bushes, in the midst of which a vast old oak tree stretched up to the very roof of the forest. I pushed my way into this thicket, wanting to feel the thorns and the pointed twigs tearing my skin to distract me from the greater pain inside, but all they did was pull at the loose threads of my coat and grab onto the end of my scarf. I wanted to be rid of the overwhelming black tide of guilt that was rising higher and higher in my head.

What had I done? My family was my life, I lived at the center of the four of them, I loved and protected and cherished them, I spent my every waking moment dealing with matters that related to them, and yet I had – I had . . . I had taken something good and innocent, the essence of the lives of five people, and corrupted it. Simon, my husband, whom I loved, who worked intently in his office all hours to earn the money that paid for our home, our food, our clothes – was this how I acknowledged his efforts? And if what happened last night ever came to light, what lessons would I be teaching my children about love and loyalty and the importance of a clear conscience?

I had thought I could at least briefly escape these unbearable thoughts, but, like swooping birds of prey, they had followed me, pecking and snapping at my conscience. I would see Joel and tell him that I couldn't meet him again. For a few brief weeks, happiness had lit up my world, but it wasn't to be mine. I couldn't have that happiness, and still meet the eyes of my children. I could never win. I couldn't be happy and guilty, but I couldn't live with misery and lethargy simply because it gave me a clear conscience.

I had wanted to shut my mind for a few minutes to what I had done, but if anything, I felt more choked with it in this enclosed place, this dead end, this nadir from which there seemed no way to move forwards and upwards. I found myself suddenly banging my head against the tree trunk, slowly at first, then faster and faster until the obsessive agonizing thoughts and images became lost in a fog of pain. I couldn't bear it, and yet the sense of all the unbearable inner turmoil being pushed to the back of my mind was such a relief that I wanted it to go on forever.

Then, gradually, I became aware of voices and of a vigorous rustling noise near me. A second later, coming seemingly from nowhere, an enormous German Shepherd appeared, a yard to the left of me. It eyed me curiously for a second or two, then pushed its way back through the bushes the way it had come. Ahead of me and slightly to the left, I could just make out the heads and shoulders of two middle-aged women in woolly hats walking on an unseen path on the other side of the seemingly impenetrable thicket of twigs and branches. I remained absolutely still, and they passed on without noticing me, calling occasionally to the dog.

Slowly I made my way back to where I had left Simon and Geraldine. At the top of the path, I turned to the right in the direction in which they had been heading, and came out at a point from where a slope led down through ferns, heather and gorse bushes to a railway line a couple of hundred yards away. The two of them were sitting on a bench, gazing thoughtfully at the view. As I approached, they looked up at me anxiously.

"Are you all right?" asked Simon.

Both of them were staring at me, curiosity and anxiety sharpening into bewilderment as they took in my bedraggled appearance. I glanced down. Thorny twigs with dead leaves still attached stuck to my coat like arrowheads, and when I patted my head, I felt twigs and leaves in my scarf and hair.

"Why is your face so red?" asked Geraldine.

"I've been – er – running very fast."

They continued to stare at me as if I was slightly deranged. As the afternoon wore on, and I struggled to follow ordinary conversation, to make appropriate remarks – and above all to repress the overpowering urge to bellow "I CAN'T COPE" so that it could be heard for miles – I began to wonder if maybe they were right.

By six o'clock we were home, and I was making a snack for three tired-seeming children who lay listlessly across the sofa and armchairs in the family room watching a Disney video. As a special treat, I brought their food in and allowed them to watch it in front of the television. Then I went upstairs and sat on the bed with my head in my hands.

"What is it?" asked Simon, when he found me there a few minutes later.

I removed my hands and sat up to face him. "How can we possibly do it? How can we possibly win? Us, you and me, against a whole swath of bureaucracy that can spend any amount of money they like on lawyers, psychologists and all kinds of experts. We haven't a hope."

He sat down beside me and patted my knee.

"Of course, we have hope," he said, making a brave attempt to pump confidence and conviction into his tone.

"I know of many challenging, nonverbal, incontinent children whose parents went through due process hearings.

They all lost. Why should we win?"

Simon took my hand. "You've got to stay strong, Lucy. You've amazed me with your strength and determination. You've been such an inspiration. Please try to hold on to that just a bit longer."

I stared at him in amazement.

"I've been an inspiration to you?"

"Yes, of course."

"Well, why on earth haven't you told me that before?" I snapped. But I wasn't angry. I was frustrated, frustrated at our continual lack of communication. I could have taken a degree in non-communication. I was a past master at it. And Simon and I together were the dream team of non-communication. My supreme abilities in non-communication were exceeded only by my skill at apologizing. I was a world-class apologizer.

"It would have meant a lot to me to know that. It would have helped to keep me going in times when I was at my lowest," I said, fatigue making me sound irritable.

"What are you getting at me for?" Simon countered.

"Sorry. I'm so sorry."

I had several calls during the evening from friends seeking to bolster my confidence by giving a similar message. Geraldine said, "Keep your nerve. I know you can win. Don't let yourself be overwhelmed."

My mother and Veronica phoned to wish us good luck, and Karen Hinton called and said, "I shall be thinking of you tomorrow."

"Thanks. Oddly enough, that's a help."

"I'm sure lots of people will be thinking of you tomorrow."

Even Joel risked phoning from his hotel in Boston. He said a whole lot of things. But at the end he said, "You are far wiser, more intelligent and talented than you believe yourself to be. Hold on to that knowledge."

I bathed Hollie, changed her into her pajamas, put a drink and a small bag of chips on her bed, and then closed the bottom half of her gate.

Then I read Joshua and Lisa a longish bedtime story, encouraging them to look at the pictures and pointing out words they might recognize, enjoying their pleasure and enthusiasm for the story. Afterwards I got out my notes, files, notepad and pens and put them on the hall floor, ready for the morning. Then I walked to the kitchen and pulled out the brandy bottle. I stared at it for a minute or two, then put it away. I needed the clearest head possible for the morning. Perhaps I should have coffee. No, too stimulating. Water, maybe. Then it came to me that I was finding excuses for jobs to do because it was impossible even to imagine trying to relax.

I went to Hollie's wooden gate and peered over. She was sitting on the floor surrounded by stacking cups of different sizes and colors. She was putting the smallest cup inside each of the larger cups and rattling it around. Each time she heard the rattling sound, she giggled. She looked as if she had the energy for several more hours of vigorous play, and it was already ten o'clock. Simon came to stand beside me.

"We didn't tire her out enough this afternoon," I commented. "She doesn't look as if she'll be asleep for hours yet."

"Let's just hope for the best," he said, peering in anxiously.

I walked wearily after him back to the family room and sat down. Simon flicked through the TV channels and found an old American war film that interested him.

"Relax," he said. "You look as if you're at a job interview."

I glanced down and found I was sitting ramrod straight on the edge of the chair.

"Sit back. Put your feet up."

But instead I found myself rising to my feet.

"I'll just go and check."

And that was the pattern for the next half hour. Every five or six minutes I was crossing the hall to glance through the gate to Hollie's room, and when each time I found Hollie innocently playing, I would return to sit tightly on the edge of my chair again. When I stood up for the sixth or seventh time, Simon, exasperated, said, "I'll go this time. For heaven's sake, sit back properly in the chair."

I expected him to reappear half a minute later, declaring everything was fine, but instead he called urgently:

"Lucy, come here."

Alarmed, I half ran along the corridor and found Hollie standing on the other side of the wooden grill that enclosed the top space above the gate, holding something in her hand. Simon was pleading with her, "Hollie, give it to me, give it to me now," thrusting his hands through the bar. But immediately she flicked her hand away from him.

"I'm afraid she'll throw it," Simon said, nervously.

"What is it?"

"Can't you see?"

I looked more closely and saw it was a cricket-ball size lump of feces that she must have reached in and pulled out from inside her diapers. Her favorite method for disposing of objects she no longer wanted in her room was to hurl them as far as possible through the wooden grill, and her right fore-arm was already poised for action.

"Hollie, give it to me," I demanded, as I thrust my arm through, but immediately she shot her arm back an inch or two.

"It's no good trying to take it from her," Simon declared. "We need to be ready in case she throws it."

"I'll stand over here," I said, moving to the left of the door. "Do you think this is the best place?"

"Well, think," he protested. "You've been here when she's done this at other times. Where is she likely to throw it?"

And then the absurdity of the question and of the whole scene hit him, and he began to laugh.

"You want exact bearings, do you? Calf, knee or thigh?" I countered, and we both doubled up, helpless with laughter. I laughed so much that my insides ached. Simon, still red-faced and shaking, made an effort to stand upright before exploding with another fit of laughter and doubling up again. Finally, my insides still aching deliciously, I managed to pull myself upright. Simon was standing immediately in front of the door.

"Hollie, give," he demanded.

And then, in a sudden movement, she slipped her hands through the bar and handed the ball directly to him. Simon glanced at me, raised his eyebrows, and again we fell apart, except that this time we were laughing with relief.

Chapter Eight

My sleep, not surprisingly, was poor. It seemed that every hour or two I came slightly to the surface of consciousness, only to feel, in those first few seconds, that I was in a dark, dark place, hurtling toward an invisible brick wall. I would then lie fully awake for whole intervals of time – sometimes a few minutes, sometimes an hour or more – when the sense of being propelled toward some grim terminal would make my heart race and my skin prickle with panic. Each time this happened, I had to get up and walk around the house for a while to try to empty my mind. After the fourth or fifth time of colliding with wakefulness – at about six o'clock – I finally gave up the attempt at sleep.

I showered, dressed, made toast and coffee and opened the file to read through my notes and my speech for one final time. I had already produced countless drafts of my points, but in an attempt to make the most of the time and to drum the order of argument further into my mind, I wrote it out again more neatly. I inserted titles in large capital letters, summarizing paragraphs, in the hope that, while speaking, I would remember at a glance what came next, and could thereby concentrate my energies on emotional impact.

I also spent about twenty minutes collecting some old cardboard boxes, cereal boxes and the like. Three or four days ago Miss Campbell had sent home a note asking parents to send in such items for a recycling exercise. But with Hollie being especially messy and destructive, and me existing on starvation sleep rations, I had not had the time or the energy to do anything about it.

At seven I woke up the children, dressed them and gave them breakfast. As I stood with Hollie on the frosty pavement waiting for the bus to arrive, I muttered "Wish us luck, Hollie."

Later Simon and I left in plenty of time to take Joshua to school and Lisa to preschool. In Joshua's school Simon stood stony-faced and silent, so anxious that he could not even smile or utter a greeting. I forced myself to concentrate on helping Joshua to hang up his coat and to put his lunchbox and drink on the correct shelf, and on issuing gentle reminders for him to concentrate, pay attention and share nicely with the other children. Then I approached Miss Campbell, who was in conversation with Mrs. Bishop, the teaching assistant.

"Are you still after cardboard boxes? I've got a bagful here."

They both looked at me and gave me that alien-landed-from-outer-space look that I knew so well. Slowly they turned and looked at each other. Then they burst into loud hysterics. I stared at them, painfully aware that the joke was probably all at my expense.

Miss Campbell was still in stitches, but Mrs. Bishop composed herself well enough to say, "Thank you very much, Mrs. Roseman, but the recycling was a few days ago."

Miss Campbell cobbled together a mock-serious expression. "Yes, the other children lent some of their boxes to Joshua so that he wasn't left out of things."

I kept a tight hold on my misery and managed to offer the two women a blank expression.

"I see," I said.

Never had I wanted so badly to find a way of explaining in a nutshell . . . Where was Lord Voldemort when I needed him?

But as I walked out at Simon's side, I realized that the altercation had served one purpose: I had actually forgotten about the hearing for a few brief minutes.

It was a day of sharp outlines; a black and white day. The leafless trees on the road out of Brackley looked stark and dead against the winter sun. As we descended the hill into Shalham, the jutting towers and harsh contours of the apartment buildings, the concrete offices and the modern cathedral looked as jagged as the edge of a saw against the cloudless sky.

The hearing was to take place in the conference room of the White Horse Hotel, a squarish 1930s sandstone building. As

Simon parked, I was shaking with nerves so much that I scarcely had the energy to push the car door open or swing my legs out. The dark green jacket and matching skirt I wore – which I had worn regularly when I worked full-time over ten years ago – felt strange on me, tight on my shoulders and on my stomach. I kept tweaking at it, where I most felt the pinch, wondering if I was to be saddled for the rest of my life with wearing only baggy, easy-to-wash jogging suits.

The receptionist directed us to the end of a corridor, and peering ahead, I saw the familiar plump, bespectacled figure of our attorney, David Greenham, holding a coffee cup and saucer and talking to someone screened from view by his enormous bulk. A second later he turned, saw us, exchanged a further brief word with his companion, and walked forward to greet us. I thought once again what an awe-inspiring figure he made in his sharp, pinstripe suit, partly because of his size, but mostly because his intelligent, thoughtful eyes, his firm mouth and slightly protruding chin contributed to building a commanding presence. His companion, who also approached us, was Beth Johnson, looking businesslike in a grey flannel suit, her hair pulled into a tight ponytail.

We all shook hands in turn.

"All ready?" David asked, smiling.

"I don't feel in the slightest bit ready," I said. "But then I don't think I would feel ready however much time we had."

"We just want to get it over with," said Simon.

"Now, do you remember the format?" David asked. I tried

to concentrate on what he was saying about the layout of the room and the order of the speakers, but most of this vast tide of words swirled past me unintelligibly. "Let's go in," David said. Beth Johnson glanced up at me and gave me an encouraging smile.

"You'll be fine," she said, but I worried she was just speaking empty words to encourage me.

The room was large and square, with windows straight ahead. In the middle, four long tables were arranged so that the ends joined, forming a square. There were already several people in the room, well-dressed, imposing-looking people, standing in two groups, well set apart from each other, talking in urgent undertones. As we entered, they looked over at us, exchanged glances with each other, then moved to pull out chairs along two sides of the square.

On the side of the square of tables nearest to us were four name cards, one for each of the members of our team.

The man at the center of the trio who sat to our left, a grey-haired man with steel-rimmed spectacles, now cleared his throat. His tone was brisk and businesslike.

"Hello, everyone. Let me introduce myself. My name is Paul Young, and I am the chairman of the hearing committee. My colleagues here are Jean Collins" – he looked to his right, to a lady with grey, page-boy-styled hair, who nodded to us without smiling – "and Peter Brookes." In pronouncing the latter name, he looked to his left to an elderly man wearing a tweed jacket, who had a walking stick propped at the side of the desk. He, too, nodded briefly in our direction, without actually looking us in the eyes.

Paul Young continued, "I would like to ask all of you to introduce yourselves, beginning with Hollie's parents, Mr. and Mrs. Roseman."

Simon coughed and said quietly: "I am Simon Roseman, Hollie's father."

Now it was my turn. I looked at the command printed at the top of my pile of notes. It was written not just in bold type, but in italics and heavily underlined. "You know your case is just. Show them this in your manner. Be poised, calm and confident." I sat up straight and pulled my shoulders back.

"I am Lucy Roseman, Hollie's mother," I said, my voice shaking.

Then David said: "I am David Greenham, Mr. and Mrs. Roseman's attorney."

The three people sitting opposite, who had not yet introduced themselves, exchanged knowing looks.

First Beth said: "I am Beth Johnson. I am an independent educational psychologist acting for Mr. and Mrs. Roseman."

The first of the three people opposite was a woman with a plain, short, hairstyle and no makeup, wearing a simple grey dress. She coughed to clear her throat:

"My name is Stella Wright, and I am a speech therapist employed by Windleshire school district."

I had met Stella Wright on a couple of occasions. I tried to catch her eye in order to smile and acknowledge that we knew each other, but I got the feeling that she was deliberately avoiding my gaze.

Next to Stella Wright sat a balding man with a thin, pointed face. His voice was high-pitched when he spoke:

"I'm Daniel Smith, and I'm the Windleshire educational psychologist who works with students at Petheril School."

Not only did Mr. Smith not look us in the eye, his gaze swung in an arc some way above our heads. I had met him before, and I didn't trust him. He had told me to my face that Hollie needed boarding school, and then written in his report to the district – a report he did not expect we would ever see – that an ordinary school dealing with general disabilities was all that was needed.

The third person was a tall, broadly built man of about sixty. I knew who he was, though I had never met him. This was the man whose name was on the top of all the district letter heads.

"I am Roger Stevens, head of special education for Windleshire," he said.

His tone was brisk, and there was something in his manner that suggested a cold, clinical intelligence and detachment.

After these introductions, Paul Young coughed importantly and began to speak again.

"Our aim in meeting here today is to decide what Hollie Roseman's educational needs are, and how they can best be met. We have read the reports that you have sent in, and there are certain aspects of the case that we want to cover. We will ask the opinion of all of you at different times, and you may ask questions, or make points, at any time. But I would like to emphasize here at the start of the proceedings" – he looked around at all of us – "that the panel's decision is final." He paused and looked down at his papers. "Perhaps we can begin by asking Hollie's parents to describe Hollie, and why they feel the Leo Kanner School is the appropriate placement."

Simon looked at me intently and nodded his head encouragingly.

This was it. The moment had finally arrived. I skimmed the paragraph titles printed in different-colored inks, so that I could see them at a glance. Then I summoned all my mental energy. I felt again the desperation, the exhaustion and the enforced neglect of our other two children. Once more I experienced the panicky feelings that I had known so often at midnight when there was no prospect of Hollie going to sleep for hours, and there were vast mountains of wet bed clothes to be washed, and endless corners of stale, mouldering toast and chips to be scrubbed. I felt the determination anew. It was almost visible, almost tangible in front of me, like a newly honed gleaming sword that could slash through all the verbiage and the prevarication.

I stood up slowly.

"Hollie was sixteen months old when she was diagnosed," I began. "After that, she seemed to deteriorate week by week, as the autism took her over. She spent her days hiding behind the closet in our bedroom, playing with three small play bricks, one yellow, one green, one blue, endlessly battering them together, then watching them fall on the floor. If either of us tried to approach her, she cried. She slept about four hours a night.

"It was the bleakest time I have ever known. We looked for something – anything – we could do to help, but everywhere we went, all the so-called experts said that there was nothing that could be done. The words 'lifelong' and 'incurable' kept being thrown at us. When I asked about therapies, I was told categorically there were none.

"Then other parents began to tell us about therapies from America that were helping autistic children to make vast progress. When Hollie was two, we were able to come up with the necessary funds and took her and our new baby to America to be trained in these therapies. The details of these therapies are in our reports.

"With this special teaching, Hollie learned a lot. She learned to make eye contact, she learned to concentrate and pay attention. She became less afraid of people and learned to take our hands to lead us to what she wanted. She even acquired a few simple words, 'more,' 'juice,' 'choc,' and a few others.

"We worked hard to win a place for her at Petheril School, the only school for children with autism in Windleshire, and we were ecstatic when we found we had succeeded. But after two years there, Hollie has lost all the skills we worked so hard to teach her. She no longer uses the few words she had learned, she can no longer concentrate or make eye contact, she is frustrated and shows this in her destructiveness; she is hyperactive and has no outlet for her endless energy.

"The decision that Petheril School made to remove Hollie is the right one, but what she does not need is to go to a school with even less specialization in autism. At schools for children with severe learning difficulties, the environment is deliberately made as bright and eye-catching and exciting as possible to try to stimulate the children. But autistic children are bombarded by mental stimuli all the time anyway, which they cannot interpret or categorize or understand.

What they need is a plain, uncluttered environment with just one activity put before them at a time, so that they can shut out distractions and concentrate. Children with mild autism can be educated very successfully with non-autistic children. However, children with severe autism, like Hollie, by the very nature of their disability, cannot share education with children with other disabilities. I went to visit Browns, the school to which the district has assigned Hollie, and, loving and caring though their staff are, they have received a mere week's training in autism."

My voice was becoming hoarse. David Greenham slid a glass of water along the table. I paused and took a sip, before continuing.

"The district could best meet her needs by adopting a different approach. The approach that seems to work best for Hollie is one with plenty of physical education and outdoor exercise that reduces her hyperactivity, calms her and soothes her anxieties. After she has been swimming or running in the park or playing on the swings, she is less frustrated and destructive and less hyperactive. For some reason . . . " I paused for effect, and glanced around at all the faces ". . . then, and only then, is she able to communicate – to give eye contact and to understand some very simple phrases.

"A school that utilizes such an approach would give her some hope of reaching her full potential, of finding a life where she is happy and satisfied, as well as one that gives us some time for our other children, time to do something other than clear up Hollie's messes. And we have found that school, the Leo Kanner School in Newshire. We are appealing for the chance to send our daughter to the only school we have seen that uses an approach that might get through to her."

"Thank you, Mrs. Roseman. I would now like to ask the district educational psychologist to explain why it was necessary for Hollie to leave Petheril School, and why he thinks Browns School is the best place for her."

Daniel Smith shuffled his notes, then began to speak in clear, businesslike tones.

"Petheril School has decided that Hollie's placement there is no longer meeting her educational needs, as her extremely low level of functioning does not enable her to access the curriculum offered there. Her high degree of mental impairment and her severely challenging behavior mean that one staff member has to be permanently devoted to attending to her and keeping her on task, a level of support that the school cannot provide on a long-term basis.

"Let me now explain why I think that Browns School – the local school for children with severe learning disabilities – is the right place for Hollie. It is a school that has a long experience of caring for children at the – er – lower level of functioning. It has very caring teachers, and several autistic children with severe learning difficulties are already attending. Indeed, one child from the school eventually went on to complete a degree in art.

"Hollie has severe learning difficulties as well as autism, and Browns will be able to address those difficulties as well as her autism, unlike Petheril, which specializes in teaching more high-functioning children with autism. Browns has specialized strategies to deal with children at the – er – lower end of the ability spectrum. It uses sign language, speech therapy is offered, and the children enjoy lots of craft activities and days out."

Stella Wright, the speech therapist, now spoke: "During the two years I've worked with Hollie at Petheril School, she has made little progress; indeed, in many ways she has deteriorated and can no longer use the one or two attempts at words she was employing two years ago. Children at the lower functioning end of the spectrum tend to be well cared for at Browns. Many of the children there also do not speak, and the pace of teaching is set at a slower, simpler level to accommodate them."

At this point, Paul Young turned back to us. "Mrs. Johnson, as Mr. and Mrs. Roseman's educational psychologist, perhaps you would like to give your opinion of Hollie's educational needs, and how these could best be met."

Beth's voice shook as she began to speak. "Everything that Mrs. Roseman has said is absolutely correct. The kind of busy, stimulating atmosphere in a school for children with learning disabilities – where pictures and collages are crammed in every corner of wall space – is utterly wrong for autistic children, who are bombarded by sensory stimuli that they have trouble interpreting and shutting out. Autistic children need teaching environments that are as plain as possible, with only the items required for the task on hand on show. The Leo Kanner School understands this, and the teaching environment is designed with the aim of being as non-distracting as possible.

"Hollie has become as destructive as she is through frustration. When I went to observe her one morning in her class at Petheril, I detected an air of boredom and irritation from the teachers and aides in that particular class – I know this is not typical of autism teachers – which I'm sure Hollie also sensed. If work was presented at a level that she could understand,

and her teachers were able to create a patient, caring atmosphere in which she felt comfortable, I'm sure she would make excellent progress. She has a capacity to learn, shown by her enjoyment of the simple teaching tasks Mrs. Roseman has done with her at home. But she is a child who needs what is referred to as a twenty-four-hour curriculum. Teaching needs to be undertaken at every available opportunity, throughout the day, in order for what she is being taught to make an impression on her. The Leo Kanner School could have been designed specifically with Hollie in mind."

Paul Young now spoke: "Mr. Greenham, are there any questions you would like to ask the district's team?"

David nodded.

"Miss Wright, you said in your submission as speech therapist that Hollie had made no progress at Petheril, and indeed that she had actually deteriorated in many ways. Would you not agree that this shows that Petheril was deficient in its approach to Hollie and to children like her, rather than showing that Hollie does not have the capacity to learn?"

Stella Wright seemed flustered. "It could show that," she began, "Except that other children . . . "

"But we're not talking about other children, Miss Wright. We're saying that Hollie, and possibly others like her – children at the lower end of the ability spectrum – are not reached by Petheril's approach, but that they could make progress with a different approach in a different environment."

"I suppose so, but . . . "

"The fact that Hollie has actually lost some of her skills while at Petheril is a bad indictment of Petheril, surely, rather than a sign that Hollie is too mentally impaired to make progress anywhere. She had certain skills, and she lost them during her time at the school. The fact that she lost those skills is not a reason to send her to a school with virtually no expertise in autism. It is a reason to send her to a school with extra specialized teaching."

"I suppose it is possible that Hollie has some untapped ability, that she is a rare case, a child who does not fit into the Petheril model – " Stella Wright began to say, uncertainly. Roger Stevens coughed loudly. She looked over at his stern expression, and a torrent of words suddenly fell from her lips.

"But Browns is just the school to bring out that ability. It has plenty of children there at the lower end of the spectrum, and plenty of experience in dealing with them."

"So I keep hearing," David Greenham said, calmly. "But no one has yet explained how putting Hollie with a lot of other severely autistic children in a school with almost no expertise in autism is going to help her."

David now turned to Daniel Smith, who was looking distinctly uncomfortable at the turn the argument was taking: "Mrs. Roseman has provided fairly compelling evidence that a school offering a concentration of vigorous physical education as part of its curriculum would be the right place for Hollie, wouldn't you agree?"

"Well, er – no, not necessarily. Browns School has a lot to offer children as well. Obviously it has a PE curriculum, the children go swimming, they offer after-school activities."

David picked up a typed sheet.

"I have here a weekly timetable for the fourth-grade class at

Browns that Hollie would enter. It offers two half-hour PE sessions a week. You mention swimming. The swimming pool has actually just been closed because it is too old, and not worth repairing, and the new pool will not open for three years at least. So how can Browns offer Hollie the high degree of vigorous PE that she needs?"

David now turned to Roger Stevens, who, unlike his two colleagues, was still maintaining an air of calm analysis and detachment: "Would you say that the point about Hollie's lost skills proves that Petheril was deficient?"

"Actually, it doesn't prove that Petheril was deficient," Roger Stevens said crisply. "Plenty of other children who, like Hollie, were at the lower end of the spectrum, have made excellent progress, and indeed have surprised everyone with how much they have learned and how much more effectively they have been able to communicate after some years there. It's more likely that if just one child loses skills, that shows a problem with that child rather than the school."

"Other children may have made progress," countered David, "but that still does not prove that the Petheril approach works for all children. The Petheril teachers want to keep up their record of apparent high achievement, so they ask parents of lower functioning children to remove them."

Roger Stevens looked angry. He now spoke with extra volume and force:

"While it is true that we are here to consider Hollie's educational needs, we have also to consider in this hearing whether the choice of a particular school is a good use of the district's limited funds. A place at Leo Kanner School costs £100,000 a year, whereas Browns cost £15,000. If a disproportionately large amount of money gets spent on a child such as Hollie, that leaves less for all the other children in the county. The choice of Leo Kanner is not an effective use of our very limited funds."

I could see Paul Young nod slightly at this argument. Jean Collins looked around at her colleagues and raised her eyebrows, obviously impressed. Peter Brookes looked up from where he had been writing notes and studied Roger Stevens. I could see, indeed, everyone present could see, that the three of them were swayed by this argument. It was, unfortunately, a factor that the authority had the right to bring into the equation. We could well lose the whole case on this one argument. Indeed, it seemed to me a miracle that any parents could ever win a hearing when the district always had this trump card up its sleeves.

Roger Stevens could see that the panel was moving toward his side of the argument. He pressed home his advantage.

"We have heard a lot about the difficulties in caring for Hollie. If we were to arrange for long-term foster care for Hollie, that would take away the burden of caring for her and allow the Rosemans time to care for their other children. That might be possible to arrange."

Hearing this suggestion, I felt the ground, indeed the whole room, shifting sideways for a moment. I was rocked with disbelief at his obtuseness. Simon's mouth had fallen open. Beth looked so perplexed that she was lost for words. But I could see David coolly thinking, and I thanked God over and over again that we had chosen, or been guided toward, such an articulate expert. Once again it was Joel I had to thank.

When David spoke, there was utter silence in the room.

"Mr. and Mrs. Roseman are no doubt exhausted from the constant demands of coping with Hollie's disability, and they do indeed need time to be a typical family and to care for their other two children. But the answer to this problem is not to remove Hollie from the care of the two people who have shown such overwhelming love for their daughter. Mr. and Mrs. Roseman have devoted hours of their time to teaching this child one-to-one, and hours of their time to come up with funds so that they can pay for other teachers to join this teaching program. They spend hours exercising Hollie, taking her swimming or for long walks because she enjoys it, and because that makes her calmer and happier and so easier to deal with.

"Hollie's parents want what all parents want, which is the best for their child, and that, in this case, is a school that can teach her at a level that she can understand, every minute of the day. They do not want to make another mistake with her schooling that will lead to her losing more of the skills that they have spent years teaching her. At the Leo Kanner School Hollie can learn much that will help her in later life while at an age when her brain is still forming and she can gain most benefit from it."

Stella Wright coughed and began to speak: "But we have to consider all the other children too. There is only a limited pot of money. An expensive placement at a school like the Leo Kanner greatly depletes our resources, and leaves us less money to care for all the other thousands of children with disabilities in the county."

Roger Stevens leaned forward with his hands clasped together on the table in front of him. He looked around at us all. His air of cold analysis and detachment had mellowed a little.

"As my colleague says, we have a set, very limited budget to serve all our special needs children. There are two million pounds worth of cuts to be made this year from the overall education budget, and half a million pounds of those cuts have to be made from the special education budget. We are less able to afford such placements than we have ever been. It would take only a few children being placed in such expensive schools, before our entire budget would be wiped out. And then what would happen to all the other students who also need help?"

I didn't know what to say. I thought of all the other thousands of families who would never receive this help, because they didn't have the energy or knowledge to fight for it, and because the resources for it simply did not exist. I didn't want to win at their expense, but the issue was clear-cut. We won, or we failed to survive. We received this help, or we went under.

Roger Stevens rubbed his forehead hard with his fingers. In place of that air of cool detachment that he had shown so far, his manner now conveyed an openness and earnestness that we had not so far seen from him. "I know we seem like the bad guys here. Of course, we feel enormous sympathy for Mr. and Mrs. Roseman, and for all the other parents in their position. But we are forced to make hard decisions. And, sadly, autistic children at the lower end of the spectrum, like Hollie, are unlikely to make much significant progress whatever the educational input. Only five percent of these children are likely to achieve much significant speech or to raise their IQ by more than a handful of points."

"Even a handful of points can make a huge difference to desperate parents," David began, but Stevens interrupted him. I realized, with a sensation of ice creeping down my spine, that Roger Stevens was actually getting the better of David.

"There can be no justification for spending a vast proportion of our budget on highly impaired children, of whom the best that can be hoped is that five percent may make very minimal progress. It is not an effective use of what are, as I have explained, very limited funds. It is, when all is said and done, a numbers game."

At that moment I saw red. For all his talk about sympathy and hard decisions, and concern for the other children, he still viewed the issue – whether he was forced to or not – as a numbers game. A numbers game. *A numbers game*. It was exactly the same phrase that Joshua's teacher had used to justify holding him back a year.

Paul Young turned to me:

"Mrs. Roseman, have you anything final to add?

"Yes, I have," I said, shaking with rage. For a moment I didn't trust myself to speak. I was afraid of spitting out all the acid words that were right on the tip of my tongue, and thereby lose the argument and the sympathy of the listeners. At all costs, I had to be cool, clear and striking. I rose to my feet.

"I know money is a consideration. I know the other children have to be thought of. But please . . . " For a moment I could not find the words. I saw the exhaustion and wretchedness and frustration of the past. I saw the hopelessness of the future. I sweated it; I breathed it from my nostrils; I felt it in every pore. "We need this school for Hollie. If you had seen her, at two years old, hiding behind the closet, screaming if anyone came near her . . . And then, if you had seen her at four, seen her calmly and happily complete a teaching session simply because we had taken her for a run in the park to calm her, you would not believe it was the same child. If you saw her holding out her hand for more when her brother plays a game on the palm of her hand, when a few months before she didn't even appear to know he existed, you would not believe she was incapable of being educated. If you had seen how readily she sits down to work after swimming or skipping or jumping about in the garden . . .

"Please – Hollie desperately needs this chance to learn. We can no longer offer her anything because we are utterly exhausted from nine years of constant care. My son has been held back a year at school because – we are told – he hasn't learned to concentrate properly. Small wonder he can't concentrate. All his life, whenever we've sat down to play a game or read a book with him, we've had to leap up every thirty seconds to stop Hollie from doing something destructive or dangerous. Our younger daughter is so disturbed that she walks into preschool with her hands over her face because she doesn't want anyone to notice her. We've not had time to inculcate even a basic self-esteem in either of our other two children.

"We are not talking about a numbers game here; we are talking about children we have loved and nurtured every minute of their lives. I'm not prepared to sit here and be given a lesson in statistics when what we are discussing is whether they have any possibility of a future."

I sat down again. I didn't dare to look at anyone, indeed I had to concentrate my energy on controlling my shaking, and preventing myself from bursting into embarrassing sobbing. After a minute Paul Young coughed and said:

"What we have heard today," he began, but his words flowed over me unintelligibly. I gathered that he was giving a summary of the evidence and concluding the proceedings. I came to sufficiently to take in his final remark that the result of the deliberations would be sent through the mail in about ten days.

"Come on, love," I heard Simon's voice saying in an unaccustomedly gentle way, as he rested his hand gently on my arm. I looked up and found that everyone had stood up. The three committee members had already left the room, and the three members of the district team were standing in a small huddled group talking animatedly in low voices. I felt for a moment that I could have given anything to have heard what they were saying, but then almost immediately I realized that it was undoubtedly far better for me not to know. Beth was collecting all her papers into various plastic folders. David gathered his papers and clipped them into a briefcase, before approaching Simon and me.

"You were marvelous, Lucy. You spoke very powerfully all through, but that last speech was clinching."

"Do you think so?" I said, looking at him appealingly. I felt too drained and exhausted to smile. I hardly had the energy even to remain standing.

"Yes, I do," he said firmly. "I was doing my best, but . . . "

"You were marvelous, David. You made many persuasive points, you pointed out the inconsistencies in their evidence."

"Maybe. But your final argument is what they will take away in their minds."

Despite his words, his expression was grim.

"It wasn't enough, though, was it?" I said. "The argument was moving their way. There was that unanswerable point about the cost and use of resources." I stopped and looked into his eyes. "You don't think we'll win, do you?" I could hear my voice becoming unpleasantly strident.

"How can I say? If the argument was beginning to move their way, it was you who stopped it, Lucy." He stared at me, and particularly at my head, which was shaking uncontrollably, with the exhaustion, and with the effort of trying not to burst into huge sobs.

"Let's adjourn to the pub across the road," he said, looking from me to Simon, to Beth. "Let's get a drink and something to eat."

But in the pub we were a low-spirited group. David ate fish and chips and Simon a baked potato, which they washed down with plenty of beer. Beth sipped orange juice while she quickly ate a plate of vegetable lasagna. I drank two glasses of wine in quick succession and picked at a plate of cheese sandwiches. The other three went over all the arguments at length, speculating on how the panel had reacted to them. I contributed nothing to the conversation. I sank into a miserable lethargy. I accepted a third glass of wine when it was offered, and then a fourth. What sort of future did we have now?

Still in my despairing state of suspended animation, I walked with Simon to the car. I was aware that he spoke a couple of times, while he negotiated his way through the Shalham traffic and back to Brackley, but it was as if he were speaking from hundreds of yards away and I wasn't able to take in the words. Eventually, I was aware of his taking my right hand in his left hand and squeezing it.

"I'll drop you home," he said. "You lie down. I'll pick Joshua and Lisa up from school."

At home he came in with me, his arm around my shoulders, and led me into the family room, to the couch. I lay down, as he bid me, then he got a blanket and covered me. A few moments later a cup of tea appeared on the small coffee table beside me. "Thanks," I murmured automatically. Then I heard the front door slam.

I lay still. I felt the familiar sense of foreboding as the colors of the carpet and the walls began to bleach and dim, and the outlines of the chairs, the table, the lamps, the bookcases became blurry and ill defined. The grey mire of depression was taking hold once more. Somehow I had to prepare the children's snack. I had to make Joshua sit down and do his homework. I had to fill the washer. And then I had to meet Hollie from her bus, knowing that I was going to have to do this every day now for years on end. How? How was I to do it? How was I to manage?

Some time later – it seemed a long time later, but it can only have been a few minutes – the telephone rang. It was Eileen Atkinson, Hollie's principal.

"Mrs. Roseman, it's Mrs. Atkinson, from Petheril School."

I sat with the telephone receiver glued to my ear, but no words came from my mouth. Instead, my head bent toward my chest as if it were an intolerable weight. Oh no, I groaned inwardly, what's happened now? Has she behaved so badly that the school is not even prepared to keep her until we find some other placement for her?

"Mrs. Roseman, I'm afraid I have some very worrying news."

Chapter Nine

"Mrs. Roseman, I'm afraid I have to tell you that Hollie escaped from school this afternoon, and so far we have been unable to find her."

"What?"

"The moment we found she was missing, we sent out search parties, which have been combing the woods around the school boundaries."

"How did she get out?"

"Through a foxhole. We check the grounds regularly for breaks in the fence, but a foxhole . . . Only a child as slim as Hollie could have managed it. It was most unlikely to happen."

"But it has happened."

"We can't be expected to patch up every hole an animal makes, Mrs. Roseman . . . " The principal's voice droned on.

I heard the key turn in the front door lock. The door opened, and I heard Joshua and Lisa run across the hall to the kitchen. "Simon!" I yelled, "Simon, come here!" I turned my voice to the telephone again. "So what happens now?"

"We've called the police." Mrs. Atkinson went on matter-of-factly. "I'm sure there's no reason to worry and that she'll be found very soon. But obviously it's best to be on the safe side."

"Of course. Who's in charge of the search?"

"Detective Wells of Shalham police department. He has told me that there are two officers on the way to talk to you."

I put the phone down. "My God," I said to the open air in front of me. Simon appeared in the doorway.

"What's the matter?"

"It's Hollie. She's escaped from school. They don't know where she is."

"What do you mean, escaped?"

I watched the color drain from his face.

"She escaped through a foxhole under the fence during the afternoon play time."

"Well, why on earth weren't they watching her?"

"Well, I think they were. They always have several teachers on duty. But you know how quick and nimble she is."

"This is ridiculous," he exploded. "What are we supposed to do?"

"I don't think we can do anything, love," I said, touching his arm. He jumped away.

"There are two police officers on the way," I added helplessly.

At that moment, the doorbell rang. Simon looked at me, his eyes full of panic.

"I don't think I can cope with this, Lucy," he said.

"They'll find her. She'll no doubt be found in the next hour or so. She's very distinctive, a pretty girl with blonde hair and a bright green coat. They'll find her soon."

"But what if someone else finds her first?"

It was a thought I had been refusing to acknowledge.

"We mustn't panic," I said, forcing my voice to sound calm. "Let's hear what they've got to say."

I flung open the front door. There were two police officers standing there, a man and a woman.

"Good afternoon. I'm Officer Ridley," the man said. "And this is Officer Allen."

"It's Mrs. Roseman, isn't it?" Officer Allen said, smiling. She was young and efficient-seeming, but there was something about her that inspired great confidence. She seemed not only sharper but more likeable and sympathetic than her male counterpart.

"Yes, please come in," I said, surprised at how calm and matter-of-fact I sounded. I felt neither calm nor matter-of-fact inside; inside I was a slimy, miry mess. But I realized that the busier I was, the more potentially helpful people I could talk to, the more I could keep up this machine-like mode of operating, and thereby keep my panic at bay.

"Do sit down," I said, as I led them into the family room. Simon was standing in the center of the room. He stared at both the police officers, then at me. He opened his mouth, but nothing came out.

"Sit down, Simon," I snapped. He sat down in the nearest armchair. The police officers sat down on the couch.

"You have been told about your daughter's escape from school," Officer Ridley said. "We can assure you that the woods around Petheril School are being thoroughly searched, but no trace has been found of your daughter so far."

"Aren't there any footprints?" asked Simon.

"The hard frost hasn't helped. There are no obvious footprints, and the woods around the school are a popular territory for dog walkers, so even if we found footprints, they wouldn't necessarily tell us anything."

"Those woods join on to Pershore Forest, don't they?" I said. I had a momentary sense of teetering on the edge of a precipice. Pershore Forest was a dense, wild area of ancient woodland. Hollie could be lost there for . . . for . . .

"She won't have had the chance to get into the heart of the forest," Officer Allen said quickly. "We have about a hundred officers searching the woods that link Petheril School to the forest. She won't get that far without one of our people finding her."

She looked at me and smiled. "Please try not to worry. I'm sure she'll be found very soon. Can you give us a couple of photos of her?"

"Of course."

I rummaged quickly in the box of photos under the bookshelf and found some of Hollie. Officer Allen looked at them and smiled again. She had a warm, enveloping smile and exuded such an air of calm capability that I found it hard to believe anything terrible could have happened.

"What a beautiful little girl," she said.

"Oh, she is."

As they left, Officer Allen promised she would call every two hours whether there was any news or not. As I shut the door behind them, the outlines of the furniture and house blurred into a blinding whiteness. I felt I was losing my grip on everything around me.

Over the next few hours my spirits leaped and plunged. There were short periods of wild hope, even certainty, that the next phone call would bring news of Hollie being found, followed by much longer periods of torment, of cold shivers, panic, when I knew that no one, absolutely no one, knew where she was. Every minute came to seem unbearable, and was succeeded by another unbearable minute. The idea that the minutes might stretch out into hours was too excruciatingly painful to contemplate.

I had to maintain the cold, machine-like effectiveness I had adopted when the police arrived in order to keep going with everyday jobs. Joshua and Lisa watched a TV program, then put their coats on and ran around in the yard for a while.

When they came back in, I had to feed them. I then had to take this automatic level of functioning to a further extreme at which I operated almost like a military commander, subjugating my feelings, while I conducted a vital strategy. This frame of mind, which required all my powers of concentration, I was able to maintain for what seemed hours, though it was probably only a few minutes, while I informed the children, and then both Simon's and my parents, that Hollie was missing.

I played the gravity of the situation down to the children, just telling them that Hollie had escaped from school, that all her teachers and some nice police officers were looking for her, and that she would be a bit late. They accepted this at face value, though they were surprised, asking some extremely concrete questions, such as when would Hollie have a snack, and then got on with the normal business of the evening.

I had to brace myself far more to call our parents. Veronica started shrieking "Geoffrey! Geoffrey!" as soon as I told her, and my mother kept repeating over and over, "Oh my goodness, oh my goodness, what are you going to do?" Both worked themselves into a panicky state, as I knew they would, but I exerted all my willpower, refusing to allow their breakdown to light the fuse of my own infinitely greater panic. At all costs, I had to shut my mind to thoughts of Hollie cold, hungry and alone in the darkness.

Julie Allen was as good as her word, ringing every two hours. In her final call, at ten o' clock, she told me another officer, Officer Evans, would call at eight in the morning.

"Do you have any sleeping pills?" she asked.

"I do."

"Make sure you take one. Or else have a large brandy in some warm milk. Please try not to worry too much. You know she escapes easily. There's absolutely no reason to believe anyone has taken her. She'll be found by morning, just you wait."

"Yes," I said emptily. Then I put the phone down. I hadn't had a drink at all that evening, partly because I had felt I had to keep my wits about me, but mainly because my anxiety levels, when they had slipped out of the clutches of my machine-like self-control, had soared inaccessibly into the outer atmosphere, where no amount of sleeping pills or alcohol could touch them. Nevertheless, I climbed up to the top shelf of the cupboard, dug out the sleeping pills and swallowed one with a glass of water.

But as I had predicted, even with the sleeping tablet, sleep was still hard to come by. I wandered around the house, drinking milky drinks in the hope that they might help me sleep, though I knew very well there was little chance of it. I stood staring at the phone for minutes at a time, then wandered to the window, lifted the curtain and stood staring into the darkness of the front yard, hoping against hope that at any moment police car headlights would turn into the driveway and Hollie would emerge.

In the meantime, Simon drove to the police station several times, which served no purpose at all except to make him feel he was doing something. At about one, he retired to bed and lay reading a thriller for an hour or so. Then he turned the light off, but I heard him tossing and turning whenever I came upstairs to shuffle around on the upstairs landing.

At about five I gave up on the milky drinks, and began making strong coffee. Not that I needed it. I was so hyper, so tensed up, that I didn't need extra stimulants. At eight o'clock

Officer Pat Evans called, as Julie Allen had said she would. She sounded bright and cheerful, but I could tell immediately from the slightly forced edge to her voice that she did not have good news.

"You haven't heard anything, have you?"

"Not yet, Lucy. But it's the start of the day. We have eight hours of daylight ahead of us, whereas last night it was almost dark before we even started looking. We have a team of a hundred officers already scouring the woods. I'm certain we'll find Hollie very soon."

"Of course."

"I'll call every two hours, and Julie Allen will take over later in the afternoon. But I'm sure we won't get to that point. There will be announcements on the local news this morning. We'll find her very soon."

I hung up the phone, aware of that gaping precipice opening up around me once more. I got the children up, prepared their breakfast and got them ready for school, all on automatic pilot. Simon took them to school, then went off to join the teams of police taking part in the search.

"They've got at least a hundred officers searching the woods," Geraldine said. "Lots of ordinary people have joined in the search too. Joel Warnock called me about it first thing this morning. He heard about it on the news. He's going to help. She'll be found any time now, you'll see." She was looking pale again. She had stopped by briefly to see how I was, before she went off to the opening ceremony for Welshney Castle.

I managed a couple of spoonfuls of cereal before I pushed my plate away. "Of course," I said blearily.

I dropped a plate as I cleared up the breakfast things, and I began to scream and flail my arms as I looked at the cold cereal sludge flecked over the floor.

"I'll clear this up, then I'll have to get off to the opening," Geraldine said quickly.

"Of course, it's Bella Haughton's big day," I said. My former meetings with Bella seemed as if they had occurred in another lifetime.

Geraldine looked at my face. "Look, why don't you go out?"

I had the unpleasant feeling that she was humoring me, talking to me as I sometimes talked to the children when they were upset. I had to get away.

"Yes, I'll go and join the search teams."

"Why don't we go for a short walk first, to help calm you?"

"I might have a very short walk first. But just by myself, if you don't mind."

"Of course, I don't mind," said Geraldine.

"I'll take the mobile phone, and a flashlight, just in – just in case."

"I think a walk is a brilliant idea," she said, again with that slightly humoring air.

I smiled weakly. "Thank you."

Geraldine came into the hall and found my coat and scarf for me, much as I had done for Lisa an hour before.

I drove to the outskirts of Pershore Forest, parked in the empty parking lot, and walked uphill through an arc of bare, intertwined birch and ash tree branches. About halfway up the hill, the path stopped zigzagging through the trees and emerged into the daylight, under a murky, overcast sky. I sat down on a bench, got the mobile phone out of my pocket, and checked it to be sure it was still on. Then I looked around. It was colder today, and though there was, thankfully, no frost, the ground remained hard from the frost of a few days ago. It was the very dead of winter. No clouds moved, and the air was absolutely still. Even though there must have been creatures moving about in the lower part of the forest spread out in front of me, I could hear nothing but the chirping of a few birds in a distant thicket. It was as if there was no one alive on the planet but me. I felt momentarily oddly detached from the grief and terror, almost as if it was all happening to someone else, a friend I cared deeply about, and whose suffering meant a great deal to me, but from which I could still slightly detach myself. It was as if it had been simply too much to bear, and I had to stand outside it all for a while.

Looking around in this oddly detached mood, I took in a large and very old oak tree on the other side of the path. Decades of wind and rain had eaten away at the soil surrounding it, and now the magnificent interlaced pattern of roots was largely exposed to the sky. Something of the child in me wanted to jump across from one large root to another. Part of the trunk of the tree had eroded away at its base, making a gaping hole, which, when I got up to investigate more closely, I saw made almost a small cave. How the children would love it, I thought. Then two thoughts seized me at almost exactly the same moment. The first was that Hollie may have taken shelter for the night in exactly such a small cave, perhaps not far even from where I sat. The second thought was of the wild boy who lived all those years in the forest. Where exactly had his camp been? Could Hollie – I could scarcely breathe, I was so excited by the idea – could Hollie conceivably have found his camp and taken shelter there?

I was on my feet in a second. At last there was some positive action I could take. I could find John Chard and ask him. He would know where the boy's camp was, if anyone knew. I scurried along the path and down the slope again, slipping on a patch of stony ground. Then I drove to the house in Pershore and knocked on the door. The cleaning lady answered it, wearing a bright red apron and clashing pink rubber gloves, her face a mask of boredom. My heart sank when she shook her head and said, "He's not in."

"Do you know when he'll be back?"

"I'm sorry, no."

I must have looked as despairing as I felt, because her rather matter-of-fact expression softened, and she said, "He said he was going to the Welshney Castle opening, so you might find him there."

"I can't thank you enough," I cried, turning on my heel and running for the car, jabbing at the numbers on my mobile phone as I did so. Pat Evans answered.

"No, Lucy, there's no news yet, but we're all very hopeful there'll be a breakthrough soon."

"Why . . . " I began, and then stopped. There was no point in asking why she thought there'd be a breakthrough soon, as it was perfectly obvious she didn't really expect one and was just saying it to boost my spirits.

"I'm going to the Welshney Castle opening ceremony," I said. "It's just occurred to me that someone I know who'll be there, John Chard, is an expert in local history . . . Oh, it's hard to explain quickly, but he knows the details of the story of a Victorian boy who lived for years wild in the woods near where Hollie disappeared. I'm wondering where the boy's camp was, and if Hollie might have found it and be hiding out there."

I could hear the cynicism in Pat Evans' voice as she replied carefully,

"It's worth looking into."

I realized she probably thought that fear had propelled my mind into temporary insanity. But she had obviously resolved to humor me, since some mental and physical activity would help to take my mind off the unbearable absence of news.

"Yes, why don't you go? You've got your mobile on all the time still?"

"Of course."

"I'll call you the moment I hear anything."

"I know."

I dropped the phone on the passenger seat as I jumped into the car. I drove the three miles from Winnersh to Welshney Castle, which was on the outskirts of Pershore Forest. I parked in the parking lot, slipped the phone into my pocket, jumped out and locked the door. The parking lot was the size of about three tennis courts, but nearly every space was occupied.

I could hear the buzz arising from hundreds of people talking as I ran up to the party tent erected for the occasion. To the right of the entrance stood the brand new kiosk, with wide doors that would normally be open to admit the public, and a small glassed-in booth where the ticket seller would sit. Behind the kiosk I could just about make out a gift shop, all mahogany and large picture windows.

It was about eleven-thirty and the function had begun at eleven, so there were still a lot of guests arriving, all very sophisticated people dressed up in suits and jackets, the ladies with polished high-heeled shoes and handbags matching their outfits.

I went straight up to the security guard, a man of about fifty, with slicked-back hair parted at the side.

"Good morning, madam," he said politely, though I sensed his disapproval as he took in my far-too-casual clothes. "May I see your invitation, please."

"Look, please, this is a matter of great urgency," I babbled. "My mentally handicapped daughter has been lost ever since yesterday afternoon. You may have heard about her – Hollie Roseman – I know it's been mentioned on television and radio. The police are out searching for her now. I wanted to speak to John Chard, who I believe is a guest here. To cut a long story short, he is an expert in local history who knows about ancient hiding places in the wood. It's just possible Hollie could have taken shelter in one of them."

"I'll get Miss Rochelle," he said immediately. "She'll know where this John Chard is. Come in."

He pressed some buttons, then spoke into his mobile phone, turning as he did to take the tickets of a middle-aged couple approaching the entrance to my left. Desperation overcame me. "Oh please, hurry!" I cried out.

"Don't worry, madam, she's coming now," he said, kindly. Then, over the man's left shoulder, like an answer to a prayer, I saw Paula emerge from between two groups of people who stood talking and laughing She looked poised, in a bottle-green dress and jacket, her hair clipped back in a matching comb. I waved frantically. A look of surprise flashed in her eyes before being quickly replaced by her familiar smooth, businesslike air. She hurried over.

"Lucy, tell me what I can to do to help. You need to find John Chard, is that right?"

"Yes, it's incredibly urgent."

"Come in. I last saw him over near the back."

It took me about twenty seconds to spot John Chard, looking very dignified in a suit, his thick iron-grey hair combed back so that it almost reached his collar. He was standing near the back talking to an elderly couple. I touched Paula's arm and said: "Thanks Paula, I've found him."

"That's good. I'll be over there near the stage getting everything prepared for the speeches if there's anything else I can help with." She pointed to a raised area that formed the stage.

I pushed my way through the crowd, muttering "Excuse me's," ignoring all the annoyed and indignant looks. Finally, I touched John Chard's arm.

"Please, John, I'm so sorry to interrupt." He looked at me in amazement. The elderly couple stared at me, open-mouthed.

"Lucy, what on earth are you doing here?" John Chard asked. "I heard about your daughter. Is she found yet?"

"No. But I have an idea about where she might be, and I was hoping you could help me."

He looked perplexed. "Anything. Anything at all."

I took a deep breath, and then the words gushed out. "It suddenly occurred to me – this probably sounds mad – that she could have found the wild boy's hiding place. I mean, I don't know where he lived, but I thought you might. Some sort of cave or broken-down ruin, I mean –" I stared at him, desperately willing him to agree with me. "I mean, it's not impossible."

"No, it's not impossible at all," he said thoughtfully. He then turned to the elderly couple. "Will you excuse me? This lady's daughter has been lost since yesterday afternoon. Obviously, I want to help her."

"Yes, yes, of course, you go," muttered the lady, still staring at me, wide-eyed.

"I'll take you straight there, Lucy," John said, putting his hand on my arm and leading me back through the crowd.

"Is it nearby, then?"

"Yes. Just half a mile or so through the forest. We could walk it easily in twenty minutes."

As we approached the opening, a woman's voice hissed urgently:

"For God's sake, Lucy, what are you doing here?"

I turned and found Geraldine staring at me in disbelief. She looked immaculate as ever in a navy-blue pant suit and crisp white blouse. But her face, in spite of heavy makeup, still looked unnaturally pale. She obviously thought anxiety had made me deluded, for she took my arm and said:

"Come. I'll take you home."

"No!" I blurted out. "I haven't gone insane, Gerry. Mr. Chard is taking me to a place where I think Hollie might be hiding. He's a local historian; he knows all about ancient hiding places in the woods, hiding places used centuries ago." John nodded to Geraldine, who eyed him curiously. "It suddenly occurred to me Hollie might have found one of them and be sheltering there."

Geraldine's face cleared of confusion. Her expression was sharp and alert.

"Good idea. I'll come with you."

"Are you up to it?" I said, looking at her closely. "I'm not sure if you're well enough to be here at all."

"I probably shouldn't have come. But I'm here now, and nothing's going to stop me from helping to find Hollie."

The three of us made our way through the side exit. To our left was a red-brick tower with small windows; a brand-new sign had been nailed on to it in honor of the official opening reading "Summer house." Underneath was printed a paragraph of local history. We half walked, half ran down a gravel path strewn here and there with clusters of damp, mildewed leaves. Above us the dead-looking branches of the beech trees that lined each side of the path twisted and appeared to interlock, forming a vast cathedral-like canopy. At the end of the beech avenue, there was a garden to the left, the flower beds empty, the bushes and shrubs neatly pruned and clipped, while to the right, beautiful wide flat lawns stretched down to the lake. Ahead of us was the seventeenth-century mansion, the original main section fronted by large grey pillars, with large wings added to the east and west. We hurried along the side of the house, then across the lawn toward a wilder, more overgrown area. Here a path led away between tall bushes and waist-high grass and nettles to meet a turnstile, another brand-new feature added in honor of the official opening. We climbed over the turnstile and found ourselves in the forest.

We hurried along a path, thick woodland on either side of us, a few trunks of fallen oaks and beech trees lining the path. After about ten minutes of fast walking, we came to a kind of clearing. Trees grew very close together up to the edge, and even in the clearing there was a large amount of undergrowth. On a hot summer's day it would no doubt be a shaded and peaceful woodland dell, but under this grey, leaden sky the overhanging branches made it gloomy and oppressive.

On the far side of the clearing the undergrowth was at its wildest and thickest. John Chard strode across and began lifting the lowest of the overhanging branches.

"There is a kind of underground cave under here," he said. Geraldine and I began feverishly moving branches aside. The three of us realized at the same moment that many loose, dead branches had been laid across the overhanging branches.

"Odd," said Geraldine, as she lifted up an armful and flung them aside.

"Yes, someone has definitely been here recently," John Chard said, pointing to some leaves that appeared to have been brushed into piles.

"Could it have been Hollie?" I asked, shakily.

"I don't know," John Chard said shortly, still laboring to lift aside branches.

Of course, I realized that a child, an autistic child, would never have undertaken such a deliberate plan to move so many dead branches to screen a hiding place. But she could have squeezed underneath a screen of branches constructed by others, kids building a den in the forest, perhaps.

John thrust aside another armful of branches. A moment later, with grey daylight falling into the newly cleared area, the three of us were looking at the clearest possible evidence that whoever had been this way, wasn't Hollie.

"Someone's had a fire here," said Geraldine

In front of us lay blackened bits of newspaper and the charred remains of dead sticks and branches.

"The cave where Adam Smithson lived was under this tree," said John, looking at the trunk and exposed roots of a giant oak tree about eight feet behind the remains of the fireplace. He started to lift up a very large branch from some sort of evergreen tree that lay horizontally over some of the roots. As he pushed it to one side, it was obvious that there was indeed a cave underneath the roots. The entrance was small – the wild boy would have had to climb through a hole about two feet long and ten inches wide.

"I wish I'd brought my flashlight," said John Chard. "I left it in the car."

"I've got one, I've got one here," I cried.

"Great."

I pulled the flashlight from my pocket, turned it on and handed it to Chard, who pointed it into the darkness of the cave. Almost immediately, it shone on something that moved and turned. Geraldine and I let out a scream. Chard, who was in a crouching position, fell backwards. For what the torch had revealed was a face, a wizened old face framed by wild matted hair, a face that stared back at us in terror.

Some ten minutes or so later we were hurrying back to the party. I hadn't been able to tell at first whether the face was that of a man or a woman, but the strange moaning sound as the figure backed away into the darkness had definitely been masculine. Chard had gestured to Geraldine and me to move backwards in an attempt to make the person in the cave less fearful of coming out, so that the two men could hold a conversation. And a momentous conversation it had turned out to be. The most crucial revelation – for Geraldine and me at least – was that he had seen Hollie. She had come up to him the previous night, and he had offered her food, some bread and cookies, which she had grabbed and run off with. He hadn't seen her again. I was in a daze of excitement at this news, feeling certain that she must be found very soon.

The old man returned with us of his own accord, and he seemed to know the way better than we did. He said almost nothing, just a few "yeses" and "nos" and grunts. I realized almost immediately that I had seen him before, on the day of Philippa Haughton's wedding, once at the churchyard, when he was being escorted out as I arrived, and once during the reception in the garden of the Windleshire Hotel. As we entered the tent, I noticed that the old man remained outside, where he lit a cigarette and took a few puffs, as if to give himself confidence.

Inside the tent, a small group of people had left the main party throng and were approaching the stage. In the middle of this group was Bella Haughton, carrying herself with her usual air of steely-eyed superiority. In her wake came Paula, two men and the woman I recognized to be Bella's secretary, who all seemed to be listening to Bella's instructions. The group came to a standstill by the stage, whispering earnestly to each other before climbing the steps. Paula, the secretary and one of the men, an elderly man in a grey suit, who had a decided air of importance, sat down on some chairs to the left of the stage. The other man, in his mid to late forties, was evidently the master of ceremonies. He approached the wooden lectern. With Bella standing expectantly to his right, wearing her professionally charming smile, he cleared his throat and looked out across the audience.

"Ladies and gentlemen," he said. The buzz of conversation died down a little, but did not altogether stop. "Ladies and gentlemen," he called once more, and the buzz died into silence.

"Ladies and gentlemen, to greet you on this most exciting occasion, I give you our hostess, Mrs. Bella Haughton."

As he stepped to the right, and Bella moved to take his place behind the large stand, Geraldine and I shifted quickly backwards until we merged into the crowd.

Bella coughed loudly, and beamed again.

"I am very glad to see you all here today," she began, and went on to greet the audience and thank everyone for coming. Geraldine was looking paler than ever. As I looked at her, she grimaced with pain.

"What is it?"

"I've been getting these pains today in my stomach on top of everything else. All I feel like doing is curling up in bed with a hot water bottle."

"Well, go home and do it then."

"I will. I'll wait until the end of the speeches. It's just a few minutes."

Up on stage Bella had finished greeting and thanking everyone for coming.

"It was my dear father's wish for many years that Welshney Castle be opened to the public," she went on. "He wanted as many people as possible to enjoy this splendid garden with its lovely lake and beautiful lawns. Unfortunately, he did not live to see this happen, but it has been my wish since he died three years ago to realize his ambition.

"I lived at the castle as a child, and I have lived at the castle as an adult for almost twenty-five years. We came to live here when my two daughters were tiny, and they have had the joy of growing up here, exactly as I did. They had woods to explore and hide in, a lake for swimming and boating, and wide expanses of lawn on which to play tennis and golf and any game they chose."

I noticed the tramp entering the tent through the left-hand opening. Standing on his own, away from the crowd, he was staring up at the stage. He was about a third of the way back, and therefore had a clear view. John Chard soon entered through the same door and went to stand to the right of the tramp, slightly closer to the main body of the audience.

Bella was still enjoying happy reminiscences.

"They were very lucky children to have a lovely house, with many rooms in which to play, and the run of such a wonderful estate. They had cellars to play in, a grotto, an ice house. They had everything any child could possibly want – "

"Except a father," boomed a man's indignant voice.

Gasps of horror could be heard from all around, and everyone turned to see who had spoken. Bella was looking stunned, as if she hadn't quite taken in what had been said.

"I'm sorry," she murmured. "Where was I? Oh yes, this is such a beautiful place, and I hope many more children will be able to visit – "

"They didn't have a father," Chard cried, louder still. "You sent your husband away, when the girls were tiny. The marriage was deteriorating, and he had a mental breakdown. He had become an embarrassment to you, so you gave him a large sum of money and told him to disappear and never come back."

Bella appeared to have lost the power of speech. Her gaze was fixed on the tramp, who stared back at her, muttering to himself.

"She looks as if she's seen a ghost," I whispered to Geraldine.

"She has."

"Robert?" Bella whispered, staring at the tramp in absolute disbelief.

Chard carried on slowly and emphatically.

"You have no understanding or empathy for other people and their problems, Mrs. Haughton. It would be a bad day for the less fortunate members of society if you ever became mayor."

Murmurs of horror and dismay were growing in the crowd.

The master of ceremonies kept his head. He grabbed the microphone from Bella, and began talking into it loudly, with an air of calm authority.

"Ladies and gentlemen, sorry – " he gave a quick laugh – "Sorry for the interruption. Let us carry on with our program. I now give you Paula Rochelle, our wonderful public relations consultant, who has so expertly controlled all the various aspects of this mammoth production."

Paula stepped forward hastily. She was obviously aiming to hurry matters along and give the audience something new to think about, so that the embarrassing interjection could be quickly forgotten. She appeared to have not even a trace of nerves. She smiled briskly at the audience, looking more beautiful than ever. And when she began speaking, it was with an air of intelligence and authority.

"I must first of all acknowledge all that Mrs. Haughton has done, and all the fine qualities she has shown," Paula began in her perfectly modulated voice. "Her vision, her energy, her determination are all admirable. I speak on behalf of the whole team when I say that we have been delighted to work with this intelligent, high-powered woman."

The tramp began to make the loud moaning sound again.

"All – all," Paula stuttered. She paused, took a breath and began again. "All of us have been committed to the idea of this outstandingly beautiful garden being appreciated by as many people as possible."

I could see the whole team of VIPs on the stage praying for a miracle, something to take the crowd's attention away from what was happening, and miraculously at that moment it came. As if in answer to their prayers, a loud moan came from right beside me, as Geraldine collapsed on the floor, her face contorted with pain.

"Gerry!" I cried, and immediately I and half a dozen other people standing near bent down around her.

"Terrible pain," she groaned, her eyes tightly shut.

"Where?" I asked, and she rubbed her hands over her stomach.

"I'll call for an ambulance."

I grabbed at my phone and jabbed at the buttons. A lady ran off to the back, and a moment later two St. Johns emergency techs arrived. They helped Geraldine to her feet and stood one at each side supporting her. "There is a medical tent at the back, madam, where you can lie down until the ambulance comes."

For a moment or two the crowd around us stared, then a buzz of anxious conversations broke out.

"I'll come with you," I said, as the two men half led, half carried Geraldine to the back.

As I turned to follow them, I saw Joel walking up the path toward me. He was wearing faded jeans, a thick polo neck sweater and black leather jacket.

"Lucy, what are you doing – I didn't expect to see you here," he exclaimed, clasping both my hands in his, stroking, massaging the backs of my hands, the tips of my fingers.

"Lucy, she's found. The police have found her. Hollie's been found, and she's okay; she's really absolutely okay!"

I must have continued to look totally blank and confused, because he went on:

"I've been helping the teams searching this morning. The reports on the radio asked for help . . . " He stared at me.

"Come here," he said gruffly, and suddenly he was holding me so tightly in his arms that I could hardly breathe. For a few blissful moments all the unbearable thoughts were blocked out as I held him back so tightly, not wanting, ever, ever to let him go. For a few seconds I forgot where I was and he, if he thought about it at all, no doubt assumed that we were hidden by the crowd from anyone who might recognize us.

But Paula was up on stage, with a clear view over everything. She was attempting to continue with her speech, and it was the unexpected sound of her stumbling on her words that drew my attention back to her.

"All the team members have wanted others to have the opp-opp-opportunity to enjoy this oasis of tranq-tranq-calmness and loveliness," she faltered. I felt Joel release his grip on me and turn to face the front, realizing too late what had occurred, his expression now guarded and watchful.

"Up until today," Paula went on, her gaze fixed exactly on the spot where Joel and I stood, "I have thought this place the most inspiring, uplifting place imaginable, but now . . . " she broke off and choked on her words. I wanted to sink to the floorboards, certain she was about to make some cataclysmic public announcement.

"But now," she continued, getting some control once more over her voice. "Now I feel above all, it is a place I shall never forget as long as I live."

She took a step backwards, tripped slightly, then righted herself, her face flushed. A section of hair fell from the impeccable arrangement inside the green comb. She brushed it back, grabbing at it so roughly that she inadvertently loosened more strands, which fell forwards over her face, obscuring her view.

The elderly man in the grey suit, who had been sitting at the side of the stage next to the secretary, now stepped up to the microphone and began to speak:

"As chairman of the shareholders who have invested . . . "

"I've got to go!" I cried.

But at that moment my right forearm was grabbed painfully tightly, and I was dragged sideways so suddenly that I lost my balance and staggered for a second, tripping over my feet.

"What are you doing?" cried a strangulated male voice that was extremely familiar, yet sounded strange. I pulled myself upright. Simon was standing at the door of the tent. The shadows under his eyes were dark as tunnels; his hair, which was always neatly combed sideways across his forehead, now flopped into his eyes.

"She's found, she's found," he was yelling, "Not that you evidently care much."

"Oh thank God, thank God," I wailed, clapping my hands, then covering my face with them, then wringing them tightly together.

"Oh, you're now going to start pretending you care, are you?" Simon was shaking, and his voice trembled with controlled anger. "Why did you come here if not to see him?"

"Look," Joel broke in, exasperated. "She's found. Hollie's been found. Surely that's what's important?"

"Nothing is more important than you and her explaining what's going on," said a harsh female voice.

By now Paula had emerged from the crowd to my left. Her pretty face was twisted with fury; her hand quivered as she reached out and thumped Joel on the chest, not hard enough to hurt, but hard enough to show that her supreme self-control had deserted her.

"Do you think I couldn't see from up there?" she spat. "I was making a speech, for God's sake, and I had to remember my words and keep talking as if nothing had happened while you had your hands all over her."

"What?" Simon blurted out. He was shaking now too.

"I didn't have my hands all over her." Joel was somehow still managing to sound calm and controlled. I sensed his deep certainty that what had happened would best be dealt with in a dignified way. His quiet strength inspired me. "I gave Lucy a hug, that's all"

"That was no ordinary hug," Simon croaked, and Paula snapped out, "Do you think we're stupid?"

But at that moment I looked outside and saw Officer Allen and two uniformed officers coming toward me up the path. Behind them two police cars drove up immediately in front of the tent, lights flashing and sirens wailing.

It was one of the police officers who spoke first.

"Mrs. Roseman, we have some news for you. We've found your daughter."

Chapter Ten

It was on the Wednesday of the following week, when we had begun to recover from the turbulent events of the previous few days, that I decided I wanted to know more of the exact details of how Hollie was found. I drove to West Shalham police station, parked in a visitor's space, and walked into the reception area. There was a young police officer on duty, who called straight through to Julie Allen. After two minutes she appeared, her round face relaxed and smiling. She led me into a small waiting room, where she filled a kettle and spooned coffee into a couple of mugs.

"It's great to see you again, Lucy. How's Hollie?"

"Oh, she's in great spirits."

"No bad after effects?"

"Oh, no. From the moment she returned home with us, after we picked her up here, she behaved as if nothing had ever happened. She played quietly with some toys on her bed for a while, then she had a long bath. For hours she took no notice of any of us. Then, after the other two children were in bed, she began banging on her wooden bedroom gate. I let her out, thinking she was hungry. But do you know what she did? She came into the family room, sat between Simon and me on the couch, and rested her head on my lap. She's never done anything like it before. I stroked her hair while Simon massaged her feet. The three of us sat there for about half an hour. Then all of a sudden she decided she'd had enough. She stood up and walked back to her bedroom and gestured for the gate to be put back up. And since then she's been completely her usual self once more, acting as if we don't exist."

Julie was looking at me, shaking her head in puzzlement. "I just can't imagine what it must be like, living with a child like that all the time. Still, I suppose you've come to terms with it."

"Oh, no, no. Don't think that. You get on with it every day, but you never come to terms with it. I'm always seeing children of her age, winning running races, playing football or giggling with friends, and I think, that's what Hollie should be doing."

I took a sip of coffee and set the mug back on the table.

"Have you got over the events of the last few weeks now?"

No, I wanted to say. Absolutely no! I – we – will never get over this. When it came to real practical help, or even solid moral support, almost everyone we knew had fallen by the wayside. Even Simon had hidden in his study, with his program designs, unable to deal with what was happening. Geraldine had cared, but even she had been a watcher from afar. I had sought help, sustenance, comfort from the only person who had freely offered it. And I'd fallen deeply, hopelessly, passionately in love.

Over the past week Simon had spoken to me as little as possible. He had made a few curt requests at the dinner table for me to pass him things. Accusation, resentment had glared from his eyes if I had happened to intercept his glance. We were broken. We had been crushed, anyway, by the strain of the previous months and years. Until I had met Joel I'd limped from one crisis to another, every day more cowed, more weighed down, until I was almost prostrate. For a few magic weeks I had not only walked tall again, I had flown. And I was to pay the price for that for the rest of my life. I had lost my husband, I had lost my family's future – and I had lost Joel. It needed only the arrival of the confirmation that we had lost the due process hearing, and the forlorn, empty future that beckoned would have arrived. Oh no, we had not gotten over it at all.

Tears spilled from my eyes. I wiped them roughly with the back of my left hand, and bent toward the coffee mug, hoping Julie wouldn't see. She reached out and put her hand over mine where it rested on the handle of the mug.

"You still feel very emotional about everything that's happened?"

"Oh, yes."

"I tell you what," she said, trying to sound bright and cheering. "You wanted to know the details of how and where Hollie was found. It was my colleague Officer Jeff Watson who was first on the scene that morning, and he's on duty today. Let me go and find him."

She rose and slipped quickly out of the room. I pulled a couple of tissues from my coat pocket and blew my nose noisily. I had no choice but to carry on. I made myself sit up straight. I took several sips from my coffee mug. It was a few minutes before Julie returned, and when she did, she was accompanied by a young officer.

"This is Officer Watson, Lucy. He'll tell you more about what happened that morning."

She smiled and went out of the room.

"Let's see what I can remember," the young man said, sitting down opposite me. "We don't know where Hollie slept. She was found late Tuesday morning wandering around the middle of the forest. She looked a bit cold, and she ate about half a loaf of bread when it was offered to her, but apart from that she seemed fine. There's not much more I can tell you."

I don't know what I was expecting to hear, but I felt hugely disappointed. Maybe I hadn't so much wanted to know more details of what had happened to Hollie, as to have somewhere – anywhere – to go that wasn't home.

"Thanks," I said, standing up. "Thanks for coming to talk to me."

"That's all right. The little girl's okay now?"

"Oh yes; none the worse for what happened."

I looked at my watch. It was ten past ten. I couldn't relax. There must be other places I could go; anywhere that wasn't home. I didn't want to go home at any time, under any circumstances.

I decided to go and see Geraldine. I had visited her in the hospital every day since her collapse, and now she was at home, being nursed by her mother. I bought some grapes and drove to her home. Mrs. Moore greeted me with a big smile when I arrived

"She's a lot better today, Lucy. Come in and have coffee with me until she wakes up."

"Thanks."

In Geraldine's bright kitchen, Mrs. Moore put the kettle on. She spooned coffee into two mugs on the counter, and into a third mug, which she placed on a small round tray with a lace cloth on it.

"You can take this one to her when she wakes, if you'd be so good."

Geraldine's mother had always loved such little gestures and luxuries. They made everyday actions such as drinking coffee together seem like special occasions. I wished I could feel that one day I would do that for Lisa. But there would never be time. I felt my eyes smarting with tears.

Mrs. Moore handed me my mug and took a sip from hers.

"Ooh, too hot," she said, and bent to retrieve the milk from the fridge. The milk was in a pretty blue jug, not straight from the bottle.

"Where's the cover for this?" she muttered to herself. She opened the third of a set of four drawers, rummaged for a few seconds and pulled out a small lacy cloth with beads around the side, which she slipped over the top of the milk jug. She seemed very at ease in her daughter's kitchen, certain where everything was.

"Mom," came a voice from the bedroom. "Did I hear the doorbell?"

"Yes, dear. Lucy's here. Wait a minute," Mrs. Moore said in her comfortable, easy manner. She poured boiling water into the mug on the tray and stirred in some milk. Then she lifted my mug and put that on the tray too.

"Would you be good enough to take that in with you, Lucy?"

"Of course."

I carried the tray to the door of Geraldine's bedroom and said, "Hi, it's me."

"Come in, Lucy."

Geraldine leant over and switched on her bedroom light. I walked across the soft carpet and put the tray down on the nightstand.

"Would you open the curtains, Lucy?"

Several vases containing beautiful arrangements of flowers were sitting on the windowsill. I pulled back the pink and yellow curtains. It was a heavy, grey, mid-winter's day. I turned around and restrained a gasp. I had visited Geraldine every day, but I had always seen her in the hospital. Seeing her here in her own home for the first time, I noticed how pale and thin she had become. Her hair, normally so impeccably styled, was plastered flat against her head, from her having spent so much time in bed. I looked for some sort of comment to make to hide my dismay.

"A miscarriage!" I exclaimed, looking across at her. "I still can't believe it; you of all people. You've always said you were never going to have kids because of the risk of passing on Huntington's."

"Well, accidents happen to the best of us," she retorted, with a trace of her old spirit.

"But why did it never occur to any of us? You were feeling sick and dizzy and lacking in energy – all the classic signs of pregnancy. But we all began to panic and fear it was Huntington's. Even though at your age it would have been unlikely, we all still feared the worst."

"I was certain it was Huntington's. I couldn't believe the cruelty of it happening, just when I was beginning to relax and feel safe."

"It must have been Colin's, was it? You went out with him last summer."

"Yes, I was with him for about six months, and the dates are right."

"You haven't told him?"

"No. There was no question of his ever leaving his wife. I didn't want him to."

"Have you seen Martin Wiseman at all?"

"Yes, I went out with him the Sunday night, after you and I had that drink with him the night before. He's sent flowers, those over there" – she pointed to a beautiful display on the window sill.

"He knows about the miscarriage?"

"Not yet. He just knows I've been ill. But I will tell him. You know, Lucy, I'm beginning to feel I will always be straight with him. There's something about him, he sees straight to the heart of issues, and he's very clear-thinking and – well – wise. Perhaps he's right. Perhaps my unfortunate circumstances didn't justify me in behaving in a way that was immoral and unfair to others."

"You're talking as if all that behavior is in the past."

"I think it is. I feel the miscarriage has drawn a line under that old behavior of mine. I feel it's about time I became an adult and behaved responsibly. I also feel somehow this miscarriage has laid the ghost of Huntington's to rest. I'd been thinking for a couple of years that I'd got away with it, that I wasn't going to develop it, and then, when I started to feel so ill, I was certain I had it. Now I feel I can stop worrying about it. And in that case, I no longer have an excuse for living as if there's no tomorrow and having affairs all the time, and for carrying on with my old philosophy of 'eat, drink and be merry for tomorrow we die.'"

"I'll bet Martin is also partly responsible for your new determination to behave like a grown-up."

She smiled, and her face flushed with color for the first time that day. "Yes, he's wonderful. There's something about him that's so discerning and far-sighted. I feel he sees straight through me if I'm not being straight with him. Do you know what I mean?"

"Oh yes, he's quite an unusual guy," I smiled. "Strong, self-assured and independent. Someone who thinks for himself and isn't swayed by the opinions of the herd. I think you've met your match there, Gerry."

"Maybe," she laughed. Then she went quiet, and I noticed she was looking pale and washed out again.

"Do you want to sleep now?"

"I think so."

I squeezed her hand, then got up and left.

Geraldine's apt description of Martin made me think of another man who was similarly wise and independent-minded. I hadn't seen John Chard since the Welshney Castle opening, but he had been very much in my thoughts. In fact, I had been plagued by all sorts of unanswered questions about him in the intervening days.

I had a quick sandwich and orange juice in a café in Winnersh while weighing whether or not it would be a good idea to visit him. I decided, on the whole, that I couldn't think of any reason why he might object. It was only a couple of miles from Geraldine's flat to John's house, and I was there inside ten minutes.

I stood tentatively on the doorstep for half a minute or so, summoning the nerve to ring the doorbell. John Chard had been so full of anger at the castle opening ceremony, so unlike the gracious, charming man I had encountered at our two previous meetings that I now felt rather in awe of him. But then, what was there to lose? If he was unwelcoming, I would make my apologies and go – there was little chance of us ever bumping into each other again. I reached out my hand and pressed the door bell.

For a few seconds nothing happened. Then the door was pulled quickly open, and John was standing there in an open-necked shirt and jeans. There wasn't even a hint of surprise in his face as he smiled, genuinely pleased to see me.

"Lucy, how lovely to see you. I've been hoping you'd call. I've found some more information for you. Do come in."

"Thanks."

I followed him across the hall and into the room with the large picture windows.

"Please, sit down. I'll make some coffee."

I sat down in one of his old-fashioned, high-backed armchairs.

John made a pot of coffee and set the tray down on the coffee table before collecting a file of notes from the oak desk in the corner. He sat down opposite me.

"Has there been any backlash against you after the Welshney Castle opening?" I asked, coming straight to the point.

"The local paper wanted to talk to me," John began, flicking through the file while he spoke. "I refused. Bella Haughton called me up and began berating me on the phone. She told me I didn't know what I was talking about. But everything Robert Haughton said rang true. I'm certain he was telling the truth."

"Do you know what's going to happen to Robert?"

"I think they're going to find some sort of home for him to live in. He still has severe mental problems."

"So where's he been living all this time?"

"I couldn't make too much sense of it. As far as I understood it, he spent a long time living in India. I think he's slept on the streets in London, too."

"And what about Bella? Has she still got ambitions to be mayor?"

"She probably still hopes to eventually. But it will take a long time for her to feel that people have forgotten that disastrous ceremony."

He smiled. "Now, on a quite different subject. I have something here of interest for you to read."

He looked down at the open file on his lap. He raised his eyes again and gave me a penetrating look. Then he smiled, a slightly teasing smile that was full of significance. I knew he had found something important. He handed me the file, and I immediately started to read.

"Chapter Five. The story of the legendary wild boy of Pershore is justifiably famous. He disappeared from the small village of Petheril in 1859 at the age of eight or nine. He wasn't found again until 1863 when some farm workers taking a shortcut through the woods came across him. He had hair half way down his back, and his clothes were almost in rags. He was painfully thin and was covered in mud and dirt from head to foot. He wouldn't talk and only made frightened grunting noises, even after he had been returned to his family and looked after for some months."

"What an amazing story," I said, looking up.

"Read on."

"But what isn't so well known," the account went on, *"is that parish records and the written diary of the vicar of Petheril, Daniel*

Linden, kept in the years 1852-67, show that Adam Smithson, the fifth, and much, younger child of a blacksmith's family, had never spoken or made eye contact with anyone even before he disappeared into the forest. He had always been a lost, lonely soul who lived in a world of his own."

My heart thudded in my chest. I turned to face John, the enormity of what I was just comprehending really hitting me.

"Good God."

John was looking at me intently.

"He was autistic, wasn't he? His non-communicativeness wasn't the result of his isolation in the forest. He had always been autistic, even before he became lost?"

John was smiling and nodding. "It could even be what led to his becoming lost, if he didn't understand about staying with those he knew and couldn't ask for help."

I stood up and went to look out at the garden. There was no sign of life. No birds singing, no flies buzzing, and no wind to sway the bare twigs and the few evergreen plants and bushes.

As I hugged and kissed John goodbye, I thought about all the lost children, of Adam Smithson, the wild boy of Pershore, of Geraldine's miscarried baby, and, most of all, of Hollie.

I went to find Joel next. I went only to say goodbye and thank you. There was no way we could ever see each other again.

The receptionist at the Peterson Warnock offices told me that he was upstairs at a meeting, which was not due to finish for some time. I sat for a while pretending to look at magazines, then, when she disappeared for a few minutes into another room, I raced up the stairs to try to find him.

I wandered back and forth along the wide, thickly carpeted corridor for about ten minutes, and was just beginning to think it was pointless waiting any longer, when about a dozen people began to emerge from one of the rooms. Joel was the last to appear.

He came straight up to me and took my hand. "Hello, Lucy."

"Hello."

We walked along the corridor, but were jostled by large groups of people; there seemed to be nowhere to talk. Joel gestured to a grand oak staircase that led upwards. The center of the staircase was thickly carpeted, and there were oil paintings of eighteenth- and nineteenth-century landscapes on the oak-paneled walls that reached up to a vaulted stone ceiling. Upstairs the corridor was empty. We walked slowly along, our arms touching. Without talking, we gazed out of the windows over the shopping center, the elegant, pristine office blocks with fountains splashing outside, all the way to the hill at the northernmost point of the city, where the cathedral looked imperiously down on endless rows of small houses.

We were silent for a while. Then Joel reached out to take my hand again. He continued to look at me, as if he had never seen me properly before, and would never see me properly again.

"What a fiasco. At the opening ceremony, I mean," I said.

"Yes, you could say that." He laughed. "Actually, it's not funny. Bella's thinking of giving up politics as a result of what happened. And as for Paula . . . She feels her reputation and her standing have been greatly damaged, even though she personally had nothing to do with it. Indeed, she did everything she could to dissuade Bella from inviting John Chard. Six months ago it seemed like an inspired career move to accept a temporary appointment as Bella's PR officer, overseeing the castle opening. After all, Bella was clearly a high-powered, intelligent woman with a wide influence in local politics. Many people thought she would be mayor in a year or two. It was said even that the local Conservatives had talked to her about the possibility of her running for Parliament. Accepting a role as her public relations officer seemed like an infallible way of extending Paula's own power and prestige.

"The trouble is, Bella's intelligence and ability are accompanied by obstinacy and arrogance. A certain amount of obstinacy is understandable, even desirable, for someone in her position, in order for her to make things happen. But when it's accompanied by blind arrogance, by a sense of total superiority and a belief that you are always right, it's bound to lead to disaster. Paula knew that inviting John Chard was a serious error, but Bella was determined to have this prestigious, up-and-coming historian at her function, and couldn't see that he was volatile and unpredictable and liable to make a scene of some sort.

"Now Paula's name, as well as Bella's, is tarnished by having been associated with that calamitous ceremony. She had nothing to do with Chard's outburst, and it in no way reflected on her abilities, but what happened has been as damaging as a piece of malicious slander. The vast majority of people can't think for themselves, blindly accepting the public image presented to them."

He took me in his arms and ran his hands up and down my back briefly. Then he held me tightly, so tightly I had to gasp for breath. After a minute or two he released the pressure slightly, and looked down into my eyes.

"I love you, Lucy. I loved you when I first saw you, and I'll never love anyone so deeply, so completely, again. But you'll never leave your family, and the guilt and the deception – for both of us – are too much to bear."

The world outside the window seemed to darken and harden into a black and grey cityscape of concrete skyscrapers and faceless office blocks. All the softer, more natural aspects – the surrounding hills, the distant mass of foliage and greenery that formed the park, the little oases of greenery around the castle and the leisure center – faded into the gloom of the approaching midwinter evening.

"I know," I muttered, "I know, I know, I know . . . "

I tried to look at him, and felt again that familiar sense of the walls and floor, and the world outside the window, shaking on their foundations, while Joel alone remained still. I couldn't bear to look at him. I couldn't bear to lose him. I couldn't bear any of it.

"Can you and Simon rebuild your marriage?"

It was like trying to find words in some unpronounceable foreign language. I had to drag each word from the furthest reaches of my mind, and then strain myself to find the next one.

"Hollie's being found helped us a bit. And when I tell him that you helped in the search to find her . . . "

I couldn't finish the sentence. He let his arms fall from where they enclosed me. He took both my hands in his and squeezed them. Then, continuing to hold my hand in his, he led me back toward the grand staircase.

"Paula and I will be married, I think," he said, very gently. He was silent for a moment. He, too, seemed to be groping for words, and then finding them too excruciatingly painful to utter.

"There's something else I have to tell you . . . " But whatever it was, it was too difficult to say, for he stared at the ground miserably and said nothing.

Suddenly a harsh voice bellowed below.

"What are you doing, talking to her?" Paula's voice came contemptuously. She flounced up the steps, looking slimmer and more sophisticated than ever in a black dress and elegant blue and black jacket. Joel gazed at me intently for the briefest of moments, then turned and plodded heavily down the steps. On the middle landing they met and talked in urgent whispers for a few moments, then Joel passed her and trudged down the lower flight before turning to the left and out of sight along the lower corridor, back toward the main entrance. He did not look back.

Paula, in contrast, almost flew up the final flight. All the time her eyes blazed on to mine. She drew level with me.

"He's not coming back," she snapped. "I sent him on to get away from you. He's gone to the car to wait for me. For me, not you."

"Paula, you won't believe this, but I'm so, so sorry for having hurt you."

"Don't go thinking I'm taking this calmly, because I'm not," she snapped. "Joel is everything to me."

How could I ever explain? It had seemed a morning like any other, that bright, blustery September day when I had driven to Shalham for a meeting, my thoughts locked securely on how we were to pay for the impending hearing. Time had stood still that day for one brief interlude (had it been minutes, or just a few seconds?). And in that brief space of time I had recognized so many things. That Joel was in a different league than all other human beings. That there was an unsuspected substratum to life, an intoxicating, tantalizing, ravishing place of enchantment where emotions hit you like tidal waves, and a hitherto unknown person could seem omnipotent. That this place of mystery gave a depth and resonance to life that made all the everyday confusion, isolation and smallness of spirit that had characterized my life seem suddenly like a habit that I had carried around with me like a bad set of clothes.

All those things I had known in that moment, and I knew they would never leave me, even though, as was abundantly clear, I would never see him again. There were no words that could come close to explaining how my guts had contracted each time I saw him or heard his voice. Nothing would change that, not time, not distance, nor the hostility of all those around us. If we were separated for twenty years, and I heard the sound of his deep laughter coming from another room, my consciousness would still telescope to that spotlight around him in which he moved, breathed, spoke, listened and effortlessly charmed all those lucky enough to fall in his path.

The disdain in Paula's gaze deepened into contempt, and even malice.

"I wanted to tell you that we're moving. We're going to New York. Not for a vacation. We're going to live there."

The bottom of my world that still remained after the trauma of the past few days rocked and then cracked beneath my feet. Everything I could see – the oak-paneled walls, the staircase – went white, as if in a polar landscape. Ice-cold knives slithered through me, cutting me to the core.

"Why? How?" I blustered. "What for?"

"I had an offer of a job there a couple of months ago. I wasn't going to take it. But now, with the fiasco of that opening ceremony . . . Bella might regard it as the end of all her ambitions to be mayor, but I'm not going to let it finish my career. Joel will restart his business over there – he has plenty of contacts, and he'll make loads more."

I stood my ground. Gradually I gained control of myself.

"I'm surprised such a strong-minded man is prepared to meekly accept your sort of dominance," I said. The words came out in a rush before I had time to think. It was simultaneously awful, and yet an intense physical relief, as if a typhoon that had been trapped inside me had suddenly been released.

"You mean you're surprised he'll honor my wishes when he won't take yours into account? Well . . . " She smiled, haughtily. "Let's face it, Lucy. I'm twenty-three. I am a top PR officer running countrywide projects and campaigns. I have been head-hunted three times this year for jobs with salaries of over £50,000 a year. I can take my career anywhere I want. On the other hand, you are just – " she coughed and then gave a little smirk" – the little woman who stays at home."

I felt myself floundering. It was hard to tell which feeling was uppermost – injustice, misery, the unbearable sense of loss. I simply had too much to contend with. But things had changed. I was no longer to be despised and belittled as I had allowed myself to be in the past. However low I appeared to sink, I still had the energy and strength and the vision of myself that Joel had given me to buoy me up. I squared my shoulders. I looked her in the eye.

"On the contrary, I have had to fight to keep the spirit of my family alive, when the weight of government authority was against us, and when almost everyone else we knew had turned their backs on us. I know far more than you do, Paula, about living on your wits and planning campaigns and making the most of every particle of energy that you possess. Believe me, the stakes have been far higher for me. If you fail, you simply move to New York. If I fail – as is more than likely – not only will my autistic daughter be subjected to a life of continued frustration, my two other children are likely never to acquire the self-esteem and confidence that is the starting point for succeeding in life."

My eyes smarted with the effort of maintaining eye contact. "No, no, Paula, I am not the little woman who stays at home. I am the woman struggling at all costs to save her family."

Paula shrugged and looked away. It was becoming clear to her that she wasn't gaining the easy victory that she had expected. But her surprise and bafflement lasted only a few seconds. I registered the exact moment when the final, clinching move occurred to her. Her gaze hardened, and I caught a flicker of exultation. She stroked the lapels of her jacket and patted the immaculate sleeves, almost as if the trump card was waiting there, ready for her to produce.

"Whatever you say makes no difference, Lucy. Accept it. We're flying out in a few days to choose an apartment. But we won't be giving you the address, and we won't be coming back here." The ice-cold glint of malice in her eyes became solid as a knife.

"You see," she went on, and a smile flickered at the corners of her mouth, "I'm pregnant. I'm having Joel's baby."

She looked me full in the face, iridescent with triumph, her smile spanning from one ear to the other.

"You'd better sit down before you fall down, Lucy."

I wavered and tottered. The drop beneath me, into which the grand staircase descended to reach the floor below, became an abyss. I had no control over my body. I couldn't feel the ground beneath my feet, and I wondered if I had lost my footing already, except that I didn't appear to be flying through the air or crashing to the bottom of the stairs. I couldn't focus on anything. I was aware of only a confused, wavering mass of brown, which was the oak paneling of the walls seen as an out-of-focus blur as I whirled about. Then a long pink limb stretched out in my direction, an arm, and I caught sight of the painted fingernails reflecting the bright fluorescent overhead lights as the hand became a palm facing toward me, ready to push. At last, my right hand connected with one of the wooden banisters at the side of the staircase. Feeling that the world was doing somersaults, I turned and staggered down the first flight of stairs.

Paula, twisting the knife, shouted after me.

"It was a bit of a shock for both of us. It wasn't planned. It was very much out of the blue. But" – she spoke the words extra loudly and clearly – "Joel is absolutely delighted about it."

I collapsed on the first step of the bottom flight, then immediately picked myself up and hurtled down the final few steps. To my left I spied a bookshelf. I stumbled toward it and rested both arms on top of it, afraid that I might be sick. Then I turned and ran down the corridor, looking for somewhere where I could get away from that taunting, triumphant tone. I saw a toilet, crashed through the door and threw myself at the sink where I started to vomit copiously. Two women came out of stalls and fled as quickly as they could, without stopping to wash their hands.

I splashed my head with cold water, then I stared at my deathly white face. This baby was plainly no accident, not as far as Paula was concerned. I thought of all the women throughout the ages who had gotten themselves pregnant in order to hold on to a lover. As the time-honored way of keeping a man you fear you're losing, it stank. It was dirty, it was low-down, it was deceitful and utterly, utterly selfish. But in this case it appeared to have worked.

I stumbled out of the toilet and found no sign of my persecutor, who had no doubt departed, enjoying her triumph. I was alone. I walked slowly along the corridor, threading my way between groups of businessmen – then out of the wide main entrance and down three large stone steps to the courtyard.

I found my car and began the drive home, though I was hardly in a fit state to do so. The traffic was heavy, and I moved slowly in the long line of cars heading out of the city. A tape – a compilation of sixties hits – had been playing quietly on the cassette player without my having even registered it. Now, with the heavy, emphatic drum beat and distinctive sixties Tamla Motown arrangement, one of my favorite songs began, but today its melancholy was almost more than I could bear. Nevertheless I turned it up, thumping my hands on the wheel in time to the beat and belting out the words, while the tears continued to stream down my cheeks. As the song came to an end, I could hardly see any more. I parked in a rest area, and sat crying solidly for twenty minutes.

Of course, I would never forget Joel. It was possible that I might learn to think of him less than constantly, but he would always be there at the back of my mind – behind my thoughts, in between my thoughts, in the corner of my thoughts, even if everyday concerns pushed him from the forefront.

But I knew how I had to think of him, and what it was best to think about him. I would probably have to tell it to myself again and again like a broken record until I came to sort of believe it. Yes, he was extraordinary, he was larger than life and matchless in every way, but it was good he'd gone, because now I could concentrate on rebuilding my family and my marriage. I had known I was never going to leave Simon, and Joel had known it too. He had served a purpose, that was all. He had merely, merely, enabled me to sparkle for a while.

There was no alternative. I had to go home and tell Simon that I was sorry for what I'd done. I turned the car engine on, pulled out of the rest area and concentrated intensely on my driving, because it didn't do to think too much about what I would say. I mean, how would I even begin to go about asking for forgiveness? It could only be done by trying to explain the background, the build-up to what had happened, all the years of isolation, loneliness and drudgery, the daily panorama of soiled sheets, upturned dinner plates and saturated, over-sized diapers, the sense of being trapped in a backwater while the main river of life flowed away in the distance.

I would have to make promises and keep them, to myself and Simon. All that embittered bile had to go, and there would have to be a not-so-fond farewell to Lord Voldemort. I would have to start seeing people again as my younger, less cynical self had seen them, in terms of their kindness, warmth and good qualities, instead of in terms of how much they had or hadn't helped us. I had to lay aside my jealousy for the relatively easy lives most of them led; these view-points had served only to increase the isolation that came naturally from living in the world of disability. I had to recover some of my former openness and generosity of spirit, which had thrown up their hands in horror and run away as soon as Lord Voldemort had begun to raise his disagreeable head.

After all, there had been some sort of redemption. I had developed stamina and determination, and, above all, a stronger belief in myself. I had to hold on to the good stuff and throw out the bad. Only then could we move on.

I picked Joshua up from school and Lisa from Isobel's house. I parked in the driveway, and they scampered out and up to the front door. Before forcing myself out of the car I sat for a moment, wishing I was anywhere else, and then thinking, Where on earth else could I go? I plodded up the path and jabbed my key into the lock, but before I could turn it, the door opened. Simon stood on the threshold, looking at me with an expression that was hard to read. He didn't smile, but something told me there was less hostility in his manner than there had been all the other days of this interminable week.

The children raced past me, dumping bags, coats and shoes

on the way.

"I visited a client this afternoon, and it didn't seem worth going back to work," Simon said, in answer to my unasked question. "So I've been doing some work from home." He paused, and added, with more than a hint of suspicion: "Where've you been?"

I shut the door and hung my coat up.

"I've called on various people today. I called on John Chard, that historian, and I called on Geraldine at her flat. I went to the police station and talked to Julie Allen." I paused for a moment, choosing my words. "And I called and saw Joel and Paula. To say goodbye."

"Why did you do that?" he flared. "It wasn't necessary."

I walked across the hall and into the living room. I stared for a few moments at the bare branches of the apple tree and the heavily pruned shrubs in the back yard, sensing Simon standing just a yard or two behind me.

"I've said goodbye now. There'll be no need to have any contact with either of them again. They're going to America. Paula's pregnant. That's it."

I sat down on the edge of the nearest chair. Simon didn't smile, but an unmistakable wave of delight crossed his face.

"I have something to tell you, too," he said. "Or at least to show you. But first of all I just want to say something."

I prepared myself for another diatribe. But it didn't come. Simon paced in front of the windows staring from the wall, to the floor, to the garden, and then to me.

"I've felt so lonely these past months," he said.

I stared at him, open-mouthed. He gave a half smile.

"You didn't realize that, did you? That's the trouble; we could never talk. You were so exhausted and so busy, and I always felt I shouldn't burden you with my feelings."

"You should have. Not burdened me, of course, but talked to me. Things might have been very different."

"It was all too hard to talk about. I felt so hopeless and so trapped. I never, ever believed we'd win, and I was afraid of you getting your hopes up and then being disappointed. I know I often appeared to say discouraging things, but I was trying to save you pain in the long run."

I was too weary to be angry.

"But don't you see, without hope I wouldn't have had the energy to fight. You need hope, even if it's completely daft and stupid and unrealistic, to have any chance of succeeding. You shouldn't have tried to rob me of that, Simon." I thought for a few moments. "I suppose that was why you seemed so cold most of the time."

He began pacing more quickly, up and down the length of the living room.

"I know I seemed cold. I was full of rage at what was happening to our family because of Hollie's disability – I just couldn't express it."

"I wish you'd tried. I could have related to that, being full of rage myself, much more than I could relate to your silences." I paused, remembering. "There was that time you said you admired me and my strength. I was so amazed; it meant so much to me. If only you'd said it before, things might have, well, they might have been different."

"I know. I've seen all that clearly today for the first time. And that's why –" he stopped pacing and stared at me, the lines on his forehead deep grooves of pain. "And that's why, though I'm – though I'm – " He turned away and walked quickly over to the windows again, where he stood with his back firmly turned.

"That's why, though I'm very, very hurt and angry about what you did, what you've done, I can sort of, just about, begin to understand it. We weren't communicating. We'd been totally pushed apart. We were too busy, too stressed and too plain exhausted to do anything about it."

The tears were back again. It seemed I'd only just stopped crying, and now I was off again.

"Thank you . . . I'm so sorry . . . thank you."

I pulled tissues from my pockets, but they were sodden and useless. I stood up and lifted the tissue box down from a shelf. Simon turned and walked slowly and uncertainly toward me. He stood for a few seconds in front of me. Then he reached out and put his arms around me. I put mine around him, and we held each other, not tightly, but comfortingly. Then I remembered something.

"What was it you wanted to show me?"

He pulled away and gave me a half smile. "You might be angry with me now. But it was important we had this talk before – before we looked at it. Afterwards it might have been difficult to see things clearly."

"Before what? Before what, Simon?" I could hear my voice rising unpleasantly.

Simon moved quickly to the mantel. Behind the wooden clock on the shelf above there was a large, thick, brown envelope.

"It's the results of the due process hearing, isn't it? Good God, Simon! How could you?"

"Open it, go on. You open it."

I gave him a furious look. I slashed at the flap with my forefinger and ripped it apart. I pulled the letter wide open in front of Simon and me. I couldn't read the swimming, jumbled up words.

"What does it say?" I asked pathetically.

Simon took the letter from me. I watched his face, expecting the sternness to harden into miserable resignation. But it didn't. Instead his whole face seemed to lift and lighten. He was smiling. Indeed, he was glowing.

"I can't believe it."

I snatched the letter and read it. "Is it true? Does it really say what I think it says?"

"It says we've won," he said, simply. He looked at me, and his face looked younger and more animated than I had seen it for a very long time, all the condemnation of the past week, all the fatigue and hopelessness of the past months and years almost miraculously smoothed away. He reached his hand out a few inches toward me, then quickly drew it back again.

"Tell me what it says. The exact words, please."

I reached my hand toward him, then I drew it back.

"It says, the committee has agreed to placement at the Leo Kanner School," he said, his gaze fixed on the letter.

I could feel my mouth gaping.

"Does it really say that? It can't. I don't believe it. Please read it again."

"It says – it really does say – the committee has agreed to placement at the Leo Kanner School."

He looked up from reading and held my gaze steadily. I reached my hand out, this time a few more inches, and touched his arm.

"Thank God. Thank God," I muttered, half smiling, half crying. He looked at me and laughed.

"What's there to cry about?" he said, having trouble getting the words out himself. Then he took me in his arms and hugged me. And I hugged him back – as if it were the simplest and most natural act in the world.

"You know what this means, don't you?" I asked. He nodded. But we didn't understand. Neither of us knew really what it would be like to be able to explore as a matter of course all those remote, exotic places – the movies, the beach, the swimming pool – that had previously been as inaccessible to us as the Great Wall of China. I could help Joshua with his homework. Lisa and I could complete that dollhouse skeleton that had remained untouched in the closet for the past weeks. And Hollie . . . Hollie would at last have the round-the-clock program she needed. The calm, structured, totally consistent approach that would help her to begin learning.

Joshua came running in, with Lisa close behind him.

"What is it?" he asked. "What's happened?"

"Hollie's going to a special school." I heard my voice speaking the wondrous words as if it were a stranger talking or a newsreader making a pronouncement on television. I knelt down and took Joshua's hand in one hand and Lisa's hand in the other. When Hollie returned on the school bus in a few minutes, I would do the same with her, because I always tried to explain things . . .

"It's the best special school in the country," I explained. "There are beautiful grounds and wonderful sports facilities where Hollie can have lots of exercise, which will help her to feel calmer so that she will be in the right frame of mind to learn. There will be excellent teachers, so she can have a lot of individual help. She'll come home for long vacations and holidays, and we'll go and visit her each weekend. She won't be frustrated or destructive any more, she won't break your toys and she'll be able to look at us. She might even learn how to talk."

I squeezed their hands.

"Is she going to be a real girl now?" Joshua asked.

I smiled and bent over to kiss his cheek.

"We will see. This is the best chance she'll ever have to be who she is. But I can promise you one thing . . . "

"What's that, Mommy?"

"From now on we will be a real family."